BANTAM **B**OOKS

NEW YORK   TORONTO   LONDON   SYDNEY   AUCKLAND

BRUCE STERLING

ZEITGEIST

ZEITGEIST

A Bantam Spectra Book / November 2000

SPECTRA and the portrayal of a boxed "s" are trademarks of Bantam Books,
a division of Random House, Inc.

Book design by Laurie Jewell.

Library of Congress Cataloging-in-Publication Data
Sterling, Bruce.
Zeitgeist / Bruce Sterling.
p.   cm.
ISBN: 0-553-10493-4
I. Title.
PS3569.T3876 Z45 2000
813'.54—dc21   00-029270

Published simultaneously in the United States and Canada

Bantam Books are published by Bantam Books, a division of Random House,
Inc. Its trademark, consisting of the words "Bantam Books" and the portrayal
of a rooster, is Registered in U.S. Patent and Trademark Office and in other
countries. Marca Registrada. Bantam Books, 1540 Broadway, New York,
New York, 10036.

PRINTED IN THE UNITED STATES OF AMERICA

BVG 10 9 8 7 6 5 4 3 2 1

ZEITGEIST

ONE

SUMMER IN ISTANBUL. ROSES IN A HAMMERED silver urn. Fresh-ground coffee in a shiny brass hand-mill. The rich tang of fertilizer and fuel oil hung over the damaged café. Starlitz could smell the hot caramel aftertaste of the car bomb, right through the baked metal, smashed cement, and burnt upholstery.

"Where are the girls?" said the Turk.

"The girls are in Cyprus. They're partying."

"With Greeks?"

"Oh, heavens no," Starlitz assured him. "The girls are in the *fun* part of Cyprus. *Turkish* Cyprus."

The Turk smiled. He picked open the lid of the coffeepot and deposited a heaping spoon of brown sugar.

Starlitz leaned back in his wrought-iron chair and folded his plump hands over his lilac waistcoat. He and the Turk sat in companionable silence, with hooded eyes behind their designer shades, and watched the pot reach a boil.

The Turk, who called himself Mehmet Ozbey, was young, and rich, with a film star's good looks. In his Italian leather jeans and camel-hair jacket, Ozbey was the picture of masculine chic.

Starlitz felt at peace. Local events were going very much his way. There had been a time in his checkered career when he would have shown up in Istanbul two days *before* a car bomb. He would have hit town with the plan, and the contacts, and the agenda, and he would have found the old city strained and jittery with fatalistic Ottoman tension.

Here at the tag end of the twentieth century, however, Starlitz was pampered by circumstance. He had arrived in Istanbul two days *after* a car bomb. The catastrophe was behind them now. They had entered the professional realm of consequence management. Bored Turkish cops measured their new monster pothole with yellow metal pull-tapes. Indifferent janitors swept up the scattered tonnage of broken glass. Istanbul downtown girls, in their chunky gold chains and Chanel suits, were trying to window-shop through the street's battered length of plywood sheeting.

Mere domestic terrorism could not cause Mehmet Ozbey to break a business appointment. The shrapnel-damaged café was almost deserted, but the young pop promoter had arrived bang on time, clean, shaved, sober, and toting a white calfskin valise. The café Ozbey had chosen was lovely, though its windows had all been shattered by the car bomb's concussion. The café staff doted on Ozbey, touched by his loyalty during their trying circumstances. They kept tiptoeing up to offer lacquered trays of sliced melon and baklava.

A young woman passed the damaged café and caught sight of Ozbey. Instantly entranced, she stumbled headlong into a striped police sawhorse.

"My little girlfriend Gonca," Ozbey remarked solemnly, "would very much like to meet your G-7 girls."

"I'm sure that can be arranged."

"She's especially fond of the French One."

"Everyone has a favorite G-7 girl," Starlitz allowed.

"The French One has the most talent," said Ozbey judiciously. "She can almost sing."

Starlitz nodded. "Yeah, that's her Left Bank café chanteuse riff."

Starlitz and Ozbey watched the pot foam up, once, twice, and the full and traditional third time. Starlitz was pleased to have stolen this moment from the onrushing millennium. It was important to pry these little breathing spaces from the final hum of the dying century. It was good for him, like oxygen.

Ozbey removed the curved pot from its flickering burner, and with exaggerated hostly care he began to pour.

"Why is there no Russian G-7 girl?" Ozbey said, setting the pot aside. "Because it's the Group of Eight now, officially. With Russia."

"That's an odd thing," said Starlitz, accepting his cup. "No one ever asks me why we have no Russian girl in the group. Unless they're Russian."

"You don't like Russians, Mr. Starlitz?"

"I fucking love Russians," Starlitz said politely, "but Russians just don't get it with the tie-in merchandising angle. They still think that a pop group has to sell music."

Ozbey removed his shades, folded them fastidiously, put them in an inner jacket pocket. He lifted his gleaming demitasse and gazed at Starlitz across its gilded rim. " 'Selling the whole concept,' " he quoted.

"Right you are." Starlitz savored a sip. He rinsed his molars with the coffee grounds. That subtle flavor of cardamom. Business was good.

Ozbey cocked his freshly coiffed head. "We sell the big picture. We sell the whole bag of wax."

"It's the spirit of the times." Starlitz nodded. "It's the soul of postmodernity."

"We sell little plastic dolls, for instance."

" 'G-7 action figures,' " Starlitz corrected.

"They're very popular with children. And the lip gloss. The candies. Those very big shoes that they wear."

"Yeah, G-7 WonderBras, G-7 pantyhose—the tie-in apparel thing has definitely been a breakthrough area for us."

Ozbey put his cup down and leaned in intently. "Who is your supplier? For the clothes."

"Indonesia, mostly," said Starlitz. "Before the currency crash."

Ozbey placed his jacketed elbows on the polished marble tabletop. "My Uncle the Minister," he announced, "has many interests in the Turkish apparel trade. He is very influential in domestic Turkish manufacturing."

"You don't say." Starlitz scratched his double chin thoughtfully. "That's very interesting."

"My Uncle the Minister has extensive interests in the Turkish Republic of Northern Cyprus."

"The Republic is a very interesting place," said Starlitz, leaning forward in tandem. "After just one week on the ground in Turkish Cyprus, I could tell that it's a country of tremendous opportunity."

Starlitz lifted one meaty hand in mock demurral. "Yes, I know—some people claim that the Greek half of the island has a better tourist industry. But if you ask me, the Greek scene in Cyprus is yesterday. They're all overbuilt and tapped out. All those nightclubs, and the rave scene, and the big cruise ships in from Beirut . . ."

"Let me show you the Meridien," said Ozbey. "Turgut Altimbasak's casino in Girne. That establishment is very . . . what is the English word?"

" 'Suave'?"

"Yes! Very suave, very international-playboy. Mr. Altimbasak is a friend of my uncle's. You could gamble freely there, Mr. Starlitz. You could run a big tab."

Starlitz considered this bold proposal. It was very much to his liking. "Call me Lech," he said.

"Okay!" grinned Ozbey. "You call me 'Mehmetcik.' Mehmetcik, it's like 'Johnny.' "

"Mehmetcik, my friend, let's be frank together," said Starlitz, steepling his big blunt fingers. "In the past we in G-7 were very displeased with our offshore accounts in Jersey and Bimini. But then you brought those Turkish Cypriot banks to our attention. Your Uncle the Minister had a few helpful words there. It's all very smooth now. That broke up the red tape. My accountant's very happy about all this."

"It's good to have happy accountants," said Ozbey. "We should all have happy accountants."

"We can all be very happy doing business together," Starlitz said. "As long as we always remember the number-one G-7 rule."

"The number-one rule is that everything shuts down before the year 2000."

Starlitz leaned back in contentment. "Mehmetcik, I knew you were special from the first time you sent us fan mail."

Ozbey nodded intently. He was shifting gears now, onto his favorite topic, himself. "People tell me that I'm special," he concurred. "My Uncle the Minister, my wife, my girlfriend, my many good friends in the pop business world—they all say I have a very special gift."

Starlitz watched as a starstruck Turkish housewife entangled herself in a flat yellow strand of police tape. "Yeah," he offered.

"I have a gift. Don't you agree?"

"Absolutely, Mehmetcik. It's written all over you. It couldn't be more obvious."

Ozbey sat up. "And you, Lech. You are also a gifted man. Obviously."

Starlitz shook his head.

Ozbey's dark eyes gleamed. "Don't be shy! People tell me

things, behind the scenes. They tell me: This man Leggy Starlitz, he is more than just a businessman. He is an imam. Like
they say in Silicon Valley, he's a business guru."

"Aw, forget that industry scuttlebutt. Musicians are way
superstitious. They're full of New Age crap."

"Do you know the future? They say that you do."

Starlitz shrugged. "Sure I do, sorta. I'm into consumer
trends, man. It's all about pop, right? Demographic analysis.
Demand curves. Stoking the hit machine. It's an Internet
thing, basically."

"Then you *do* know the future."

"Aw, crystal balls are for suckers." Starlitz scowled. "You
want some supernatural powers, pal? Find a money laundry.
You can work miracles with those things."

Ozbey frowned. He daintily lifted a wedge of sliced melon,
changed his mind about tasting it, and tactfully put it back
down. "To speak life's deepest truths across two languages . . .
It's very hard to speak about these secret things. There are so
many important secrets in life—realities that are never said."

Starlitz very loudly said nothing. To fill the silence he
watched a Turkish crow pick its way across the café's rooftop.
The dusty bird, its trash looter's eyes like two bullet tips, was
shivering with greed. Starlitz surreptitiously dropped a chunk
of melon.

Ozbey toyed with the ornate coffeepot. "Please tell me
that you somehow understand these secret truths I cannot
speak."

"Mehmet, just put a lid on it, okay? Don't even go there."

"But we are business partners. I must be sure you understand. I must be very clear from the beginning." Ozbey sighed
and lowered his voice. "I am a powerful secret master of the
modern world's deeper reality."

"I'm hip!" Starlitz insisted, wincing. "I'm so hip that you
didn't even have to tell me that you weren't saying that."

"You and I can both break the laws of nature at will. We

are great adepts with supernatural abilities that fools would find fantastic." He examined Starlitz with frank concern. "Am I saying too much?"

"Mehmetcik, that dervish crap moves a lot of product in your part of the world, but I'm in a global outfit, so I'm not in the market for it. You're a heavy operator with a lot of local connections. I know that, I respect that. That and a hand-shake, that oughta be enough for both of us. Let's leave the deeper reality under the rug where it belongs."

Ozbey seemed disappointed, but he was bearing up. "I see you came to my town of Istanbul to talk about the rug business. Yes? It's nothing but business with Leggy Starlitz. Very well. I am your host, I will be polite. Say no more."

Starlitz said nothing. The air was heavy with coffee and roses.

Ozbey reached deftly across the table and plucked up Starlitz's coffee cup. "Since I am your host, let me entertain you. We have an old tradition here in Istanbul. We can read a man's future in his coffee cup."

"Hey, I was drinking that," Starlitz protested.

"I'm very good at this," Ozbey insisted. He brandished the demitasse with an aggressive grin, ritually swirling the coffee grounds. "What is your future, Leggy Starlitz? Let us see."

"You don't want to try that with me," Starlitz told him.

"Don't tell me what I want," said Ozbey calmly. "Save that for teenage girls. I know very well what I want. I know it much better than you." Ozbey cradled the coffee cup in both his hands. Then he gazed inside it, with a careful squint.

The cup was empty. It was perfectly clean.

THE BLACK RUBBER PLATES OF THE LUGGAGE CONVEYOR track moved with eerie mechanical ease. Jet-lagged passengers appeared in silent clumps, awaiting their gear like the bored parishioners of some failing religion.

An apparition sidled silently past Starlitz. Floppy gray fabric hat, long translucent raincoat over bony shoulders, two camera cases and a folded tripod bag, a lumpy photographer's vest and multipocketed khaki trousers. The ensemble ghosted through the airport on a pair of high-ankled Adidas monkey boots.

Starlitz tossed aside his glossy copy of *Mixmag* and rose from his red plastic seat. "Hey, Wiesel."

Wiesel rotated his narrow head, his pale eyes like gimlets. The paparazzo's blank face swam into focus then, and it registered resigned distaste. "Leggy, what are you doing in Istanbul?"

"Is this Istanbul, man? All airports feel the same to me."

Wiesel shrugged uneasily. "Where are the girls?"

"The girls got a few days off. They're poolside in a secret hotel. Naked and covered with cocoa butter."

Wiesel's sallow face showed a flicker of reflexive interest, but it faded rapidly. "G-7 are yesterday."

"They're yesterday in London, man, I agree with you there. In the London scene, fuckin' tomorrow is yesterday. But spangled hose and lip gloss are the coming thing in Teheran."

Wiesel examined the passing luggage, feigning indifference. Starlitz, who knew better, watched him weakening.

Wiesel's eyes flicked up. "You mean to scam the mullahs, Leggy?"

"New regime in Iran, pal. Big window of opportunity there. I need your help again."

Wiesel detached one swollen camera bag from the shoulder of his flimsy raincoat and set it with care on the floor. "Give it a rest! You and your boss man have nothing left to work with. The gimmick's two years old. Fuck, they're not even a *band*. They can't sing. They can't dance. They lip-synch. To tapes."

Starlitz shrugged.

"They don't even have *names*," Wiesel insisted. "They're seven random birds you picked up with adverts."

Starlitz nodded. "All according to plan."

"You're gigging the arena circuit for chump change, in deepest, darkest Eastern Europe. There's just nothing there, lad. You can't make big stars out of nothing at all."

Starlitz sighed patiently. "Who needs big stars? Big stardom is poison. This is all about the *marketing concept*. The first pop group that won't sell music. The first pop group with an expiration date."

"Like I said, gimmicks."

"Lemme tell you about this upcoming Istanbul gig. It's the first leg of our big Islamic pop tour. The setup behind this one is a thing of genius."

Wiesel was visibly twitching. Celebrity bored him, but the lure of a well-planned hustle was more than Wiesel could withstand.

Then something caught Wiesel's gimlet eye, and an expression of relief flooded his face, giving it an almost human cast. He rotated smartly on his rubber heel.

A motorized wheelchair had arrived at the baggage claim. It bore a woman in an off-the-shoulder Lycra stretch dress. She wore a blond wig: a bubble-headed cut with a broad wing of bangs. She had big blue eyes, and enormous breasts, which rose from her torso with the taut inflated look of sports equipment.

The wheelchair eased to a buzzing halt. Its female occupant looked Starlitz up and down, taking in his lime-green linen suit, the diamond pinky ring, the Gucci shoes.

Slowly, she emitted a stream of smoke. "Friend of yours, Benny?"

"It's business, Princess." Anxious to please, Wiesel stiffened. "This is Leggy."

"Lech Starlitz." Starlitz cordially offered his hand. The woman switched hands with the cigarette, absently wiped ash into the glittering Lycra fabric on her meaty thigh, and gave Starlitz's fingers a damp, condescending squeeze.

"You can call me 'Diana,' " she told him. "Most people do."

"Is it dystrophy?" Starlitz asked her.

She smiled. "Nah."

"Multiple sclerosis?"

"Nope!"

"It couldn't be BSE."

"Aw, fuck no! I don't eat hamburgers, I'm a fuckin' dancer!"

"It's autoimmune syndrome," Wiesel offered. "She's allergic to herself." He jerked one thumb at the luggage track. "I got her CAT scans with us. I got her full NMR scans. You should see all my prints, Leggy. They're beauties."

The woman pointed one lacquered finger. "My bags, Benny. Go get the damn bags."

"Yes, Your Highness," Wiesel said. He sidled off through the crowd and began to wrestle with an extensive set of yellow hard-shelled cases.

"Lotta luggage," Starlitz remarked to the Princess.

"Yeah. We're moving. We're leaving London, we're off to play housie together. Me and the king of voyeurs there."

"Any idea where you're going, Your Highness?"

She puffed her cigarette, and looked up, squinting. "You ever been to Goa, Mr. Starlitz?"

"Goa's very happening," nodded Starlitz. "Got its own sound named after it."

She blinked. "What sound's that, then?"

"Well, it's the 'Goa Sound.' "

"Well, what *is* it?"

"There's a big trance-and-dance scene in Goa. A lotta techno action there."

The Princess just wasn't getting it.

"Techno, you know? I mean electronica."

No comprehension there at all.

"Music," Starlitz insisted. "Party tracks that people play off tapes and mixers. Sampling. Break-beat." Starlitz went up a final level. "In Goa they play a lot of disco."

She brightened. "Oh, yeah. Party music."

"Yeah. That's the big trendy pitch there in Goa, that's the story."

"Any strip clubs in Goa? That's in India, right? Do they do exotic dancing there? Any specialty impersonation acts?"

"Lotta nude beaches in Goa."

She sighed. "Friggin' hippie amateurs are always spoilin' my scene."

Wiesel pulled over one of the big yellow cases, lugging it two handed. The grainy plastic case was covered with duct tape and bungee cords, and its sides bulged ominously. "They have Ayurvedic medicine in Goa," he puffed. "Ayurveda, that's the herbal wisdom of the ages! It's real progressive!"

"Yeah, I've heard a lot about that Hindu herbal stuff," said Starlitz helpfully. "They use a lot of cow urine. Make real sure they sterilize those puncture needles." He held up two fingers, four inches apart.

Then Starlitz gazed down with fatherly concern into the wheelchair. "You know what you need, Di? For an autoimmune disorder you need a major detox. All natural. They got this woman's Turkish bathhouse in Edirne. All marble inside, all female staff. Medicated mudpacks. Special mineral water. Hasn't been a man inside that building in four hundred years. They staff the place with these Assyrian nurses out of the mountains of the Caucasus, where people live to be a hundred and twelve."

The Princess blinked. "Cor."

"It's all about the yogurt, you know? And the massage."

She had a last puff and dropped the smoldering butt near Wiesel's shoe. "Where did you say this was?"

"Nearby. Outside Istanbul. Of course, they're booked up years ahead. They're very strict Moslems, they don't do Christian women. You gotta be the Sultana Valide Roxana to book a room in that joint."

"We're booked for Goa," Wiesel insisted, loyally stomping the Princess's cig stub.

"Oy," the Princess protested, "I can go for Moslems! If they've got heaps of money, that is."

Starlitz gripped the bony shoulder of the paparazzo's flimsy raincoat. "Wiesel," he told him soberly, "you see that luggage conveyor track? There just might be an unmarked black valise waiting for you there. With twenty thousand dollars U.S. in it."

Wiesel and his Princess exchanged significant glances.

"But there isn't." Starlitz reached into his lime-green waistcoat pocket, and came out with a gold plastic rectangle. "Because cash is yesterday. Customs people are very down on cash now. So instead I brought you this handy Visa card. It's made out in your favorite name. With a twenty-thousand-dollar line of credit from an offshore bank in Turkish Cyprus."

Wiesel reached out reflexively, then restrained himself. "How do I know that's true?"

"You can call their toll-free number, pal. It's printed here on the back of the card. Cyprus is a Commonwealth country, so Cypriot bankers always speak great English. You can call the bank first thing, from the suite that I booked you at the Istanbul Pera Palace."

Wiesel grunted. "Christ."

"The Pera Palace is a way photogenic hotel, man. Built in 1892 for the Orient Express. All mahogany, Turkish tile, slanting light through the shutters, and Sidney Greenstreet's drinking arak in the bar. It's perfect for you, Wiesel. You're gonna love this assignment."

Wiesel produced a pair of reading glasses from his vest. He set to work on them with a patch of high-tech lens cloth. "What's the pitch, Leggy?"

"I've put the itinerary here on this diskette for your Palm Pilot." Leggy handed over a fresh square of data-soaked plastic. "But here's the executive briefing, man. You call your paparazzi contacts. And I don't mean the good ones. I mean the worst and scabbiest freelancers you know. Guys with no

brakes. Guys who bribe waiters and hide inside trash cans.
Guys who bust into rest rooms with shoulder cams. The loose
cannons of paparazzidom. You tell 'em the 'bloids are going
ape for the G-7 performance in Istanbul. They're paying top
dollar for pix of the girls."

Wiesel sighed. "Why would anybody pay for that?"

"Romantic rumors, man. We've built a whole set of hot
leaks, cut for national demographics. The French One is having it off with a soccer star who won the World Cup. The
American One's got a Republican congressman on the line."

"It's the usual, then."

"No, man, these are good rumors this time. We invested
some effort. The best part is that we actually *pay for the pictures.* See, we're not asking you to stiff anybody. You're actually
gonna buy all their photos! You give them their money, straight
across."

"Look, the tabloids won't run any of that crap! You
scammed them already, way too many times!"

Starlitz sighed patiently. "We're aiming for the *Turkish* media, man. The Turkish tabloids, the Turkish fashion rags, and
especially Turkish TV. They all ignore conventional Western
promotion. They're kind of stuck up about it. But when they
see your boys turning Istanbul upside down, they'll catch up
on our buzz in a hurry."

Starlitz lowered his voice. "We just want the girls to be
seen in the clothes. That's all we want. We want screen time
and column inches for the clothes and the shoes. We got a
buncha sweatshops gearing up in Anatolia, that used to do
Versace forgeries. They're gonna flood the Turkish market
with G-7 glitter crop-tops and platform sneakers. So we can
pay your foreign paparazzi top dollar, because that outlay is
gonna be maybe five, six percent of our revenue. Not to mention that we're laundering the works offshore in Turkish
Cyprus, so it's totally tax fucking free!"

Wiesel's eyes grew round as lens caps. "Damn."

"So here's your angle, man: you hire 'em, you deal with 'em, and you pay them off for us. You're my cutout, Wiesel. They never know about me, ever. So whether your boys kick you back a commission, that's your own business, I don't care about that, you are the boss there." Starlitz drew a breath. "So, you want in on this lig, or what?"

"Nobody ligs like you do, Leggy," Wiesel said. "But I don't need any business now. I'm settling down, see? I'm looking after her health. What about my wife?"

"We're not married," the Princess said hastily.

Wiesel winced. "We're formally engaged. Awright?"

Starlitz beamed at them. "You kids ever try a Turkish marriage? You can repudiate it just by saying, 'I divorce you,' three times in a row."

"Whoa," the Princess said, blue eyes gleaming. "That's something nice, that is."

Wiesel recognized defeat. Then he rallied himself. "So what about this Turkish health spa you were talking about?"

Starlitz offered a troubled frown. "Well—I sure would have to pull a lot of strings. . . ."

"Then you better do that, Leggy. You cut my Princess in on the action, or it's no deal."

"This isn't like you, Wiesel. You're twisting my arm here, man." Leggy glanced into the wheelchair. The byplay wasn't fooling the Princess any, but she looked rather pleased about it anyway. She was touched that Wiesel would take the trouble to bullshit her.

"Okay," Leggy said. "Have it your way, man. I can handle that. Princess Di goes first class, all the way down."

DRIFTING OVER THE TERRACE WALLS, THE CYPRIOT BREEZE carried a sensual reek of oleanders, seaweed, and badly tuned cars. Ozbey signed the chit for another round of margaritas for the boys.

Turgut Altimbasak's sprawling casino favored heavy plungers. The sprawling seaside establishment was especially attractive to swingers like Ozbey, moneyed gentlemen from Istanbul or Ankara, traveling with squads of armed retainers. The casino's Byzantine wings and high-rise floors could be sealed off like a card-sharp's Führerbunker.

Mehmet Ozbey's private thugs always clumped up at crucial business junctures. Drey and Halik and Aydan, their scarred mugs gleaming with sweat and booze, had never looked happier. The boss was in an expansive mood.

Ozbey gazed dramatically past the white masts clustered in the Girne harbor, past the old Venetian villas and the blue romantic hills, and into the lucid depths of the slightly discolored Mediterranean. His handsome face took on a visionary cast. "Our business deal is sure to prosper."

Starlitz propped one Guccied foot on a whitewashed plaster wall. "Absolutely. You got the big ticket, man." Now that he was back in air and daylight, Starlitz felt better. The dank interior of the casino, with its solid harem walls and distinct lack of clocks, had given Starlitz an oozy sensation of chronic liquidity. "You define reality," Starlitz pronounced. "You got the press in one pocket, and the cops in the other. Cops and the media, that's all the reality most people will ever need!"

Ozbey nodded. "We have kidnapped the spirit of the times! We are manufacturing reality!"

"Well, pop hits come and go quick, that's the beauty of pop. But the *money*, right? That money stays just as real as money ever is!"

"And money is never real inside a casino," Ozbey diagnosed. "Casinos are factories that make money less real."

"Exactly, man. Now you're getting it." Aydan and Halik and Drey couldn't follow English, but they were fascinated anyway. As Starlitz and Ozbey pontificated for them, they had the look of New Guinea tribesmen exposed to video porn. "You see," Starlitz said loudly, "casinos have a very hot product. Casinos sell people their own greed. 'Greed' is one of those way-hip meta-commodities, like 'access,' or 'click-through,' or 'bandwidth.' That's like this fabulous new-economy thing, and—" Starlitz stopped short, staring in astonishment.

Ozbey rose from his chair. "Here comes Gonca. Late, as usual." He spoke briefly in Turkish, and air-kissed the actress's roseate cheeks.

Gonca daintily adjusted Ozbey's white boutonniere. Then she offered Starlitz a paralyzing dark-eyed glance and emitted a bright contralto stream of lilting Turkish.

Ozbey offered his girlfriend a private briefing and then switched to English again. "Leggy, this is Miss Gonca Utz. She was Miss Turkish Cinema 1997."

"Charmed," said Starlitz. Miss Utz offered her hand. Starlitz took the risk of briefly gripping her perfectly lacquered fingertips. Then he had to sit down and exhale.

"Miss Utz has no English," said Ozbey.

"That's a pity."

"She has excellent French," Ozbey bargained. "She grew up on the Syrian border."

"*C'est triste,*" Starlitz said, "tough choice of imperialists there."

Gonca Utz lifted the gilded hem of her midnight-blue Saint-Laurent gown and did a slow and exquisite twirl. A group of stunned Bruneian oilmen at a nearby table burst into spontaneous applause. They subsided rapidly under the sudden feral glares of Drey, Halik, and Aydan. It was a very large casino, but it was a rather small terrace.

At a twitch of Ozbey's eyebrow one of his muscle guys hustled aside to give Miss Utz a chair. The actress did the chair the supreme favor of sitting in it. She began the elaborate ritual of producing a cigarette.

"Miss Utz was in one Italian coproduction," Ozbey said, leaning forward deftly with his platinum Zippo. "Her film role came with the beauty contest. But that film was domestic release only. Turkish cinema is no longer what it was, back in the glory days of Muhsin Ertugrul. Too many foreign cassettes, you see."

Starlitz adjusted his sunglasses and watched Miss Utz breathing smoke. Gonca Utz was a sleeping geyser of primal feminine charisma. The woman was all steam and seltzer-bubbles.

"She dances, right?" Starlitz said.

"Of course she dances."

"And she sings?"

"Like an angel."

"I can see where this is going, Mehmetcik." Starlitz leaned forward, frowning. "Your problem here is that you have very good taste. This woman is a natural. She's a true star. In any country with a functional film industry she would be huge. She's got way, way too much talent to be in a teenybopper pop act."

"She's young," Ozbey offered. "You need an Islamic G-7 girl, Leggy. To sell your concept in Teheran."

"Oh, yeah. I'm with that approach big-time. I'd love to have an Islamic G-7 girl. Hoofin' it up with the others in her spangled chador, man, I guarantee you the sparks would fucking fly. The thing is, she's got to be a *genuine fake,* just like the other G-7 girls. She's got to be a *random, everyday* Islamic girl. The kind of girl who could be *any* Islamic girl, if she took a few lessons and had a pro do her makeup."

"Not like a true star, you mean."

"Exactly, not like a star. But, see, the demographics of Islamic chicks are very badly surveyed. There's just no standard for the Islamic female consumer in the fifteen-to-twenty-one age bracket. We're talking the Mahgreb to Malaysia! That's at least a hundred million girls, in thirty-something nationalities, and a couple of dozen major language groups."

"But Gonca's so pretty," Ozbey said wistfully.

"I concur, man. She's fantastic."

"Why can't it matter that she's pretty?"

"Oh, she could matter all right. But you got the wrong scene for that. G-7's about marketing, it's absolutely not about mattering. You want to matter with a pop group, you are talking a different reality."

Despite his feigned indifference Ozbey was visibly vibrating with the urge to lunge for commercial daylight. "Tell me about this so-called reality. I need to know that. It's important."

Starlitz scratched his jaw. "Let me get you up to speed here, man. You wanna know who *matters* in Islamic pop music? Fuckin' rai musicians in Algeria, they matter. They've got a backbeat and electric guitars, they sing about sex and drugs. All the Algerian fundies want 'em dead, blind, and crippled. Cheb Khaled, for instance. You ever heard of Cheb Khaled?"

"No," said Ozbey thoughtfully, "I never have heard of this Khaled."

"Khaled matters big-time. He has to live in Paris, 'cause they burn his records back home. Cheba Fadela, she sang 'N'sel Fik,' right? Biggest rai hit ever recorded! She and her main squeeze are beatin' the streets in exile in New York now, looking for a Yankee record deal. And they're hoping they don't get what John Lennon got."

"I have very much heard of John Lennon," Ozbey said alertly. "Oh, yes, I remember him well. One man on the street, with a pistol."

"Lennon mattered. Lennon mattered even when he didn't want to matter anymore. See, there's *no expiration date* with mattering. That's the basic problem there."

"What if I *want* to matter? I have the money to matter. I have the business contacts too. With Gonca I have the talent. Maybe I would like to matter."

"Go ahead! Give it a try. But you're never gonna get there with *my* act, because we fold our tent for good on Y2K Day."

Ozbey smiled bitterly. "The number-one rule. Of course,

you have my word about your number-one rule." He lowered his voice. "But what can I do with my little friend? She's so pretty, and so ambitious."

Starlitz nerved himself and gazed at length upon Miss Gonca Utz. It was like staring into sunlight on water. "You want my professional advice there, Mehmetcik?"

"Yes, of course!" said Ozbey, leaning back. "As long as you're not telling me to give her up and go back to my wife."

"Television personality," Starlitz prescribed at last. "Turkish game-show hostess."

"Television?" Ozbey considered this proposal. "That's your answer?"

"Fuckin' A, man. Cinema is dyin' everywhere that can't afford digital special effects. So it's gotta be Turkish national TV, definitely. TV will overexpose her and burn her out, but TV is big stardom."

Ozbey nodded. "Hmmmm."

"And when she starts to lose her looks, go for elective office."

Ozbey brightened. "Politics?"

"Absolutely. After TV, that's the only media outlet big enough to hold her. Yeah, I mean run her for Turkish Parliament. Center-left party, very mildly progressive, a women's-issues scene, plenty of time on the stump, a lot of public baby-kissing. But with, you know, some hidden steely depths there. Kind of an Iron Lady riff. Know what I mean?"

"Yes. You mean Mrs. Tansu Çiller."

"Mrs. Tansu Çiller is not Turkey's prime minister by accident, you know."

"Yes, I know. I know very well about all of that." Enlightenment was visibly breaking over Ozbey. He was definitely with the program; he was moving it to the top of the wheel in his mental Rolodex. "I know Mrs. Çiller," he confided. "My Uncle the Minister and I, we had dinner with her, in Ankara, last month. And also her husband, Mr. Ozer Çiller: the prominent businessman, and party financier. Mr. Ozer Çiller is a very clever fellow."

"You're kidding. You know the prime minister?"

"We're all very good friends! We're very close! I spent two semesters at her alma mater in America. That's where I learned my American English."

Starlitz considered this revelation. It was explaining a lot to him. "You're an ace guy to know, Mehmetcik. I'm very pleased with these informal exchanges. This is leading us to a new world of expanded market potential and multicultural amity."

Ozbey spread his hands. "Business is good! G-7 will be big in Turkey. As big as you let me make it." He narrowed his eyes. "If you can deliver the seven girls. On time. Dressed in the proper merchandise. Ready to dance and sing."

"No problem, man. The girls love Cyprus, they are tanned, rested, and ready. I got all their roadies and trainers in town, they're rehearsing their little hearts out."

Ozbey gazed on Miss Utz with jaded Asiatic sentiment. "Don't tell me 'no problem,' because I don't believe it. Woman is always a problem for man, it is her nature. Seven girls! Ha! I have just two girls in my life, and I am a busy man."

Gonca erupted with a sudden petulant demand. Ozbey listened to her with a pious show of gallant attention. Then he turned to Starlitz again. "When will Gonca meet the French One?"

"Tonight," Starlitz promised, "in the casino. It's cool, man; the French One is okay. The French One's mom is a little off the wall, but the French One is good with her fans."

Gonca had grown impatient. It was simply not in her nature to wait in anybody's wings. "I gotta go, man," Starlitz said politely, rising and glancing at his faked Korean Rolex. "Gotta take a meeting tonight."

"Tonight? I booked a table at Niazi's."

"Sorry, man, can't make it. I gotta see a Russian about some hardware."

This remark touched Ozbey. His reaction was very much

as Starlitz had predicted. Despite his cosmopolitan airs, Ozbey considered himself a Turkish patriot of the very first order. In strict precedent Ozbey fiercely despised Greeks, Kurds, Armenians, Arabs, Iraqis, Serbs, Iranians, Jews, Circassians, and Croats. The Russians were also among Turkey's blood enemies, but unlike these other nationalities the Russians had never been a subject people in the Ottoman Empire. So Ozbey tempered his partisan disgust for Russians with a certain curiosity.

"You must have noticed all the Russian whores in this casino," Ozbey offered smoothly.

"You bet, those Natasha hookers are way hard to miss."

"Many Russians in the Turkish lands these days. Russia is Turkey's biggest trading partner. As my Uncle the Minister always likes to tell us."

Starlitz rose from his seat and nodded at Miss Utz. Miss Utz aimed, assembled, and fired a dazzling smile.

STARLITZ LEFT THE GROUNDS OF THE CASINO. HE STROLLED past a harborside café, with its scarred tables and cigarette-ad umbrellas. He carefully unchained his hired bicycle. Before reaching Turkish Cyprus, Starlitz hadn't been spending much time on bicycles. It was alarming how his spreading ass fell over both sides of the narrow seat.

Obvious as neon in his big green suit, Starlitz slowly pedaled the narrow streets of Girne. After five minutes he descended from the bike, left the street, and walked the bike down a flight of stairs. This allowed him to lose his Turkish tail without being impolite about it.

Ozbey had a lot of guys on his payroll. Ozbey had a lot of mouths to feed; Ozbey had to keep all his people occupied. It was natural for him to have Starlitz tailed. Starlitz was prepared to be understanding about this.

Starlitz had come to be enormously fond of Turkish Cyprus. The TRNC was truly his kind of place. The little pariah state was often described as "unspoiled," but this couldn't capture the full glory and wonder of its anomolous position in the world. Turkish Cyprus was not "unspoiled." It was *counter*spoiled; driven into limbo by twenty-five years of political impasse and frantic ethnic hatred. Its pygmy regime was formally unrecognized by any state but Turkey. The invisible hand of the global market couldn't get a proper grip in this thorny little locale.

The truth was visibly written all over the Cypriot landscape. For instance, the local ruins. The Turkish Republic of Northern Cyprus was one of the last spots in Europe where the Ancient Ruins © ® ™ were actual, fully authentic ancient ruins. These ancient ruins had never been lacquered over or tidied up. They had never become monuments or public attractions. Instead, they were horribly old and neglected things that had fallen apart. The tumbled walls and columns simply lay there in their wreckage: Greek, Roman, Arab, Crusader, Ottoman; whatever, whoever, whenever. Broken history, quietly soaking up dew and baking in the sun.

During rare moments alone Starlitz liked to sit inside the various ruins of Cyprus. It did him good to abandon the buzzing, frantic G-7 entourage and ease his increasing bulk on these old Cypriot stones. He took a strange tenuous pleasure in this, like pressing on an aching tooth. When he faded among those forgotten, weed-grown rocks, time simply ceased. There was no speed anymore, nothing going on, no vector of development. Inside these moments of freedom Starlitz could literally feel himself vanishing.

Cyprus had suffered an evil summer. The summer heat of 1999 had set new records worldwide, and there was still a bad drought on. The island's ancient aquifers, badly overtaxed, were failing day by day. The local vineyards were dusty and limp, the sheep pastures were brown and crisp. It didn't help that the local Greeks and Turks struggled valiantly to steal one another's share of the island's water table.

The strangest part of Cyprus was the island's twenty-five-year-old cease-fire wilderness. The frozen battlefront of the Green Line slashed completely across the island, over hill over dale, straight through the divided capital, from one end of Cyprus to the other. The no-man's-land—up to five miles across in spots—was lavishly lined with rusting land mines, corroding barbed wire, amateur trenches, and militia bunkers. The overgrown limbo was patrolled by UN blue-helmet troops, while rifle-toting Greek and Turkish draftees manned their rickety watchtowers.

Thanks to many illegal sewage dumps, the Green Line was very well watered. It thrived because it was freed of the cruel burden of humanity. It was an involuntary wilderness, a kind of postmodern Neolithic. But even the Green Line had suffered in the pitiless weather: the impromptu forest had caught fire on several occasions, blowing land mines like popcorn and shrouding the whole island in smoke.

The island's overlords, Greece and Turkey, engaged in constant proxy culture war over their dual minorities. The Greeks possessed the louder propaganda machine, but the embattled Turks were closer to the homeland, and seemed to feel the outrage more keenly. The Turks were more tormented, more extravagant.

During the evil summer some unsung genius in the Turkish environmental ministry had come up with a drought-rescue scheme. The Turks had created a model fleet of giant polyvinyl water balloons. These blimplike contraptions were towed to Turkish Cyprus by big Turkish tugs, out of the Turkish ports of Antalya and Hatay. Pumped tight with fresh water, the monster plastic bags rolled and steamed to Cyprus like sea-shouldering whales.

Local fire departments brought up their pump trucks, to add the water to the TRNC's municipal tanks. So the imperiled minority in Turkish Cyprus possessed the living gift of Turkish water. Majority Greek Cyprus had to make do with water rationing, angry radio broadcasts, and Russian-surplus air-defense missiles.

Naturally, there was a further wrinkle to the scheme. As it happened, the poppy-strewn area around Hatay could give the Golden Triangle a run for armed dope corruption. It hadn't taken ten minutes for the locals to grasp the profound opportunities involved in bulk submarine transport.

Starlitz, pedaling along peacefully past the outskirts of Girne, found the lucid Mediterranean twilight fading into luscious starry dark. At length Starlitz spotted a security blockade on a narrow beach road: bored Turkish paramilitary kids were checking ID. Starlitz dismounted and silently walked his bike past the roadblock. He then coasted down a sandy hillside to the beach. He carefully chained his bicycle to a concrete telephone pole, taking care to wrap the thick steel links through the frame and both the wheels.

Starlitz meandered downhill to the tire-torn sand of the beach. The nighted sand was crowded with old cars, rust spotted and duct taped. Their trunks yawned open, and their occupants were doing a brisk business, by the mellow glow of their trunk lights and dangling kerosene lamps. Charcoal glows rose here and there, where entrepreneurs were selling lamb kebabs. These smugglers were all men, middle-aged hustlers mostly, in the local uniform of baggy gray pants, checkered shirts, belly-hugging woollen vests, and little cloth caps. Many were carrying shoulder-slung shotguns, but there was very little menace to the scene. It was just business.

No one seemed surprised to see him. No one would arrive at a rendezvous of this sort without a good reason to do it.

Starlitz was searching for his contact, a Russian emigré named Pulat R. Khoklov.

He located Khoklov, not far from a loudly laboring tow truck. The big wrecker had its rear wheels jammed deep in the sand, fixed with big chocks of brick and driftwood. A taut steel cable strung far out to sea, humming with tension.

Pulat Khoklov was an Afghan war veteran, a former Soviet fighter pilot, now in his early forties. The Russian had made a halting effort to adapt to Cypriot conditions: he wore a black fisherman's cap, an open-weaved tourist shirt, shorts, and sandals. Khoklov was badly sunburned, and gaunt with illness. The braided rim of his hat showed pale wisps of hair, with the fluffy, damaged look of chemotherapy.

"How's life, ace?" said Starlitz in Russian. "Long time no see."

"Why are you dressed like this, Lekhi?" Khoklov said. He examined Starlitz's bright green suit. "You look like a Popsicle."

"It's good to see you, too, Pulat Romanevich." Starlitz gave the man a bear hug. There wasn't a lot left to him. The bones of the Russian's wasted rib cage were flexing like Teflon.

Khoklov smiled sourly and held Starlitz at arm's length. "You seem so fat and happy."

"I'm in the muzik biznis," Starlitz told him. "Not like the old days. I'm peaceful and civilized now."

Khoklov dropped his arms and lowered his voice. "Give me a cigarette?"

Starlitz patted his pockets and shrugged. "I quit, ace. I quit. I finally kicked the habit."

"Me, too, damn it." Khoklov sighed, and coughed a bit, painfully. "Well, you need to meet my sister's boy. He does a lot of my legwork these days."

They found Khoklov's nephew gnawing a spear of kebab, sipping a Fanta orange pop, and staring out to sea. The young Russian was wearing a Toronto Maple Leaf hockey jersey, and rave-kid jeans, with pant legs so enormous that they could have fit a Kenyan bull elephant. Khoklov's nephew sported a patchy goatee and short blond dreadlocks. His drug-addled eyes were like two dinner plates.

"Viktor, this is Mr. Starlits," Khoklov said patiently. "Lekhi Starlits is an international financier and musical impresario."

The kid staggered to his sneakered feet and knocked sand from his ass. *"Da,"* he remarked. Viktor looked all of seventeen. He offered Starlitz the fixed, ingratiating grin of a heavy dosage of Ecstasy.

"This is my nephew, Viktor Mikhailovich Bilibin," said Khoklov. "He's from Leningrad."

"Petersburg," Viktor corrected pleasantly.

"We've been on the Baltic circuit together," Khoklov said. "Finland, Germany, the Kaliningrad enclave . . . I had a little banking start-up in Kaliningrad, much like the one we tried together in the Alands. Vinogradov was backing my scheme. You know of him, Vinogradov? One of the legendary Seven Bankers."

Starlitz nodded. "The Seven Gnomes of Moscow, huh? You sure can pick 'em, ace."

"But I wasn't feeling well. And then came the big Russian market crash. Vinogradov washed out, the Gnome went down with all hands." Khoklov shrugged his emaciated shoulders. "The south, the warm and kindly Mediterranean . . . Cyprus is a better place for my health."

"I heard you'd been killing some time up in the former Yugoslavia," said Starlitz.

Khoklov scowled. "Yes, I was there."

Starlitz nodded. "I kept meaning to go up to Yugo-land. Wanted to make that scene all through the nineties. Never could quite make the proper opportunity."

"You don't want to go there," said Khoklov, his face grim. "Trust me on that assessment."

"It's fun there," offered Viktor suddenly in English. "The son of Milosevic owns the biggest disco in the Balkans! Marko Milosevic is a very hip fellow. He's like you, Mr. Starlits, the noted musical impresario."

"You've got pretty good English, kid," said Starlitz indulgently. "That's good to hear, because that's good for biznis."

"Viktor's my English translator," said Khoklov. "He grew up

with Radio Free Europe. And many pirated punk and rave cassettes." Khoklov grunted. "But in Petersburg the Tambovskaya gang set fire to Viktor's kiosk. So it's not healthy for Viktor in Russia now either. So now my nephew and I are a team. We are international biznis consultants. Engaged in much romantic travel in exotic vacation spots."

They scuffed casually back toward the laboring tow truck, with Viktor trailing cheerfully and gnawing his greasy kebab.

"I got a biznis pitch for you, ace," said Starlitz. "It's pretty heavy duty. You want to hear about this?"

Khoklov scowled. "I've known you for a long time, Starlits! Ever since Azerbaijan. Also, that banking debacle in the Aland Islands . . . I don't think I've ever profited by knowing you." Khoklov sighed, his bony shoulders rising and falling in his cheap tourist shirt. "When I first met you, I was flying MiGs out of Kabul air base. Then I was a happy man. I was young then, I was a warrior for socialism. Those were the happiest days of my life! It's all been downhill since those days."

Starlitz frowned. "Do you want to bitch about your lousy fate, or do you want to hear my proposal?"

"Now I'm a lonely exile," Khoklov continued, ignoring him. "The maphiya sons of bitches are eating the corpse of Russia. They shoot the mayors in the street. They poison the biznizmen. They ruined every one of the banks. Yeltsin is drunk and he's dying. The Russian army eats dog food! Russian soldiers are starving to death in their barracks!"

Starlitz reached into his jacket, produced a fat cash clip, and crisply removed five American hundred-dollar bills. "Here," he suggested. "Shut up."

Khoklov peered at the bills. "So, these are the new American hundreds? The ones they can't forge yet?"

"Yep."

"Okay." Khoklov pocketed the cash.

"Give me some," Viktor said, skipping alertly forward.

"Later, kid." The sound of the tow truck changed suddenly,

from a grumble to a high-pitched whine. The truck's crew broke out in excited Turkish. They gunned their engine, with big blue gusts of combustion.

A lively crowd gathered at the waterline, carrying lanterns and longshoreman's hooks.

"This must be our bag," Starlitz remarked.

"Viktor," Khoklov snapped, "wait. Watch out for these Turks, boy; Turks carry big sharp knives."

"It's beautiful out here," Viktor protested, eager to rush forward with the jostling crowd. "What a beautiful night! Look at all the stars."

"We're among Moslems here, boy. Pay attention."

Viktor glanced at Starlitz, with an apologetic chemical grin. "My uncle is old-fashioned," he explained. "He's a patriot."

"I'm new at this myself," Starlitz said. "How do we collect our merchandise in a setup like this?"

"You'd be surprised how neatly they run these things," shrugged Khoklov. "This is the submarine arm of the heroin network. These heroin people have bought their own bus lines now, they own their own truck lines. . . . There are huge new drug maphiyas in Azerbaijan, Tajikistan, Turkestan. . . . There's nothing left to the old borders now. The heroin people are very efficient, very free market. They even have postal codes."

Men with long iron hawsers splashed into the surf. It had grown quite dark. Yo-ho-ho-ing in a concerted muscular effort, the Cypriot smugglers slowly rolled and tugged their giant water balloon onto the beach. In the patchy lantern lights the gleaming, deflated bladder resembled nothing so much as a giant used condom.

Starlitz and his two companions crept up for a closer look as the smugglers broke into their shipment. The giant bladder had a waterproof interior sac of some kind, a big plastic cyst sewn into it. Armed men with automatic rifles appeared, to oversee the divvying up of the smuggled goods. The riflemen were escorting a video cameraman.

"Hey!" Starlitz said, recoiling as if stung. "What's with the videocam? I don't like that."

"You don't want to fuck with the heroin postmen," Khoklov advised. "The camera's good for biznis. The people respect a security camera. It calms them down." Khoklov unbuttoned his shirt. A large bandage was taped to his prominent ribs. He dug inside the bandage with one bony finger and produced a cardboard claim chit. "Here you go, my boy."

Viktor looked at the ticket numbly. Viktor was wrapped in an Ecstasy rush moment, when the user feels quite superb but has lost all concept of initiative.

Khoklov scowled. "Don't drop that claim check! And don't drop the package either. Go on down there now, hurry. Try to be careful."

Viktor scampered down the beach.

"He's better when he's high on the drugs," Khoklov said in frank despair. "He's happier. When the boy gets all depressed . . . Well, you don't want to see Viktor depressed. Then he gets all poetic."

"Kids." Starlitz grunted. He put his head in his hands.

The local syndicate had disemboweled their bladder now, and they were dragging the shipment into the swarming light of handheld lamps. Starlitz could smell the unholy weight of the packaged white powder: the bone-warping gravity of smack. The almighty presence of the world's most fiercely sought commodity. Cordite for the weltanschauung. Whole kilograms of fiercely concentrated damage. Reality had a new lacquer on it suddenly: the cold blue shimmer of junk sickness. The consumer God of Pain and Fear from the red-hot spoon, scourge of and from the century's boards, syndicates and governments, filthy deals consummated in a million lavatories, the needle people the insect people the vegetable people, hi-fi junk note metal fixes on a twentieth-century nod-out. . . .

Khoklov looked at Starlitz in surprised concern. "You understand about children, eh, Lekhi? You have a child of your own." Khoklov was struggling to achieve some sense of human engagement. "How is she? Tell me, how is your little girl?"

"I have no idea," Starlitz said, lifting his sick head with an effort. "I don't hear much lately, out of Mom One and Mom Two. It's kind of a bad scene there, over in New Age Lesbian Land."

"I'm sorry to hear that." Khoklov drew a deep breath and winced. "That's a shame for you. Life is hard."

"Well, there's always some kind of trouble, ace. Only people out of time have no troubles. But, hell, life doesn't have to be so hard." Gathering strength, Starlitz straightened. "Because I've got a major revenue stream with backing at the highest levels of the Turkish government! It's taken me three years to develop this thing, but it's the sweetest scam I've ever pulled. I'm living large, pal. I'm so rich right now, it's almost legal."

Khoklov was astonished. "You're telling me you're *rich*, Lekhi?"

"Yeah, that's the story line, man. I got a full-time accountant and thirty employees."

Khoklov's threadbare eyebrows buckled on his sunburnt forehead. "That's interesting news. I hadn't expected that from you."

"I'll tell you all about it. See, I finally wised up. We had it all wrong in the past. You don't make a big commercial success by engaging in all kinds of underground intrigue and taking big brave risks."

"No?"

"No! You don't even *want* to be the cool guy in on the heavy spy action. That's all for kids and suckers! You don't want to be exciting. You don't want to be a man of mystery or a front-line hero. You just *make people want things*, and then you *give them what they want*. That's the secret, man. That's the secret of success."

"What are you talking about?"

"It's as simple as that, ace. You create demand, and you supply it. Then people give you a truckload of money, and they're proud and happy to do it. They love you for it. They want you to have a car, and a house, and a girl. They want you to be on the city council, they want you to be a congressman. They'll powder your ass and publicly kiss it. It's amazing."

"So you became a big commercial success?"

"Exactly, man. I'm a hit maker."

Khoklov considered this. "I don't trust the Turks. I don't like Moslems, and I never have, and I never, ever will."

Starlitz nodded helpfully. "I don't trust anybody either. That's why I've got a job here for you, Pulat Romanevich. Distrust. That's your angle, flyboy."

"So it's a security job?" Khoklov winced. "Lekhi, I can't do any muscle work. I have one lung left."

"So did Doc Holliday. This is not about muscle. It's about nerve."

"Who is this Doctor Holliday? Is he a cancer specialist?"

Starlitz shook his head. "Look, I know you're not the guy you once were, when you were flying hashish out of Kabul for the nomenklatura. But I'm not asking you for any supersonic airstrikes here. This is a very simple gig. It's all about seven girls who sing and dance. I just need a street-smart guy who can watch my back, while I'm taking these Turks for some cash. And I'm taking the Turks for a reasonable cut of the gross. So it's not something that the Turks need or want to get all upset about."

Khoklov thought it over. "There's a lot of money in this?"

"Enough. And it's tax free. I need you to do two things for me, ace. Use your instincts, and look like you're willing to kill some people. I know that you have instincts. And you *are* willing to kill some people, so this should all work out just dandy."

Viktor now returned with a large white carton, neatly wrapped in waterproof duct tape. It had a bar-coded tracking tag and a paste-on address label in Cyrillic, Turkish, and Arabic.

"You got a pocketknife?" Starlitz asked Khoklov.

Viktor groped down the leg of his enormous jeans and produced an eight-inch steel pigsticker with its handle wrapped in string. With clumsy enthusiasm he chopped and slashed his way through the watertight wrappings.

Inside the wrapping was a flip-top Soviet ammo case. The metal case was lavishly stuffed with finely shredded Cyrillic newspaper. Viktor dug in with abandon, gleefully scattering packing-trash across the beach. He finally produced a large glass bulb.

"You know vacuum tubes, kid?" Starlitz said.

"Sure," nodded Viktor. "I used to deejay at 'Fish Fabrique' in Petersburg. I know all about tube amps and tube mikes."

"Swell. So are those babies true-blue, sixties-vintage, Soviet 'Svetlana Five eighty-ones'?"

Viktor shrugged. "It's too dark to read the labels."

"They're military vacuum tubes, all right," Khoklov assured him earnestly. "Straight from the tracking computers in Magnitogorsk. They sell everything out of the missile sites now, the chips, the connectors, they sell everything they can steal. They cannibalized all the ballistic routers." Khoklov coughed. "If we want to nuke New York, we'll ship the warheads over in a rental truck."

Viktor looked up. "I count nine of them. We said ten, but nine is close enough. So where's our money?"

"Not so fast, Vik. I gotta make sure all this rough handling hasn't fucked up those delicate diodes and triodes. Where you guys staying?"

The two Russians exchanged glances. "You could call it a beach house," Khoklov offered feebly.

"If you're on the G-7 payroll, you'll be in the Meridien Casino in Girne."

"We could live in a five-star casino," Khoklov said. Viktor shrugged and slapped the case shut.

"Consider yourselves hired." Starlitz looked at them. "Now listen. There's one crucial G-7 rule. I take that back. For you two guys there's *two* crucial rules. Number one is that the whole enterprise shuts down before New Year's Day 2000. Absolutely, no exceptions. Rule number two is no hard liquor before seven P.M. You guys got any problem with those rules?"

"Yes," said Viktor.

"No," said Khoklov. "He meant no."

"You guys got a car?"

"We hitchhiked," Viktor said artlessly.

Starlitz loosened his tie and scratched his neck. "Well, let's see if we can pay off some local to sneak us past the militia. And for Christ's sake, don't drop that case."

G-7 SPECIALIZED IN PROMOTIONAL STUNTS,
since they never bothered to sell their music.
Six hundred people were attending G-7's Cyprus farewell bash. The casino mogul Turgut
Altimbasak was a lavish host. Tonight Altimbasak was laying it on with a wheelbarrow and
trowel. Most of the guests were young, and
new to the ancient temptations of casinos.
Leggy had seen to it that the band received a
tidy cut of the night's slot and roulette action.

Altimbasak's favorite high rollers all had
gilded invitations to the bash. These cheerful
losers were mostly Lebanese and Gulf Arabs.
At any public appearance by a glitzy Western
girl-group, these playboys could be counted on
to hoot and chew the carpet, with all the eye-
popping gawk of Tex Avery cartoon wolves.

At the carpeted edge of the glittering ball-
room lurked a damp cluster of Turkish Cypriot
party apparatchiks. They were all political
clients of Ozbey's uncle, Lefkosa ward heelers

in glasses, mustaches, polished shoes, and cheap suits, attempting with mixed success to get down and boogie. The Turkish Cypriot press had also turned out in force. Like journalists anywhere, they were cordially ignoring the main attraction and methodically filling their pockets with hors d'oeuvres.

Kiddie toy store people wandered along the flocked velvet walls, enchanted by the splendid ranks of beeping, blinking poker slots. Clothing retailers from the local bazaars had also succumbed to the G-7 lure. A couple of Turkish radio DJs had flown over from Istanbul to cover the scene, live.

The neon bar was heavily clustered with hard-drinking Finns and Danes from the UN peacekeeping contingent. Amid the crowd of muftied blue-berets, teenage contest-winners were sneaking free brandy sours. These underage girls were the core G-7 demographic. It was the pink pocketbook of their generation that was basically supporting all this hustle. The girls looked suitably impressed and disoriented.

A cluster of Eurotrash rave kids had sneaked past the casino security. These tattered, sunburnt youngsters were dominating the dance floor, since they had all the best Ibiza party moves. They gorged themselves on Lucozade and chopped squid, between bouts of energetic writhing.

The legendary G-7 girls were, of course, attending the event by stark necessity. The American, British, French, German, Italian, Japanese, and Canadian Ones were painstakingly tarted up in their trademark spandex-and-cleavage national costumes. As they'd done in a hundred towns before, the G-7 girls were gamely mugging, vamping, and pawing one another, their antics drenched by flashbulbs.

The girls were the formal focus of attention, but they were just the buxom front-women, a kind of glitter-clad visible iceberg for the dark looming bulk of the G-7 enterprise. The act's hard-bitten working staff included a dozen G-7 roadies, a sound man, a voice coach, two choreographers, the makeup crew, and a gaggle of lighting guys. The seven girls themselves further supported a hopping flea circus of personal assistants, suck-up cronies, stage moms, and boyfriends.

The true linchpin of the G-7 crew, however, was Nick the G-7 Accountant.

Nick the G-7 Accountant commanded the full personal attention of Starlitz, because Nick was signing the checks. The girls and the road crew were expendable commodities, but Nick possessed a core skill-set and was hard to replace. Nick was a thirty-two-year-old London banking whiz who had run into a dire spot of trouble in the Bangkok derivatives market. Nick was very gifted financially. He was seriously overqualified for the cheesy business affairs of a dodgy midlist girl-group. But G-7 was favored with Nick's exclusive services anyway, because Nick faced swift arrest for embezzlement if he ever set foot in any locale with a hotline to Scotland Yard.

Starlitz was holding court behind a long banquet table draped in red linen, where cut-glass platters the size of roulette wheels held generous heaps of dolmas and pastry rolls. Starlitz spotted Nick the G-7 Accountant as Nick emerged unsteadily from the men's room.

Starlitz beckoned him over. "So, Nick, how's the nut hanging?"

Nick wiped his cocaine-crusted nose and sipped his Italian spumante. "Well, our funds look very sound, as long as we don't export them off this island."

"Come closer, Nick, I can't fuckin' hear you. Sit down over here, man. Eat something."

Liam the G-7 Soundman was violently pounding a medley into the crowd. Over three years of steady touring the act had compiled an extensive signature playlist. Tonight Liam was spooling the G-7 catalog through a full set of his specialty remixes: trance, trip-hop, Balearic, jump-up, Chicago house, hard-step, speed garage, and various other species of the digital-disco jungle.

Though their music was not for sale, G-7's mixes were

rather well known on white-label vinyl twelve inches, East European pirate cassettes, and MP3 pirate audio Websites. G-7's sampled sonic product was infested with other people's cool, stolen break-beats; it had more catchy hooks than the barbed wire around Verdun. The best-known G-7 hit worldwide, which Liam was pitilessly pumping into the crowd at the moment, was the anthemic "Do As I Say (Not As I Do)."

Tonight's G-7 playlist also included the insistent "Speak My Language." The upbeat "Free to Be (Just Like Me)." The pulse-pounding "We've Got the Power," and the ominous, techno-heavy "Remote Control." The girlishly assertive "It's the Only Way to Live" had won many converts worldwide in the eight-to-twelve age bracket. G-7's showstopping encore, a regional hit from Taiwan to Slovakia, was "Shut Up and Dance." (The forthcoming G-7 effort, destined for their Teheran debut, was a crossover Iranian folk/calypso number called "Hey, Mr. Taliban, Tally Me Banana.")

"Eat some baklava, Nick. Try some of this walnut chicken." Starlitz forced a fork into the accountant's jittery hand. "Any more trouble shipping the boss's cut to Hawaii?"

"Yes, that's very troublesome!" shouted Nick politely. "The shell companies, no problem! Fund transfers to and from Istanbul, no problem! Tax avoidance, no problem!" Nick helped himself to a grape-leaf dolma. "Large sums of Euroyen from the Akdeniz Bankasi to a Japanese bank branch in Hawaii, yes, that is a definite challenge!"

Starlitz grew intent. "We need you to handle that, Nick."

"The locals don't like it!" Nick objected. "I don't like it either!" Enlivened by the excellent dolma, Nick leaned forward to spear an aubergine in peppered olive oil. "Japanese banks are dreadful this year! They're held together with sticking plasters! They have coppers coming through the front doors and VPs flying out windows!"

"All the more reason that the boss needs ready money. Screw anybody you have to, Nick, screw the Turks, screw the girls, screw the road crew, but don't ever screw Makoto. I want Makoto fat and happy, man, I want him in his aloha shirt puffing Maui Wowie."

Nick scowled. "Makoto's a bleedin' rock musician. He never checks his books, he can't even read them! We could take Makoto for anything we want! He'd never know, and he doesn't even care!"

"Nick, that's a great wideboy's analysis there, and I agree with you totally. I love you for that, Nick; I'm glad we have a relationship here. You're a pro; you're the tops. Just one thing." Starlitz plucked the fork from Nick's hand. "You do what I fuckin' tell you, or you'll be eating off a plastic tray in Wormwood Scrubs."

Nick laughed nervously. "Look, Leggy, I have it under control, okay? Istanbul will work out for us! Even Iran looks all right! It's all in line, no problem!"

Starlitz nodded tautly. He left Nick and worked his way through the party toward Liam's mixing station.

Starlitz plowed through a crowd of young, sweating, half-deafened Cypriots. These kids had the dazed, rootless, half-breed, malleable look of core G-7 fans. Half the population of Turkish Cyprus lived in London. The children of exile had one leg perched on each island; they were teenagers who were uniformly surly and unhappy anywhere in the world. The little hybrid kids were bopping like maniacs, gamely struggling to follow a global beat.

Liam the G-7 Soundman lurked in the shadows behind his massive blinking stacks and keyboards. Liam was a fat, balding musician in a backward baseball cap and a dashiki, with a Players A smoldering in his yellowed fangs.

Starlitz picked up a padded headphone-and-mike rig and plugged in to Liam's system, so that they could talk inside the almighty din.

"How's the new hardware, Liam?"

Liam turned and grinned at him. "Can't you feel that,

man?" Liam patted his bulky gut, which was visibly shaking with the bass track.

"I'm tone deaf," Starlitz reminded him. "Tell me about the vacuum tubes."

Liam flicked switches and turned down their headphone treble to a muted squeak. "Legs, for two years I've been limpin' along with friggin' Mullards and Tung-Sols! I'll never use that shit again! Listen to the rich, brilliant spank off these Russki missile tubes! They got big fat midrange furriness, and a big girthy magic down in the low ends!" Liam knocked the side of his skull with his nicotine-stained knuckles. "The top end still sounds a bit thin, but that's because they haven't burnt in proper yet!"

"So the tubes are okay?"

"They're brill!" Liam gurgled. "I put one tube up for auction, on-line. Just to see what the pros would do for it, eh? Latest bid is five thousand!"

Starlitz raised his thick brows. "Five thousand bucks for a friggin' vacuum tube? Jesus, I'm in the wrong business."

Liam grinned hugely. "Five thousand *pounds,* boss! Yankees don't know from tubes!"

Starlitz offered a hearty thumbs-up. He plugged out, submerging himself in the racket again. Liam was useful. Liam was predictable. Once upon a time Liam had toured four continents, lugging his guitar as a Tantric monk of British psychedelic blues. But Liam had survived the sixties; Liam was past the fame, long past the groupies, he had even survived the awesome Niagara of drugs and booze. Liam had fully recovered from rock 'n' roll, except for one fatal addiction: his equipment jones. Being a career musician, Liam didn't require a salary, a roof, dental care, or health insurance. But he couldn't face himself without an exclusive kit.

Liam owned a lacquered 1957 hollow-bodied Gibson in an exclusive run of twenty-five. He had bass strings made in total darkness by blind Portuguese gypsies. He owned Turkish cymbals made in a five-thousand-year-old Bronze Age foundry. Liam's G-7 road kit included a cherry Roland 303, a vintage Mellotron, even an Optigan. Liam was getting his own way in the service of G-7. Liam was the picture of fulfillment.

The time had come for a check on the girls. Leggy did not deal with the G-7 girls personally. He recognized this as unprofessional. For the artistes "Leggy the G-7 Manager" had to be a remote, mystifying figure, a creature of high-level deals and cryptic Masonic handshakes. Leggy would look in on the girls periodically, to distribute knickknacks and petty cash. He left the day-to-day discipline to the middle layer of G-7 management: the G-7 voice coach, the two G-7 choreographers, and especially the group's chaperone.

Tamara the G-7 Chaperone had joined the team from Los Angeles. She had skills and a personal background that were hard to match. Tamara had first become an Angeleno way back in 1990, after fleeing in abject terror from Soviet Azerbaijan, where the collapse of her husband's Communist regime had made her a nonperson. A courageous emigrant in search of freedom and a better life, Tamara had arrived from the long shadows of the Kremlin onto the bright neon streets of Hollywood, alone and friendless, with no resources other than her Swiss bank account, a small valise crammed with gold bars, and three prime kilos of Afghani hashish. Despite these disadvantages Tamara had gamely worked her way up through the Armenian California mafia of gasoline pirates and chop shops. She'd established a thriving used-car business in Brentwood Heights. Finally, with her English fully polished and her seams straight, Tamara had infiltrated the glamorous world of "Irangeles."

Los Angeles, California, was the entertainment capital of the Islamic Republic of Iran. Once upon a time, in the distant royal 1970s, Iran had possessed a Westernized pop culture rather similar to Turkey's. Iran had nightclub music on vinyl, punch-'em-up black-and-white action adventure movies, belly dancing on TV, quavering male heartthrob pop singers, and so forth. This pop scene had all been scraped painfully off the face of the country and flung overseas by Khomeini. The Ayatollah had installed a fifteen-year pop-music regimen, exclusively consisting of martial songs and folk hymns.

However, Iran's numerous exiles still required something to play on the stereo and watch on TV. There were a million Iranian emigrés, scattered all over the planet. Germany, Turkey, Britain, and Sweden all had extensive communities, but Los Angeles boasted an Iranian contingent that was eighty thousand strong. So the Iranian entertainment biz had grown and flourished beneath the Great Satan's palm trees, attracted there inevitably, not by creative freedom, of course, but by Hollywood's unrivaled recording and distributing infrastructure.

With the passage of the years and a slow thaw back in Mullahdom, Iranian pop was seething back into the homeland, its tendrils weaving a vigorous smuggling network through the Arab Gulf States. After twenty bitter years of Yankee exile, Iranian pop was lean, mean, and beautifully produced, with big digital sound studios and genuine Hollywood set design. Los Angeles talent such as Dariush and Khashaiar Etemadi were hot property in every Teheran bazaar. If not for the fact that their work was pirated (for the Islamic regime brooked no royalty arrangements), these guys would have been the Ratpack.

Mrs. Tamara Dinsmore (it had been a green-card marriage, but Tamara was a stickler for the niceties) had become a major fixer in the Irangeles pop scene. Tamara was a natural for the work of Hollywood, since she had once been married to the Azerbaijani Communist party chairman. Tamara had gamely undergone the obligatory L.A. tucks and face-lifts, and wore tall clacking heels and an Armani suit. Once a woman of rare, exotic beauty, Tamara was in midlife now, rather past mere exoticism and well on her way to the bizarre.

Leggy found Tamara giving a brisk dressing-down to the German One. Though the German One somehow attracted scoldings from everyone around her, the German One was basically all right. She was trustworthy, clean, and obedient. The German One was G-7's originally installed German. Nothing if not persistent, she had lasted out three entire grueling years.

Leggy cherished the German One. He took the trouble to stay up to speed with all her various loony flirtations. He was best acquainted with her French self-declared fiancé, a minor-league Belmondo type who showed up every bank holiday with chocolate, champagne, and a sports car. The German One was always coolly polite and considerate to her French beau, but tattered, worthless stage-door Johnnies were the guys who infallibly won her ditzy little Love Parade heart. Sensing a soft touch, these ex–Warsaw Pact hustlers tracked the German One from gig to gig, sending her long ardent faxes in obscure local languages with acutes and circumflexes, and begging her for expedient loans. The German One had given her girlish all to the big blustery blond Polish kid. She'd fallen under the intellectual spell of the mild and acerbic little Czech kid. Worst of all was the crazed, pistol-toting Serbian kid, who had gotten her into big trouble.

Now the German One was meekly sniffling under Tamara's dressing-down. It had everything to do with some Turk.

Leggy patted the German One's dirndled shoulder. "How's life treating you, German One?"

"I love him." She sniffled.

"I see. And what does your mom say about that?"

"Mamma hates him!"

"Well, see, that's your story all over. Nothing new there." He turned to Tamara. "How's she holding up?"

"I guess she's all right," shrugged Tamara, "she's just young and stupid."

"Come on, German One," Leggy coaxed. "We're depending on you to pull us through. You're our rock, girl. You're our locomotive! Nobody holds your past problems against you anymore! You're all grown up and responsible now! You're as sound as the mark! You've become our Sensible One."

The German One wiped her eyes, disturbing thirty dollars' worth of layered gloss, mascara, and metallic dust. "You think so?" she said, touched.

"Absolutely, babe."

She scowled. "I'm all right. But the American One's acting like a stupid bitch!"

"Not again," Leggy said.

The German One stamped her dainty leather boot. "She's high on coke and she owes me a lot of money, Leggy!"

"I'll straighten that out for you, German One. Chin up! Shoulders back! Big smile! I need a word with Frau Dinsmore here." Starlitz took Tamara aside.

"It's true. The American One is impossible," Tamara hissed.

Leggy considered this. It was bad news. "How many American Ones does this make for us now?"

"This is your sixth American One, you big fool! Why can't you get us an American One who can do the job? Do something right for a change! Try something different!"

Leggy was perturbed. Despite his best, repeated efforts, he somehow had never been able to get an American One to fully click with the group. Maybe it was the fact that America was basically nine different cultural regions. Big continental empires always had weird demographics. "How bad is she?"

"She is totally terrible! The American One is sloppy, rebellious, lazy, and disrespectful!"

"Oh, well."

"And she believes her own press releases."

Leggy was startled. "Christ, that's serious!"

"I'm sick of your stupid American One! It's time for you to

do something! We have a big event coming in Istanbul, and she's dragging all the other girls down."

"Tamara, I'll look after that problem. There's gotta be some kind of workaround there. Cheer up. I've got a big new development in G-7 backstage personnel."

Tamara looked skeptical.

"This is gonna be a big personal surprise for you." Starlitz offered Tamara a friendly leer. "Does the name 'Pulat Romanevich Khoklov' ring a bell?"

Tamara considered this, her tight face bleak. " 'Khoklov'? Is that a Russian name?"

"Of course it's a Russian name! I'm talking about Pulat Khoklov, the romantic war hero. The flying ace! He used to fly Ilyushin-14s out of Kabul."

Tamara was skeptical. "Why are you telling me about some pilot?"

"He's not *some* pilot, Tamara, he's *your* pilot! Khoklov used to work for you and your husband! He flew contraband into Azerbaijan, during the war! He's your kind of guy, babe!"

"Leggy, I have plenty of men already. I have too many men. I don't need your 'my kind of guy babe.' "

"But you and Khoklov were a hot item! He fell for you like a ton of smack! Last time you saw Pulat Romanevich, you were humping him in the back of a bus!"

Tamara's taut face grew stiff. "I don't like that kind of language!"

Starlitz was pained. "Look, Tamara, I wouldn't make this up—I was *there in the bus with both of you.* Think back! Nagorno-Karabakh in the eighties, remember? A handsome, charming Russian guy! White silk ascot and a cool battle jacket full of medals!"

"I never think back." Tamara's voice was wintry. "Those days are dead. I never think about that place anymore."

"But he's here, Tamara. Khoklov is here in Cyprus."

Now Tamara was nearing panic. "There's a Russian here?

There's a Russian in this casino? Someone who knew me? Someone who could talk about me?" She stared at Starlitz, unable to conceal her terror. "Did you tell him about me?"

Starlitz lowered his voice. This wasn't working out the way he'd hoped. "No, Tamara. I didn't get around to telling Khoklov about you. Khoklov doesn't know."

"You're lying," she concluded in anguish. "Of course you told the Russian about me. Now some Russian is here to chase me, with his big Russian tongue hanging out. Oh, my God!" She put her hand to her forehead. "Men are so stupid!"

The extent of his misstep was now clear to Starlitz. The scattered, decentered entity that was Tamara Dinsmore simply couldn't assemble a cogent narrative. There was no continuity in Tamara's late-twentieth-century film-script. No rewind button in there.

"The Russian doesn't know about you," Starlitz promised quietly. "I don't have to tell him a thing."

"Khoklov is here in the casino, yes? Where is he?" She began to gaze around in agitation. "*What* is he? He must be Russian Maphiya by now. . . ."

"Look, Tamara, I can handle all that, okay? Relax. You're a Yankee businesswoman now, you're Mrs. Dinsmore from Los Angeles. Pulat Khoklov is this washed-up gun from Petersburg who's running around on one lung. Pay no attention to him. He's not even in your universe. This thing you once had with Khoklov, it's gone, it's not even of this world anymore. It's yesterday. No one cares, no one's counting."

Tamara wasn't mollified. "Why do *you* still remember?" she demanded shrilly. Her doelike eyes beneath their eyelid tucks were full of obscure pain. "Why do you remember all of that old time and that old world? Why do you lick your lips like that, why do you roll your eyes, why do you laugh at me? I hate you."

Starlitz sighed. "Tamara, try and understand. You're a pro and a trouper, a major asset to my operation. But if you wanna stay on my payroll, you just gotta come to terms with me being me. Okay? Being me has got its downside, I admit that. But I'm me right here and right now, I was me back then and back there, and I'm *always* me, and I plan to *stay* me."

Starlitz held up his hand modestly. "I got sentimental about the Russian. That was lame. I was totally out of line there. We won't discuss it anymore; it's completely off the agenda. In the meantime, girl, mellow out! It's cool, because you're from L.A.! Take a couple of Halcion."

At this sermon's conclusion Tamara rallied herself. "Do you *have* some Halcion? I'm all out of Halcion."

"Yeah, okay." Starlitz quietly pressed two pills into Tamara's taloned hand. "I was kinda saving 'em for the Italian One, but yours is the greater need, babe."

Tamara signaled a bow-tied waiter and selected a double brandy sour. "No more surprises in personnel. All right? I *hate* surprises."

"Right."

Tamara drank and looked up wetly, her upper lip grainy with sugar. "Surprises never make me happy, Leggy. I had too, too many surprises in my life."

"No problem, Tamara. I'm cool with that."

"And fire the American One! Fire her tonight, while we still have a chance to hire a new one." Tamara tossed back the pills and drank. Then she stalked away, clacking.

Spotting her own opportunity, the French One sidled up to confront Starlitz. The French One was the group's sophisticate. She had a good line in press repartee, and unlike her G-7 colleagues she fully understood how to sing and dance. The French One wore a ribbed designer bustier, a tricolor miniskirt, and a little red Marianne cap. She knew that the group's stage gear was hopelessly louche and déclassé, but she was a pro, she was putting up with it.

The French One had brought the Canadian One in tow. The tartan-clad, toque-wearing Canadian One spoke a little

French, which naturally endeared her to the French One. The Canadian One was polite, modest, and self-effacing, practically invisible in the group's affairs. She was blond and petite, the third Canadian installment. (Two earlier Canadian Ones had angrily dropped out, once they'd realized that the act had no intention of breaking in the USA.)

"*Comment allez-vous, la Française?*"

The French One put on her vinegar face. "Stop hurting my language."

"Right, okay. Not a bad night, Canadian One, eh?"

"We need a favor," said the French One primly.

Starlitz was properly cautious. "Just tell me what you want."

"We want the Turkish girl to sing tonight," announced the Canadian One.

"Gonca Utz? Wow. Why would you wanna do that?"

"I talked to Gonca tonight," said the French One. "She can't get a break in the music business. It's sad. We're famous musicians, so we want to help her."

"Look, you know that Gonca can't be in G-7, right? Gonca's got no English."

The French One nodded impatiently. "English, English, I know, I know. Who needs a Turk in G-7 anyway? Not me! But Gonca speaks French! Good French with good grammar, much better than her."

"Hey!" scowled the Canadian One.

"Gonca sings in Turkish. She had classical Turkish voice training and can sing all the old songs. So I think, if Gonca sings here at Mr. Altimbasak's big casino, then she could get a good chance later. A radio spot. Or a nightclub."

"Mmmnh." Starlitz turned. "Well, if you girls were performing tonight, I'd never allow some local amateur to go onstage, but . . . What do you have to say about this notion, Canadian One?"

The Canadian One was very pleased to be consulted. She

drew herself up to her full height. "I concur with the French One! Minority voices deserve some time allotment! Besides, we own all the microphones anyway, so it doesn't cost us anything."

"I like the way you put that, Canadian One. That was very worthwhile. Now tell me something. Did you ask Mehmet Ozbey about this?"

"Mehmetcik loves the idea!" said the French One. "He said we were very generous."

"Mr. Ozbey cares about us," said the Canadian One, her blue eyes glistening in big powdered pools of eye shadow. "He knows all our songs by heart!"

Leggy soberly rubbed his double chins. "Well, you can't just shove this guy's girlfriend up onstage, and jam the mike in her hand. There's a certain operational protocol involved here. We gotta walk carefully, because this can be kinda political." He paused. "What's your analysis there, French One?"

The French One leaned back on her platform heels. "My mother says that Mehmet Ozbey is a typical Westernized Third World elitist who is bound to carry out the interests of his class and gender."

Starlitz nodded thoughtfully.

"My mother also says that Turkish cabaret music is an authentic form of proletarian expression despite its many patriarchal overtones."

Starlitz scratched his neck. "Okay. I guess that settles it. So can your pal Gonca rap over a backing track? We're kinda low on Turkish cabaret musicians, at the mo'."

The French One reached into her Liberty hat and produced a C-30 cassette. Starlitz, who was not wearing his bifocals, squinted to read the label, which was hand scrawled in green ballpoint pen. " 'Muserref Hanim Segah Gazel.' Oh, brother. Did you listen to this?"

"Why should we listen to old Turkish cabaret?" shrugged the French One. "No commercial potential!"

"Backing tracks are Liam's job!" the Canadian One insisted.

"Okay, you talked me into it," said Starlitz. "I'll run the tape by Liam. In the meantime, you tell Ozbey that he needs an MC who can do her intro in Turkish."

Starlitz delivered the tape to Liam and smoothed arrangements with the lighting guys. He appreciated Ozbey's tact in arranging things in just this manner. A direct request on Gonca's behalf would have smelled too much like a strong-arm. But exploiting the artistes to get his way, well, that was something that everyone did in the music biz. With this arrangement, if Gonca suffered a flop night, it was nobody's fault. There were face-saving positions all around. Lots of win-win options and interlocking benefits. Ozbey was a professional.

With the situation under control, Starlitz went in search of the American One.

The American One had abandoned the party in an angry, dope-addled huff. As usual the British One was trying to cover for her.

The British One had been working very hard on her own public image. Somehow, against all customary grain and expectation, the British One had become very buoyant and light of foot, almost as stagily vivacious as the Italian One. It seemed that some psychological barrier had finally snapped inside the British One. She'd burned her last royal rags of imperial dignity, abandoned all icy reserve. She was blatantly reveling in exhilarating sleaze.

Leggy collared the British One for a private conferral. "Okay, British One, what the hell's going down with the Yankee One?"

The British One's face fell. "Don't take it out on her, Leggy. She has a good heart and she always means well."

"Look, just tell me where the American went."

"The American One is perfectly fine! Look at the Japanese

One," the British One insinuated. "*She's* the one losing her grip."

Leggy shot a quick suspicious glance at the Japanese One, who was listlessly mugging for a camera in her autumn-leaf minikimono. The Japanese One had been suffering a prolonged attack of glum introspection. However, unlike the American One, the Japanese One always delivered the goods on time and within specs. "Okay, so the Japanese One is a little down lately. There's nothing wrong with her that Wonder bread and a candy bar wouldn't fix."

"She's clinically depressed, if you ask me."

"No one's asking you. We're depending on you to talk sense into the American One. You're the pro at doing that, you know. So what has the Yankee done to herself, huh? Is it the dope again?"

The British One pursed her glossy lips judiciously. "I suppose that's part of it."

"What do you mean, 'part of it'? The Yankee One snorts more coke than the rest of you girls combined."

The Japanese and Italian Ones eagerly horned in on the conference. They could smell that something was up.

"She's just ambitious," said the British One, her narrow shoulders hunching in apology. "She's always inventing some big project for the gang of us. Then, when we won't do what she says, she just borrows a lot of money from us and does it all by herself."

"American One is not a team player," scowled the Japanese One, scuffing at the carpet with her platform geta clog.

"She's a very very big prima donna," said the Italian One, with a dismissive flick of her fingers.

"Where'd she go?" Leggy insisted.

The British One sighed in defeat. "Oh, she ran off to snort more coke and cry."

"Where?"

"Wherever there aren't any cameras. The private pool, I presume."

A Turkish radio MC took the stage to announce the imminent debut of Miss Utz. He struggled visibly to feign enthusiasm, over an unruly shriek of microphone feedback. Leggy left the party.

He discovered the American One lying in a white plastic lounge chair by the drained and empty swimming pool. She was still wearing her star-spangled miniskirt, and snuffling into an imported Kleenex.

"What's the problem, American One?"

The American One looked up. "Stop calling me that! I have a name, you know."

Starlitz sat on the popping edge of a plastic lounge chair and knotted his beefy hands. "What's got you down tonight, Melanie?"

She looked at him through red-rimmed eyes. "This just isn't working out the way you said it would."

"Money's good," Starlitz offered.

The American One blew her nose.

"Nice hotel, right? Balanced diet. Plenty of aerobic exercise."

"When you told me, when you first hired me, that G-7 was all just a big fake, and totally just for the money . . ." The American One drew a tremulous breath. "Well, I just didn't realize what that *meant*."

"Look, isn't it obvious? That's gotta be very obvious, right?"

"Well, I didn't know you were *totally serious!*"

Starlitz shrugged. "We're cashing in on a pop scam here! Why should that bug you? You're the American One, for heaven's sake."

"But it's not even fun! I thought it would be fun, but being a total fake is like a big boring drag! It's like we're selling hot dogs. I hustle off the plane, and I hustle off the bus, and I hustle off the limo. I shake my ass onstage, and I sing all those stupid, *stupid* lyrics!"

"Look, G-7's lyrics are a genius creation, babe. Verse-

verse-chorus from every international pop hit in the twentieth century, filtered through a four-hundred-word basic-English translation engine. That is totally high tech and wicked."

"I memorized all the damn lyrics, okay? I can do all the dance moves too. But what about me, huh? What about *me*?"

Starlitz shrugged. "What about you?"

"What about *me*, me the artist, Melanie Rae Eisenberg?"

"Look, Melanie, the G-7 enterprise was never about you. The whole business shuts down sharp on the very first day of 2000. Then you fly back to Bakersfield with a big cashier's check. That was our deal, remember?"

"Well, that stupid deal doesn't ever let me be me! I'm like a kid's cartoon! I'm like a blow-up doll or something."

"So what? You're a pop star! You get limos and a masseuse."

"Well, I could be me, and I could be a big star too."

"Nope! Sorry." Starlitz shook his head emphatically. "Forget about that. That is totally impossible, by definition."

Melanie stuck out her lower lip. "Well, that's what *you* say. That's what *you* think. I've been in the music business now, and I know better than that."

Starlitz scratched his head. "Melanie, you're cakewalking toward a swift career guillotine here, so let me clue you in. You don't want to become a solo singer-songwriter. You're just not up for that life. You're very normal and average."

"Sure, *once* I was normal and average. That was before *you* got hold of me. Now I've toured Poland, and Thailand, and Slovenia. . . . My life is totally freaky and weird."

Starlitz drew a long breath. "Look: I want to help you out here. I tell you what: I'll run a futurist scenario for you. That'll make your options perfectly clear."

Starlitz sat up straight and cracked his knuckles. "So, just as a premise for extrapolation, let's pretend that you have big talent, okay? Let's take it as a given that you're a female singer-songwriter with tremendous musical gifts. You're smart, you're dedicated, you're blond, you're Californian, you got cheekbones to die for. You win some Grammies. The critics adore you. You move a lot of plasticware."

"Yeah?" said Melanie, sitting up with interest. "That sounds *great*! That would be perfect."

"But time moves on, that's the downside. You gig and you gig, and you give and you give, until your looks go, and your voice goes. By then you're forty. Being a woman, you got forty-five long years left to live. And those years don't look good, babe. You're stuck in your mansion in Malibu, smoking Thai-stick and doing bad abstract paintings to keep your head together. You're ghosting around in there like Howard Hughes, listening to old Billie Holiday albums and pondering cosmetic surgery."

Melanie shrugged. "But I'm forty by then, right? So what? That's old."

"No, it isn't. You're not really old. You're just really over. Magazines don't want you on the cover anymore. Your idea of a hot night is firing your maid. Because you're past the pop life, and nobody's listening, nobody's buying it. There is no demographic for heartfelt folk-rock songs by embittered, aging female millionaires. So you're suing your label, you're dissing your critics, you're firing your agent and publicist. You've got more grudges than Serbia. It's just you, and the mean old clock, and the big yellow clipping book. And that would mean *success*, okay? Because you were a genuine pop artist! You kept your integrity, you were always true to yourself."

"You're just trying to make it sound bad. I wouldn't end up that bad."

Starlitz stared at her, then shrugged. "Well, you're right, Melanie. That would never happen to you. Because you have no talent. What's more, you're poorly educated and you have a substance problem. But that's all okay! You're young, and you have sixty long years of another century waiting ahead of you.

G-7 screwed your head up, but it hasn't done you any perma-
nent harm. You can work your way around this little episode."

Dark suspicion struck her. "What are you talking about?"

"I'm telling you how your future could work out for you.
How you could set it up with no regrets. How you could actually *benefit*. Finish the G-7 job with us. Get to Y2K day. Take
the big money. And just go home. Marry a medical student."

She gaped. "What?"

"Marry a doctor. That's a great option, babe. It's a great ex-
ploitation of your pop career. For the rest of your life you'd be
the glamorous star who gave up show biz, just for him. You'd
have enough ready cash to put him through med school too.
So it's like a double ego gratification for this guy. That's a terrific package deal. You could pick out most any med-school
grind you want. He would totally go for that, I almost guarantee it. You'd be in clover, babe."

"I'm supposed to turn into some *housewife*? I'm a star!"

"Put all that crap way behind you, Melanie. Go have kids.
You're very, very low on reality right now, but kids will give you
all the reality you can stand. When you're a woman with kids,
you always know who you are and what's required of you. That
works out really well for average people. Two or three kids, in
a nice house, with a guy who's really grateful and thinks the
world of you. You'd have roots, you'd be human, you would
matter to people you care about. It's happiness."

"You're scaring me," Melanie said.

"That's your best-case scenario. That's the straight pitch.
Don't even get me started on your worst-case scenario."

She sat up on the poolside chair and confronted him. "I
know what you're up to. The others don't know it, but I know
it, I know it in my heart. You're stealing something from me. I
don't know what it is you're stealing, but I can *feel it*. You've
gathered us all up, and you jammed us together, and you promoted us and you sold us, but we're never, ever real. We just
don't matter. You never let us be anything important."

"You've got a problem with that?"

"Yeah, I do, because it's all phony! It isn't real! It doesn't matter! I don't care how much money there is. Fuck the money, I just can't stand it any longer!"

"Okay." Starlitz drew a weary breath. "Let me tell you what I'm hearing from you, Melanie. What you're telling me is that you require some personal integrity."

"Yeah." She brightened. "That's exactly what I'm saying."

"You want to be true to yourself, and put aside all this empty, meaningless, venal hustle."

"Yeah!"

"Well, you're never gonna do that in my outfit. I made that clear from the very beginning. So, you're fired."

"You can't fire me! I quit!"

"Great. That's even better." Starlitz dug in his back pocket. "I can't give you one thin dime from the G-7 account, because Nick the Accountant just wouldn't hear of that. But I'm a good sport, so I'll do you a personal favor. Here's a hundred bucks. That'll get you to Istanbul. They got planes to all over from there, so call your parents and get a ticket to wherever."

She looked at the crisp hundred-dollar bill in disbelief. "Hey! Wait a minute! You can't just kick me out of the act and leave me in a strange country!"

"Of course I can. Do it all the time."

"Hey. I'm not like the Japanese One, okay? I'm the American One! I'll sue you."

"You wouldn't be the first to try, but I wouldn't waste Mom and Dad's money in the Panamanian court system. Go be true to thine own self now, babe. You've screwed up my operation, and created a lot of extra work and hassle for me, but I'm cool about that. No hard feelings. So long."

Starlitz left her fuming. He sought out Turgut Altimbasak and had all the keys changed in the rooms of the American One and her layabout personal entourage.

The casino owner was totally obliging and agreeable. "I understand the difficulty, Mr. Starlitz. We'll do just as you say."

"Mrs. Dinsmore and her assistants will be throwing quite a bit of luggage into the street tonight. Tell the bellhops to pay no mind."

Altimbasak pawed at the leather thong of his worry beads. "Is Mr. Ozbey happy tonight?"

"Why ask me?"

"If you could speak with Mr. Ozbey about me . . . You are his business partner, I know that he listens to you. . . ."

Starlitz frowned at him. "You got Ozbey the best penthouse suite in the joint, right? Adjoining rooms for his boys? Private boudoir for the girlfriend? Limos standing by, fax machines running, a big booze tab?"

"Yes, yes, of course we did all that. Of course!"

"Well, if the red-carpet treatment doesn't mellow him out, nothing will."

"Mr. Ozbey's friends are very powerful." Altimbasak lowered his voice to a reedy whisper. "He has many friends in the MHP . . . and the ANAP. . . . I don't want him to think that I might be in DHKC! Or, my God, that I have anything at all to do with the PKK!"

"Yeah, yeah." Starlitz nodded helpfully. "Well, those sound like legitimate concerns. I'll have a word with Mehmet tonight, and see if I can't get that straightened out."

"Thank you so much." Vague hope was dawning in Altimbasak's glassy eyes. "That would be so wonderful. . . ."

Starlitz briskly returned to the evening's festivities. Gonca Utz was doing her closing number. She had a backing track, a bread-loaf microphone, and a white satin gown. Gonca required nothing else. Finally given the spotlight she deserved, she had publicly flung open the depths of her being.

Gonca slid into the song's secret depths like fingertips filling a kidskin glove. Glittering eyes half-lidded, she emitted a soulful ululation that set men's hair on end all over the building.

Starlitz fought his way into the room and across the grain of Gonca's voice. He managed to reach Ozbey, where the Turk stood, arms folded, in judgment, amid a pack of his armed retainers.

"The song is old-fashioned," Ozbey remarked.

"Damn," Starlitz gritted.

Ozbey smiled triumphantly. "It's a shame she has so much talent," he said. "It seemed like such a good idea, to find a Turkish girl with the true talent. But now that I find such a girl, what am I to do with her? You see, she is a voice of the people."

Starlitz forced a nod. "Yeah."

"They are a very great people, the Turks. You see that now, don't you? A people's soul, that is what I found in her."

"Oh, yeah," Starlitz said, coughing. "I grasp the situation, man. It's way hard to miss."

"I'm glad that you agree with me. Of course you do. You are a man of perception. Gonca Utz, she is a true Turkish star. She's like another Safiye Ayla. Or a second Hamiyet Yuceses."

"Yeah, you've got a very serious problem on your hands here."

Ozbey's face grew clouded. "I shouldn't have made her my mistress. That was a mistake. Now I am very involved."

"You're in deep water, brother."

"Yes," said Ozbey, his liquid eyes frank and confiding. "The omens are very bad. Great art, great destiny . . . great tragedy. The Turks are a tragic people. A great singer knows much unhappiness. But money, business . . . these are not important things in life. There is honor. There is pride. Who am I, to steal the destiny from the people's artist? Listen to her sing!"

Gonca wound it up in a final anguished quaver. Her audience was reduced to mulch. They were beyond mere enthusiasm. Their lives had been fundamentally altered. The rave kids stared at the stage, arms hanging limp in utter disbelief; they were unable even to register the experience. The Finnish UN guys had all turned their backs to the bar: they were too astounded even to drink. Middle-aged Turkish politicians were weeping openly.

Gonca swanned off the stage with a radiant smile. She was leaving them hungry for more. Gonca could have sung all night with ease. She could have sung for years on end. She could sing off dusty vinyl, and years after her death people would sit up straight in astonishment and grip the arms of their chairs. But, now, thankfully, Gonca had departed to a dressing room.

"Mehmetcik," Starlitz said, "I'm pretty sure somebody's doomed to pull the carbon rods out of the pile there. But it doesn't *have* to be you."

"Yes, of course I know that," said Ozbey nobly. "I know I have a choice. If I'm doomed by my love and devotion to the cause of my people, then I must *choose* that doom."

Starlitz said nothing.

"A great man," Ozbey mused, "the man of destiny, the master of events . . . He must be a lion. He can't afford to be a pig. Don't you agree? That's the truth, isn't it? It's the deeper reality."

Ozbey turned aside for a moment as his pet bouncer, Ali, delivered a message at his ear. Ozbey nodded, delivered a few judicious words. Ali left, freighted with an errand. Then Ozbey straightened again and bored in.

"Speak up now, Starlitz. Give me some counsel. Tell me what truly matters in this life, tell me what is real. There must be something in your life beyond cash. Something that you would give your life for, that you would die for. Yes?"

"I dunno, man. I guess I take your point, but I don't die easy." Starlitz shrugged. "And dying for some pop musician? Come on. That's for kids."

"What about your homeland? Does your fatherland mean anything to you?"

"People are people all over the world, man."

"We can't all be devoted patriots," said Ozbey tolerantly. He signaled a waiter and accepted a martini glass with a lemon twist. Ozbey sipped, stared into the middle distance for a moment, sighed with satisfaction, took a deep breath, and began to radiate charisma.

"At first," Ozbey confided, "I thought you must be CIA. Who else would haul a troupe through so many worthless countries? But then I saw your old Russian bandit, sneaking around this casino. The old, sick man with no hair. . . . My boys don't like the Russians, Leggy. Communists annoy us."

"G-7 is a stone multinational. We got personnel from all over the world. That's the new way to do biz, you know? You gotta stop being picky. You're part of the steamroller, or you're part of the road."

"Why give me these clichés? You're not being serious with me. A man of your abilities could matter. You could change the destiny of this unhappy world."

"That's just not my angle, man. We got the act started on a bar bet in Guam . . . got it incorporated in a brass-plate front in Panama. . . . No, the act's not important. I admit it, it's a scam. But you know something? I like the work. I enjoy it. We make platform shoes in Shenzhen. We sell glitter tube-tops in Turkmenistan through the Nakhichevan Corridor. I like making those connections. I enjoy running the network. It suits me. I don't ask for much else."

"What kind of man are you, anyway?" Ozbey said mournfully. "What do you call yourself?"

"Well, man, if I had to pick just one term, I think I'm best described as a 'systems analyst.' "

Ozbey emptied his martini glass and held it out to an eager flunky. "All right, let's talk business, if you must talk business. This is our business: you could do much, much better with this act than you are doing. For all your business talk, you are not very efficient. You run your act like a silly private joke. You don't make all the money that we could make. You don't move all the goods that we could move. I worry about you, Starlitz. I worry that you don't take our bargain seriously."

"Why do you say that, man?"

"Why did you fire the American One? Why did you throw her out of the hotel tonight? She was central to the G-7 act! Everyone looks at her! Because she's the American One!"

"I can get us another American One."

"In three days? How can that be? Do you have a girl in your pocket?"

"I'll hire another American girl. That demographic bracket has fourteen million women."

"Not here in Turkish Cyprus."

"Well, I got very good instincts in finding personnel."

Ozbey rolled his eyes in contempt. "Why don't you put Gonca in the act? Gonca knows the G-7 dance moves. You could dub her voice in English."

"The gig doesn't work that way."

"Make it work that way."

"Sorry. It's not possible."

Ozbey sighed. "I want to see Gonca happy. If only for a little bit. One day. Maybe two days. When she is happy, she is very generous with me."

"Mehmet, you're an ace guy, and I get it with the romantic problems. But don't tell me how to manage my act. You don't see me complaining about your end of the deal. Like, say, your setup with the local casino owner. That guy's seeing double and his knees are shaking."

Ozbey's handsome face darkened. "Did Turgut Altimbasak complain to you?"

"I wouldn't call that 'complaining.' I would describe it as 'panic-stricken begging.' "

"Mr. Altimbasak's stupid stubbornness has been interfering with the affairs of my Uncle the Minister."

"Mehmet, I don't need any explanations. You don't owe me that, and I don't even care. That's your end of the deal. PKK, MHP, that's a Turkish internal affair, not my problem. I wouldn't pry, okay? I wouldn't be that discourteous."

Ozbey digested this, glowering. At last he spoke up. "You'll have the act in Istanbul, ready to go onstage?"

"That was our deal, man. If I fall down on my end, you'll be the first to know. I appreciate your investment. You've put a lot of effort into this. I want to see you as happy as I can reasonably make you."

Ozbey was not taking this at all well, but he was taking it. "It doesn't matter. It's not allowed to matter. It's all over in the year 2000, anyway."

"Exactly. You could hold your breath, and get there from here."

"Very well," said Ozbey somberly. "For you I will hold my breath."

AT HALF PAST ONE IN THE MORNING STARLITZ STEPPED OUT on his third-floor balcony, ripped open a pack of red Dunhills, and lit a cigarette. If he smoked outside his room, it was almost as if he weren't smoking at all.

After the second lingering puff, dormant centers of addiction leapt to juicy life in the inner depths of his skull. Starlitz slid a little sideways, the brown study of the drug throwing a new cast over his difficult night. He scratched at his bulging, hairy belly as he stared over the empty parking lot.

He hadn't gotten it about the singer/actress. He hadn't made himself fully open to the scary depths of narrative vitality there. G-7 was supposed to slide right *through* Turkey. The whole Turkish scene was supposed to be extremely meaningless and temporary. If the situation somehow stalled, the consequences could become extreme.

A taxi arrived and pulled up below him. The driver flung his door open, scrambled out, fled headlong across the parking lot, and crashed through a line of oleanders. He vanished, stumbling, into the shadowed, treacherous mess of a seaside construction site.

Starlitz tossed the cig, grabbed a shirt, and headed downstairs.

The Cypriot taxi was still parked, its motor running. Starlitz peered warily into the backseat. Sprawled limply across the backseat was a large plastic garbage bag. The big gray bag had the wrinkled, fetid, overstuffed look of a torso murder. It was topped with a pair of broken sunglasses and soled with rotten tennis shoes.

Starlitz yanked the taxi door open, grabbed the bag, and shook it violently. "What is with you? Get a grip! You're scaring the straights."

"She didn't make it," the trash bag muttered. It began to sob bitterly.

"What the hell happened?"

The trash bag lifted one gray wrinkled arm, found its shattered sunglasses, and placed them onto its slack, shriveled face. The apparition flexed and wriggled somehow, into a better light. It became apparent that it was Wiesel the paparazzo. Wiesel was a shadow of his former self.

Wiesel groaned in anguish, his voice like a distant, desolate wind. "I took her to that Turkish bath. They cleaned her! They cleaned her all up!"

"Who? What?"

"Princess Diana. She's in the trunk."

Starlitz gripped the taxi driver's dangling keys and shut off the engine. Then he circled the vehicle and carefully opened its trunk. An unspeakable stench roiled forth, the sickly, funereal reek of an entire nation's worth of dead roses.

Amid Wiesel's heaped-up camera gear Starlitz found the kitsch little tomb of the Princess. She'd been stuffed inside a little suitcase, like a hat case for a grown-up doll. Starlitz touched the slick plastic handle and snatched his hand back, fingers tingling. He swore quietly.

"It was fucking stupid to do this!" Starlitz said, moving to the open door again. "What did you do, check her onto a plane?"

"Yeah." Wiesel groaned.

"And she got through the security scan? I can't believe this. . . ."

Wiesel wrinkled his empty, paperlike forehead. He began to sob again, his rib cage rustling audibly.

Starlitz absently flipped the driver's keys over thumb and forefinger, like a set of worry beads. This was a very bad scene. He hadn't seen one this intense in quite a while. "Too bad," he said at last. "Shit happens."

Wiesel pulled his broomstick legs from the back of the taxi seat and dropped his rotting rubber shoes, one-two, onto the hotel's tarmac. "She died so happy," he mourned. "You should have seen her smile! Like she just . . . faded. My little angel . . . God, the camera loved her so much!"

"I knew she'd never make it through Y2K," Starlitz said slowly. "I didn't say anything to you . . . but I mean, how could she? How the hell could she?"

"I always tried to keep her out of fast cars," Wiesel confessed in anguish. "And Paris. I never took her to Paris, ever."

"Look, you can't blame yourself, man. Sometimes the narrative just shuts down, you know? There's no sequel possible. You can't extend the franchise."

"I know that," Wiesel said in black despair. "It's Y2K, boyo. It's that bleedin' glass wall. . . ."

"Well, then."

"I'm not gonna make it either."

"The fuck you talking about? Of course *you're* gonna make it! The next century, that's gonna be the golden age of surveillance. You're much better off without her, man. After Y2K you're finally coming into your own."

"No, that isn't true. This isn't my time anymore. It's not my wonderful time. Me and the scooter boys, back on the Via Veneto . . . When a paparazzo took a picture back in the sixties, we *wanted* to take a damn picture! The public *wanted* to see the pic! There was *stars* then, there was *faces*, there was"— Wiesel drew a tortured breath—"there was *desire*. If you ever saw a candid photo in the 'bloids, somebody *wanted* that picture, somebody had to *take* it. . . . But it's all about *machines* now. It's all bleedin' automatic."

Starlitz was silent. He had no ready counter for this assertion. There was no workaround for it. Wiesel was dead right. It was one of those two-in-the-morning, midnight-of-the-soul things.

"Well," Starlitz barked at last, "what the fuck are you doing *here*, then? Why didn't you just stay in Istanbul? What are you doing in this cheap-ass Cyprus casino? I'm trying to get some goddamn business done around here!"

"I need to put the Princess to rest. Because . . . at the end of the day . . . I was all she had."

"In *your* condition? You're a fuckin' specter! How'd you let yourself get this bad, anyway? It's not professional."

Wiesel laughed hollowly. "Just get me on my feet, Leggy. Put her in my arms." Wiesel was stirring now, bracing himself with his last foul dregs of initiative. "Point me to the no-man's-land. The Cyprus Green Line, between the Greeks and Turks. So many lovely flowers there, behind the barbed wire. There's constant UN surveillance . . . it's perfect for the two of us."

"Look, you can't do that. What about your equipment?"

"You keep it. I'm so tired, Leggy. I'm sick of myself. I swear I'm ready—I *want* it to be over."

"Look, man, you're not over. *She* is over. All you need is a new assignment."

"I tell you I'm sick of the whole world. I'm sick to death."

Wiesel leaned suddenly over his skeleton knees. His

death-pale face ripped open, like a slit in a taut bedsheet. Money vomited out of his mouth.

First came a dense, choking wad of sepia-colored Turkish lira. Wiesel spat the cash onto the pavement, drew a desperate breath, and violently heaved up a wet torrent of British pounds.

Starlitz looked around himself. This was a crisis: Wiesel was going down hard. The situation seemed hopeless. Only a sudden, dramatic intervention could save them now.

Greatly to his own surprise, Viktor Bilibin suddenly manifested himself in the hotel's bushes. "Mother of God," Viktor said in Russian, numbly trying to zip up his jeans. "Where is my room? Where's my toilet?"

"Get over here," Starlitz commanded him in Russian. "Put down that vodka."

"This is not vodka," Viktor said reasonably, staggering out of the vegetation and brandishing his bottle. "It's Cyprus brandy. It's very good."

"My friend has had too much tonight, Viktor," Starlitz crooned, the voice of clear and lucid reason. "So now you're going to help us with his luggage."

"Okay," said Viktor, staggering over. He casually set his brandy bottle on the roof of the cab.

Wiesel grasped at the taxi's door frame with tormented, skeletal fingers. He heaved, retched, and blew a foul torrent of deutsche marks over Viktor's Nike-clad feet.

"He's badly off," said Viktor agreeably. He gripped Wiesel's hollow shoulder and levered him up with one hand. "Come on, old man. Don't bend over when you puke. You can choke to death that way. Come on, up on your feet." He heaved Wiesel out of the car. "Walk! Walk it off, you can do it."

Viktor tugged Wiesel's entire limp body-husk over his own shoulder, as if trying on an overcoat. "He smells like a whorehouse," Viktor complained. "What's he been drinking, eau de cologne?"

"Something spilled inside the trunk," Starlitz said. "Have you got a good grip on him there? I'm gonna fetch all his camera gear."

"It's all right," Viktor assured him, "it's not the first time that I've done this."

A Meridien Casino bellhop belatedly appeared. "Is it all right?" he said in halting English.

"He's drunk," said Viktor calmly. He kicked at the wet cash on the tarmac. "The taxi driver left. Can you do something about this dirty money here?"

The bellhop gazed at the pavement. His attention was suddenly riveted. "Oh, yes," he said. "Of course."

Starlitz tucked the yellow case into the bellhop's slack hand. "Could you hold this case in the checkroom for me? Mr. Starlitz, in room 301."

"Of course, Mr. Starlip."

Starlitz slung a tripod over his back.

They entered the Meridien's lobby through the sliding double glass doors. "Where do you want him?" said Viktor, expertly shuffling the unconscious paparazzo.

"Let's put him inside the elevator."

Viktor plucked a stray twenty-dollar bill from Wiesel's slack lips, wiped the photographer's mouth with it, and tucked it fastidiously into Wiesel's gray raincoat. The elevator opened promptly, and the three of them staggered inside.

Starlitz pressed a button for the penthouse.

The elevator rose. "Did you ever read Pelevin?" said Viktor conversationally, flopping Wiesel against the mirrored wall and propping him there with one elbow.

"Should I?"

"Pelevin's from Moscow. He wrote *Omon Ra* and *The Yellow Arrow*."

Starlitz nodded helpfully.

"I mention that," said Viktor thoughtfully, "because this is a very Pelevin-like moment."

Starlitz scratched at his head as they cleared the sixth floor. "Is Khoklov around anywhere?"

"I don't know. I don't think so."

"Your uncle hasn't been drinking, has he?"

"You said that we could drink in the evenings," Viktor pointed out.

The elevator opened with a wheeze. The casino's penthouse landing was lushly carpeted and lined with fine blue-and-white Turkish tiles.

"Your friendly Turks don't like me very much," said Viktor.

"Just pretend you don't speak any language they can understand," Starlitz told him. "You can get away with anything then."

Ozbey's pet thug Drey was standing guard at the penthouse door, but Drey recognized Starlitz, and let the three of them in. Ozbey and his entourage were enjoying a little after-hours party. The air was thick with blue cigar smoke, and someone had put on a Tony Bennett album.

"Here, let me take him," Starlitz told Viktor. He propped the photographer's dead-eyed husk against the striped wallpaper. "Dig in that Nikon bag on my back, and gimme his thirty-five-millimeter."

Viktor did as he was told. Then Ozbey appeared, toting a demitasse and puffing a cigarillo.

"What happened?" Ozbey said, eyeing Wiesel skeptically.

"This is Mr. Wiesel from the British *Vogue*," Starlitz said. "He's a fashion photographer."

"Is he dead?" said Ozbey with interest.

"Rough flight from Istanbul," Starlitz said. "He didn't know there are no direct bookings to Turkish Cyprus. He kinda overdid it on his motion-sickness meds." Starlitz glanced up. "You get the story?"

"It's a shame about the flight embargoes here," said Ozbey. "But he looks very dead."

"Stop saying that," Starlitz insisted. "I brought him into

town to shoot your girlfriend. So I did you a favor, okay? So do you wanna see Gonca in a two-page spread, or do you want to keep her tucked inside your hat?"

Ozbey smiled in apology and gestured into the depths of the suite. "Well, she's never looked prettier."

"Get this man a mineral water," Starlitz grumbled. "He's jet-lagged to shit. Get him some dex or some coke. He's up for it."

"We'll see what the boys have down the hall." Ozbey shrugged. Ozbey was bored now, so he vanished.

"Look, this isn't going to work," Viktor hissed. "Because he's dead."

"Shut up, kid."

"Here's an empty liquor box," the young Russian said alertly. "Let's just crumple him up, and stick him inside it."

"Give me his goddamn camera," Starlitz insisted. He had spotted Gonca in a crowd of men across the room. She had accumulated a little claque of politicians and a couple of awestruck radio guys; Gonca was laughing, with her chin up and her throat vibrating like a nightingale's. She paused to tear coquettishly into a salmon-colored cube of Turkish delight.

Starlitz adjusted the focus. Then he squeezed Wiesel's papery mitts onto the camera and lifted the machine to his face.

A soft moan emerged from behind the lens.

Starlitz pried the camera away, just a bit. "She's hot," he confided. "Go ahead, man, *look*."

Starlitz lifted the Nikon again, like a nurse lifting a mug of warm cocoa to the lips of an avalanche victim.

Rapid clicks emerged from the camera.

Wiesel's spine straightened suddenly. He peeled from the hotel wall like an origami trick.

"C'mon baby," Wiesel whimpered. "Give!"

Viktor gazed at Wiesel nonplussed. He leaned in as Wiesel's desolate face filled out with a sudden flush of health.

Wiesel gave the Russian a swift stiff-arm. "Get out of the shot, punk!"

Viktor staggered back with a surly knitting of the brows. Wiesel fired off the last of the roll and reached into his pockets reflexively. His hands came up empty. He gave a hiss of anguished need.

Starlitz quickly handed him a plastic film canister, without a word. Wiesel champagne-popped the cap with an instant stab of his thumbnail, then locked-and-loaded the film. Starlitz gazed across the suite at the actress. Gonca had fallen silent suddenly. She was still unaware of them, but a puzzled, thoughtful look had touched her radiant brow.

Wiesel sidled along the wall behind a hatstand, took a shooter's stance, lifted his machine, and began absorbing images. Gonca, lost for a moment, reached for a cigarette. She lit up with trembling hands, and bit her lip.

Wiesel sighed in deep gratification.

"Easy, boy," Starlitz told him.

"The lighting stinks in here," Wiesel complained, edging back out and groping in his bag for a meter.

"I can get you a private session," Starlitz told him. "I can book you a whole afternoon."

"Yah. Great. Super," Wiesel said, pale eyes gleaming like lacquered glass. "I'll need a studio. . . ."

Ozbey returned to the suite, flanked by a friendly pair of thugs. He stared at Wiesel for a moment, then shrugged. "Your friend looks much happier now."

"He always rallies once he's on the job. Fashion people are way temperamental."

"Tell him to be careful where he points that big camera. There are special friends of my uncle with us tonight."

"Hey, I'm not her manager, you are," Starlitz objected promptly. "You want to set ground rules for the foreign press, go tell him yourself."

Wiesel strolled over and busied himself yanking equipment bags from Starlitz's bulky torso. He shrugged into them hastily. The net of fat nylon bag-straps seemed to squeeze Wiesel right back into shape. Wiesel burrowed into his ditty bag, found a fabric hat, and whipped it over his head at a cocky angle.

Gonca rose from her seat suddenly, calling out for Ozbey in Turkish. She had gone pale.

Ozbey laughed in surprise. "Stage nerves! I was starting to think little Gonca didn't have any nerves."

"You her manager?" said Wiesel abruptly. "You gotta be, right?"

"Oh, yes," smiled Ozbey hospitably.

"Let's have a word about the property, okay?"

"It's late, my friend. You're tired from your long flight. Let's have a drink together."

"Capital idea," said Wiesel, his face plump and meaty. "Make mine a double." He slung a last bag across his shoulder and strode off toward the bar without a second look.

Starlitz turned to Viktor. "Okay, we're done, we can go now," he said in Russian. He left the suite.

"Just a moment," said Viktor, tagging after him down the tiled and shining hall.

"You got a problem?" said Starlitz, turning.

"No," said Viktor. "Not so much a problem as a philosophical matter."

"Find a mosque and ask an imam."

Viktor stepped into the elevator with him. The kid's clothes reeked of brandy and cheap cigarettes. "I want to know," he insisted, "what happened to me. I was in my own room, after a hard night. Suddenly I found myself downstairs, standing in the bushes, pissing all over my own shoes."

"That's simple, boy. You're stinking drunk, so you don't know where you are, or who you are, or where you're going."

Viktor grunted. "Well, I may be drunk, but I know where *you* are going."

Starlitz glanced at him in surprise. "Yeah?"

"Yes. You are going downstairs now, to deal with that terrible biznis inside the yellow hat case. Whatever that biznis is."

"That biznis is only one of my many burdens and responsibilities, kid."

The elevator doors opened again, onto the lobby. "Life is like that, isn't it?" said Viktor wisely, stepping out. "You have one of those bad nights, when something unspeakable happens. . . . It's never just *one* strange thing. The surface of life breaks open . . . and the depths come pouring through."

Starlitz glanced through the glass doors of the deserted hotel lobby. The abandoned taxi was still sitting there; the panicked driver had not seen fit to return. Someone had stolen Viktor's abandoned brandy bottle from the roof of the car. "You ever discuss these matters with your uncle?"

"No. He's a brave man, Pulat Romanevich. . . . He has killed more people than I can count. . . . But, no, he doesn't understand life. Not anymore, not this modern life. No, not at all. He's a lost soul."

"Where is he tonight? I have some uses for him."

"He left for the airport this afternoon," said Viktor. "He said he had a surprise waiting."

"What kind of surprise?"

Viktor shrugged. "A surprise that flies, I suppose!"

Starlitz banged the bell at the concierge stand. "Listen, kid. How'd you like to make some serious cash tonight?"

"Not particularly," Viktor allowed, leaning on the counter. "No?"

"No. I don't need money. I'm intelligentsiya. I cannot be measured by any common yardstick."

Starlitz looked at Viktor with care. The kid was wearing bloated pants, a stained wife-beater with an anime cartoon on it, and a zip-up athletic jacket made of recycled polystyrene bottles. He had fake Turkish Nike joggers and both his wrists bore little bracelets of woven tatty yarn. Both Viktor's ears were cauliflowered with badly healed piercings.

"You got any cigarettes?" Starlitz said.

"Yes, I do," said Viktor, patting his pockets. "Turkish Camels."

"Come on with me, then. It's gonna be a long night."

THREE

STARLITZ ACCEPTED THE REEKING YELLOW
hat case from the yawning concierge. He left
through the glass doors, pulled the taxi keys
from his pocket, and put the case in the taxi's
trunk.

"Get in," he said.

Viktor slid into the taxi's passenger seat.

"Not back there! Get up in front."

"I'm more convincing as a passenger," Viktor objected. "If they see me in front with you,
they'll *know* we stole this thing."

The kid had a good point. Starlitz slammed
the doors, gunned the complaining engine, and
pulled out of the lot.

Starlitz drove past the moth-beaten neon of
the Meridien's hotel sign. He turned onto the
coast road, heading east. Like most Turkish
Cypriot taxis the car had an evil-eye charm,
made of cast blue glass. It dangled on a leather
cord from the rearview mirror. Starlitz yanked
the blue eye loose and tossed it out the win-

dow. After a moment's thought he followed it with the driver's dash-mounted cellular phone.

"Cigarette?" said Viktor cheerily, passing a Camel to the front.

"Great," said Starlitz, accepting a light and puffing energetically. If he didn't actually ask for a cigarette, it was almost as if he weren't smoking.

Snapping a key loose from the driver's chain, Starlitz opened the taxi's glove compartment. He removed a British-printed road map of northern Cyprus, a cheap German handgun, a Cypriot union card, a dog-eared pack of risqué playing cards, and a much-depleted Baggie of Lebanese hashish.

Starlitz tossed the Baggie into the backseat.

"Thanks!" said Viktor, pocketing it.

It cost Starlitz an effort of will to drive British style, on the left-hand side of the road. As was common on the island, the Cypriot taxi had its steering wheel on the wrong damn side of the car.

"Where are we going?" said Viktor calmly.

" 'Yasak Bölge Girilmez,' " said Starlitz.

"Ah, yes," Viktor quoted, " 'Forbidden Zone, Interdite Zone, Verboten Zone.' " Every local tourist came to know the bright-yellow Yasak Bölge Girilmez signs. Turkish Cyprus brandished hundreds of them in the face of every visitor.

They passed night-shadowed coastal villages. On the rocky slopes of the Pentadactylos, big, showy hillside villas loomed under their blue security lights. The ancient landscape boasted many half-completed modern projects, abandoned by offshore developers when some inflation crash had hit the Turkish market. Their grimy slabs and concrete pillars littered the countryside, instant prefab ruins.

They skirted sprawling Turkish Army bases, walled twelve feet high in chain link and razor wire. They rolled past the sealed-up, shadowed hulks of cheap tourist kafeteryas. They drove past square yellow postboxes that were not included in the global postal networks. Past gloomy roadside palm trees, and minareted village mosques. Past sleeping, dusty, drought-stricken orange groves. Past dreaming fields of yellow asphodel. Past writhing, crooked olive trees that could have sheltered Odysseus on a bad sailing day.

Starlitz pulled onto a tiny country lane. After an extensive travail of bumping, scrunching, and weaving, he finally parked the taxi by a mossy, half-collapsed stone wall. He killed the engine, got out, and stretched.

Viktor emerged with a bold flutter of denim pants legs and lit a fresh cigarette.

The dirt road had ended suddenly, in an evil cornucopia of rotting cardboard, rags, and bottles. At the crest of a nearby hill was a sleeping briar tangle of rust-eaten barbed wire. The snarled barricade was lavishly shrouded with snagged and windblown plastic trash. It resembled a laundry clothesline from hell.

The no-man's-land between the Greek and Turkish Cyprus factions was twenty-five years old. By its deadly nature it was utterly unlivable, so it had promptly become the island's premier dump. The deep ruts in the back road had been cut by illegal sewage tankers, who made it their habit to water and fertilize the septic, forbidden wilderness. The Green Line had responded with gusto: three briar-strewn lumps nearby were a dead British fridge, a defunct French stove, and an entire overgrown Volkswagen.

Starlitz opened the taxi's trunk. He removed the yellow case with queasy care and set it gently on the road. The flower smell seemed fainter now: more rotten, and yet, at the same time, somehow more poignant.

"You want that case dumped in the no-man's-land?" said Viktor curiously.

"Not dumped. I want it buried." Starlitz produced a pick-ended tire jack.

Viktor's glowing cig-end wobbled as he nodded in the dark.

"Tell me something," said Starlitz. "You ever crawl through a barbed-wire border in the middle of the night?"

"Can't say I have," said Viktor. "Barbed-wire borders, that was a nineteen sixties biznis. Much before my time."

"Oh, yeah, the Green Line here, it's way sixties," Starlitz agreed. "There are sixteen thousand land mines scattered around in there. Lemme tell you something about land mines, okay? Land mines are like videocams, they are way objective and technical. You can't talk your way out of a land mine. They don't give a shit who you are, or what you are, or where you're from. They will blow your ass up even if you married the Prince of Wales."

"Oh, give me the stupid case." Viktor yawned. "I can't let some fat man of your advanced years blunder around in there all night. This is a young man's job."

"Don't light up in there," Starlitz counseled, handing over the case and the tire tool. "The Greeks keep moving their sniper posts, and the UN has infrared cameras."

With a wry smile Viktor searched various pockets, and obediently handed over one, two, three, four, and five ragged packs of smuggled Turkish cigarettes.

"One last thing," Starlitz told him. "Don't open the case. Just bury it good and deep."

Viktor left, his Nike track shoes crunching through the brittle weeds.

Starlitz sat inside the darkened taxi. He clicked the ignition and turned on the car radio. With a little effort he found a powerful offshore pop station. The Turks were still very big on Turkish-language heavy metal. Heavy metal rock held on like a barnacle in the planet's various backwaters. Metal had an inherently polyglot character. Any language screamed with the amps at eleven became a universal language.

Two hours crept by. It grew colder. A light fog crept across the briar-strewn landscape. Then footsteps approached. Starlitz flicked on the headlights, casting a stumbling Viktor into the glare. Stenciled out of darkness, Viktor stood there, dazed and shivering.

Starlitz went to join him. Viktor's baggy pants were wire snagged and dew soaked. He still clutched the dirt-smeared tire tool.

Viktor was coated head to foot with a substance like light greasy smut, a kind of radiant floral garbage.

Starlitz put one hand on Viktor's damp shoulder. Beneath his grip Viktor's flesh made an ashen, crunching sound.

"You had to open the case," Starlitz said kindly.

"Of course," Viktor muttered. His pale Slavic eyes looked quite blind.

"Get in the car," said Starlitz. He led Viktor forward.

At Viktor's uncanny presence the taxi groaned in mechanical protest. Its shocks popped audibly. The paint blistered. A stick of chrome trim snapped loose.

Starlitz got in.

"Give me a drink," groaned Viktor.

"That won't help you, kid. Not in these conditions."

"I've seen death before," said Viktor hollowly. "But *never* death like *that*."

"There's death, and there's death," Starlitz told him. "When you bury a century, a whole lot has to go down with it. Spirit of the times, brother."

"Yes," Viktor said weakly. "My artist friends in Petersburg always say that. 'Even spirits die.' That's what they say . . . my friends, the Necro-Realists."

"Spirits die *first*." Starlitz started the engine, laboriously turned the taxi in the narrow, rutted lane, and flicked on the radio again. Their situation called for something nice and loud. Something mawkish. Something mundane, that would restore them to the default position of human banality, circa 1999. Celine Dion singing the theme from *Titanic*. Perfect.

"You wanna to stay off the booze and the dope for a couple

days," Starlitz advised. "Just be normal, okay? Order room service, and watch bad TV in a cheap hotel."

"Will that help me?" Viktor croaked.

"Absolutely. Just ride it out, man. We'll be leaving this island soon. Once we're out of here, none of this will matter. Because it's over now. We buried it. It's off the agenda. Not on the record. It's yesterday."

Viktor's teeth were chattering. With a visible effort he got his jitters under control. As they passed the pale lights of Lapta, something like a human color was returning to the resilient flesh of the young Russian. "I can't let my uncle see me like this," he said. "There would be questions."

"Not a problem. I'll check you into a hotel in Lefkosa. I gotta do an errand in that town, anyway."

Viktor leaned his shaggy head against the window glass and stared into the night. "Is it always like this? So horrible?"

Starlitz turned around over the driver's seat, slinging back his elbow. "How do you feel, kid? You feel like you're gonna die?"

"No, I'm a Necro-Realist," Viktor said stoutly. "I know what death is. But I don't die easily. Dying is for other people."

"Then, no, it isn't always this horrible." Starlitz turned back with a grunt. " 'Horrible' would be too simple. The world isn't simple or pure. It isn't any one thing. The real world, the true reality . . . it literally isn't what it is. 'A is not A,' right? In the real world A can't even fuckin' bother to be A. You ever read any Umberto Eco?"

Viktor stirred restlessly. "You mean those big, fat popular novels? No, I can't abide that sort of thing."

"How about Deleuze and Guattari? Derrida? Foucault? You ever read any Adorno?"

"Adorno was a fucking Marxist," Viktor said wearily. "But of course I've read Derrida. How could one not read Derrida? Derrida revealed that the Western intellectual tradition is riddled with logical aporias." Viktor looked up. "Have *you* read Jacques Derrida, Mr. Starlitz? *En français?*"

"Uh . . . I don't exactly *read* those guys," Starlitz confessed. "I had to pick it all up on the street."

Viktor grunted in disdain.

"I do read Jean Baudrillard sometimes. Baudrillard's a real comedian."

"I don't like Baudrillard," said Viktor, sitting up straighter. "He never made it clear how a political intervention can avoid being recuperated by the system. 'Seduction,' 'fatal strategies,' where does that get us?" He sighed. "We might as well go get drunk."

"Well, see, the basic deal there is," mused Starlitz, "that when the master narrative collapses and implodes, everything becomes undecidable."

Viktor leaned forward intently. "Tell me. Where does one find this 'master narrative'? I want some of it. Do you *buy* it? Is that the secret?"

Starlitz waved one meaty hand. "Millennium's almost over now, kid. The narrative is increasingly polyvalent and decentered. It's become, you know, way *rhizomatic,* and all that."

"Yes. So they tell me. All right. So what? Where is my part of the action?"

"Well, I dunno if you've got any action or not, but you're not gonna find it here in Cyprus. This is a tiny, unrecognized, outlaw republic. We're among the excluded, out here. We are very, very peripheral. And besides that—there's a big cusp coming. A major narrative crisis. It's gonna wipe a lot of slates clean. Bury the walking zombies."

"You mean Y2K," said Viktor, leaning back.

Starlitz nodded silently. The night was going well. The kid would be okay now. The kid had made his bones tonight. Now he was in the know.

STARLITZ PARKED VIKTOR BY THE HOUR IN A FLEABAG Lefkosa *pansiyon.* The place was locally known as a "Natasha house," thanks to its staff of expatriate Ukrainian working girls. It was five in the morning. The staff were all asleep. They were exhausted from their bone-grinding, hands-on labor, underpricing Turkish whores.

Starlitz dumped the taxi in the tall weeds of an abandoned Turkish trench works, west of the capital. As he walked back toward the divided city, a Homeric dawn gnawed at the Nicosia skyline with her rosy gums.

Starlitz lit one of Viktor's cigarettes, put his hands in his pockets, and began to drift.

Midmorning found Starlitz sitting on a bus bench, eating from a large bag of chocolate croissants and sipping a Styrofoam Nescafé. Urban crowds went about their business, men in flat hats and patterned sweaters, women heaving baby carriages along the black-and-white-striped curb.

A rust-spotted jitney pulled over. A backpacking American woman climbed out of it. Her skin was the color of a Starbucks frappuccino, and she had black, kinked hair in big clusters of thread-knotted twists. She wore a nylon tropical shirt, knotted at the midriff, and chocolate-chip desert-camo cutoffs, unconvincingly cinched up with a gleaming concho belt.

Starlitz rose from his bench and trailed her.

The Yankee tourist opened a small gate and walked up the steps of a whitewashed suburban home. A plaque at the door read BARBARLIK MUZESI. She read a framed, typed announcement on the wall, and pulled a change purse out of her bellows thigh pocket. She carefully counted the zeros on a slender stash of Turkish lira. Then she scuffed her lug-soled boots on the welcome mat, yanked the iron-grilled door, and stepped inside.

An aged museum guard silently accepted her money. Starlitz pulled a fat money clip from his pocket and paid up as well.

Lefkosa's Museum of Barbarity had once been a private home. A famous Cypriot atrocity had taken place inside it.

The place had been consecrated to the murders. It had become a neat and dainty little atrocity exhibition.

The walls were hung with pedantic care, with many period photos showcasing a stark variety of Greek inhumanities to Turks. There were many burnt and bulldozed homes, schools, mosques, and shops. There were profaned flags, smashed windows, and vile graffiti. There were dead people dug out of pits, with filthy improvised clothesline still binding their mummified wrists. Even Turkish statues had been shot in the head.

Starlitz edged a little closer to his target.

The woman spoke first. "I sure ain't with this! Why didn't we cluster-bomb these sons of bitches? How hard could that be?"

Starlitz proffered his bakery bag. "Chocolate croissant?"

"Yeah!" She dived her hand into the bag, removed a flaking pastry, and munched with gusto. Then she jabbed at a ghastly photograph with a tooth-severed croissant horn. "Look at them dead kids! Where was CNN when that was goin' down? Fuckin' media creeps are never around when you need one!"

"Been in-country long?" said Starlitz.

"Nope! Just cruisin' by to see the local sights."

"Where you from?"

She shrugged. "All over! I'm an army brat."

"What do your friends call you?"

She stared at him. "My *friends* call me Betsy. But *you* can call me 'Mrs. Ross,' fella."

"My name's Lech Starlitz, Mrs. Ross." Starlitz dug into his pocket and removed a hundred-dollar bill. He smoothed it between two fingers and handed it over.

"What's this about?" she said warily.

"It's for listening to me for a minute."

"Okay." She tucked the bill in her pocket. "Talk."

"You ever heard of a girl group named 'G-7'?"

"Heck, yeah, I heard of G-7! I'm down with all that shit, NATO, UNPROFOR, Gulf Coalition, you can name it!" She scowled. "You're not dressed well enough to be a pimp, mister. You look like you slept in those clothes."

"I have a business proposal for an American female expatriate. Somebody just like you."

"So what's the deal with you, you some kind of intel puke?"

"I'm a pop-music producer, Mrs. Ross. I manage a touring act."

Mrs. Ross blinked in surprise. "Huh."

"I need you to be a performer. You get gophers, a makeover, hair extensions, and a total new wardrobe. Plus limos, big hotels, free food, free travel, and big screaming audiences of teenage girls. The works. I wanna make you a star."

"Ooh-rah," she said slowly. She looked him up and down. "What's your real problem, exactly? You're insane, right? You're mental."

"Nope. No bullshit. It's a serious offer."

"Well," she admitted slowly, staring at the photo-studded wall, "I gotta admit it, that would be me all over. That is my *vida loca*, right up and down. Me, the overnight sensation."

"Here," Starlitz said persuasively. He handed her another hundred dollars.

"You mean it," she realized.

"That's right. And there's lots more where that came from."

She narrowed her eyes warily. "Well, what's the mission assignment, then? You better make it well defined, bubba."

"You have to sing and dance. In public."

"Well, I can dance. I dance great. I'm not real big on singing."

"That's okay. The G-7 act is a road show. It's all done with tapes and computers."

Mrs. Ross stuck her thumbs in her armored concho belt and rocked back onto her bootheels. "Come on, homeboy. I can tell you're up to *something* you're not telling me." Suddenly, she grinned. "You're not the bad boy that you think you are, know what I'm sayin'? I've seen worse dudes than you. I've even *done* worse dudes than you."

"Get a grip, Mrs. Ross. I manage the G-7 act. I am the boss. I'm all about the game plan and the money. There are six other girls on the bus with you. You are just one of a crowd."

Mrs. Ross looked down at the museum floor. The humble wooden boards were deeply scuffed with thirty years of constant foot traffic. Then she looked up resolutely. "How much money are we talking? Because I owe my hotel some money. Kind of a lot."

"Not a problem, babe. We pay off hotels every day. We even wreck hotels, sometimes."

"I had to pawn some shit too. Some personal shit."

Starlitz nodded. "I will assign you a personal assistant, who will retrieve your personal shit."

"I make a lot of long-distance phone calls. To Bosnia, mostly. Because my ex-husband's in uniform there."

Starlitz grinned. "Phones, we got." He was really touched by the armed forces ex-wife thing. There was a very good, convincing smell about all this.

STARLITZ TOOK MRS. ROSS OUT FOR AN EARLY LUNCH. FOOT-loose, broke, newly divorced, and half starved, she fell on her lamb kebab like a timber wolf. They dawdled over hot Turkish coffee until a large white limo arrived for them from the Meridien.

Once they were safely back in Girne, Starlitz handed the newly recruited American One into the capable hands of Tamara.

Tamara undertook a brief inspection of the merchandise, with all the delicate tact of a Balkan horse dealer. Then Tamara passed Mrs. Ross on to the G-7 makeup people.

"There isn't much time," she told them coldly. "Do your best with her before you pack for Istanbul. Hurry."

The new American One was rapidly hustled out of earshot. "So, what do you think of this one?" Starlitz asked Tamara. "Not bad for such short notice, eh? Great muscle tone."

Tamara shrugged. "I like her skin. Very Jody Watley, very Mariah Carey. It's a nice American color."

"You seen Mehmet Ozbey around? Ozbey was bitching at me earlier. He didn't think I could find a new American One overnight." Starlitz chuckled falsely. "Shows what he knows."

"I knew you'd get someone," she told him, bored. "You always get somebody. I hope you didn't get us another crazy one."

"Any problems dumping the last American One?"

"Of course not. I took care of all that. She's gone." Tamara's tight eyelids narrowed. "There is a new problem, with the Italian One. An Italian man is here, someone who knows her. I don't like this Italian man. We're trying to pack for Istanbul, and he's bothering the staff."

"Okay," said Starlitz. "Send this problem to my office. I'll square it away."

Starlitz went to his hotel room and showered. He ripped the dry-clean plastic off a Carnaby Street bespoke ensemble in vivid chartreuse. He dressed and went to his office at the Meridien. It had a spectacular view of the rocky Cypriot coast, over a handsome balcony at the rim of the hotel gardens. Reaching across the rail to a straggling hibiscus, Starlitz snagged a boutonniere. Then he sat behind his borrowed desk, opened a drawer, and removed a large glass ashtray.

The Italian arrived. He was a silver-haired and courtly gentleman, who walked with a slight limp. He was wearing a Borsalino hat, a tailored seersucker shirt, and a pin-striped Milanese sport jacket. He carried a nifty Hugo Bosca hand-stained leather valise.

"Mr. Sarlinz?"

"*Si?*" Starlitz half rose.

The man delivered a business card. "I represent a protective service. We are international security experts. . . ."

"Take a seat!" said Starlitz. He examined the card and tucked it in the desk. "Cigarette, Signor Patriarca?"

"No, thank you." His visitor coughed politely. "I had to quit."

"You don't have a spare lighter, do you?"

"No."

Starlitz hunted through several drawers and found a paper book of Meridien hotel matches. He lit up with a flourish. "So, what can G-7 do for you?"

Mr. Patriarca perched neatly on the edge of his chair. "Travelers have many hazards. It would be a shame if your company had an accident. My people, we can help you. We can insure that you have no security problems."

Starlitz exhaled and scratched his head. "So is this, like, a *kryusha* pitch you're giving me here?"

"What?"

"*Kryusha*, you know. Like, *Tambovskaya kryusha*, or *Fizba kryusha*?"

"What are those words, Russian words? I don't understand Russian."

Starlitz smiled helpfully. "Sorry, man, I just assumed a protection racket *had* to be Russian. So, who are these insurance people of yours? Ndrangheta?"

Patriarca scowled. "The Ndrangheta are Calabrian!"

"How about Camorra?"

"The Camorra are Corsicans!"

Starlitz stared at him in wild surmise. "Don't tell me you're Sicilian Mafia."

"We never use that word, *Mafia*," said Patriarca with dignity. "That is an old, ugly word, invented by police! We are businessmen of honor. We have many restaurants, shipping companies, construction companies. And we have excellent insurance policy—just for you."

"Wow! Really? This is too good! Just one moment. Let me contact my business associate." Starlitz picked up the desk phone and dialed the penthouse. After a brief interregnum with Ozbey's staff he got through.

"Leggy," Ozbey grated, his voice thick with hangover. "How glad I am that you returned to us. I was concerned."

"Mehmetcik, you're not gonna believe this. I got a soldier from the Sicilian Mafia down here. Right here in my office, right now!"

Ozbey was skeptical. "In Turkish Cyprus? Is this a joke?"

"No, man, he's serious! And he isn't Turkish 'Maffiya' or Russian 'Maphiya,' this guy is good old-fashioned, traditional, *mafia* Mafia! He's shaking us down!"

"What a surprise!" said Ozbey, his voice rising in an eager arc. "I have to see this Mafia man right away!" It had clearly been a long, eventful, decadent night for Ozbey, but the new business prospect was cheering him right up.

Starlitz hung up. "My associate wants to discuss your proposal."

"Is he bringing money?"

"Money? You bet! He's very well to do. Has checkbooks like you wouldn't believe. Has his own banks, even."

Starlitz tapped ash from his cigarette. Then the office door slammed open. Frosted glass shattered and fell out of it. Three of Ozbey's goons catapulted through the doorway, carrying Israeli-made Uzi submachine guns. They were breathless from racing down the stairs, but they gave Patriarca three cheerful grins, so redolent with evil that the room's stuffy air seemed to crystallize.

Drey held up his right hand, making a gang sign with his scarred fingers: the two middle fingers touching the thumb for a muzzle, and the forefinger and pinky lifted for the wolf's ears. Drey gazed at Mr. Patriarca quizzically as Patriarca went pale with recognition and terror. Then Ali, lumbering silently forward, punched Mr. Patriarca in the head. Patriarca fell from his chair. The three Turks stomped him lavishly and removed two handsome pistols from his belt and his armpit. Drey took his pulse, and then they stomped him some more.

At this point Ozbey arrived from the elevator.

Ozbey chided the boys gently in Turkish. "Sorry about the glass door, Leggy."

"I'll have Turgut Altimbasak look after that."

"Mr. Altimbasak is not with us anymore. Get a better office. We leave Cyprus soon anyway." Ozbey looked down at the prostrate Patriarca. He bestrode him. He prodded him with a polished shoe. " 'Sicilian Mafia.' The very idea." Ozbey shook his head. "How old and tired he looks! He's very weak. And so dishonored! This is sad." Ozbey glanced up, brown eyes gleaming. "Isn't it? It's sad!"

THE HOTEL'S MANAGER HAD VANISHED DURING THE NIGHT. Khoklov was also nowhere to be found.

A brand-new crew of Turkish hotel consultants had flown in overnight from Istanbul. To judge by the terrific racket, they were already fully engaged in remodeling the casino. The local Cypriot staffers were petrified by this powerful offshore intervention. They were hunched and hopping like rabbits, scampering from wing to wing and room to room.

Starlitz, adapting to the confusion, helped himself to a fine new suite on the second floor of the seaside wing. He called the operator to have his phone rerouted. No one was working the phones. Instead Starlitz found himself confronting the hotel's voice-mail service.

The digital phone service spouted a brief canned intro in Turkish, and then horribly disgorged its mangled contents.

A woman's intonation, her voice chopped and jerky.

Bouncing off the ionosphere. Blistered by buckling software. The nemesis voice of a pursuing Fury:

". . . in an area of total killer creep conditions—the agency of shadow stock bubble—cut evil empires gray dust of broom heavy—heavy blue twilight exit visa smoke bones—cut you . . . in for suckers dirty marks expelled the airport laughing and pointing come and get . . . set your watch by it, Leggy . . . ohmigawd are we ever in Hicksville . . . <click>"

Starlitz put the phone down, hands tingling with dread.

Starlitz sat frozen behind his empty desk, feeling dislocated terror sink into his flesh. A thumb had come from dark futurity to nail him. There could be no safety here. There could be no such reprieve.

Itchy urgency overcame him. Spooked and restless, Starlitz began to tour the hotel. Mrs. Ross was undergoing radical image surgery, but the other G-7 girls looked okay. They'd been burnt out like matchsticks when they'd first hit Turkish Cyprus, but they were bored by their vacation now, they were jittering to hit the stage again. They'd packed up for their final limos to the airport, while their groupies engaged in the traditional status battle to see who got to sit next to the star. The sound and lighting guys had been the first G-7 agents to go; they were already settling into the Istanbul Stadium Hotel, flopping down the jaws of their cell phones, demanding fifty-amp fuses, manufacturing brand-new road hassles.

Ozbey was in fine fettle. He was keeping the Meridien's penthouse on indefinite personal loan. The next floor down had been freshly given over to a brand-new, gathering thundercloud of Turkish television technicians.

Down at the front desk the Meridien's guests were being reshuffled en masse. They were cheerful about it, since the new owners were canceling their outstanding bills, in an eerie gush of sinister generosity.

It all looked far too good. Starlitz ground his teeth and returned to the emptiness of his new office. There was no Khoklov, and no Viktor. And no answers. Time was short, and he could feel the pressure building steadily.

After a stiff interior battle Starlitz plucked a crisp *meishi* business card from the innermost depth of his wallet. He made a phone call.

The phone was answered in Japanese. It was one of the eccentric millionaire's glamorous uniformed staffers.

Starlitz requested an audience with Makoto.

"How it hanging, Reggae?" said Makoto. "Is there good news?" Makoto had amazing, uncanny English. Makoto's grasp of English grammar was a little uneasy, but he was the world's most polished vocal mimic of American pop-music diction. Give him a glass slide and a cheap guitar, and Makoto could outslur Robert Johnson. He could sound more lonesome, tunesome, and tubercular than Jimmy Rodgers. He even had better slack-key guitar and falsetto Hawaiian pidgin than Bradda Iz. Makoto was perfectly capable of calling Leggy "Leggy." He called him "Reggae" just for old times' sake.

"No, Makoto, there's a problem. A big problem. I can smell it. Is there something awful on your end? Anything really weird happening? Major earthquake, nerve gas in the subways, something like that?"

"No, no! Everything beautiful here!"

"Then, yeah, it's just like I thought," Starlitz said. He stared out his new window at the tops of the swaying palms. "The time has come for me to pay some kind of dues."

"A money problem? Don't worry so much about money! Because we are friends."

"It's not the money, no. That would be too simple."

"A talent problem. I'll send you new Japanese One. Someone cute and shiny. I keep telling you, Reggae, hire real musicians! Pay scale! You know? It's easier."

"The girls are fine. The act is fine. No, this awful thing, it has gotta be"—Starlitz sighed—"a *personal* problem."

There was a long silence on the line. Makoto was stunned.

"But you are *Reggae!*" he protested at last. "You don't *have* personal! No personal at all."

"Well, normally that's true. But this is a funny time, man. It's the end of an era. This is, like, my Y2K personal problem. It's, like, looming up here."

Makoto sucked air between his teeth. "Well! I don't know what to say."

"This is dead serious, man. I'm not sure I can hold up my end. I might have to take some kind of . . . leave of absence."

" 'Leave of absence'? What is *that*? That's not in our agreement, Reggae."

"I know that. That's why I'm calling you, right now. You are the honcho, and I'm the line worker. I gotta have a vacation. That's my pitch. I need some personal time. How about it?"

"Okay! No problem! Come to Kauai!" Makoto coaxed. "Good vacation here! Sandy dancing on beach. Barbara taking hula lessons! Barbara love Hawaii, I love Barbara, so it's beautiful Pacific paradise."

"Later, man. I just want you to know that I haven't forgotten that mah-jongg game we had in Guam. I might have to drop a stitch or two with the G-7 act, but I'm standing by that bet we made."

"Of course you are stand by our bet," said Makoto pleasantly. "You are my friend, you are honest."

"Right."

"Why worry? You worry too much."

"No, I don't," Starlitz muttered. "I should have been worrying a lot more, earlier. I forgot what time it was."

"The Man can't bust our music, babe," crowed Makoto eerily. "If you bereave in magic, in the young girl heart!"

"Yeah, sure, Makoto. Whatever works for you, man."

"You call me again, when you more one-love, upful, righteous positivity." Makoto hung up.

STARLITZ CALLED THE PANSIYON IN LEFKOSA TO SEE IF
Viktor had survived the night. He had a long, fatally confusing
phone encounter with a young hooker from Belarus whose
parents had been jailed by the Lukashenka regime. This Belarus girl had one of the most interesting Russian accents
Starlitz had ever heard, but she had never heard of 'Viktor Bilibin,' and she couldn't find anyone who had. As for Khoklov, he
no longer had a room in the Meridien. Khoklov wasn't even in
the hotel register. Khoklov had become a Turkish Cypriot nonperson.

The sense of impending doom was acute. Starlitz abandoned his office and sought sanctuary in the Meridien lobby
bar. He ordered a double shot of port-finish Glenmorangie
and bought two packs of red Dunhills. He patted his pockets.
No matches.

"Here." A female tourist in a baggy dashiki passed him a
Cricket lighter.

"Thanks!" Starlitz lit up, exhaled gratefully, and stared at
his benefactor. "Christ!"

She tucked a witchy mass of gray-blond hair behind the
earpiece of her wire-rim glasses. "Have I changed that much,
Leggy? You didn't even reckanize me."

"No, Vanna," Starlitz lied immediately. "No, you look
great."

Vanna picked morosely at her damp paper napkin. "Yeah,
what a bullshit artist."

"When did you get into town?"

"Aw, just this morning. I've been in Budapest. Trying to get
my head together, with some net dot friends from the 'Faces'
list. . . . But you wouldn't know about that."

"Yeah, no, maybe," Starlitz hedged, sipping his whiskey.
Now the situation was falling into place. It was tumbling onto
him with bone-snapping force, pinning him to earth, like a
great, boxed, avalanching closetful of aging *Ms.* and *Playboy.*

Starlitz knew instantly from the crushed, portentous look

of Vanna that this latest development was about as bad a thing as he could imagine. He could already feel it, ruining everything he had worked for and cruelly derailing his life. But at least, knowing that it was Vanna, getting some working parameter on the wrecked and wretched story line, that was a major relief. The panic was behind him now. He would just have to deal with the consequences.

"They're 'cyberfeminists,' " Vanna continued.

"It's been a little hard to keep up with developments," Starlitz said stoutly. "Press of business and all."

"Oh, yeah. Sure, man." Vanna sucked down the frosty dregs of her brandy sour and rapped the bar with her plastic lighter. "Hey, you, Mister Turkey-guy! Gimme another one of those chick turista drinks! And put more sugar in it this time."

The Turkish barman gave Vanna a skeptical frown. In his local version of reality, women didn't order their own booze. Least of all jittery, baggy-eyed, makeup-free, West Coast hippie women who were sixty pounds overweight and wearing drawstring stretch pants. Starlitz quickly made the universal money-pinching gesture and tapped himself on the chest. The barman nodded reluctantly.

"So," Starlitz said, passing cash and tapping ashes, "how's life on the separatist commune?"

"That life's all over. They busted us."

"You're kidding. With your White House connections? How the hell could that happen?"

"Aw, they set us up like a bowling pin. We were dealing Viagra point-and-click off the Website. Why we got out of RU-486 and into boner drugs, that I'll never know. Those silly bitches in the central committee, it was all about return on investment all of a sudden. . . . I mean, once the Movement's just about the money . . . It's *over,* that's all. It's just all over." Vanna's slack face clouded behind her bifocals. She looked ready to cry.

"Aw, c'mon, Vanna," Starlitz said consolingly, "even Clin-

ton got set up in a fundie sex-bust. It's kind of an honor, really."

"I don't even want to talk about that. It's all over, it's yesterday." Vanna shrugged in anguish and lit a vile, clove-
flavored cigarette. "So, do you really know this Russian guy
Khoklov? The guy with the private airplane?"

"I didn't know that Khoklov had any airplane, but, yeah, I
know Khoklov."

"Khoklov flew me in today! That's some super weird airplane that Russian dude's got. He set us down right on the
beach. He told me he couldn't go inside this hotel, though. He
said there were people in here trying to kill him."

"Well, the band's just now checking out of the joint," Starlitz elided, ordering another Scotch. "We got a major gig coming up in Istanbul."

"Yeah, the band, the band. I never hear the end of that.
You, managing a girl group. Who'da thunk?" She blew a trail
of herbal smoke at the bartender, who flinched away in alarm.
"So, are people trying to kill you too?"

"No, not really, I'm not Russian."

"Okay. Yeah." Vanna sank deep into her second brandy
sour, then swiveled on her stool to look him over. "So, you look
to be doing pretty good for yourself now, Legs. You're sure
dressing better than you useta. Those are like *banker* shoes."

"Yeah, these *are* my banker shoes, actually. Bought 'em in
Zurich. You want something to eat, Vanna? The food's really
great in Cyprus. You can't get a bad meal in this country."

Vanna said nothing. A large wet tear appeared on her
lower lid, brimmed, and ran slowly down her cheek.

Starlitz sternly commanded the barman's attention and ordered some mezes. With any luck the casino's kitchens were
still functional. Vanna slowly lowered her pale, disheveled
head. She was drunk now, maybe badly jet-lagged. Starlitz
reached out with the care of a snake charmer and placed his
hand against her batik-covered shoulder blade. Solid human

flesh in there. She was badly off, all right, but she was still his Vanna.

"Okay, you and me, we go way back, right?" Starlitz told her. "Ten years now?"

She looked up blearily. "More like thirteen."

"So, okay, spill it. Level with me. Lay it right on me."

Vanna braced herself with another sugary gulp. "Well, when the commune broke up, Judy and I had this, like, ideological discussion. . . ."

"A big fight."

"Yeah, one of those, and seeing as there was this dope warrant out on Judy, she decided to split for a while to one of those places where, like, evil, global, neoliberal capitalism doesn't have any pull. . . ."

"Yugoslavia?"

"No."

"Lebanon?"

"No."

"Paraguay? Belarus? Yemen? Chechnya?"

"Shut up! No, West Africa, stupid! West Africa, with the antimutilation campaign."

"Oh, yeah," nodded Starlitz. "A women's-issues thing, I shoulda known."

"So, Judy was out there, hanging with the sisters of color, doing some consciousness raising. . . . And it looked like they were going for it, you know? Until she, like, got to the genuine issue at hand down there."

"The cops got her?"

"No, the *women* got her. Because she gave 'em a basic health lecture. She talked about female anatomy. These women were totally shocked. So they just picked up, like, broomsticks and pot ladles, and they beat the shit out of her."

"Dang."

"They beat her real bad, Legs. I got the U.S. embassy to fly her back in. When the dope cops saw her in rehab, they dropped all the charges against her. She's still in the clinic in Portland. Tryin' to walk." Vanna bit back a sob.

"When the hell was this?"

"Three months ago."

"Three *months*! Why didn't you call me?"

She looked up teary eyed. "Well, we can't depend on you. You know that."

Starlitz was angry. "Well, of course you can't depend on me! But I got capital now like you wouldn't believe! I'm running a major-league hustle here! I coulda bought you a stack of Band-Aids the size of a house."

Vanna's face crumpled. "Oh, don't unload on me! I've had so much of that, I can't stand any more! You don't know what Judy's like now. It just made her so bitter. She just can't bend at all, it's all one little narrow thing with her, it's all just like one little tiny righteous fucking thing."

"Well, with an attitude like that, she's not gonna make it through Y2K."

"And don't start on me with that crap, either! I'm up to here with fucking Y2K! I read fifty megs of CERT dossiers on UNIX date bugs. I already burned my stupid Windows box." Vanna reached unsteadily off the barstool, pulled up a knit Guatemalan shoulder bag, and produced a brand-new cell phone the size of her forearm. "Instead, I got me this k-rad Motorola Iridium."

"Damn," said Starlitz, gawking. "That's the first one of those I've seen!"

"Instant global access," Vanna announced, bravely sniffing back her tears. "It's linked up, like, literally out of this world."

"Yeah, that gizmo is totally not of this century. It's got the *new* stuff!"

"Calls cost six bucks a minute!" she said proudly. "If you pay for 'em, that is. Of course, this unit's been phreaked."

"Well, of course."

Starlitz stared in silent hunger at the satellite telephone. The device stank of futurity. They would probably go broke, being so far ahead of the curve and all, but the gizmo was an utter harbinger of things to come, like discovering a fossil in reverse. Starlitz felt a powerful urge to grip the phone, caress it, perhaps bite it, but he restrained himself. Vanna was sure to take that gesture all wrong.

A platter arrived from the kitchen. This was fortunate, for Vanna was visibly weaving on her barstool. It was easy to underestimate a brandy sour; under their sugar and lime the things had the reeking kick of a Cypriot mountain goat.

"You know this Russian kid Viktor?" said Vanna, innocently spooning up a clotted salad of sheep's brain in olive oil. "Kind of a doper rave kid?" She paused, surprised. "Mmm! This is tasty!"

"Yeah, I know Viktor."

"Viktor's okay, right?"

"Viktor's on the hustle. I dunno. He's smart. Khoklov and Viktor, they're smarter than they look. Totally inept, but, you know, really Russian and gifted."

Vanna chewed and swallowed. "I've been hangin' with some Slavic 'kyberpheminists.' . . . They're sure into weird shit now, the Russians. There are sisters in Petersburg who are like way-heavy theorists on the Syndicate list."

"Russians are people. They just had one fuck of a twentieth century, that's all."

Vanna licked her spoon and enthusiastically munched a cabbage dolma. "Well, that Khoklov guy did me quite a favor, flyin' me in under the radar. My documents being, like, not exactly in order and all. . . . But I had to leave 'em both with Zeta."

"With what?"

"With Zeta. You know. Zenobia. Zenobia Boadicea Hypatia McMillen. Our daughter. Okay?"

Starlitz was thunderstruck. *"You brought the kid here?"*

"Yeah. That's right. Our kid's running loose in Cyprus with those Russian pals of yours. I sure hope they're all okay."

A rolling flash of lightning lit his mental horizon. His world was filled with new and savage clarity. "Damn, Vanna. The kid! I never even heard her full name before. 'Zenobia,' I knew that part, but I never knew your slave name was 'McMillen.' "

She shrugged eloquently. "It's just legal shit. It's on her birth papers."

"You say her full name's 'Zenobia, Boadicea, Hypatia McMillen'? The State of Oregon accepted that?"

"Yeah."

Starlitz considered this. "So what's *your* full name, then?"

"Look, just keep calling me 'Vanna,' " she told him, stubbing out her reeking clove cig so she could eat with both hands. "That's my hacker handle, okay? Everybody always calls me 'Vanna.' "

Starlitz shook his head in wonderment. "I can't believe you finally broke down and brought the kid to meet me."

Vanna sighed. "I just plain broke down. That's all."

"So she's what, ten years old now?"

"Eleven. But don't blame *me* for that! *I* never cared if Zeta met her father! It was *Judy* who was dead set against it. But now . . . Well, my coven hates me. My marriage to Judy, well, that's all ruined. I got the dope cops down on me at home. I'm dead broke. I got huge medical bills, and no house. And I'm clinically depressed! I'm all *fat* and I'm *old*!" Vanna's voice broke. "I'm strung out on Zoloft! I got heart fibrillations! My daughter can't stand me! She's having fifty-seven screamin' kickin' fits every day, about you and that stupid, stupid band! Zeta's *driving me around the bend*!"

Starlitz looked up from his chickpea dip. "You're telling me Zeta's a G-7 fan?"

"The biggest. She's a fanatic." Vanna clutched her brandy glass in anguish. "I can't handle this, Leggy. I can't handle it, I can't handle her, I can't handle my life! It's the end of the world!"

Starlitz drummed his fingers on the laminated bar. "Huh! So that's the story, huh? Well, how about *me*, then? You haven't seen me in years. You think you can still handle me?"

"I dunno," Vanna said, wheezing. "I don't even care. You're all I've got left." She smiled tearily. "You're my last hope, Obi-Wan Kenobi."

"Well, it's good to see you, Vanna," he said sincerely. "You look great."

"Oh, hell, I know I look awful, I look like hammered shit," she muttered. "I *deserve* to look this bad. You got no idea what I've been through."

Starlitz lowered his voice. "You're just strung out, that's all. You need a major change of pace. Just, you know . . . to get over the ol' millennium hump. Reassemble your life."

"Look, I've been tryin'. *Real* hard. Nothin' helps. It always just gets worse."

"Well, you came to a nice place. Parts of this hotel aren't bad. I got a nice room in here. And I run a free tab."

"Yeah?" Vanna swigged the crushed ice in the bottom of her glass.

"Yeah. So, I tell you what, Vanna. Let's you and me go up to my room. Right now. Let's have a roll in the hay."

Vanna choked on her drink. She set it down with a thump. She gazed at him red eyed. "Are you out of your mind? You can't tell me that!"

"Well, why not? C'mon."

"I'm a lesbian!"

"I don't think once every twelve years is gonna kill you. How long has it been since you *had* any action, anyway? At least three months, right?"

She scowled. "More like three *years* . . ."

"Okay. Point made. We're both here, we're both drunk now, we're in the mood, and I've got a room. No matter what, we're kind of family, we got a kind of history together. Right? So let's get it on."

They weaved their way up to his room. With some care and difficulty they engaged in middle-aged sexual intercourse.

"Man, that was great," Starlitz crowed, rolling off her and blowing steam. He strolled into the bathroom and rid himself of a Turkish prophylactic.

At the gurgling flush of the hotel toilet Vanna stirred. "Gimme a cigarette," she groaned. "Got any aspirin?"

"Got Zoloft!" he announced.

"Wow. Zoloft would be great."

Starlitz opened the room's bar fridge and fetched out a Turkish mineral water, plus a multicolored Baggie of mood-commanding substances. He plucked out a pill from a crowd of its brethren and brought it over.

Vanna bolted it down and thirstily chugged half the water bottle. Then she sat up wearily in the rumpled bed, crossed her cellulite-spotted legs, and tucked in her cracked heels. "Mother of God, I was plastered."

"It's okay. What's the harm. It's just us."

"I can't believe I did that. Why did I do that? I'll never do that again."

"Aw, give it another twelve years. Then make up your mind."

"Could you put on some pants?" she said plaintively.

"Yeah, sure."

"And a shirt. No offense."

"Whatever." Starlitz whistled to himself as he stepped into his boxer shorts. "I feel young again," he announced, tunneling into his suit trousers. "I mean, too much booze, and spontaneous sex . . . This is really doing it for me. I feel like it's 1977."

Vanna looked up doubtfully. "You're *happy* about this?"

"Yeah, that's right. Life is great!"

"Well, if *somebody* got off, I guess that makes it worthwhile. . . ."

"Sure it does! Why shouldn't it? Sex is like that all over the world."

Vanna drank the rest of the water and put the bottle aside. "Y'know, that was totally super icky, but . . . maybe you're right. I think I may have bottomed out, just now. 'Cause . . . y'know? *How* could it get any *worse*? I feel . . . like I'm all *drained,* somehow."

"Yeah! You look swell! You're all ethereal."

"That's some word," Vanna said suspiciously. She tugged at her lower lip. "Remember that kinky threesome we had in the rubber hammock, way back when? They say that it changes your luck. . . . Boy, that sure changed mine."

"Same here, I guess."

Vanna rose, staggered into the bathroom, ran tap water. Then she glanced into a mirror and emitted a shriek. "Mother of God! What's happened to me?"

"You've gone all lucid. You have an inner glow."

"I can *see right through my own skin*! I look like a frosted lightbulb!"

"It's this Mediterranean sunlight," Starlitz assured her glibly. "Cyprus is the birthplace of the goddess Aphrodite. So, no matter what it is, it must be like a totally natural, beautiful, empowering, New Age thing."

"I think I'm dying! Is this some kind of dope-booze horror? Will I puke? I better lie down." Rubber legged with shock, Vanna collapsed into the bed. She breathed hard for a few minutes, hiding under the reeking bedclothes and stirring restlessly.

Humming to himself, Starlitz combed his hair and knotted a tie.

Then Vanna's tangled head emerged. She spoke up again, in a new voice. "Legs?"

"Yeah?"

"I gotta tell you something about Zeta. 'Cause I'm gonna leave Zeta with you."

"Yeah, that's what I figured," Starlitz said equably. "I thought that had to be the story. Because that girl . . . Well, that little girl is the one thing I did in the twentieth century that I can't get away from."

"What?"

"It makes perfect sense that she'd show up at Y2K. Because she is the one consequence that is gonna outlive me. I can't dodge her or deny her. I can't crawl under her, and I can't jump over her. If I'm gonna be who I am, then I gotta deal with this—I gotta go right through this thing, to get to the other side."

"Listen, I'm her mother, and I love her. But Zeta's really weird."

Starlitz said nothing.

"I don't mean *cute* weird. I mean, yeah, sometimes she's cute weird, but mostly, she's like, *poltergeist* weird."

"Eleven-year-old girl, right? Like, real hung up on pets and horses, really picky eating habits . . ." Starlitz decided that a shave was in order. He ran hot water over his Bic razor.

"No"—Vanna sighed—"I mean more like flying out of four-story windows. Breaking TVs by looking at them. That sort of thing."

Starlitz waved one foam-covered hand. "Aw, kids always fake that poltergeist shit, you know? Kids are really clever."

Vanna groaned. "Oh, it's no use! It's no use even talking to *you* about it. If there's anybody in the world who would never get it, it would be *you*." She drew a ragged breath. "I tried, okay? Just remember that I tried."

Starlitz leaned into the mirror. "You're right, babe. The less said, the better."

"I hope she hasn't done anything to those poor Russians. All that plane travel makes her really hyper."

"Aw, the boys are on the payroll. They can handle it."

"I'm giving up," Vanna declared. "This is finally it: I'm giving up." She sat up. "I'm past caring! I just can't go on! It's the end of the road." Suddenly, she smiled.

"See," said Starlitz, "you're better already!"

"I tell you what I'm gonna do, Leggy. I got myself a new plan. It's like a whole new program. It just came to me like a rush, while I was lying there sick to my stomach, with that pillow over my eyes."

"Roll it on out."

"I'll go up to Vancouver Island. To Canada. I know some cool tree-spikers up there. Good people. They got a big survivalist tree-house. I'll just . . . eat my sprouts. I'll do yoga. Yoga and yogurt, that's the plan. I'll get up with the sun, and cook lots of veggies. I'll get my health back."

Starlitz nodded in encouragement. "Yeah, that's a good strong narrative."

"I'll clean all out," Vanna insisted, her voice growing firmer. "I'm gonna kick the antidepressants."

"Definitely couldn't hurt."

"No more baby-sitting, no more yin drama. No more net-surfing either. I'll read the *Bhagavad Gita*. I'll kayak every day. I'll realign my chakras. When Y2K hits, we'll cut a big totem pole, and we'll dance around it, and everybody'll sing."

"Tremendous. That's the ticket. Drop the hell right out. Find your inner self again. Get a firm new grip on your cool little alternative thing."

"You really think that'll work for me? It'll get me through Y2K?"

"Absolutely," Starlitz said. "That was a brainstorm, it was great. It's totally you, babe. So: can I have your satellite phone?"

Vanna considered this. "Nope. No way."

STARLITZ DISCOVERED KHOKLOV AND ZETA, SITTING TO-gether in Girne, in the Cockney Harbour Club. They were at an outdoor table under a big tattered umbrella, eating two plates of fish and chips.

The little seaside eatery catered to elderly British retirees. Ten or fifteen of them were lounging there now, absorbing sun and shandies in their senile Shangri-La. Khoklov, all avuncular jolliness, had a rubber-band sheaf of hundred-dollar bills. He was passing them to the girl, one by one.

Zeta was wearing a cheap blue jumper and had her hair in a French braid. Leggy stood and watched her. A sensation utterly new to him washed through him. It was a feeling of tremendous, transformational potency. She didn't look much like himself—she had Vanna's long bones and fair skin—but then she bent her neck to pluck up and devour a French fry. Starlitz took stunned note of the squat, solid, cannonball shape of her head. In a single instant he knew with profound mammalian certainty that she was his issue.

He drew nearer.

Zeta was examining Khoklov's bills and arranging them in two neat stacks. "This one's good!" Zeta said to Khoklov. "This one's no good. . . . This one's okay. . . . Gosh, this one's really terrible!" She lifted the bogus bill into the air and made a face. "Who drew this one? He stinks!"

Khoklov beckoned him to the table. "Don't make her lose count," he cautioned in Russian. "She has such a talent for this!"

Starlitz pulled up an injection-molded white plastic chair. He had no idea what to say. He'd never before confronted any human being with Zeta's particular qualities. He felt very much at a loss. "So, where'd you get all the counterfeits?" he said at last, in Russian.

"From a Lithuanian. He paid me to do a Cyprus laundry cash-run for him."

"I thought Lithuanians were way up to speed with Yankee currency."

"He was a Russian-ethnic Lithuanian."

"Yeah, well, that would account for it."

Zeta aimed a friendly smile at him, with a childish rack of gappy teeth. "Hi, mister!"

"Hello."

"You said 'hello' to me! You have some English, huh?"

"Yeah, I do English."

"You have some funny money too? Well, give it to *me*! 'Cause I can tell 'em apart really good!"

"Good for you," Starlitz said meekly. "You oughta work on that, it's a useful skill."

Khoklov laughed at him. Khoklov was wearing Italian aviator shades, a linen ice-cream suit, and a natty straw boater. There was a new trace of color in Khoklov's seamy cheeks.

Starlitz felt the inherent limits of the day bursting wide open. For the first time, as he sat there at the wobbling table, Starlitz realized that the little town of Girne had a truly beautiful harbor. It was small, twinkling, compact, and sunny, full of handsome yachts. The Girne harbor was the kind of place that might reconcile a man to a hostile universe.

"Look at you!" Khoklov chuckled. "I've never seen you like this!"

"Like what?"

"You're *happy*."

Starlitz said nothing. But it was true. So that was it: that sinister, untoward feeling of fantastic, soul-unfolding power that was stealing through his flesh. That alien sensation was simple human joy. Khoklov was right: he was happy. He felt happy and proud to be sitting there with his daughter. Starlitz could even feel his face changing shape—there was an expression stamped on it now that had never before crossed his features.

Khoklov pulled off his shades and smiled. "It's a good surprise for you, eh, Lekhi?"

"Yes. It's a really good surprise. Thank you, Pulat Romanevich."

"Shall I tell you how I managed it?" said Khoklov, leaning back. "It was quite a story."

"No, not yet. I just want to look at her for a while."

Khoklov signaled the waiter. "Tell her to hide all that cash for a minute. I'll buy you a nice Turkish beer."

Zeta contentedly stuffed the cash into her pink vinyl G-7 backpack. Starlitz saw at a glance that this was the Korean model, featuring the seven girls as dancing anime cartoons, their eyeballs big as manhole covers. Quite the fan collector's item. There was always some consumer bleed-over around the Pacific Rim markets.

Zeta picked the fried crust from her fish and swallowed a wedge of flesh. "I only eat the white part," she volunteered.

"You like that band, G-7?"

Zeta nodded violently, braid flapping at the nape of her slender neck. "Yeah, Mom One and Mom Two, they bought me all their white labels!"

"I never thought your daughter would be so pretty," said Khoklov in Russian. "She's a pretty, young American girl! You know who she reminds me of? That youngster who flew to the Soviet Union, for peace."

"Matthias Rust?"

"No, not him! He was German, he was insane! I mean that little American pilot girl."

"Oh, yeah! The one who died in the plane crash later. I've forgotten her name."

"I've forgotten her too," said Khoklov. "That sweet little girl—poor thing. It was a Cold War biznis, so now she is all yesterday. . . ." He looked at Starlitz intently. "You have to cherish them, eh? You have to look after them, while you have them."

The waiter arrived with two bottles of Efes Pilsner. Khoklov paid. "You want something else?"

"I had a little something in the hotel just now, but . . ." Starlitz examined the tabletop menu. "Yeah. Bring me some prawns. And, uh, some mutton chops. Is the baklava good? Bring us some of that. We're celebrating."

Khoklov had a long, nourishing draft of cold beer. He

pointed at Zeta's backpack. In his fragmented English he told her, "Girl, give me that nice money."

"Sure, okay!" Zeta handed over two neatly sorted wads of good and bogus bills. Sitting up straight, she began thumbing her way through the rest of the stack, counting under her breath.

"What an excellent young lady." Khoklov grinned. "She has won my heart, I like her very much. In English how do you say: 'This is your father'?"

"You say, 'This is your father,' " Starlitz told him.

"Girl," said Khoklov sternly. "Zinovia! 'This is your father.' " He pointed.

Zeta looked up. "*This* is my *father?*"

"Yes. This is your father: Lekhi Starlits."

She gazed into his eyes. "*Are* you?"

"That's right, Zenobia. I'm your dad."

Zeta lunged forward and flung her skinny arms around his neck. Starlitz patted her back awkwardly. Her long, flat, pre-teen torso was full of startling muscular strength. Zeta was lean and mean, she was like a little growth stock.

Starlitz pried his throat loose from her forearm. "It's really good to see you, Zeta. I think you'd better help Uncle Pulat with his cash there. It's starting to blow away."

"Oh. Okay." She sat down again. "Gimme some more, Uncle Pilot!"

Starlitz cleared his throat. "You and me, Zeta, we're gonna be together for a while. Okay? We'll get to know each other."

"Do I get to meet the band?"

"You bet. Absolutely."

"All the girls? Every one?"

"Every one. Autographs, T-shirts, you'll be just like a radio call-in winner."

"Oh that's just so GREAT!!" Zeta screamed.

"I ought to go back at the hotel now," Starlitz said in Russian. "I need to knock heads, and settle accounts, and get them all packed. There's always some crisis, there's always some loose end. . . . But you know what? To hell with all that."

"That's the spirit."

"I got better things to attend to now. I never saw anyone like this before. She is amazing. This is someone who *exists* because of me."

Khoklov politely handed another sheaf of bills to Zeta. "Young girls are very good at this detail work," he said. "It's time to teach her to cook. Borscht, that would be a good start."

"Oh, hell, Khoklov, what do you know about it? You don't have any kids!"

"How sadly true," sniffed Khoklov. "Of course, there is my useless nephew. . . . But until this moment I never missed fatherhood. I never married. There were plenty of girls, naturally. . . ." Khoklov shrugged casually. "You can't help that, when you're a jet ace. But I never found the right woman."

"They're hard to find. So they say."

Prawns arrived. "You want some of these?" Starlitz asked his daughter.

"Okay, yeah, no, maybe, I guess." Zeta carefully peeled away the crust to look at the shrimp's insides.

"I wasn't looking very hard, to tell the truth," said Khoklov. "I once asked a woman to marry me—a very rich niece of Berezhovsky's. She wouldn't have me, though. Very wise of her. Besides, she was Jewish."

Starlitz watched Zeta as she sampled a white dab of cabbage. "I never married her mother."

"No? Why not?"

"Well, for one thing, there were two of them. Two women in the bed at the time."

Khoklov raised his brows in disbelief. "You seduced two women at once, Lekhi? *You?*"

"Yeah. Except it wasn't a bed, it was a hammock. And they were lesbians."

"Hey, Dad," Zeta piped up.

"What?" said Starlitz.

"Hey, Dad."

"Yes, what?"

"Hey, Dad!"

"What is it, Zeta?"

"Have you ever been inside this guy's airplane? It's super cool!"

"What is she saying to you?" said Khoklov.

"I didn't know you had an airplane here," Starlitz told him.

"It isn't exactly mine," said Khoklov, tilting his beer. "It belongs to President Milosevic."

"What, from the Yugoslav Air Force?"

"No, no, it belongs to the president of Serbia personally. He's a very clever man, you know. A great man, Slobodan Milosevic. He can change history. The twentieth century doesn't breed men like him anymore."

Starlitz nodded thoughtfully. He slid the prawns toward Zeta and attacked the spiced mutton chops. "I hear his wife's a real piece of work too."

"Oh, yes," said Khoklov sincerely. "Mirjana Markovic, she loves to live dangerously. She's an old-school Bolshevik Communist girl, Mirjana's some kind of woman." He sighed. "It's not that I don't love women, you know? They're sweet! It's *me* that's the problem! I just can't imagine being Mr. Husband, that boring fellow behind the newspaper. That family dad, eating at the breakfast table. When I'm with a woman, I want to be *exciting*, I want to be *thrilling*! The man with the scar on his cheek and the cold blue eyes!"

"Absolutely. That's you to a T, flyboy."

Khoklov sobered. "One day, though, I had a kind of revelation. . . . I should tell you about this now, Lekhi, I should confide in you. This is important. It's about my role in the world, my personal role in Slavic history. . . . It was at the Davos Economic Forum, in those beautiful mountains, in Switzerland. . . . Are you going to eat all those prawns?"

"Have a few, Pulat Romanevich. You need the protein."

"I was in Berezhovsky's entourage at the time. He was conferring with the other Seven Russian Bankers about the Yeltsin reelection campaign. I myself, I was getting the secret plane built for Milosevic, at a certain aviation base in Switzerland. . . . We all went out drinking with George Soros, and his capitalist dissidents. You know those Soros network people?"

"What," said Starlitz, chewing, "the rogue billionaire's hippie media freaks? Oh, yeah, they're way hard to miss."

"They're not spies, exactly. A network without national allegiances. A 'Nongovernmental Organization.'"

"'*Post*governmental Organization.'"

"Yes, that's right, exactly. So I was drinking with this Soros operative, one of those 'economic analysts' that our country is infested with. The 'English-speaking thieves.' He began to confide in me. . . . Out came this *document* he had prepared. . . . All about our Russian *demographics*."

"Uh-oh," Starlitz said.

"Yes. He explained it to me. It was horrible beyond words. Our soaring Russian death rate. Our crashing Russian birth rate. Alcoholism. Outmigration. Life expectancy for Russian men, fifty-seven years. Much worse than under the czars! We are finally free, democratic, in command of our own destiny— and we are emptying the nation. We're liquidating ourselves."

"Aw, that's NATO scare talk. He was pulling your leg, ace."

"No, he wasn't lying to me. He was very drunk and honest, he went to puke five minutes later. No, that was *my own portrait* that little functionary had in his little papers. *I* drink too much. *I* rob the Russian nation. I'm in the bankers' maphiya, so I shoot the stupid people who get in the way of the big thieves. And then, I myself, I abandoned Russia. I erased myself from my Motherland. I'm over here, lost in a foreign country, drinking beer in the sunshine, and running some silly hustle, while the Turks are trying to kill me."

"Hmmmph."

Khoklov lifted his poet's eyes at Zeta. "It would be different if *I* had a child. I know that now: if I had a true stake in the world, if I had a future that mattered, then somehow my life would become different."

"Maybe."

Khoklov's fond gaze soured. "But then there would be the mother. Oh, my God. I can't imagine that: chained for life to some aging, sagging, boring woman. . . . I love them when they're pretty and eager, but what if they were . . . old, and wrinkled, and bitter! Or desperately pasting themselves together, like that evil Dinsmore woman in your entourage. . . . Oh, my God, if a woman I had loved turned into something like that. . . . That would be my worst nightmare."

"I *like* ugly women," Starlitz blurted.

"Really?"

"Yeah, ugly women are my type. Because I'm an ugly guy."

Khoklov examined him, full of thoughtful pity. "I suppose that, in some very basic, animal level, they are all the same in the dark. . . ."

"No, man, that's not it at all. It's a lifestyle choice." Starlitz finished his beer. "If you're a wandering guy like we are, and you're bound and determined to screw so many different women that you lose count . . . Well, there aren't many ways to love 'em and leave 'em without hurting their feelings. The best way is to leave them thinking: *I could have had all of that I wanted, but I had too much self-respect.* You know? That's what always works for me."

"You never tell them: 'I must leave you here in comfort and safety, darling, to return to my harsh life of danger'?"

"Come on! Let's face it: if they're spreading it for some character like me, they're desperate and courting ruin. Fuck, I *am* their life of danger."

"Hey, Dad," said Zeta.

"What?"

"Hey, Dad."

"What is it?"

"Hey, Dad!"

"I'm listening, Zeta."

"I'm stuffed now. Can we go? I wanna see the band!"

"We'll leave in just a minute. You need to go to the bath-room or anything?"

"Yeah, maybe."

"Okay, the bathroom's in there," said Starlitz, pointing into the pub. "Make sure you don't have any of this guy's crappy C-notes left inside your backpack, okay? I got plenty more for you back at the hotel."

Zeta bumped her plastic chair back and left at a skipping trot.

"She likes you," Khoklov observed.

"Not really, man. She's just suckin' up to me because she's dead tired of living with Mom."

"No, she *does* like you. She even *looks* like you. I didn't see the resemblance at first. Mostly it's that cunning monkey look she gets on her little face when she's trying to puzzle out what we say."

"Speaking of which, where is Viktor?" Starlitz said.

"Oh, yes," said Khoklov glumly, "the Viktor issue." The de-parture of Zeta had changed Khoklov's mood. Khoklov was vis-ibly collapsing, as if he had sprung a slow leak. He reached inside his jacket and began counting cash into his lap.

"Is Viktor okay?"

"At the moment Viktor's up on those castle ramparts," said Khoklov, glancing across the harbor at the postcard-worthy stone bulk of a twelfth-century Crusader fortress. "He's watching over us, with his binoculars."

"Why would Viktor wanna do that?"

"Because I told him to stake out this rendezvous and watch out for trouble. But also because he's been stupid." Khoklov sighed. "That first day you met him, at the beach, when we acquired those vacuum tubes . . . Well, there were ten tubes in the shipment, not nine. Viktor filched one of them."

Starlitz blinked. "No kidding."

"Yes, and later the rascal secretly sold it to that musician in your entourage, for a full fifteen hundred dollars!" Khoklov shrugged in pained embarrassment. "It was bad of Viktor—though it was good to have the cash. It let me get my little plane back. Then, I did some flying money-laundry work for the Lithuanian, and I picked up your girlfriend and daughter as well. So now, we're back in Cyprus safe and sound, and here is your money back. Fifteen hundred."

"Viktor fenced that vaccum tube for one thousand five hundred?"

"Yes! I could not believe that English fool would pay that much money! Western musicians, they're all drug addicts, they're totally addled."

Starlitz accepted the cash and jammed it into his clip. "Next time, check out the auction scene on eBay dot com. Those matryoshka dolls, the little Kremlin badges—you savvy hustlers could clear some big money that way."

"I apologize for Viktor's stupid act of thievery. He did it without my permission."

"I accept your apology, Pulat Romanevich. Consider the matter closed."

Khoklov brightened somewhat. "You're not going to shoot him? I told him you'd be within your rights to shoot him."

"I'm not saying I would never want to kill Viktor, but I'm not going to have him whacked over some fucking piece of stereo equipment. For one thing, I got too much dignity. And for another, that's the exact sort of shit I used to pull when I was Viktor's age. The old palm-it-and-pocket routine—man, those were the days! Christ, when I was Viktor's age, they didn't even have tracing tags."

"That's very good of you, Lekhi! I wouldn't have thought you'd be so indulgent about this. I know that Viktor is reckless hooligan scum, but I think, perhaps, he's improving a little. Viktor's quite different since you took him to that brothel in Lefkosa." Khoklov grew thoughtful. "You showed him some of the ropes, eh? You knocked some of the snot out of him."

"Oh, yeah. No question there."

"It's good of you to take such personal trouble with my sister's boy. I appreciate that. I wanted to do this little favor for you in return, eh? I wanted to do a favor for you that was just between the two of us, man to man. Not about the cash. Not part of the stinking market." Khoklov turned his pale, chiseled face to one side, elegantly raised the brim of his hat, and spat on the pavement.

Zeta emerged from the pub, shrugging on her backpack. As she walked to join them, a taxi driver arrived at the pub, searching for his client. The driver called aloud, at the slumbering crowd of Britons. "Mister Hawcliffe?"

" 'Mister Hawcliffe,' " said Khoklov, rising from the table and brushing crumbs from his pants. "That would be me."

"You called us a taxi?" said Starlitz.

"No, that would be Viktor. Viktor has a new cell phone."

"You know something?" Starlitz said. "I think that kid of yours has got the stuff!"

FOUR

STARLITZ AND HIS DAUGHTER CLIMBED IN THE back of the taxi. Starlitz handed Zeta a tooth-pick and a mint. Khoklov rode shotgun.

"Ercan," Starlitz ordered.

"Why the airport?" said Khoklov.

"To catch the girls before their flight to Is-tanbul. The kid wants to see the property." Starlitz grinned and lit a cigarette.

Khoklov frowned and rolled his window down.

Starlitz sheepishly flicked the burning cig on the taxi's rubber mat and mashed it under his heel. They jounced uphill, away from the harbor. Despite the island's lasting drought it was a pretty day. With many a honk and pot-hole crunch the cab left the outskirts of Girne. They wove their way up across the spine of the island, toward the highway pass through the Pentadactylos.

Zeta tongue-levered her toothpick through her missing canine tooth.

"So," Starlitz offered in Russian, "I understand you've been having trouble with Ozbey's boys, back at the hotel."

"That's true," said Khoklov.

"Ozbey's boys are too enthusiastic."

"Yes, they are."

"How'd you get in so much trouble with Ozbey? I mean, how could you even manage to bother him? You've been flying to Budapest when I was paying you to watch that guy."

"Watching Ozbey required specialists," Khoklov told him. "I found a subcontractor for the job. I hired a Turkish Communist who is nostalgic about the KGB."

Starlitz stroked his rubbery, freshly shaven chin. "There are working Communist cells around here?"

"Of course! There are thousands of Communists in Turkey. Turkey is a land where it's always the 1960s. An international, proletarian revolutionary . . . it's a fine career. I hired a Communist gentleman from the violent, leftist Devrimci Sol movement. In fact, since he worked so cheap, I hired his entire Devrimci Sol cell. The Communist cell watched Ozbey for me. They were willing to do that for ideology, but they were happy to do it for cash."

"And?"

"Well, how much do you want to know? A trip to the airport only takes twenty minutes."

"Frankly, I don't want to know very much. It would just spoil the beauty of the deal." Starlitz lifted his meaty hands. "I mean, the magic of a hustle like G-7—it's all about skipping right across on the surface, very light and easy. Too much involvement on the ground, and it gets all grimy."

"All right," said Khoklov, shifting in his ragged taxi seat and coughing into his fist. "I'll tell you one important detail. Why Ozbey's boys want to shoot me. It's about the casino owner, Mr. Altimbasak."

"Yeah? What's Altimbasak's problem?"

"Well," said Khoklov, "he was a very kind host, and he told

me some useful things about the situation here. But he was also a leftist, you see? So, his body is inside his crashed Mercedes, at the bottom of a cliff. But Mr. Altimbasak's *head*— well, his head had several bullets in it, so his head is in a bucket of cement."

Starlitz said nothing.

"Have you ever heard of the 'Turkish Gray Wolves'?"

"They shot the pope," Starlitz recited by reflex.

"Yes, Mehmet Ali Ağca. That business was about banks. The Vatican's Banco Ambrosiano. A very holy bank. They were laundering money for the Polish anti-Communists, while they also brokered arms for the anti-Communist Turks. They got very excited about Poland, and neglected to pay the Gray Wolves. So, the pope was punished for defaulting."

Starlitz grunted.

"Ozbey gave Ağca the pistol that shot the pope. He didn't call himself 'Ozbey' then. Ozbey has at least six official identities. I know for a fact that he has six Turkish diplomatic passports. He also commonly uses special passports from intelligence agencies in Azerbaijan and Turkmenistan. Mr. Ozbey has outgrown the old Gray Wolf militia. He has prospered in his investments, and moved into the highest circles of Turkish government. Nowadays he does a great deal of oil, guns, and drug biznis in the formerly Soviet Turkic countries. His 'Uncle the Minister' is the chief of clandestine operations for MIT, the Turkish Central Intelligence Agency."

"I could have glided right past all this," Starlitz mourned. "This didn't even have to come up on the agenda."

"There's more. There's much, much more. My Turkish Communist revolutionary friends have been fighting their government for fifty years. They have been losing, because their truck bombs are always badly parked. But they have many secret dossiers on Ozbey. They have dossiers on his friends, his donors, his sponsors, his mentors. They keep all their files in computers in Holland, because inside Turkey the MIT has the Communists jailed, tortured, and shot."

"Hey, Dad," said Zeta. "Hey, Dad!"

"Hey what?"

"Hey, Dad, how come you talk so much Russian? I feel carsick!"

Starlitz gazed at her in alarm. Zeta spat out her half-sucked peppermint; she had gone all pale and greenish. "If we stop the car," Starlitz told her, "we might not make it to the airport in time to catch the G-7 girls."

Zeta's brow knitted crankily. "Well, I can't *help it* when I'm *feeling carsick*! I feel like I'm gonna *throw up*!"

"Stop the car," Starlitz told the driver. They pulled over by the long stone railing of the pass through the mountains. Zeta flung herself out of the taxi with comic-opera emphasis, as if nausea had turned her bones to rubber.

Starlitz and Khoklov stepped out for a breather. The spectacular Cypriot vista showed glamorous villas, gleaming swimming pools, the tall green spikes of many cedars-of-Lebanon, and the sprawling, elaborate campus of a phony-baloney offshore university. To apologize for the wait, Starlitz slipped the young driver several hundred thousand lira. The driver shrugged philosophically, opened his glove compartment, and had a long, thoughtful shot of Beefeater gin.

Starlitz cupped his hands and lit a Dunhill.

Khoklov watched the little ritual with an addict's desperate eagerness. "Those cigarettes will put you in the hospital."

"No, they won't."

"*Yes, they will*. They may not look evil, but trust me, they are."

Starlitz blew smoke and gazed into the lilac-blue Cypriot distance. "He's outmaneuvered me, hasn't he? He's cut me right out of the loop."

"Well, Lekhi . . . You're a friend of mine, but your little music biznis is not a match for Ozbey's biznis, understand? This fellow calling himself 'Ozbey,' he's a career secret agent. He runs death squads. He has a national apparat behind him. He's not a 'pop music promoter'! He only looks like one."

"Well, I only look like one too."

"You don't look *very much* like one," Khoklov said sourly. "Ozbey looks much more like one than you do."

Zeta spoke up suddenly. "Secret agent," she parroted in Russian. "Death squad, national apparat."

Starlitz rolled his eyes. "Zeta, don't interrupt us grown-ups when we talk business, okay? It's rude."

Zeta scowled. "Well, you shouldn't be talking to him so much! What about *me*? You can talk to him anytime! I want you to talk to *me*!"

"What did she say to you?" said Khoklov. "That sounded almost like Russian she was speaking just now."

"My daughter was telling me to pay more attention to family matters."

"That's a wise little girl," said Khoklov. "I think perhaps your time has come for some domesticity." He looked at Starlitz thoughtfully. "Some fatherly time with this lovely young girl—or your big ugly head, in a bucket of Turkish cement—I think there may be useful signals here."

Starlitz turned to his daughter. "Zeta, I'm gonna talk to you, I promise. I'm gonna tell you a whole lot of things. It's just that, well, you kinda caught your dad in the middle of something important, so I have to tie up some things first."

"Money," Zeta said.

"That's right. Money. That's why people run bands."

She looked up into his face, squinting. "Is *that* why people play music? Just for money?"

"No, no! I said that's why people *run bands*."

Zeta shrugged her skinny shoulders and looked at her shoes. "Okay, Dad. If you have to."

Starlitz looked at her with the first pang of sincere guilt that he could recall in his adult memory. It struck Starlitz suddenly that little Zeta was bearing up extremely well, considering. Hauled all over the world, dumped on his doorstep like unclaimed luggage . . . He was being clumsy. Starlitz put on his best, firmest, dealing-with-teenybop-fans voice. "You feel better now, Zeta? Not so carsick?"

"I feel okay now that you're talking to me."

They slammed the taxi doors and resumed their trip. "You know, Pulat Romanevich, it's not the first time you and I have dealt with a heavy spook. There was Raf the Jackal, back in Finland. That guy was quite a piece of work."

"Are you joking? I'm *still* dealing with Raf the Jackal. That's one reason why I'm anxious to leave this lousy Turkish island, and get back to the comfort and safety of Belgrade. Raf is in Belgrade—he's working there now. It's been peaceful too long in the Balkans. Something will tear loose soon. Then, Russians will be very popular in Serbia. Every time the Serbs go crazy, they discover that they love Russians."

"Yeah, I've noticed that."

"Soon they will love us, and then, the president of Serbia will forgive me for running off with his special airplane."

"I gotta hand it to you, Pulat: that pitch makes a lot of sense. So, is there any pop band action in Belgrade? Or Novi Sad, maybe? I mean, besides all those Slavic turbo-folk chicks like Ceca Raznjatovic? We already did Croatia and Slovenia."

"Lekhi, take my advice: put the music biznis behind you. Don't fight Ozbey: just sell out to him. He can pay you well; he has the Turkish state behind him, he can afford to be generous. The G-7 band is worth much more to Ozbey than it is to you. An international touring act is a perfect cover for a Turkish secret agent who needs to run arms and drugs. Those girls can carry him through the Mideast, the Balkans, all over Central Asia, just like seven camels."

"Yeah, sure, maybe—but, hey, scouring the marginal, emergent markets with a Spice Girls copy band, that was *my original concept*."

Khoklov looked at him with limpid eyes. " 'Your concept.' Is this a professional talking?"

"I also have a mah-jongg bet riding on it."

Khoklov shrugged, defeated. "There's no accounting for you, Starlits. Sometimes you talk perfect sense, and sometimes you're like a block of wood."

As an outlaw state the Turkish Republic of Northern Cyprus had no flight clearance with the world's many grim, self-important civil air authorities. So the republic's primary airport was, by necessity, a rather modest place. The terminal was flat and dusty, and surrounded by unkempt flowering shrubs. The airport's rusty radar scanner resembled a barbecue grill.

Starlitz abandoned Khoklov with the taxi. Starlitz and Zeta walked together, hand in hand, through the terminal's cracked glass doors.

The floor of the Ercan airport had a fine layer of wind-blown yellow dust. There was putty and duct tape aplenty on the magazine kiosks and the tatty souvenir stands. The little airport's battered X-ray machines looked entirely decorative.

Starlitz bought his daughter a whopping shrink-wrapped box of assorted Turkish delights.

"Do people eat these?" Zeta said skeptically.

"They're like marshmallows."

"I only eat *white* marshmallows."

"Then only eat the white ones."

Starlitz spotted Wiesel, sitting on a stool at the airport bar.

Wiesel was sipping fizzy gin-and-tonics, with big green wedges of the local limes. His sallow face was greasy with suntan oil; his upper lip was sprouting a new mustache. Wiesel sported a new haircut, new glasses, and brand-new equipment bags. A red-and-white Turkish Airlines ticket packet peeped from the pocket of his trench coat.

Wiesel was visibly startled, but he braced himself. "Legs! Fancy meeting!"

"How's business, Wiesel?"

"Lovely! Smashing! Can't thank you too much for introducing me to Mehmetcik. Fellow's got all kinds of photo work for me. His uncle's a big wheel in Turkish media, you know."

"Yeah."

Wiesel displayed a laminated G-7 access tag, on a beaded neck chain. "He's got me covering the band throughout the Turkish tour. It may not be the world's biggest pop scene, but you know something? The Turks, they still *care*."

Wiesel retrieved a Turkish pop scandal-rag, which had been lying on the bar with a pile of its gleaming, pulpy brethren, beneath a plastic-bagged light meter and a fresh pack of Craven A's. "Check out these candid Turkish shots! They peep down necklines, they peer up skirts. . . . If a star is in bed with a fellow, the Turks still make a big deal of it! It's all straight out of *La Dolce Vita*!"

"Don't get stuck in the sweet old past, man."

"I'm not stuck. I'm *floating serenely*. I'm on the dodge back there. The past will help me." Wiesel emptied his glass. "It'll help me to forget."

Starlitz thought about the paparazzo's strategy. "Yeah. Maybe. Switch from gin to arak. Use vintage flashbulbs. Date babes in foundation garments. Y'know, that could work."

Wiesel nodded across the length of the airport's seedy, red-velvet lounge. Gonca Utz was perching quietly among Ozbey's bodyguards, wearing a fabric couture hat the size of a bicycle wheel, and paging through notes on a clipboard. "That girl has the voice, the moves, the face. . . ." Wiesel's face lit up with hunger. "Leggy, I can feel it."

"Where are the G-7 girls?"

"They just boarded." Wiesel grinned. "Trace of lipstick, all that's left. Down the runway in a cloud of glitter dust. . . . Ha ha ha! How about a drink?"

"Are they *gone*?" said Zeta, stricken.

"Yeah," said Starlitz sadly. "Sorry, sweetheart. We just missed 'em. They're flying off to Istanbul to do their next concert."

Wiesel looked down at Zeta. "What's this then, a little fan? Another sweepstakes winner?" He dabbed a hand in his stiff new shoulder bag and came out with a silver Japanese blob. "Give us a nice big smile! I'll take your picture, precious."

"Make them come back again!" Zeta insisted, hopping in place in her anguish. "I want to see them!"

"I can't do that," said Starlitz regretfully. "Once they seal the doors and start taxiing, it's a total security thing."

Zeta clutched at her sweets box with a wail of despair.

"Oh, don't cry now, darling!" said Wiesel hastily. He aimed his pocket camera. "Here, give us a smile! I can put you in newspapers!"

Zeta shot Wiesel a poisonous glare. Wiesel pantomimed a shot. There was no flash. Wiesel looked at his lens in puzzlement. "Oh, hell."

"Tell you what," said Starlitz to Zeta. "You see that big ugly guy over there, with the fez and the big hammered crates? That's Ahmed, our collectibles guy. He's got all the band memorabilia. You tell him I said to show you everything he's got. All the best stuff."

Zeta blinked away tears. "Really?"

"Yeah, really. For you it's all on the account. Quick now, before he gets away."

Zeta scampered off.

Starlitz turned to Wiesel, scowling. "Why'd you sell me out to Ozbey, you dumb bastard?"

Wiesel shrank back on his rotating stool. "Because it's my way through! I *love* Istanbul—just like you said I would! It's got cafés a thousand years old. So what's Y2K to them, or them to Y2K? I'll just sit quiet under some nice awning with my hubble-bubble, till everything blows over. I'll polish my lenses, and cash my paychecks, and count my blessings."

"And what else did he hire you for, Wiesel? You're gonna be out with your big telephotos, trolling for lefties and Kurds?"

"If it pays the bill, of course I am! Nothing wrong with

working for Ozbey—because he's NATO, y'know! He's fightin'
Commies, just like the Swingin' Sixties in Carnaby Street! His
kind of work, it's all about click-click-click at Miss Christine
Keeler."

"Look, Wiesel, you and I had an arrangement."

Wiesel pawed nervously at his empty gin glass. Despite his
bluff front he was the picture of moral conflict. "Look, don't
feel badly about this. So what if you lost some stupid band?
You'll be back, Leggy. You're always back, with another daft
scam. Because you're Leggy."

"I needed you, man. I had you on personal retainer."

Wiesel sniffed, considering. "Yeah, awright," he said at
last. "Your money was good, and a deal's a deal, right? A man's
as good as his word. So, I won't let you down, Legs. I'm gonna
turn you on to someone else, you get me? Somebody really
sweet. My man Tim. Tim the Transatlantic. Tim from ECHE-
LON. You got a biro?"

Starlitz handed him a chromed fibertip.

Wiesel reached into his wallet, plucked out the dog-eared
business card of a London camera repair shop, and flipped it
over. "So here you go," he said, scribbling. "Beeper number.
Twenty-four hour. Now, he's your man, our Tim. Up on all the
latest equipment. Big computer boffin, you know? 'Never Says
Anything.' "

Starlitz lifted his brows. "This guy 'Never Says Anything'?"

Wiesel put one finger along his gin-flushed nose. "Tim
from ECHELON sees all, Tim knows all! Never says a word!"

"Does Tim work scale?"

" 'Scale'? He's so far underground, he's got eyes in orbit!"

"Okay," Starlitz grunted, jamming the business card into
his pocket. "Yeah. I think I might have a use for this."

"No hard feelings, then? Shake the old hand, brother?"

"No," said Starlitz. He had just spotted Ozbey.

Ozbey emerged from behind the airport customs booths.
Even Starlitz, who made something of a habit of buying offi-

cial favors, had never seen such jolly customs personnel as these local Turkish Cypriots. They were whacking yellow chalk along G-7's untouched crates and cases, as if they were proud and privileged to have the opportunity.

Ozbey broke from their hearty grips and mustached cheek-kisses. He crossed the lounge to the bar. "Leggy, we've all been waiting."

"How's the situation, Mehmetcik? Everything under control?"

"I would say so, yes."

"Drink, boss?" offered Wiesel.

Ozbey gave Wiesel a silent, contemplative stare.

Wiesel slid a five-million-lira note across the bar, touched the brim of his hat, hoisted his shoulder bags, and vanished.

Ozbey brushed at his spotless jacket sleeves, settled daintily onto the cleanest, least-damaged barstool, and crossed his creased trousers at the knee. Starlitz had never seen Ozbey looking so dapper. Ozbey was poised, radiant, and stagy; if Starlitz wasn't mistaken, Ozbey had even gained a full two inches in height. His Cyprus jaunt had clearly been a tonic to Ozbey: he was tanned, rested, and looked ready for any conceivable form of mayhem.

Ozbey glanced back at the disbanding cluster of customs men with mock disdain. "Her Former Majesty's Former Customs Service . . . It's important to care for them properly. Turkish Cyprus is a Commonwealth country, another government service, there are certain interbureau rivalries. . . . We must remain friendly."

"Yes, I agree."

Ozbey settled confidently onto one elbow. "I have to compliment you, Leggy. The new American One."

"Yes, Mehmetcik?"

"I believed that the *old* American One was good. But no, no! That old girl was weak, sick, a loser! I *love* this new Yankee girl! She's big and tough, and as they say in America, she takes

no shit from anyone! She's like a cop!" Ozbey smiled in delight. "I love cops! A man can't own too many of them."

"I feel just the same way."

"This will be an excellent pop tour. Now I'm sure of it. I
have great confidence. I've decided to extend G-7's Turkish
program. More engagements for the girls. Bursa, Izmir, Konya,
Trabzon—even Diyarbakir!"

"You think that's wise? You don't want to wear them out
before their big Iran junket."

"Yes, of course, Iran, but . . . why just Iran? There is also
Azerbaijan. And Turkmenistan. Chechnya, Dagestan, Uzbekistan, Kyrgyzstan, Tatarstan, and the Chinese Uighur Republic. . . . A world! A world of Turkish-speaking peoples, entering
history again, waking up to the global market."

"I agree that they're just waking up, but . . ."

Ozbey lowered his voice. His handsome eyes glittered
with steely resolve. "Leggy, this is a war. A culture war. A war
for the soul of the next century. My uncle the minister and I,
we have invested very much in this. Day by day our tactics
improve."

"No kidding."

"We used to bribe journalists. How useless that was! My
uncle has a better approach. Now we buy the media! We own
two new television stations now, financed from our chain of
casinos. We are gaining extensive interests across the entertainment industry. You see? Political capital and banking capital. Very much cross-leveraged."

"That's very Rupert Murdoch of you. Very Vladimir Guzin-
sky."

"The tactic works beautifully in Turkey! Once we control
the channels *and* the content, then we can take the war inside
the homes, and heads, and hearts, of the fundamentalists. The
future of Islam is spangled brassieres—or dark little head-
kerchiefs." Ozbey looked up sharply. "Are you laughing?"

"Fuck, no, man! I totally concur with that analysis."

"I knew you would agree. Istanbul has two futures after Y2K. She could be a Moslem Rome—or the next Teheran. A great world capital—or a fanatic's dungeon. The playground of the East—or the West's worst nightmare. I know the stakes. I know the trends. I know which side I'm on. And I know that I can win!"

Starlitz sucked air through his teeth. "I gotta hand it to you, Mehmetcik: that new pitch is great! The World Bank and the IMF would totally love you for that. I bet you could do with a drink now."

But Ozbey was not to be derailed. He leaned forward intently, steepling his fingers like a talk-show pundit. "Victory centers on consumer goods and pop promotion. 'Bread and circuses,' in other words. If *that* is the battlefield, then I *know* that we can win. Can Kurdish separatists offer us platform shoes? Of course they can't! Can mullahs make a pretty girl a star? They'd rather stone her to death! But the 'military-entertainment complex'! Oh, yes!" Ozbey banged the laminated bar. "Those things together, military force and entertainment: that's the heart of modern Turkey, that works for me."

Starlitz nodded through the sermon like a metronome. "I see. Yep. That's it. I'm betting on the side with the most TVs. Every fuckin' time. Definitely."

"In a culture war you can't ask if the weapon is good or bad. The weapon exists, and the weapon works, and that is obvious. The true question, Leggy—this is our part of this story—is: Who has the best use for this fine G-7 weapon? Is it you—or is it me? And, Leggy—given your personal performance in the last few days . . . these unexplained absences from the band's important business . . ."

Starlitz held up one hand. "You don't have to go on, Mehmetcik."

For the first time Ozbey looked startled. "No?"

"No. Because I see where you're going, and I'm already there. It's true: I've let you down about the band. I didn't want to disappoint you, but I have to do it. A family crisis has come up." Starlitz drew a heavy breath. "It's about my father."

Ozbey gazed at him in limpid astonishment. "Your *father*?"

"Yeah. Father."

"Not girlfriend? Not daughter?"

Starlitz scowled. "No, man, you heard me: my father."

"When did this happen? I had no word of this."

"Well, it's like I told you earlier. I gave you a promise: 'If I can't handle the band, you'll be the first to know.' So now you're the first to know: I can't handle the damn band. I have to leave Cyprus right away. I have no choice in the matter. I understand this may be the last time I ever see my father."

"The last time to see your father," said Ozbey. "What sad news. I'm very sorry to hear that." He seemed genuinely touched.

"I'm sorry, too, Mehmetcik. It means I have to leave the act entirely in your charge."

Ozbey stroked his chin. "I see."

"I hope you're up for that responsibility. You've been terrific on the publicity and money angle: I give you every credit there. But with all this butch talk about 'warfare' that you just handed me, I'm a little concerned. They may be pop stars, but they're still young, vulnerable girls, under all those wigs and the WonderBras."

Ozbey watched him warily.

"Sure," said Starlitz reasonably, "they have big expense accounts, and they sleep with anything in pants, and they can barely dance. Or sing. But you know something? I spent three long years with this act. We toured every hellhole in Eurasia. I recruited and fired nineteen different women, out of seven different nationalities. And let me tell you something crucial. *Not a single one of them has died.*"

Ozbey considered this. The prospect was new to him. "Not even one?"

"That's right, man. There's been drug addiction, bankruptcy, jet lag, sex scandals. There was pregnancy, herpes, motorcycle spills, punch-ups in nightclubs, wigs ripped off, fan stampedes, hotel thefts, you name it. But *no dead ones.* Because *every single one of them makes it to Y2K alive.* That is a central part of the G-7 magic."

Ozbey frowned thoughtfully. "Did you say, '*through* Y2K alive'?"

"No, no, I said *to* Y2K alive."

"I see."

"Because, see, that's when we wrap it all up and put it away. Once we're past Y2K, well, who gives a shit? It's all yesterday then, it's not my problem. But *up* to Y2K, yes, that *is* my problem. And that means, now, that it's *your* problem."

"Was this really part of the arrangement?"

"Absolutely. From before the start of the band. *No dead ones.* Can you promise me that? No dead ones?"

Ozbey wasn't having it. "We're pop promoters. We're not God. We can't guarantee people's fates."

"All right, Mehmetcik, then I'll put it another way. The 'military-entertainment complex.' I get your pitch there, I'm with the program. Of course, you can be a soldier, and also be a great entertainer. That's why armies have military bands. That's why the Mafia's in show business. But if you're a professional, *you don't kill the talent.* You get me? That is my point, that's how it works. Kill the enemy, sure. Kill the audience, even. *You don't kill the talent.*"

Ozbey was uneasy now. It was clear that this new factor was disrupting his analysis. Finally, he offered a diplomatic smile. "Why so upset? They're seven young girls with no talent."

"They're still our performers. They make the act what it is."

"They know nothing about reality. They dance, they sing, they sell clothes. The culture war does not concern them. Because to them it is totally a secret war."

"Ignorance is bliss, huh?"

Ozbey nodded somberly. "It is for women."

"All right," said Starlitz. "I won't kick about that part. I just want you to promise me one thing, before I go. I want you to give me your word that you'll look after these seven foreign women"—he pointed at Gonca—"in just the same way that you look after *her.*"

"But Gonca Utz is my second wife! A great artist! And the G-7 girls are nothing but pretense! You admitted that to me."

"Of course I admit that. I know it, and you know it. But a girl is a girl, Mehmetcik. You know, democracy, human rights, Helsinki Convention, all that crap. Get with the story line here."

Ozbey was stubbornly silent.

"I'm sentimental about this," Starlitz insisted. "I worry, otherwise."

"You're trying to trap me," Ozbey said at last. "You want me to tie the future of your silly girls to the great golden future of Gonca Utz. But your girls are nothing, a trick to sell shoes. Gonca is a great artist, the soul of the people."

"So you're admitting you're not up to the job, then," Starlitz said.

Ozbey glowered. "I did not say that."

"Two minutes ago you were bragging about this great, sophisticated weapon you had. And now what do I hear from you? Instead of field-stripping the weapon properly, and learning the professional drill, you're going to rust it out and break it, and leave it on the road, like some kind of cheap Kurdish mountain bandit."

Ozbey smiled tautly. "You're trying to make me lose my temper."

"What am I asking of you here? Nothing that *I* wouldn't do! They didn't come to any harm while *I* was managing them. If you put Gonca into my care, you wouldn't have to fret about Gonca."

"You could not touch Gonca Utz. Not her sandal. Not the hem of her skirt."

"You talk a pretty good game for a beginner, Ozbey. But I think you need to decide who you are." Starlitz sighed. "Are you smart and suave and slick, like you think that you are—or are you just secret, cheap, and dirty?"

Zeta reappeared, skidding across the airport's dusty floor.

The hair beneath her snappy, glitter-shedding hat brim exploded with a rainbow set of G-7 plastic-fanged hair grips and fabric scrunchies. She wore the G-7 pink and rhinestone plastic shades, the shapeless extra-large "Turkey Tour" pullover. On one narrow wrist she swung a yellow net G-7 poolside bag, which was stuffed to bursting with G-7 lip balm, hair gel, and foot spray. Beneath the other arm she clutched the much-coveted G-7 Tour Bus Set, with its seven dolls, its driver figurine, and its working gas pump. She sported three different versions of the dainty Taiwanese G-7 "sports watch," wore the popper-bead candy necklace, and toted the squeeze-canteen blob-sack of benzoate-yellow G-7 "energy drink."

Ozbey stared down at her.

"You are right," he said crisply, glancing up at Starlitz. "They are guests, and I am their host. It's a matter of honor. I value their life, I promise: just as I value Gonca's life."

"That's all I wanted," said Starlitz. "Now you're talking like a man."

He offered his hand. Ozbey shook it reluctantly.

"When can we expect you back?" said Ozbey.

"Don't expect me."

Ozbey brightened. "You're not coming back?"

Starlitz sighed. "No, it's just that it's never any use expecting me." He put his hand on Zeta's shoulder and walked her away.

Zeta was quiet as they retreated. "He's scary," she said at last.

Starlitz grunted. He stared through a sheet of dusty glass

onto the drought-stricken tarmac. The Turkish Air flight was just getting up speed, carrying three years of hard work. He watched it climb into the sky, on dark twin rails of jet spew.

"He's scary, Dad. He's not real, and he looked right through me. He doesn't know what I am." Zeta was pensive. "I hope you're not mad."

"It's okay, Zeta. You're fine. You just gotta take it a little easy. Try not to scare the straights."

"I bet Turkey would really be fun if it wasn't for all the scary guys."

Starlitz turned from the window. "Forget about Turkey, babe. Real soon now, you and me, we're flying to Mexico."

Zeta's clear brow clouded thoughtfully. "*They're* not real, either, are they, Dad? I mean, the G-7 girls. You made them up, right? They're not real."

Starlitz said nothing.

"It's okay, Dad. I don't care. Mom One and Mom Two really hate G-7, but I knew all along that they were just pretend. I *like* G-7. I like video games, they're not real. I like cartoons, they're not real. I like John Webster's revenge plays, even though they're just make-believe."

Starlitz stood flatfooted. "You like John Webster's revenge plays?"

"Yeah, *Duchess of Malfi, White Devil,* those are my favorites!"

"I keep forgetting you were schooled at home," Starlitz said.

Zeta stared across the echoing hall. She had suddenly noticed Gonca Utz. "Who is *she?*"

"Well, that happens to be a real one."

"A *real* one! Wow! How did *she* get in here?"

"She's a star," said Starlitz. "She is a true rising star, and the world doesn't know it yet."

"Wow, she is so *beautiful!*" Zeta looked at her, goggle eyed behind her cheap plastic shades. "What should I do, Dad? Because she's a star."

"Go ask her for her autograph."

"Oh, I can't." Zeta was attacked by shyness.

"Go ahead! It's what stars live for."

Starlitz watched from a careful distance as his daughter approached Gonca Utz. Zeta bravely traipsed around the perimeter of Ozbey's thick-necked bodyguards, and intruded herself on the actress's attention. Miss Utz put down her clipboard, plucked out her Walkman earplugs, removed her Milanese sunglasses. She offered Zeta a radiant, unguarded smile that would have killed and cooked any male human being.

Zeta returned, skipping. "Look, she signed on my arm with a pen!"

"Wow."

"She was super nice to me! She wrote, like, a whole secret message on me." Zeta stared at the long Turkish script. "I wonder what it says."

"Let's go wash that off before we leave," said Starlitz.

STARLITZ AND ZETA WOKE ANOTHER CABDRIVER AS HE SLUM-
bered in the sun outside the terminal. They returned to the Meridien. Dragged from its dogmatic snooze, the hotel was suddenly booming. A new set of international flagpoles had gone up, and every banner in developed Europe snapped in the offshore sea breeze. The ancient neon had been uprooted and cast aside, while a new digital display board, four times its size, lay in the grass to await its moment. A new television logo was being painted across the hotel's top floors, while the roof sprouted a high-tech forest of spanking-new microwave horns.

A flock of limos had appeared like magic below the casino's portico, sporting plates from Istanbul, Ankara, and Adana.

Inside the place the line at registration was bustling.

"I'm hungry," Zeta complained. "I'm all hot and sweaty!"

Starlitz examined her. "Better lose that big hat and the pullover. You can change in my room."

They stepped into the elevator. Even the hotel's Muzak had transmuted, from old sixties British nostalgia hits to a snappy syndrum medley of nineties Turkish pop divas: Sibel Can, Ebru Gündes, Hülya Avsar. Zeta tapped her foot in time, with a flapping, smacking sound. She was wearing a plastic, pebbled set of G-7 beach zoris.

Starlitz tried his key. The door did not respond. He removed an American Express card and popped the lock.

The rumpled hotel bed had been stripped and not remade. There was no sign of Vanna. "Damn!" Starlitz said. "We gotta find your mom."

"Why, Dad?"

"Because she's got all your clothes and all your documents."

"But I don't have any luggage! Mom One sold all our stuff in Budapest."

"Well, I noticed she still had that big Guatemala bag with her."

"Huh." Zeta wrinkled her nose. Then she walked across the room to the phone. She picked it up entirely from the bedside: an ungainly, old-fashioned Ericsson handset.

An American passport had been taped to the phone's brass bottom, along with some baby aspirin, a folding toothbrush, three animal Band-Aids, and a set of barrettes.

"She always hides stuff under there," said Zeta practically. "Like our house keys, and our pager numbers and stuff."

Starlitz flipped through Zeta's grimy passport. He examined the grinning, pigtailed blur beneath the official lamination. "This photo sure doesn't look much like you."

"Oh, my pictures never look like me."

Starlitz examined the passport's stamped pages. "I think they spelled your names wrong. And there's no record here of your ever being in Cyprus. Or even in Hungary."

"What's that mean?"

Starlitz shrugged.

A polite knock sounded at the door. Viktor Bilibin had appeared.

"Hi, Vic!" Zeta sang out.

Viktor aimed a crooked grin at her. "Pretty clothes," he said in English.

"How did you get up here?" said Starlitz in Russian.

"Our agents are watching this casino. There is much activity. They saw you come in with the little girl."

"And what about the girl's mother? Have you seen her mother?"

Viktor was startled. "Is that ugly old woman truly her mother?" He shook his head. "No, I haven't seen her anywhere. I guess she left Girne."

"Stop talking Russian!" Zeta insisted.

"Well, that's Vanna all over," Starlitz muttered. "She was never the kind of woman who would stay where you put her."

"For you we will speak English," Viktor told Zeta gallantly. "You are ready to go inside the plane again? My uncle is waiting with the plane, to leave Cyprus."

"But I don't want to get back in that stupid plane!" said Zeta bitterly. "There's no room inside it, and it smells like plastic!" She threw herself on the bare mattress, crossed her arms, and lowered her chin to her chest.

"It's no use to stay here," said Viktor sympathetically, and switched to Russian. "Ozbey has beaten you. The band is his story now."

"He hasn't beaten me," Starlitz said. "I have other obligations."

Viktor shrugged. "You are doing the best thing." He patted his shallow chest, easing his tender Russian heart. "Forget G-7! Your own flesh and blood is more important than that silly pack of floozies!"

"Why the tough talk, Viktor? You always came across like quite the G-7 fan."

"I liked them at first," said Viktor sulkily. "But I bore easily. . . ."

"You didn't actually have sex with any of them, did you?"

"Well, only one."

"*Which* one?"

Viktor frowned. "That would be telling!"

"Oh, never mind. To hell with it. It's all part of the program." Starlitz shook his head. "The sons of bitches tried to throw me outta my own room. . . . I gotta clean out my office and get the hell off this island."

"It's too late. Ozbey's men raided your office."

"You're kidding."

"No, they took the extra sets of financial books and all the floppy disks. In all the confusion here it was easy."

"Damn," said Starlitz. "That's a real blow."

"There is also some good news. While they were busy raiding your office, I took my black bag and burgled Ozbey's office." Viktor reached into the bellows pocket of his cargo ankle-pants. "Look, here is a fine Italian pistol from Ozbey's own desk."

"Cool!" said Starlitz, accepting the loaded golden Beretta. He sniffed the chamber. The gun had seen plenty of use.

"And here is a Turkish gun permit identifying the bearer as a special weapons expert in the covert-action department of the MIT. It's stamped and signed!"

Starlitz examined the document, fingering its crisp rag paper with care. With its gilt curlicues and multicolored inks it bore the authentic musty reek of the highest, weirdest levels of Turkey's Kafkalike bureaucracy. "Now, *this* is some valuable paper, kid. This license must be worth ten times what this pistol is. The paper's no use outside Turkey, though." Starlitz handed it back. "You keep it."

"Of course," nodded Viktor, refolding the document carefully. "He has such good taste, Mr. Ozbey. . . . There was a very nice cocktail shaker. . . . Some cocaine, some amyl nitrate, some Viagra. . . . A very candid photo of the girlfriend Gonca. . . . A framed thank-you note from the female Turkish prime minister . . . Also, a complete set, in Turkish, of the works of Jan Fleeminck!"

" 'Jan Fleeminck'? Who's he, some kind of Belgian theorist?"

"No, no, the British spy, the famous imperialist warmonger."

Starlitz pondered this. " 'Ian Fleming'?"

"Yes." Viktor scowled. "Jan Fleeminck, exactly as I said. I have seen those hateful propaganda films . . . *From Russia with Love* . . . Ha! Very old, stupid movie! No understanding of my culture! Many cheap special effects!"

Starlitz was still holding the Beretta. For some reason he did not yet grasp, the dim yet potent intuition struck him that it would make perfect sense to shoot Viktor five or six times now. The Russian had trustingly handed him the pistol, Starlitz knew that it was loaded, he had the drop on Viktor, and this was the last opportunity he would have to shoot Viktor for quite some time. The act of shooting Viktor would increase the world's sum of human happiness. The planet's thin pretense of consensus reality would be far better off with Viktor Bilibin shot. The next time Starlitz made Viktor's acquaintance, it would probably be too late to shoot Viktor—considering that Viktor was an entity with such unique and rapidly developing personal qualities. A mature Viktor on the far side of Y2K would surely be trouble of the gravest kind.

But Starlitz had put that kind of thing well behind him. Shooting Viktor was more trouble to him than it was worth. It was probably *already* too late to shoot Viktor. Besides, there was a child in the room.

Starlitz carefully tucked the pistol in the back of his belt. "Viktor," he said warmly, "I know your uncle's kind of gruff, but deep down the old man must be mighty proud of you. You'll be staying in Cyprus quite a while, right?"

"Of course! I love this island! Girls, sun, music, grilled kebabs . . . It's like paradise!"

"You're not heading anywhere near the United States, right?"

Viktor chuckled. "Ha! As if they'd give *me* a green card."

"Then I guess this is good-bye, Vik. There's just one thing. I want you to keep an eye peeled for this girl's mother, okay? Try the gay bars, peace rallies, veggie restaurants. . . . If you happen to run into her, well, give her a hundred bucks and some tranquilizers. Put it all on my tab."

Viktor nodded respectfully. "Good-bye, Mr. Starlitz. It was pleasant to meet you. Thank you, that I learned so much from you. How do I call you?"

"You just keep your cell phone handy, Viktor; I'll call you. Where is Khoklov now?"

KHOKLOV WAS WAITING FOR THEM, NEAR THE ABANDONED beach in the ghost town of Famagusta. Following his phoned instructions, they'd pulled up at the entropic, collapsing corner of the defunct Greek metropolis. The half-abandoned petrol station, which dated back to the early seventies, sat just at the edge of the Verboten Zone. A dispirited, weedy line of Martian-red barbed wire stretched halfway into the Mediterranean surf.

Khoklov had brought his special airplane with him, stuffed into the trunk of a large Mercedes sedan. The petrol station had everything Khoklov needed for their escape flight: gasoline, compressed air, relative privacy, and a flat launching surface.

Starlitz gazed past the feeble Famagusta Green Line at the glassless facades of the crumbling, pastel beach hotels. The grim exigencies of the civil war had caused the Greek section of Famagusta to be entirely evacuated. The Greeks were un-

willing to return, and the Turks were forbidden to go in.
Therefore, the little pocket Riviera had turned into a creaking,
swaying, grass-covered necropolis.

The year 1974 had taken a fatal wound to the guts here;
pinned like a Cypriot moth in a cigar box, 1974 had become a
parodic derelict, blasted clean from the grip of time. Big flocks
of urban pigeons wheeled out of their impromptu rookeries.
Houseplants had eaten all the homes. Feral lemons and or-
anges supported a mini-ecosystem of rats and stray dogs.

"Nice car you got here," Starlitz remarked.

"It's Albanian," nodded Khoklov, lifting the trunk lid and
pocketing the keys. "The Albanians are the biggest car thieves
in Europe. The country's entire regime are car thieves. They
can snatch a Mercedes out of Bonn and have it in a minister's
garage in twelve hours."

"Swell racket," Starlitz allowed. "Beats smuggling cigarettes."

"Luxury car alarms don't scream aloud anymore. It's all
about satellite locators now," Khoklov said darkly. He glanced
across the tarmac. "Tell your daughter to hand me that air
hose."

Zeta obediently came forward, tugging the long black reel.
Then she returned to chatting with the gas station's attendant,
a scarred Turkish Cypriot urban guerrilla who had settled into
a kindly middle age. The mustached station manager had the
squinting look of a veteran sniper, but he had just favored Zeta
with a gratis Neapolitan ice-cream bar from his big frosty gas-
station fridge. It was clear that the old guy didn't get much
custom here at the edge of the abandoned barricade. The station was clearly a front for some other activity entirely.

"This geezer grease monkey gonna give us any trouble
here?" Starlitz said, squinting in the setting sun.

"He's on the payroll," Khoklov said patiently. "He's a Communist."

"Oh, yeah. Of course. That would explain it."

"Give me a hand with the president's airplane. This is harder than it looks, you know."

Serbia's version of Air Force One packed a lot of heft. With its ailerons, cable, and landing gear the collapsed aircraft weighed close to a ton. Getting it to the ghost town in a car trunk had been a real credit to Teutonic suspension systems.

The aircraft had been folded up with crazy Swiss neatness, collapsing in on itself with layer after flat waffled layer, like an impossible cross between an Alpine tent and a vacuum-packed box of incontinence diapers. Starlitz and Khoklov couldn't lift the entire fabric monster at once, but three men, working hard, could manhandle its polyester segments out of the bundling, and stretch and flop them into place.

It was no picnic lugging the twin twenty-eight-horsepower engines. The toughest part of the job was bolting on the tele-scoping landing gear. Compared to the delicate plastic engines the aircraft's rigid ailerons and the lean propellor blades were a literal snap.

After they had spread it out, flat as polyester roadkill, Khoklov patiently pumped compressed air into the craft. Slowly it began to rise, yeastily, flopping and straining as the laboring compressor puffed it into proper shape. A segmented, multiwaffled, ridged single-wing began to assert itself across the weedy tarmac. The inflatable aircraft was twelve meters from tip to tip, and it was sleek, shiny, and deeply anomalous, just like a beached stingray.

"You still remember DOS, don't you?" Khoklov said. "Line commands, and all that?"

"Doesn't this heap run under Windows yet?" Starlitz said.

"We only need to boot the system that controls these ten-sile cables," Khoklov apologized. "After that I can pilot it by joystick."

Starlitz pulled fat, sturdy Velcro straps over the two tiny aircraft engines. Dwarfed by their own fuel tanks, the engines seemed absurdly small and frail. But it was obvious that they could get the job done, because the aircraft itself was nothing more than membranes, air, and wire. It possessed wings, ailerons, a working rudder: with enough air pressure it was rigid enough for serious lift and speed. The polyester fabric skin was German ballistic rip-stop stuff that could probably take small-arms fire. Khoklov had a working four-man aircraft that weighed less than Styrofoam.

"What kind of octane you want?" said Starlitz.

"The highest available."

"Right."

"Don't fill the reserve tanks. With you on board we don't need the extra weight. The coast of Turkey is only half an hour away."

After a few words with the station attendant Starlitz began loading and carrying big jerricans full of gas. Once upon a time Starlitz had hauled containers this size with one hand. Nowadays, though, he waddled forth with a two-handed grip while his spine complained ominously.

Starlitz laboriously decanted the jerrican into a stained plastic funnel. "Pulat Romanevich, this is some fine Swiss craftsmanship here, but I remember you as strictly a Mach one, Mach two kind of guy."

"It's not about speed anymore, Lekhi. Speed went out with the Concorde and the cosmonauts. It's all about stealth now."

"Mmmm."

"President Milosevic and his wife, they're from the old East European school. They don't want to end up like the Ceaușescus. No MiG can protect them from that." Khoklov smiled as he patted the swelling fuselage, which now looked uncannily like a poolside air mattress. "If it comes to the worst, they want to take their famous Rembrandt painting, leave the Presidential Palace in Belgrade, and vanish completely from the NATO radar. Later they'll reappear on their private Greek island with their eight-million-dollar dacha, under the protection of the Orthodox Church. Then the

Milosevic clan will still have enough money in the banks of
Greek Cyprus to buy the son and the daughter a radio station apiece. A year or two to let things cool down, and it's
back to the Slavic revenge fantasies, twenty-four hours a
day."

Starlitz nodded. "Where do you find cool shit like this,
ace? You're way ahead of the curve here."

"Oh, word gets around among us cross-border pilots. The
concept was invented by a German pneumatics company.
They make blimps, air balloons, whole inflatable buildings
with inflatable roofs and inflatable girders. . . . You see, it's
simple. It all goes up, it all comes down. Full of hot air. No
one ever sees how it works, no one ever knows where it goes.
So it's just like a Russian bank, Lekhi."

Starlitz nodded respectfully. "I am so with that!"

A pair of Cypriot boys had arrived from the neighborhood,
pedaling bikes. They looked about six and nine, and wore
striped-sleeve football shirts and big goggling grins.

"Tell them it's a magic gypsy tent," Starlitz recommended
to the station attendant. "Tell 'em we want 'em to step inside."

Given this tale of terror, the kids vanished immediately,
peeling out so fast that their tires shrieked.

"Ladies first," said Khoklov. He offered his arm to help
Zeta climb aboard, through a long, zippered slit.

Starlitz followed.

"I *hate* it in here," Zeta hissed fretfully. She was crammed
into a thrumming fabric space the size and shape of a sleeping
bag. "There's no peanuts or anything! There's no movie, even!
Why do we have to do this?"

"He's Russian, okay?" said Starlitz. "Uncle Pulat's going
through a kind of transitional period. We gotta be polite
about it."

The twin engines started, with a cough and a startling
whine.

Khoklov wriggled aboard. He thrust his pale head into a

transparent bubble and gripped a lozenge-shaped Nintendo joystick.

The aircraft wheeled reluctantly in place. Then a laboring plastic piston came down and painfully levered the plane into the air. The propellors caught. They began to climb, and headed out to sea.

DAYS LATER, THIRTY THOUSAND FEET OVER the Atlantic, Starlitz knocked back a last sip of airline whiskey and leaned his sorry head against a skimpy pillow.

He had once heard from an elderly German that mankind's ultimate luxury was an unbroken night's sleep in a soft bed. Before that leaden, brutally sincere revelation, Starlitz had never been a devotee of slumbering. Nowadays Starlitz took sleep very seriously. Starlitz felt sure that if he ever lived as long as the old German had, his nights, too, would be flaking, restless, and broken by sinister flashbacks: not the thunder of Stalin organs on the frozen Eastern Front, necessarily, but other, more personal equivalents.

Zeta lay curled in a tight, twitching ball under her thin airline blanket. When you were eleven years old, even sleep was frenetic.

A stewardess passed down the aisle, with the trancelike step of a professional who lived between time zones.

Starlitz passed her three empty plastic liquor bottles and five disemboweled foil bags of peanuts. She collected the trash impassively, never meeting his eyes, and left him without a glance. He watched her vaguely as he secured his airline tray. Something about her hip roll and soft-footed shuffle struck Starlitz deep in his core. What was it?

Then he had it: good old what's-her-name.

That Chicago girl. She came in every night, to tidy up the lair of a Chicago machine politician. She was an office cleaner. Starlitz had been up late one sleepless night with the other hustlers, counting the kickbacks and smoking cigars, when little what's-her-name had first meekly entered his life, propelling her bucket and mop.

Little what's-her-face, though only five feet tall, was about a yard across. Anything but frail, she was as sturdy as a tractor. She could have hauled a goat carcass on her shoulders across a Mexican desert while wearing nothing but rubber hua-raches, and with never a wince or complaint. . . . Not promising material to most young guys on the make, granted. No one else in the office had even been able to see her. They had never said a word to her. No other man in the room would ever bother. She was totally beyond their ken.

But he could see her. When she realized that his eyes had focused on her body, she looked up from her mop handle and shot him an opaque, deer-in-the-headlights look. Not so much a feminine come-on, really, as a deliberate, daring step into his story line.

Now it was all coming back to Starlitz, on an interior tide of pained nostalgia and dessicating airline booze. He plucked at his sorry pillow, struggling fruitlessly for comfort. He had the bedroom they'd been in, her smell, her tatty underwear, her face, everything but her name.

As a first hook he'd told her he would help her with her English. She possessed enough bits and pieces of English to pay rent and to buy Mama's bread and sundries. But she had no real command of North American lingo, and she was never going to get any. There just wasn't any room for the world's biggest and pushiest language inside of her rock-solid head. Everything inside her skull was totally occupied with the tremendous, preternatural effort it took to adjust, oil, lubricate, and maintain her remote interior universe.

Their affair, if he could call it that, had lasted eleven months. Mulling over it in his stingy tourist-class seat, Starlitz realized that this was the longest single period that he had ever put up with anyone. After the fruitless English lessons he liked to dress her up to pass, and take her out on the town for disco nites, fine Irish whiskey, and cripplingly expensive steak dinners. It was especially good that she could not read the menus or speak English to the waiters, and yet she wore the classy, intimidating garments of an upper-class WASP matron who could buy any waiter ten times over. He would take her to Chinatown and shovel her full of rice wine and the finest pepper-blazing Szechuan. It was a visceral thrill to see her white teeth crunch through those baby-corn ears.

Twenty years on, and the vitalizing incongruity of it still made Starlitz grin. He'd cared so much about it, their little scene had meant so much to him. It had all been so much . . . *fun*. Now that he could see it in the muddled clarity of middle age, all in amber, tintype retrospect, he realized that little what's-her-name had first claim as the love of his life.

She had the most intense and utter self-possession Starlitz had ever encountered. They could barely speak to each other, but such was life. She might be ugly as a fence post. To get to second base with her was like ground war. He'd never seen her entirely naked. He didn't much want to. It was never remotely like a boy-meets-girl thing. They were two alien worlds in near collision; it was all about earthquakes, gravity, and terrifying primal forces.

Most of the time she silently fought for her virtue, and about one time in three she would switch sides and silently fight against it. It wasn't that the sex was any good, because even for a young guy, as he'd been then, sex with her was way too much like work. No, the reason that Consuelo—and yeah, *that* was it, her name was Consuelo, or something very much like it—had worked out for him was her titanic, liberating reservoir of uniquely personal dissident reality. She could never be described as hot in the sack, but it was life after the sack that amazed him. He would storm out in the middle of the night, freezing and half crippled with unmet male needs, and Chicago would almost vaporize. That enormous, gimcrack, heartland metropolis turned into van Goghian ethereal fire. He felt as if he could walk straight through the city's skyrocketing steel walls. He'd been able to live for months off the great bloody sparks she threw off, from the enormous, invisible friction between herself and Yankee reality. Being with her was like visiting the moon.

She never questioned anything he did. Nothing shocked her—or rather, everything he did shocked her equally, which was to say, not at all.

As the months wore on and his frustration grew, he got crueler and crazier. He would try elaborate gambits to disrupt her fortresslike status quo. He sensed that if he could just impale a secret hole below her waterline, elements of his universe might somehow leak through. So he experimented. He equipped her with closetsful of stolen clothes from the mansions of Oak Park. A mafia-hijacked color TV. Then a big set of zircons. A tiara. Once he stole her a mink.

She sold the clothes at rag sales. She gave the TV to her mother. She put the jewelry in a locked box, and lost it. Even in the dead of Chicago winter she wouldn't wear the mink, although he once spotted her gently stroking it with a look of sorrowful bemusement. As for the rest of it, the vibrator, the thirty-four DD push-up bra, the edible underwear, that was all part of one vast, homogeneous, demonic landscape; the obscene roiling chaos beneath the tightrope wire of decency. She was utterly commonplace, and utterly remote. Knowing her was like shaking a Coke bottle, popping the top, and having the lava of Kilauea pour out.

She wasn't nice to him. She didn't get it about boosting his ego, cadging favors, or pretending any girlish happiness. She even took out her own garbage. His role in her life was entirely symbolic. For Consuelo he was any man and every man. He represented her existential confrontation with the masculine principle. No other man was knocking to get in, and after he left her, she would just settle down with the memories. Higher forces had yanked him out of the properties backstage, and dusted him off and sent him along, because Consuelo's private mythos somehow needed an incubus.

Then, one day, he met her mother. That was all about long white hair, rattling yellowed blinds, and Olmec Santeria. He found himself clawing his way off the sacrificial pyramid in about thirty seconds flat. After that there was no way forward. So, he offered her a stolen diamond ring cut like a hockey rink, begged her to marry him (in neutral ground, a synagogue), and to fly with him to Libya. Consuelo considered this proposal soberly, reached a just and final conclusion, and said absolutely not, never ever. So he threw the diamond into Lake Michigan, wept for a few minutes, and flew to Libya the next Monday, by himself. And that was a swift and final end to all that.

Libya had been just great, everything he expected and more. Except—and he knew this now—he was never going to care about a woman that much again. He could still go through with sex, but the motive force was slacking off. He would never bang his head that hard again; at the best he would shave, dress up, hold out a wad of money, and wait. If they came, they came; and if they didn't come, they didn't come. Big deal. Anything remotely like romance was farther and farther behind him now. Sex would never have a meaning that he couldn't control, there was no danger of its having any genuine consequence for him. In the secret depths of his blood and bone there was no future.

"Hey, Dad."

"What?"

"Hey, Dad."

"Yeah?"

Zeta put her tousled head above the edge of the blanket. "Hey, Dad, my thumbs are all sore from playing Nintendo. Are we there yet?"

"We're in the middle of the sky above an ocean, but we'll get where we have to be."

THE CUSTOMS IN MEXICO CITY WAS EASYGOING ABOUT PASS-ports that looked American. Starlitz emptied his wallet at the currency exchange, taking on a ballast of pesos. He bought himself a duty-free carton of Lucky Strikes and a glass-ribbed three-quarter-liter bottle of Gran Centenario tequila. He bought Zeta a pack of Chiclets.

"I don't like these colored Chiclets," Zeta complained, her eyes red rimmed with jet lag. "I only like the white ones."

"Then only chew the white ones. We've got some shopping to do."

Starlitz threw their meager luggage, and both their passports, into a rented airport locker. He slammed the metal door with finality, went into the airport men's room, and flushed the key. He was looking for his father now. That was the central task at hand. It absolutely had to be done, and it was never an easy job. It was entirely impossible, unless you had entered the vast and shadowy realm of the Undocumented.

Starlitz bought a cheap canvas shoulder-bag with a crude four-color logo of the goat-sucking Chupacabra. He bought a woven Baja jacket with wooden toggle buttons, and with some effort he acquired a hat that was not a "Mexican" hat, but an actual Mexican hat.

"You need a total makeover," Starlitz told his daughter. "Because I'm taking you to meet your grandpa."

"Doesn't Grandpa like G-7 clothes?"

"Grandpa's never heard of G-7." Starlitz shook his head. "You see, when you meet my dad—your grandfather—you can't just 'go see him.' You have to really *let go*, and then, just maybe, you can get a glimpse of him. Because if we're lucky, and the time and the place are just right, your grandfather sort of . . . shows up."

Zeta nodded thoughtfully.

Starlitz tried his best to sound earnest. "You see, Zenobia, now that we're together, you've got to get to know my side of the family. And my side of your family really isn't much like Mom One and Mom Two."

" 'Cause they're New Age lesbians?"

"Oh, no, no. That would be way too simple."

"I'm not much like my side of the family either," Zeta said bravely. "It's okay, Dad."

Starlitz patted her band-T'd shoulder. This heart-to-heart was going rather better than he had expected. "Yeah, Zeta, and it'll help us a lot if you give up your super cool nineties clothes for a while. You need to be wearing different clothes now. Clothes that could have been worn at any and all periods between the years 1901 and 1999. Okay? There's a pretty serious locus of affect around 1945."

"Nineteen forty-five, Dad? Wasn't that World War Three?"

"World War Two."

"Oh, yeah."

"The past is a different country, Zeta. We have to be different now too. We don't take cabs anymore. We're poor people now, you and me. We're poor, and we're invisible. We don't have any ID, so we can't let cops catch us. We don't know any lawyers or doctors, and we don't have a bank. Don't talk to strangers, ever. Pretend you don't speak any English. Never write your name down, never tell anyone who you are." Starlitz drew a breath. "And most of all, stay away from videocams. If you see a security video, just get the hell away from that whole neighborhood, right away."

"What's wrong with videocams?"

"Haven't you noticed yet?"

She shrugged. "I know that videocams don't like me. I break 'em all the time. I even break cameras sometimes."

"That's because of two important things, babe. Surveillance and documentation. It's all about mechanical objectivity, proper observation, the scientific method, reproducible results, and all of that scary crap. If we're going to find your grandpa, we can't be pinned down like that, not even one little bit. We've got to be looser and farther away from the consensus narrative than you've ever gotten before. You understand me? I know this is kind of hard to understand."

Zeta wrinkled her brow. "It's like hide-and-go-seek, sorta, right?"

"Yeah. Sorta."

"We're hunting for Grandpa? We're sneaking up on him in disguise?"

"Yeah. That's the story. Pretty much."

She looked up brightly. "We've got to go underground to nail his sorry ass?"

"*Absolutely!*" Starlitz beamed. "Now you're really with it!"

BY EVENING THEY WERE ON A BUS TO JUAREZ. ZETA FELL asleep against his shoulder, a torn ticket and a half-chewed flour tortilla still in her hand. Starlitz sat chain-smoking amid his neighbors, the cheekboned widow in the frayed black shawl and the pear-shaped gent in the seersucker suit. The night outside the window was full of Central American stars.

Starlitz enjoyed a Mexico City–style coughing fit, tossed the butt, and lit another. He was dead broke now, his baggy cotton pants holding scarcely a peso, but he was far from lost in the world, because he still had cigarettes. Cigarettes, always the primal currency of the twentieth-century underground, the war stricken, the occupation forces, the resistance, and the jailed. The secret wealth of the gulag, Occupation Paris, stilyagi Moscow, of Hong Kong boat people, and a thousand county clinks and rehab clinics. He'd been smoking all day, because it hid his face, it fit him in, it made him commoner. As long as he never took the trouble to check inventory, he knew that there would still be cigarettes left, in the bottom of the bag.

Starlitz and Zeta spent nine days in Juarez, locating a coyote, and waiting for the mighty coyote to deign to take them across the Big River, to The Pass. Rio Grande, El Paso, the pass into El Norte, that vast, legendary realm of cruelty and gold.

Starlitz saw that El Norte had sent its writhing, unnatural tentacles over the border, and El Norte had come to stay. El Norte had sunk down great big solid roots here in the maquiladora country; there was no more slumbering mestizo vibe about this part of Mexico now, there was nothing here you could successfully repel with any bandolier and any machete. Japan was here building gizmos of plastic with double-A batteries, multinat Europe had blown into town with the silicon and the big wheels. This place was Mexico, all right, still definitely a wholly owned family enterprise, but it was Mexico 1999, La NAFTA, Mexico as the world's first and only Latin American economic superpower. The snake and eagle were a hiccup and sneeze away from the third millennium.

The down-market streets were full of wandering, booze-dazed Yankees, so they ate quite well and slept better after Starlitz had lifted a wallet.

Zeta looked a little downcast over her greasy stack of white corn tamales. "Dad, it's not right to pick people's pockets, is it?"

"Absolutely not!" Starlitz assured her firmly, chasing the

beans on his flowered tin plate with a Taiwanese fork. "The margins in the pickpocket racket are razor thin. Lifting wallets the right way takes organization: the bumper, the lifter, the getaway guy. . . . That's way too much labor for the rate of return. The only cats who make out picking pockets are specialists, they farm people out to hit airports and trains. It's a franchise. Forget about it."

"Is it bad that you stole that drunk guy's wallet?"

"You bet it's bad, but it's worse not to pay your coyote when you cross the big river."

"Okay, Dad." She put a semicircle of toothmarks into her tamale.

THEIR COYOTE WAS THE KIND OF SORRY, AMATEUR COYOTE you could find in a border town, on a bad weekend, with broken Spanish. The coyote was an acne-faced Tejano kid with a silver buckle and a big black cowboy hat, who figured he had *la Frontera* sussed because he carried the proverbial *pistola en la mano*.

After midnight their little cluster of the adventurous unemployed waded the concrete-lined Rio Grande, and were almost immediately flushed out by a pack of Migra with infrared cams. Luckily, thanks to a recent shoot-to-kill scandal, the uniformed agents of the INS were a little more sluggish and tentative than usual. Scrambling up the harsh concrete incline, Starlitz and Zeta hit the thorny dirt and froze in a meager patch of tumbleweed, while a thundering herd of booted feet and whining dogs passed them not ten feet away. Then they climbed and plucked and lightly bled their way through the barbed wire, and slithered and tiptoed between and among the various spotlit free-fire zones, until, finally, they emerged onto a cracked, weed-grown sidewalk of a formally American street.

"Hey, Dad," Zeta panted, picking vicious burrs out of her hair.

"Yeah?"

"Hey, Dad, you know something?"

"What?"

"Hey, Dad, you know something, I never did anything like *this* before. This is *terrible*. I'm hungry, I'm hungry all the time. I feel cold, and I'm dirty. We have to walk everywhere. We go to the bathroom right on the ground. I don't have my own house, or any water."

"Yep. That's the story line, all right."

"How come this feels so normal?"

"Because this *is* normal. Most of the people in the world live like this. Most people have *always* lived like this. Most people have always *expected* to live like this. This is the great untold back-story, it's the genuine silent majority. Most people in the world are totally poor, and totally obscure. Billions of people live like this. It never makes a headline. No camera ever looks at it, they're never on TV. Nobody who matters ever pretends to care."

They walked on silently for some time, passing cracked streetlights and shabby convenience stores boasting of lottery payoffs. "Hey, Dad."

"What."

"Hey, Dad."

"What?"

"Do poor people eat lightbulbs?"

"Why would they wanna do that?" Starlitz paused thoughtfully. "Do *you* eat lightbulbs?"

Zeta fell two steps back and muttered inaudibly.

"What was that?"

Paralyzed with shyness, she looked up. "I said, 'only the frosted white ones.' "

"Did anyone ever *see* you eat lightbulbs?" His voice grew sharp. "Did you ever *tell anyone* that you eat lightbulbs? You never ate lightbulbs in front of a camera, did you?"

"No, no, no, no, Dad, I never told anybody."

"Well, I guess you ought to be cool, then."

"Really?" she brightened. "Great."

They walked on silently. "I would watch it with the light-bulb thing," he said at last. "I mean, they're made of glass and metal, when you think about it. That's inorganic."

Zeta said nothing.

"It's okay," he soothed, "I'm your dad, and you can tell me about these things. It's all right, Zeta. It's *good* to tell me."

AN ELEVEN-YEAR-OLD GIRL HAD NO TROUBLE HITCHING rides with the kindly and supportive rural populace of New Mexico. They were a little disappointed to discover that she didn't speak border Spanish, but they wouldn't make an issue of this when she was accompanied by her large, silent, hat-wearing dad. Their migration was slow and semirandom, full of long, dusty roadside waits and many doublings-back, but the continent's crust moved below their feet, and their destination was no particular place. Their destination was a state of mind.

Except for the possible interest of bored sheriff's deputies, there was no real hazard in hitchhiking. The locals were people of the mountain-studded North American Empty Quarter. Under no circumstances would they dream of turning in Starlitz and Zeta to the loathsome minions of distant Washington. A couple of their drivers even pulled off the road, fed them chile, and picked up the tab. One generous matron offered to buy Zeta better shoes.

They slept in culverts and under bridges, slowly climbing up toward the arid, piney reaches of Socorro.

Now they walked up the side of a broken road, built for some long-forgotten military encampment. Zeta was browner and thinner. Despite their hard nights and their meager, irregular rations, she seemed to have grown an inch. She was alive, in motion, and breathing mountain air. Every day, every hour, put a new, visible lacquer of experience on the fine surface of her young soul.

"Dad, are we there yet?"

"Almost. I can feel it. We're definitely closing in."

"Does Grandpa live around here?"

"No, he doesn't live anywhere in particular, but this is the place that turned him into what he is. Or what he was. You know. Whenever."

Starlitz finally settled on a broken, paint-flaking Quonset hut, in a declining suburb of Socorro. Someone had forgotten to buy the place out and develop it; likely it was fatally out of code, commercially hammerlocked by some distant federal registry of toxic sites.

As Starlitz and Zeta settled into the place, chasing its cobwebs and dropping candy wrappers, the nature of its allure slowly clarified. This eldritch structure had once been part of a great, reality-shattering research effort, the bloody midcentury parturition of Big Science. The place definitely had the smell and taste of Major Technological Advent, a faint metallic isotropic tang of anomalous Geiger activity, from backyard lab procedures dating back to the Belle Epoque of Marie Curie, when stuff that glowed in the dark was considered a nerve tonic.

Some local mestizo junk guy had picked the metal barn up off the atomic security lot, sometime after the mighty Fall of Oppenheimer, and some small, tax-evading businessman had hammered and wire-tied the military lab back together, put up its arching iron bands and its waffled sheet iron. It had acquired a series of cut-through, tie-on, handmade wooden shacks, like a series of paradigmatic airlocks into the world of proletarian poverty.

As the southwestern decades passed, the little complex had picked up consumer detritus like the stony growth of a desert rose; a gas pump, a wooden sign, various pachuco spray-bombings, dead batteries, a new concrete floor, a dog's lair or maybe an urban coyote's; dead tractor tires, fake nylon Paiute blankets; foot-crushed, illegible, oil-stained calendar pages of zaftig beach-babes, souvenir fake-flint arrowheads chipped by retrofitted war-machines in occupied Japan, fossilized squirts of axle grease, splintered wooden pallets, frayed pulley-belts with every atom of use rubbed out of them by bitter years of high RPM; bent, dented copper rivets, heel-piercing shards of rainbow-colored, fingernail-paring-shaped lathe scrap, six wooden-handled tin buckets of paint long congealed into rubbery, colorless solids, a rat-haunted stack of ancient cedar firewood, empty, logoed flour sacks half gone to woven powder, empty bottles of Jim Beam and Dos Chamucos tequila, a curled-up, sand-eaten, fatally kinked coil of garden hose. . . .

They spent a cold night on the concrete floor, lighting a little tramp fire on the cracked cement, dancing together to try to keep warm, but there was no sign of the old man.

"I'm sorry he didn't show up," Starlitz said resignedly, in the grim pink light of dawn. "This is going to be harder than it looks. I kind of figured it might be, this being the very, very tag end of the century and all, but I didn't want us to do all that work, if we didn't have to. We'll have to try again, and this time we're gonna have to really put some effort in it."

"Doesn't Grandpa know we're here?"

"He doesn't have to know." Starlitz scratched his greasy hair. "We can try the Christmas thing. It's an entryway," he explained. "Every twentieth-century Christmas is pretty much like all the other ones. Christmas got more consumer oriented every year of the century, as the Judeo-Christian thing lost its shareholder value, but the holidays tend to work for him. The surveillance always eases around Christmas. People are sloppy drunk and fighting with their relatives, so they never look hard at strangers. The newspapers are skinnier, the TVs are full of old comedians. Back when I used to see my dad a lot, he would always show up around Christmas. . . . Kinda wander into town to see me for the holidays, you know. . . . In Florida, mostly."

"Are you from Florida, Dad?"

"Yeah, no, maybe. When I was your age, after my mom finally went into the hospital and couldn't come out again, there was this old guy from outside Tallahassee who took me up . . . the Professor, we used to call him. . . . This woman he was with—my stepmom, I guess—she used to feed us. . . . I used to help out on his great project." Starlitz rubbed his sandaled heel on an oil stain. "Kind of a child-labor, backwoods, Florida-hick thing, really."

"He had a great project? I wish I had a great project. What kind of great project?"

"Oh, the usual. Guys like the Professor, they're beyond the fringe, but there's generally some kind of huge, cranky scam going down there. . . . Guys like him generally have a great project, if they're strong enough. . . . If it's way outside your discourse, the 'great project' looks totally nuts. But if you're inside the story line, it definitely comes across as some kind of very serious world-changing scheme. . . . The Professor didn't want to be blown out of the consensus narrative, so he was really *clinging on*, you know. . . . Kinda piling up physical evidence of his own existence. . . . The Professor was putting together this, uhm, personal reality anchor. With used car parts and giant chunks of coral. . . . I mean *giant* chunks of Florida coral stone, like five-ton, six-ton chunks. . . . He used to wait till after dark, so nobody would see him pick 'em up and carry them in his arms. . . . It passed as a kind of a folk art, this wacky roadside-attraction thing, at least that's what it *looked* like, this big stone maze he built, and lots of dangling hubcaps and cypress-root sculptures. . . . That's where I lived, when I was a kid."

"Well, why don't we go *there*? I mean, that sounds like a nicer place than this stinky garage. I mean, Florida, wow—I *went* to Florida once. It's warm!"

"A tornado took it. Took him, Stepmom, took the whole compound. Mobile homes, trailer park, brochures, the souvenir stand, everything." Starlitz scratched his dirty head. "At least, they *called* that thing a tornado, after it was gone. . . . See, the poor guy just got to be *too obvious*. There was gonna be some TV coverage, and stuff. . . ."

Zeta scowled. "Why?"

"Well, that's how reality works, that's why."

"Why does it work like that, Dad?"

"It's the laws of nature. It's the birds and the bees."

"I know about *that*, Dad," said Zeta with a wince. "They made me read *Our Bodies, Ourselves* when I was seven."

"If only it were that easy. That's not 'reality.' You see: the deeper reality is made out of language."

Zeta said nothing.

"People don't understand this. And even if they say it, they sure as hell don't know what that *means*. It means there is no such thing as 'truth.' There's *only* language. There's no such thing as a 'fact.' There is no truth or falsehood, just dominant processes by which reality is socially constructed. In a world made out of language, nothing else is even possible."

Zeta searched in the dirt. She picked up a rusty nail. "Is *this* language?"

"Yep. That's a 'rusty nail,' as the conceptual entity called a 'rusty nail' is constructed under our cultural circumstances and in this moment in history."

"It feels real. It still gets my fingers all dirty."

"Zeta, listen to me. This part is really important. 'Even though her father loved her, the little girl died horribly because she stepped on the rusty nail.' That's language too."

Zeta's face crumpled in terror. She hastily flung the nail away into the darkness.

"There is no objective reality. There *might* be a world that has true reality. A world with genuine physics. Like Newton said, or like Einstein said. But because we're in a world that's made out of language, we'll never, ever get to that place from here. There's no way *out* of a world that's made of language. We can never reach any bedrock reality. The only direction we can move is into *different flavors* of the dominant social discourse, or across the grain of the consensus narrative, or—and this is the worst part—into the Wittgenstein empty spaces where things can't be said, can't be spoken, can't even be thought. . . . Don't even go there, okay? You can never *come out* of there. It's a black hole."

"How come you know so much of this stuff, Dad?"

"I didn't use to know any of it. I was just living my life. I just liked to go live at the edge of the system, where things were breaking off and breaking down. It took me a long time to figure out what I was really doing, that I was *always* in some place where the big story was turning into little weird counterstories. But now I'm wising up to my situation, because I'm old now, and I know enough to get along in the world."

Starlitz sighed. "I don't know all that much, really. There are just a few people in this world who understand how reality works. Most of them don't speak English. They speak French. Because they're all language theorists. Semioticians, mostly, with some, uh, you know, structuralists and poststructuralists. . . . Luce Iragaray . . . Roland Barthes . . . Julia Kristeva . . . Louis Althusser . . . These are the wisest people in the world, the only people with a real clue." Starlitz laughed morosely. "And does it help them? Hell, no! The poor bastards, they strangle their wives, they get run over by laundry trucks. . . . And after Y2K their whole line of gab is gonna be permanently out of fashion. It'll be yesterday."

"How come *they* know so much?"

"I don't know how they know. But you can tell they know what's really going on, because when you read what they say, it sounds really cool and convincing, until you realize that even though you know it, you can't use that knowledge to change anything. If you can understand reality, then you can't do anything. If you're doing anything, it means that you don't understand reality. You ever heard of any of those French people? I bet you never heard of any of them, right?"

"I've heard of Julia Kristeva," Zeta volunteered shyly. "She's a second-generation antipatriarchal ideologue, like Carole Pateman and Michèle Le Doeff."

Starlitz nodded slowly, gratified by this revelation. "I'm glad you know about them. . . . I'm glad they taught you some of that already, you so young and all." He shrugged wearily. "I don't spend enough time with Mom One and Mom Two. . . . We disagree on a lot of stuff. . . . We kinda try to get along, but we're always ticked off at each other, like with my arms-smuggling thing on the commune, or that dope ring out of French Polynesia. . . . We fight too much. It's sad, really, you know? I'm sad about it. I should have been around more, helping out, when you were littler." He sighed. "It was never your fault, Zeta. It was just one of those post-nuclear-family things."

"Well, you can't come back to the commune now, because they had to sell out."

"Yeah, I know that. I guess it had to happen. There's a big transformation coming. A change in the story line. There aren't many ways through it." He sighed, and stood up. "I sure hope I can find us one."

STARLITZ RESOLVED ON A FULL-SCALE EFFORT. It was, after all, a.d. 1999, a year promoted for decades as the final excuse for a twentieth-century party. He'd been foolish to hold anything back.

It took a long bus trip back to the border, and a full week's earnest effort, to locate a criminal chop shop. Starlitz ingratiated himself with the speed-crazed bike-gang owners. He carefully wrote down their requisite want-list for marketable windshields, door handles, and mufflers. Then he went out to hunt revenue-on-the-wheel.

His hot-wiring skills were sadly out of practice. In his long absence from the trade, cars had evolved a fiendish repertoire of yelping alarms, backed up with brute-force steering-column clubs. Still, a determined operator with a good eye, a steady hand, and patience was sure to bag a car eventually. It helped a lot to have an alert underage lookout.

Three boosted cars later Starlitz had acquired the requisite sum of folding money. He and Zeta returned by bus to Socorro. They methodically haunted the Goodwills, the St. Vinnies, and the dollar stores. They purchased great shiny wads of flock and tinsel, long, blackout-dotted strands of twinkly Christmas lights, an ancient turntable with working speakers, and a scratched stack of Christmas carols on vinyl. At a desolate yard sale they bagged an unused electrical generator from a despondent New Mexico Y2K survivalist. This tragic geek had forfeited his career, his marriage, and his life savings while trying to hide from buggy software.

Then came a crucial juncture of the operation: assembling a merrie crowd of Christmas revelers in the middle of autumn. Starlitz, who was driving without a license or, indeed, without ID of any kind, borrowed a junked truck from an ill-guarded wrecking yard and set out to hire help. The end result of his rattling, backfiring campaign was a spontaneous choir of local down-and-outs: six illegal-alien day laborers, seeking employment from the parking lot of the local Home Depot; four grimy, cowboy-hatted Native Americans, off the reservation and cruelly paralyzed on gin and ripple; and an ill-assorted pair of aimless, bearded, mystical drug casualties, your basic local Taoists from Taos.

Starlitz drove the revelers, in shifts and by roundabout routes, back to the abandoned Quonset garage. For the sake of the warmth he lit a hearty, mildly toxic fire in a corroded barrel. Starlitz oiled, lubricated, pull-yanked, and adjusted the survivalist generator, while Zeta strung lights and tinsel from the rust-streaked metal walls. There were glitter-coated party hats all around, and plastic-wrapped candy canes. Then, over the generator's industrial racket, they fired up the record player and belted out Crosby's perennial hit "White Christmas."

Since half of the party spoke no English, the chorus was weak. Two gallon jugs of Mogen-David enlivened the festivities considerably.

"Dad, it's super loud! Cops are gonna come!"

"Yeah, no, maybe," Starlitz shouted. "It wouldn't be the first time, given my dad. But this approach is working! I can feel it!"

The sugared booze was hitting his guests like a series of convoy depth bombs. Starlitz gazed about the fire-shadowed walls. Somewhere outside the sonic limits of their scratchy, atemporal racket, chill night had settled over the desert: the dessicated town was surrounded by silent ticking fallout and the cedar-pollen psychic dust of lost Anasazi spirit guides.

"It *is* working," Starlitz realized. "Zeta, look, it worked!"

Zeta removed her hands from her ears. "What did you say?"

"He came, he's here! Your grandpa just showed up."

Zeta looked doubtfully among the half-collapsing revelers.

"Count them!" Starlitz said.

Zeta carefully tallied their guests. "I get thirteen sad old drunk guys," she said mournfully.

"Hurray! I only hired twelve!"

Zeta examined the closed, rotting doors, which had been cinched with a kinked length of rusty chain. "Dad, nobody came in. . . ."

"Your grandpa doesn't have to come through a door. Lemme think. . . . We'll give every one of them a cigarette, just like for Christmas, okay? Kind of an ID tag!"

Starlitz worked his way through the revelers, methodically flicking his Cricket in a mass baptism of smoke. He was dragging them from the booze-sticky depths of their private realms, and into the Christmas-twinkling light of a greater awareness. Each time the lighter flared, they leapt out of their alcoholic shrouds. Teeth gone, bearded lips slack. Windburns from a lifetime of sheepherding. Grizzle and grease, the dust, the smell. Scarred eyelids, spiked eyebrows. Caries, vitamin deficiency. Rural decay, urban decay.

Then—right before him—here was the man. The man

who looked more like the others than the others could ever quite look. He had a face that was a distillation of all lost, invisible faces. He possessed a deep, pristine air of loss, a sense of disconnection so final and complete that there was an eerie joy to it, like poetry in a dead language.

Starlitz seized the shabby shoulder firmly. "Zeta! Zeta! Come quick!"

She came at the trot.

"Look, Zeta, here he is, this is him!"

The timeless bum puffed his freshly lit cigarette and bent his dirty head. He was firming up considerably now, emerging from infinite shadow into the vivid quotidian world of mass, space-time, weight, grime, grit, filth. Starlitz was astonished to see how young his father looked.

Starlitz had never witnessed his own father looking so anomalously youthful. With his black, dusty hair, unlined, supple neck, and birdbone wrists, he looked no more than twenty-five.

Starlitz's father was wearing khaki pants, canvas shoes without socks, a buttoned gray canvas shirt that might have come from jail or a construction site. All of it colorless and threadbare, bleached by a thousand suns. He lifted one grimy, gracile hand and touched Zeta's bare wrist. Zeta flinched with the jolt, but the contact visibly enlivened him. Human awareness flooded his distant, shoe-button eyes.

"O Javanese Navajo," he muttered.

"Dad," said Starlitz anxiously, "you know me, right?"

The young man shrugged, with a feeble, wavering smile.

"Hold on to his arm, Zeta. Hold on to him good, don't let go of him, not even for a second. I'm gonna turn down the music." Starlitz saw to the blasting phonograph, and returned.

"Dad," he said intently, "it's me, it's Lech. I'm your son, the son of the Polish girl, the girl at the hospital, remember? This is what I look like when I'm all grown up. And this—this is my daughter, Zenobia. This is your granddaughter, Dad."

"Can he talk English?" said Zeta with interest, still clutching the apparition's scrawny arm. "He sure doesn't *look* English."

"He can't talk English, exactly," Starlitz explained. "He has his own native language. It's one of those tribal lingos. It has, like, sixteen words for the color orange and eighteen words for deer tracks . . . but past tense, and present tense, and pluperfect and all that stuff, they never quite worked all that out, somehow. See, he never *needed* any future tense or past tense. That was never part of his narrative."

"What's his name?"

"Well, I know he had some kind of American legal name once, 'cause they enlisted him in the U.S. Army in the forties. He was in the Pacific war, with the Navajo code talkers. Later he got this broom-pusher job with some big-time feds in Los Alamos. . . . He had a military accident there, that blew his identity away, just obliterated it. . . . My mom, your grandma, she always just called him 'Joe.' Like 'GI Joe,' or 'Hey, Joe, you got gum?' So you can just call him 'Joe,' too, okay?"

"Hi, Grandpa Joe," said Zeta.

Grandpa Joe smiled at her and said something elaborate, kindly, self-deprecatingly humorous, and completely indecipherable.

"Hey, wait a minute!" said Zeta, staring at him intently. "I know who this is! I *know* him! He's that old man! He's that nice old man, that guy who used to bring me little toys and stuff!"

"No kidding? You've seen him before?"

"Yeah! But he was so much *older* than this. He was all gray haired, and kind of bent over, and he used to talk to himself in a made-up language, and walk backwards and forwards all the time. He used to come around at Christmas. He gave me, like, cool old candy with real sugar in it!" Zeta scowled. "Mom One and Mom Two, they always said I was making him up."

"Wow, Dad, good one!" Starlitz said gratefully, patting the

lost man's broomstick upper arm. "See, your grandpa Joe just doesn't have a forward gear or a reverse gear. But he never forgets what he saw in the future, just the same."

Joe nodded cordially, with an apologetic grin. Joe was still rather spectral, but he seemed increasingly pleased with himself. Joe resembled a young GI who had witnessed some unspeakable Nazi atrocity, but had swiftly restored his aplomb with a stiff rye highball and a Benny Goodman track.

"Wow, so that nice old man was my grandpa all along!" said Zeta cheerily. "That guy who brought me that old-fashioned watch that glowed in the dark."

Grandpa Joe placed a tender hand on his granddaughter's shoulder, and looked at Starlitz confidingly.

Starlitz was touched to the core. To think that his father had taken such trouble, under such difficult personal circumstances. Visiting his only granddaughter, bringing her anachronistic gifts, right there at the very edge of his wandering range, in the century's very last decade. This was truly above and beyond the call. Starlitz felt an unspoken stress suddenly easing inside himself. He knew now that he had done the right thing in coming here. No matter what past losses or future consequences, it had already all been worth it.

"Kayak," said Grandpa Joe, clearing his throat. "Kinnikkinnik. Knock conk."

"He's trying to talk to us!" Zeta said excitedly.

Grandpa Joe was gathering strength. Far less phantomlike now, he'd gone all wiry and virile, even jitterbuggy. He turned to Zeta, winked at her cozily, and jerked a derisive thumb at Starlitz. "Dolce Vita man. An amative clod!"

"Aw, Dad's okay," Zeta said defensively. "Dad's a lot of fun, when you get to know him!"

Joe sniffed sentimentally. "Ma is as selfless as I am."

"He's talking about your grandmother," Starlitz explained. "Nurse Starlitz. Agnieszka Starlitz. See, she'd been in the death camps in Poland, but once she made it safe to America, she got to where she could see Joe better than anyone else could. Agnieszka could even *touch* him. . . . They were never in the same place long enough to get married, but my mom and dad, they were pretty much two of a kind. So they kinda looked after each other."

"Can we meet my grandma too?"

Starlitz shook his head mournfully. "She's mighty hard to reach now, sweetheart. She's got her wheelchair, the remote control, her oatmeal three times a day. . . . Sometimes she's the nurse, sometimes she's the patient, most of the time she was both at once, see, kind of a phase-change thing. . . . I guess you wouldn't understand that, it's kind of a grown-up thing, but, no, you can't see your grandma. Trust me, you really don't want to be in the kind of mental head-space where you see a lot of Nurse Starlitz." Starlitz rubbed his chin. "But if anyone can get to her, it would be him."

Grandpa Joe was feeling his oats. He stood up, yawned, and stretched. The electrical generator immediately coughed and died. The Christmas lights winked out. The record player perished with a voltage-starved groan.

The few bums still singing Christmas carols quickly gave it up. The dead garage was shrouded in flickering metallic dimness, lit only by the blazing trash in its iron Bhopal barrel, but Starlitz's father did not mind this. On the contrary, the silent, mythic glow of firelight seemed to strengthen Joe considerably. He was in a jollier, almost bumptious mood.

He gazed at the nearest reveler with amused contempt. "Man." He grinned. "Eve let an idiot—a retromastoid idiot, Sam, or teratoid—in at eleven A.M.!"

"Never mind these other crazy jaspers, Dad. We're just glad to see you. You're looking great, considering that it's 1999 and all."

Starlitz rose to comfort the parishioners and deliver more wine all around. When he came back, he found his daughter and his father rapt in conversation.

"See, Grandpa, it's all about 'calling down the moon,' "
Zeta told him shyly. "My two moms do a lot of moon-worship
rites, out in the old-growth forest."

"Most naive deviants 'Om,' " Joe offered thoughtfully.

"You know what, Grandpa? I just got back from a place
where they have Moslem people!"

Joe nodded indulgently. "Nail a Moslem a camel, Soma-
lian! Ottoman in a motto."

"Wow, Dad sure gets along with you, Zeta," said Starlitz,
sitting down with his Mexican backpack. "I need to tell you
Grandpa's life story now." Starlitz ceremonially produced his
amber bottle of Gran Centenario tequila and a waxed stack of
cheap paper cups. "It's important that you learn this history,
okay? This is your heritage, girl. Grandpa would have kind of a
hard time telling the story all by himself." Starlitz pulled the
bottle's foil tab and cracked the plastic twist-off top. "You
don't mind helping me out a little with the old story line, do
you, Dad?"

"O no," Joe agreed cordially. He accepted a filled paper
cup of tequila. "Rot a gill, alligator!" He drank.

"Well, first of all, no matter what Joe says, he's not a 'Javanese Navajo,' " Starlitz said. "He's ethnic, all right—he's *extremely* ethnic—but no matter what ethnic label you pin on
him, Joe is always somebody else. And that's your true ances-
try, Zeta. You belong to the tribe of those who never belong to
a tribe."

Starlitz sipped the tequila. Gran Centenario: a vintage
century, one hell of a nostalgia kick. "Your family: we break the
mold, okay? We live in the cracks in the broken mold. Your
grandpa Joe . . . well, he was always one of 'them' who wasn't
ever actually 'them.' He's the Javanese Navajo, the overlapping
element in two different circles that are never supposed to
meet."

"Yeah! Okay!" said Zeta cheerfully. This was clearly making
a lot of sense to her. It was as if she had been waiting all her
life to hear this revelation. She shivered with delight.

"Joe got into the war early on. . . . Because wars are perfect for people like him. You always end up with, you know, totally freakish situations that nobody can explain. The freakishness doesn't even become visible till years later, because, at the time, they've been in combat for months on end, so they're way past thinking straight about anything. . . . That Navajo code-talker thing, the Japanese Purple Code in the Pacific, those prehistoric analog code-breaker computers, those weird Nazi wind-up code machines, the gay British mathematician with the secret life, all of it super, super secret, all super important, nobody hears a goddamn word about it, till thirty, forty, fifty years later. . . . Well, that situation was perfect for Joe. Even though he is what he is. . . . No, *because* of what he is. It *made* him what he is."

"Dad . . . I like this story a lot, but . . . Joe's awful *young* for a grandpa, Dad. He looks younger than you, even."

Starlitz coughed on a throat-ripping barb of tequila. "I'm *getting* to that part. They mustered young Grandpa out of the Navajo code thing—probably because that code he was speaking wasn't really Navajo—and they made him a kind of local gopher or janitor around the Manhattan Project. Where they were building the atomic bomb, getting ready to test-fire it."

Joe spoke up again at this point, with an authoritative, been-there-done-that nod. "Oh, a parabola-lob Arapaho."

"Yeah, Joe was a local Indian janitor—mostly, though, he was stealing their office supplies. Spare tires, gasoline, scrap metal, all very valuable back then, during the rationing. These atom-bomb professors had tremendous resources, billions of 1940s dollars, it was all totally hush-hush, they were in a tremendous hurry, so all kinds of valuable stuff was kinda falling off the back of the atom trucks. . . . You can take it for granted that there has to be some kind of black-market operator, in any situation like that. . . . Well, it was Joe, of course."

"Megatart's stratagem," commented Joe.

"Then the time came to actually test the atomic bomb . . . the 'Gizmo,' they called it. Out at the Trinity site, here in New

Mexico. . . . For some lame security reason they decided to set this bomb off, in a violent rainstorm, at five o'clock in the morning. So, Zeta, just imagine it: it's pitch black, there's a high wind, and the straights can't see a damn thing because they're all hiding in their bunkers a thousand yards away. . . . So that's the best excuse ever to sneak out to the shot tower, and steal a bunch of cool stuff."

"Oh, yeah," Zeta said thoughtfully.

"Tons of valuable copper wiring in there, or maybe even the plutonium core. Because, you know, with all the tremendous expense it took 'em to refine that plutonium, that stuff was the most valuable scrap metal on earth. So Joe was either directly under the Bomb, or maybe—and I know this sounds weird, but the records of the test kinda back this up—he may have actually crawled *inside* the Bomb, just before they bolted the last plates onto it. And then it blew. The biggest, most powerful release of energy that the human race had ever created." Starlitz sighed. "It blew him right out of history."

"How'd it do that?" said Zeta with interest.

"Well, see, that was a defining moment in the twentieth-century narrative. The twentieth century's core thematic moment. The Bomb was an off-the-wall, shattering, plot-smashing freak scene, straight out of nowhere, very unexpected, a ten-out-of-ten on the world disruption scale. History has never been the same since the Bomb—because history has to live under this glowing mushroom cloud that says, 'History is provisional.' Cause-and-effect just kind of lost its grip on Joe—ever since then your grandpa has been kind of smeared across the whole twentieth century, kinda like an electron fog. He's sort of everywhere in the twentieth-century narrative at once now—but he can only, well, *register,* when he's being observed. When someone's looking at him. When someone's looking *for* him."

"Like here and now?"

"Like exactly right here and right now."

"Wow. So, this is like, a super special time, then."

"That's right, Zeta. So take a good look, and try hard to remember, okay? Because this is the last time ever."

"What? Why?"

"It's a good thing that you saw him now, and that you saw him before, because in the future you're not gonna see him."

"Why not? What about next year?"

Joe shook his head sadly. "No darn radon."

"Grandpa's right," Starlitz said heavily, "after Y2K there's no way."

Zeta was stricken. "But why not?"

"It's a Bomb thing," Starlitz said. "It's the *narrative* of the Bomb. There is no 'Atomic Age' in the next century. The Atomic Age is over, it's yesterday. The meaning of the Bomb is different after Y2K. I mean, if you ever see them set a Bomb off . . . the Bomb was the twentieth-century Holy Grail, but it can only be the Holy Grail for about eight minutes. For eight incredible minutes you get to walk around with your sunglasses on in the shock wave, saying all this heavy, supermythical narrative crap like 'I am brighter than a thousand suns, I am become Death the destroyer of worlds.' . . . But when your eight minutes is up, then all you've got is *trash*. Trash by definition, okay?"

Starlitz gazed into his daughter's candid eyes: he was doing his best to level with her; it was the time for it. "Let's go back to the story of the Trinity test shot. Well, first you've got this silent flash that lights the mountains. Then, a gigantic shock wave. Then a huge boiling egg, a phoenix that rises up into the sky, and then, the desert wind slowly pulls the mushroom cloud apart. . . . But then . . . after the heat dies down . . . you got four federal guys, in hats and suspenders and uniforms, standing around these melted, screwed-up pieces of reinforcement rod. That's it. That's the Atomic story line. Atomic energy is a super cool cosmic breakthrough for maybe eight minutes. After that . . . it's radiation waste. Trash, practically forever. Trash now, trash a hundred years from now, trash ten thousand years from now. The next century lives downstream from the Atomic Age. So whenever it looks at a nuke, it never sees the original glamour, it always sees the trash *first*."

"No way! But what about Grandpa? It just isn't fair!"

"After Y2K it's just not his kind of story anymore."

Joe looked at Zeta with distant pity. It was visibly paining him to hurt her feelings. But there was just no way around the issue. Joe struggled to explain. "Miss, I'm Cain, a monomaniac. Miss, I'm Cain, a monomaniac. Miss, I'm . . ."

"That's enough, Dad," Starlitz said. "I'll explain to her some other time, all about the Bomb and the mark-of-Cain part."

"Hey, man," said one of the revelers, wandering over, "you got tequila here."

Zeta clenched her slender fists. "But it can't just be all over, just like that!"

"Kid," said Starlitz, "when it's over, it's *over*."

Zeta wasn't taking it well. Her mind raced in rebellion. She sat up with an excited grin. "But, Dad! Hey, Dad, the year 2000 is *still part of the twentieth century*! It says so in my math book! So Grandpa should get a whole other year! Right?"

"Okay, let's ask our friend here about that," said Starlitz, turning to the leaning drunk. "Hey, buddy. I'll give you a shot of the cactus juice here, but first you gotta answer me something, okay? When does the twenty-first century start?"

The derelict brushed at a desert-dusty dreadlock. "New Year's Day, man. Y2K. Everybody knows that. Planes fall out of the sky, blackouts all over the place . . ."

"Suppose you start back at the year zero, and start counting off hundreds of years. Aren't you gonna come up one year short?"

"Why the hell would I wanna do that?" He turned to the others. "Hey, *borrachos!*" he shouted. *"Tenemos tequila!"*

Surrounded by swift and boisterous demand, Starlitz distributed the contents of the bottle. It didn't take long to kill off the Gran Centenario. Straight, no chaser.

Layered onto a bellyful of kosher wine, the tequila hit the crowd like ruinous high-octane jet fuel. One of the day laborers drunkenly yanked the generator back into life. The Christmas lights flickered on. Two guys flung rags and bits of ancient board into the trash barrel, which blazed up enthusiastically, flooding the garage with a bloody glare.

Starlitz spoke up earnestly. "Dad—tell me about Mom, okay? What is she like now, in that old folks' home?"

Joe knocked back his tequila and shuddered. He nodded reluctantly, chin wobbling back and forth. It could have been a trick of the flaming light, but Joe looked a full hundred years old now. He shook his head mournfully. "Senicide medicines."

Starlitz tapped his forehead. "She's already gone, up here, for all intents and purposes, right? Y2K can't touch her now: she already left."

Joe's brown eyes glittered. Joe's eyes looked quite ageless suddenly, like two puddles of heat-fused glass. Not glassy cold, though. Lit from within by masculine will, almost a soldierly heroism, a man who had come fully to terms with every blow that life would ever be able to deal him.

Joe drew a solemn breath and lifted his shabby arm, the flag bearer at the barbed-wire brink of his trench. "Are we not drawn onward, we few—drawn onward to a new era?"

Starlitz turned his face away. He swallowed his tequila, and now the booze was on top of him, with that fatal charm of alcohol, that deadly skill the drug had of turning real emotion into sentiment. When you were drunk, you knew very well how you felt; the truth welled up from its deepest pits of repression, but the booze bleached the sharpness and the color away, it became the cheap, grainy cartoon version of your anguish. "My God," Starlitz said, "my God, I'm truly *stuck* now. A few more ticks of the old atomic clock, and I'm finally all alone in the world. I'm alone in the universe, Dad. No mother, no father. I'm an orphan."

Zeta's eyes welled up. "But *I'm* still here, Dad! Look at me! *I'm* not an orphan!"

Starlitz put an arm around her shoulder. The two of them fell silent, looking at Joe. Starlitz had never realized it, that a child could be such a source of strength. She was pulling him into the future, like hands reaching over the gunwale of a lifeboat.

The drunks were singing again. They'd found a Mexican "Feliz Navidad" record in the stack of battered vinyl, a pop track with a little more picante to it. Someone had marijuana. The juice and weed had liberated their sense of seasonal generosity. The ones who could still stand were attempting to dance. Joe looked at their staggering tea-head antics, amused, his wily face the picture of forties hepcat cool. "So!" he said. "Catnip in tacos?"

As the smoldering barrel continued to blaze, the garage filled with toxic smoke. Starlitz felt his eyes stinging painfully. Why hide anything? It was a wake, the century was a dead dog.

There was a violent banging at the broken door. "¡Policía! Police!"

"¡La Migra!" someone yelled. Instant panic broke out among the revelers.

Joe laughed in defiance as he faded from sight. He simply evaporated before the pair of them, like a veil of handmade lace in an atomic sheet of purifying flame. Starlitz barely caught his last cry: *"So crank on in, OK narcos!"*

"Dad, it's *cops!*" Zeta shrieked in terror.

"Just sit down, Zeta," Starlitz said, wiping his eyes. "Put your hands where the officers can see 'em, okay? This is just something we gotta get through."

———

STARLITZ WAS ARRESTED FOR VAGRANCY. THERE WERE POTEN-
tial charges aplenty waiting for him: breaking and entering,
trespassing, corrupting a minor, driving without a license in a
boosted truck with no inspection sticker, creating fire hazards,
attempted arson, and so forth. And so forth. But these charges
were all contingent on his revealing who he was. Starlitz had
no ID, and he wasn't answering any questions.

He got one obligatory phone call. He tried an emergency
number, got an answering machine in Washington, D.C. No
dice. Starlitz went back into the jug.

Three days passed. Starlitz wouldn't talk. The sheriff's department soon grew bored with him, but this was a question of
will. In any prison situation the bulls always had it figured that
time was theirs to give or take. Starlitz stayed out of fights,
watched prison television, kept his teeth, hair, nails, and his
uniform clean, and finally wheedled his way into a second
phone call.

This time the line picked up.

"Jane O'Houlihan?" he said.

"You got her. It's your dime."

"Actually, this is the county's dime, Jane. I'm in a county
slammer in Socorro, New Mexico."

"Yeah, that's what my Caller ID says. So who is this?"

"I can't tell you, because even county cops tap phone calls
these days. But think back to the early nineties, okay? You're
an assistant attorney general in Utah. There's a Section Ten
Thirty bust of a bunch of radical antiabortionists. Inside the
Utah state capitol. Remember that?"

"Oh, fuck," O'Houlihan said thoughtfully. "It's Leggy."

"Yeah. Sorry, Jane. Voice from the past, and all that. Guy
who knew you when. Listen, I need a favor."

"Did you leave a message on my answering machine last
Monday?"

"Yeah, I did."

"Damn, I had that figured for phone phreaks. They're all

Bulgarian now, did you know that? Shitloads of crazy Bulgarians." O'Houlihan sniffed. "What the hell good is telecom security when the fucking national phone company is owned by Bulgarian maphiya? And the little sons of bitches have got my office number too."

"At least they're not Serbian."

"You're joking, right? The *worst* ones are Serbian."

"Well, at least they're not Russian."

O'Houlihan's voice fell even lower. "In Russia the *cops* are the maphiya. . . ."

"Jane, I know you're busy, so let me cut to the chase here, okay? Things got out of hand, down here on the border. I got busted for vagrancy. I need the DoJ to yank me some big federal strings from Washington, so I can walk out of this mess."

"You're kidding, right? You expect *me* to get you out of some county jug? Sonny boy, you have no idea what kind of operational constraints we feds labor under. I gotta fill out six OMB forms and an Al Gore Website to procure a friggin' hairpin."

"Janie, you're hurting my feelings, okay? Who was it that boosted you into the Spinster Prosecutors' Club, at the right hand of Janet Reno? If it wasn't for my unique talent-spotting abilities, you'd still be busting check forgers in deepest, darkest Mormonville."

"Don't you dare tug my chain, boyo. I can reach out with my big Yellow Pages finger here"—there was a series of rapid disconnection-clicks on the line—"and you're just another sad cry for help in alt dot prison dot support. You get me?"

"Janie, *don't hang up.*"

"That's more like it," O'Houlihan said.

"Look, it's just a vagrancy rap. I was broke, and I have no ID on me, and I was sleeping in an empty garage. Those aren't even supposed to be *crimes*, for Christ's sake."

"You weren't holding dope, right?"

"No, no drugs."

"You didn't have a hot-wired laptop, or a shitload of guns, or anything?"

"No way."

"Then what was it? You're not telling me what it fuckin' *was*."

"Well, there's an underage kid involved. . . ."

"Aw, Jesus."

"She's my daughter."

"Your *daughter*?" O'Houlihan gasped in astonishment. "*Your* daughter, Starlitz? Your daughter by *what*?" She paused. "Not those little toll-fraud dyke bitches from Oregon."

"Uh, yeah, one of them."

"Why do men do this to themselves?" said O'Houlihan wonderingly. "When there are wonderful women in the world, like Grace Hopper, and Madeleine Albright, and Janet Reno. *Honest* women. Clean. Dedicated. Faithful public servants."

"It's not just asking for me, okay? It's for the kid. They'll book her in some kind of juvenile facility, and she's led a really sheltered life. She's only eleven years old."

"So what is this alleged child's name? You got her SS number handy?"

"Her name is Zenobia Boadicea Hypatia McMillen."

"Look, that's enough names for five or six little hippie kids."

"I didn't name her, okay? And I don't have five or six kids, I only have one. I'm at rock bottom, Jane. She's all I've got left in the world."

"Okay," said O'Houlihan slowly. "Maybe you got me all touched here. Maybe I can do something about dismissing a New Mexico vagrancy rap. It's not some Chinese Los Alamos atom-spy thing, anyhow. Right?"

"Yeah, right."

Her voice grew taut. "So: give over. And I'll think about it."

"What do you need to know?" Starlitz said cautiously.

"Whatta ya got?"

"We shouldn't talk about this on a tapped line."

"I'm a heavy fed now, okay? Rule number one, I don't want anything that any fucking redneck county sheriff can do or care a fucking thing about."

"Okay," said Starlitz. "If that's how you want to play it. I wanna help you out here, I'm serious. I appreciate the role of law enforcement. I got my ear to the ground. I got some pretty weird contacts. I think I could turn you on to some pretty heavy-duty, fed-style casework here."

"I'm listening," O'Houlihan said.

"Like, for instance . . . hey! Come to think of it, I know two girls who had oral sex with the President!"

"The Big Guy beat the rap in Congress. Barely. Reno's not gonna go through that scene again. She'd rather cut her own ears off."

"Okay, how about: a big commune full of backwoods, Bible-thumping, apocalypse cultists. They're totally insane. And they are armed to the teeth."

"That's an ATF job. I never work with the ninja tobacco-inspectors."

"Uh, okay . . . how about a military washout kid who's got a borderline, white-supremacist, paranoia thing? He's buying fertilizer and he hired a rental truck!"

"Tell it to Ted Kaczynski! I don't do loners. There's way too many of 'em. I need a case with some meat on it, like a good RICO thing."

"I'm with you here. . . . Okay, maybe I'm scraping the bottom of the barrel, but how about a private mafia of trench-coat-wearing high-school teenagers who want to shoot all the jocks in their gym class?"

"That is *kid stuff*! Do I look twelve years old to you? Come on, get serious!"

"Okay," Starlitz said wearily. "Listen. This is my best pitch. Turkish heroin is being smuggled into Turkish Cyprus inside giant inflatable bags of tap water."

Starlitz heard the rapid scratching of a mechanical pencil.

" 'Cyprus,' you said? 'Turkish' Cyprus?"

"Yeah."

Starlitz heard the dry tapping of a keyboard and the rapid swish of an ergonomic mouse. "Eastern Mediterranean island? Economic embargo regime? Under international trade sanctions?"

"Yup. That would be the place."

"This is heroin, though, right? And a brand-new smuggling method, right? Never discovered, never been busted by anybody before?"

"Yeah, that's right," Starlitz said, brightening. "So listen: if I'm gonna out these submarine smack guys, I need the witness-protection nine yards. Me and my kid, too, okay?"

ONCE HE'D BEEN SIGNED OUT OF THE SLAMMER, STARLITZ took a bus north to Albuquerque to spring his daughter out of the state juvenile facility. This was by no means an easy matter, since the facility had been designed specifically to repel any and all suspicious male loners who might claim that they were somebody's father.

While he planned Zeta's prison break, Starlitz kept his daughter's spirits up by smuggling in her favorite foods: tuna sandwiches on crustless bread, all-white-marshmallow bags, provolone-and-macaroni casseroles. Given that it was her first time in custody, Zeta had been bearing up well. Granted, there had been some unfortunate incidents. An episode of walking on the ceiling, the spontaneous poltergeist-style explosion of a television, a social worker's handbag bursting into flame. Starlitz was not too concerned. These things could be swiftly explained away with the normal paradigms of child misbehavior circa 1999, i.e., designer drug use and bad digital media. Starlitz knew that the kid had gumption. He was convinced that she would be okay.

When they finally met in the cheerless conference room, with its unburnable, unbreakable, tot-colored plastic furniture, Starlitz saw a lost, doubting look in Zeta's eyes. He'd never seen such a gaze of silent reproach in a human face. It lanced through him like an emotional harpoon; he found it worse than being shot. He had failed to take proper care. She knew it. He knew it. He could offer no conceivable excuse.

Starlitz social-engineered the staff by phoning and faxing in a stream of deceptive messages, adopting the guises and letterheads of a child-custody lawyer and a school psychiatrist. He extracted Zeta out the facility doors on a "day trip." The two of them swiftly vanished from New Mexico's official ken.

Starlitz had had more than enough of the local hospitality. They crossed the border into Colorado.

They finally departed the Greyhound together at Boulder. The city of Boulder seemed as good a place to stop and recoup as any, and maybe a better place than most.

Over the next week Starlitz finally buckled down to the real-life role of single fatherhood. He rented them a trailer at the Mapleton Mobile Home Park. The trailer was owned by a carpenter with a collapsing marriage, so the front and rear yards were full of unplaned boards and broken tools and mounds of rotting sawdust. A giant set of transmission towers strode through the neighborhood, through the pines, the willows, the brown Dumpsters, the kids' bicycles, the clotheslines, and the barbecue pits.

Starlitz got a straight job as a retail clerk at a convenience store, just up the street past the pediatric center and the eye clinic. He opened a bank account and acquired some training-wheel credit cards. He enrolled Zeta in sixth-grade classes at a Boulder public school. He hired a child-custody lawyer and filled out the reams of necessary paperwork.

Domestic routine invaded the lives of Zeta and Starlitz, conquering all before it. Every morning Starlitz would haul the reluctant Zeta out of bed. He would cajole some cereal into her, get her into her clothes, insist that she brush her tangled hair and greenish teeth. He would make her a bag lunch: Hostess snowballs, crustless tuna sandwiches, the palest packaged club-crackers, a banana. He would walk Zeta the six blocks down to her Boulder elementary school, unless it rained, in which case they would take the divorced carpenter's beat-up orange truck. Then he would trudge back, ride a pawnshop single-speed Schwinn to his retail job, and handle the candy, cig, cappuccino, and gasoline purchases for eight hours.

Then he would retrieve Zeta from her state-supported day care. The two of them would go back to the trailer park, with its wind chimes, dogs, bird feeders, towering aspens, and aging hippies playing mellow old Eric Clapton albums on vinyl. They would eat nuked TV dinners in front of cable cartoon programs, which featured comic ensembles of fast-talking monsters, and cosmos-exploding Nipponese anime cartoons.

"Hey, Dad."

"What?"

"Hey, Dad."

"Yeah?"

"Hey, Dad, how come I have to waste so much time in that stinkin' school with all those stupid kids?"

"Because I say so." Starlitz put down his bean-smeared tin fork and sighed. "Because I'm the dad and you're the kid. See, Zeta—it's like this. Sometimes it's a lot easier to *become* what you say you are, than it is to try and pass for it."

"But, Dad—you and me, we could pass for *anything*. I mean—you manage G-7, the coolest band in the whole world! Why don't you pass for—like—the guy who owns the Nintendo company? Then you'd be a zillionaire and I could be Japanese! That would be super cool!"

"That's just not the narrative, Zeta."

"Why not?"

Because she was the narrative. And she was not his cute

moppet sidekick, offering local color, as they jetted from city to city in the company of muso hustlers and coke-snorting pop starlets. Sure, of course *he* could pass there, that was his natural world. But it was also phony-baloney tinsel crap with no staying power.

He couldn't depart this century without becoming her father, fully and irrevocably, with everything that entailed. And that meant fatherhood. Not some made-up, sentimental, sitcom-TV version of fatherhood, where the dad figure shuffles in and out of camera range, stage left, without ever getting blood and vomit on his shirt. No, it meant no-kidding, down-and-dirty, *parental life.*

No ifs, ands, or buts. No backsliding, fast talking, or soft-shoeing. Stark confrontation with the consequences of the human condition. He had to genuinely commit. He couldn't park Zeta in the closet between camera setups, and pay other people to raise her. *He* had to raise her. *All the time.* He had to feed her, dress her, get her the obligatory booster shots, teach her to swim and ride a bike. He had to give her an allowance. He had to watch her kick, and scream, and fuss; he had to look after her, during nightmares, when picking bloody scabs off her knees, losing her teeth, breaking out in virulent spots, and running a fever of a hundred and four. He had to chill her out when she was hyper, cheer her up when she was sour. Mom One and Mom Two had done this grueling labor for *eleven solid years*—he couldn't complain, now the time had come for him to ante up. She was his child, and there just wasn't anybody else up for that job.

"But, Dad, why not?"

"Because this is the world and we live in it. I gotta show you the ropes of consensus reality. God knows your mothers never would. We're gonna get IDs, Zeta: social security, legal American passports. I'm gonna get exclusive custody, granted by the Colorado state court, signed, sealed, delivered. Paid for. Witnessed. In the files. When we're done here, we'll be real, a real dad, a real kid. We'll be *better* than real. We'll be official."

"Oh."

JUDY, MOM TWO, THE LEGAL ENTITY FORMALLY RESPONSIBLE, failed to contest the custody proceedings. Most likely she simply never got wind of them. The Colorado court gave Starlitz sole custody. He paid off the lawyer's crippling fees through merchandise shrinkage at the convenience store.

Then two grainy blue passports arrived, shipped overnight directly from Washington in a handsome string-tied manila envelope. Starlitz gazed at the documents in wonder. They were sublime. Even the kid's photograph looked terrific. The photo was nine-tenths fictional; he'd had to tart up Zeta's blurry, camera-shattering image with Adobe Photoshop; but at last his daughter, all grinning and pigtailed, had that hotly coveted prize of economic globalization, a genuine, fully attested, stamped and legal United States passport. The fact that her name was misspelled "Zinobia" was but a small gnat in the ointment.

He couldn't quite believe that O'Houlihan had gone through with it. She'd actually come up with the documents. But there was no getting around the fact: Jane O'Houlihan was an honest public official. True, she was a federal prosecutor from the Department of Justice, so attracting her sustained attention was a more dangerous and lasting misfortune than shattering both your thighbones, but the woman had her own kind of merit. She wasn't simply lining her own pockets, like most of the planet's legal apparatchiks. She was a sworn nun of American federal law and order, a stainless paladin of bourgeois constitutional democracy, one of the scariest and most authentic entities that the dying century had to offer.

Zeta thumb-flipped through her passport, bored. "Why are you so happy about this, Dad?"

"Zeta, we just joined a very privileged fraction of the human race. We are documented! And by the world's last superpower too!"

"It's a crappy little blank book, Dad. It only has one picture."

"Yeah, that's the truth, but that's a *kid's* version of the truth." Starlitz sighed. "Zeta, we need a serious talk now, okay?"

Her narrow shoulders hunched in embarrassed pain. "Aw, Dad, not another one!"

"Honey, this is vitally important. You see: we have a choice among contingencies here. You got no idea how tough it is to become fully documented, but . . . well . . . we are no-kidding legal now, both of us. It's a huge accomplishment. There's nothing to stop us from living just like this indefinitely. You can go to junior high school next year. I'll buy you cool new teen-girl subculture clothes, you know, whatever Britney Spears is wearing on MTV. I'll help you with the math homework, I'll get you a moped, I'll see you through the whole nine yards. Because I'm legal, clean, and sober. I'm holding down a straight job. I show up on time for every shift, I can make proper change, and I never rob the till. I'm a great employee. They'd have promoted me to district manager already, if it weren't for that shrinkage rate out the shop's back door."

"Dad, I dunno how much more Bit-o-Honeys I can eat. I mean, I used to love 'em, but three cases? That's a lot!"

"Zeta, we have a path forward. It's the Bill Market, here in the USA. Times are booming. Employment is sky high, inflation is dirt low, and thanks to two million guys who are stuck in the domestic gulag, crime rates have crashed all over the country. It's the fat of the Yankee land. We can move to a better apartment. I'll get out of this high-risk package-retailing on a stick-'em-up urban street corner. That's way too twentieth century, anyway. I've got some plans for us: I'm thinking: four or five personal eBay accounts, and some Internet-stock day-trading. We'll get all upwardly mobile, middle-class-American-Dream style. We can buy health insurance. We'll eat vitamins. You'll grow up tall and strong and literate, with fluoride in your big white teeth, and no scars and no criminal record. And the best part is: since we've placed ourselves in a yuppie town right into the fat center of a major demographic median, we're practically certain to *slide right through Y2K!*"

"Is all that s'posed to be *good*, Dad?"

"Well, I'm not saying we'll go totally unscathed. There might be a few power outages here in Boulder, some screwed-up traffic lights, a bank collapse or two. . . . Big deal; we'll just buy a bag of rice and some tiki torches. But see: we've established ourselves in a massively augmented part of the narrative. We've got it made now. You'll cruise right through the year 2000, just like you were always bound to do anyhow. I'll tag along with you, in my kindly supportive role of your dear old dad. I'll do only predictable, single-dad-style things from now on. Buy us a used car, maybe. Maybe I'll take up some Rocky Mountain trout fishing. Or go to some baseball games. I might even get married!"

"Dad, that is all so totally *boring!*"

"Honey, it's only 'boring' if you don't know any other life. If you thought about this from a different angle, behaving in a totally conventional middle-American way would be a huge challenge. An incredible adventure. Just try to imagine living that way with *total conviction* and without a *single moment of self-doubt*. It would be like searching for the source of the Nile. It's practically *beyond imagination*."

Zeta pondered this. "Okay. What's our *other* lifestyle choice, Dad?"

"Well," Starlitz said, his voice growing thicker and grainier, "we have new passports. So: maybe we boost some air fare, pick up our loose ends, and get back in the pop hustle. Somewhere, about a million shades of strange away from the other kids in Boulder's sixth grade, the Serbian scene is blowing big-time. NATO's a fire-breathing dragon. It is McWorld versus Ji-had, kid: it's the high-tech souped-up Lexus smashing head on into the ethnic Olive Tree. The nineties version of reality is cracking up, the body count is stacking up, and it is culture war to the knife in Kosovo, Montenegro, Greece, Italy, Mace-donia, Croatia, Turkey, Bulgaria, Hungary, Albania, and Azer-baijan. My Russian maphiya contacts are gonna be in this neck deep."

"That means you'd pull me out of school, right? Before my next report card?"

"Absolutely. I'm thinking, maybe, university extension classes and a private tutor. You'll need a laptop. I'd have to make some phone calls."

"Dad, get a satellite phone."

STARLITZ MAXED OUT HIS CREDIT CARDS AND TRIPLED HIS money in a week, fronting Beanie Babies in the Internet auc-tion market. He bought into collectible phone credit cards, and used one to call a cell phone in Cyprus.

"*Shtoh vy khoteti?*"

"I want to speak to Viktor, please."

"This is Viktor Bilibin Efendi. And you are?"

"Viktor, it's me. It's Lech Starlitz."

"Who? What?"

"Lekhi Starlits!"

"Oh, yes," said Viktor gruffly, "now I remember. My former uncle's former friend."

"You're not drunk, are you, Viktor?" Starlitz could hear a radio blaring and girls singing in the background. They sounded like Russian girls. Some kind of Balkan radio tune, lots of diatonic quavers and Yugoslav synthwashes.

"Why should you care?" Viktor demanded thickly. "Off to America! Leaving us in the lurch!"

"Uh . . . is your uncle around? Put Pulat Romanevich on the line."

"My uncle was in an aircraft hangar in Belgrade! The first wave of NATO attacks smashed everything! He is missing and presumed dead, you butcher of the Balkan nation! Bomb-flinging NATO aggressor!!"

This was heavy news. It didn't feel quite right, though. It had a certain ritualized phoniness about it. "Did you actually see Pulat Romanevich inside a zinc coffin, Viktor?"

"*Nyet.* They're still sweeping up pieces of the MiGs!"

"Then don't count him out, okay? Those Afghantsi veterans are hard men to kill. If the mujihadeen couldn't get him with Stingers, he's not gonna be knocked out by some Dutch greenhorn in a French Mystère."

"Anything can happen in a war," Viktor said glumly. "Even people getting killed."

"Tell me about the band, Viktor."

"He is huge," Viktor blurted.

"Who is huge?"

"The Turk. Ozbey. Ozbey has become huge. Since the war in the Balkans he is incredible. He's an evil genius, that man. The Turks never believed that NATO would bomb Christians for the sake of Moslems. But they were wrong, because it happened. They never believed they would catch the Kurdish leader, Ocallan. But they were wrong. Because the Yankee spies sold out the Greeks, and fingered Ocallan to the Turks. The Turkish Special Operations kidnapped the Kurd in Kenya. The Turks danced with joy in the streets of Istanbul. Ozbey and his spies are national heroes."

Viktor took a deep breath. He was on a big Slavic confessional roll now; the cork had been pulled from his neck and he was emitting a fiery stream of painful confidences. "Then, Starlits, listen to me: the Kurds broke into Greek embassies all over Europe, and set themselves on fire. Can you believe the drama? The hated Kurds, seizing Greek embassies, and setting their flesh on fire! In front of CNN cameras! Turkish cameras! It is a Turkish miracle! It is a Turkish dream! And now, as I speak to you: Turkish jet pilots are bombing a Christian air force! NATO is patting them on the back and underwriting all expenses! Ozbey is walking around like a minister! Ozbey is ten meters tall! He can't be touched!"

"Viktor, calm down. Tell me something—has there been any trouble locally with that, you know, underwater postal service thing? Like, any American antidrug people sniffing around, Interpol, anything like that?"

Viktor laughed harshly. "Hah! Can you imagine a Turkish heroin-smuggling scandal when the Balkans are on fire? No American cop is that stupid! They're crushing a heroic Slavic people in their innocent heroic homeland. Heroin means nothing to the Yankees now! Their new Yankee darlings are the KLA, an Albanian terrorist mob. They steal cars and sell heroin! It's how the KLA bought the guns to massacre pregnant Serbian women and gouge the eyes out of children."

"Yeah, that's some story, all right."

"The KLA were all trained by Osama bin Laden. You know that, don't you?"

"Oh, yeah, millionaire philanthropist and all that, he's a heavy guy, Osama bin Laden. Look, Viktor, I can see you're taking this temporary air strike pretty hard, and I'd love to discuss regional politics with you some other time. But frankly, I just called to see how the band is doing."

Viktor lowered his voice. "A lot of money in that band. Tours. New clothes."

"That's great."

"A new album. Turkish lyrics."

"No kidding."

"The French One died."

"Oh, hell. The French One? Dead? The French One was the only one who could sing!"

"Her own fault. She was stupid. She snorted the wrong kind of white powder in a party in Yerevan. Ozbey hired a new French One. A Moroccan girl from the Arab quarter of Paris. 'Cheba Angélique,' a rai singer in exile. She is hot! The crowds love her! She makes the old French One look like a week-old blancmange."

"I can't believe the French One's dead."

"She is dead, though. Very. I saw her when they shipped the body through. And the new American One! Oh, my God."

"You didn't have sex with her, did you?"

"No, but Ozbey did. And Ozbey's Uncle the Minister. And Ozbey's uncle's *boss*. The husband of the former prime minister bought her a gold Mercedes. And so did a Saudi prince. And the playboy son of the president of Azerbaijan gave the American One a hundred thousand dollars in a casino in Yerevan. She took her clothes off in the steppes of—"

"I get the picture there, man."

"She's huge. She's huge like Ozbey, only . . . like a woman, a pop star."

"You're dead sure the French One is really dead?"

"She's dead as Napoleon, Lekhi. She's deader than Minitel."

"That's a very big problem. I'll be in touch." Starlitz hung up.

AS THE PLANE ROSE FROM THE NEW AND BARELY FUNCTIONAL Denver airport, Zeta stuck her nose to the scratched and clouded glass. "Boy, you're the greatest, Dad. No finals! And Hawaii! Wow, I've never even *been* to Hawaii. Can we surf? Boy, life is just so great!"

SEVEN

BY THE DAWN OF THE TWENTIETH CENTURY every scrap of the island of Kauai had been tidily sewn up by six oligarchical clans. These were Anglo-Hawaiian plantation folks, people with the tooth-gritting single-mindedness of Scarlett O'Hara, but in sarongs instead of hoop skirts. Only a hellish catastrophe could force them to sell off the homeland.

Luckily, a horrific El Niño typhoon had ravaged Kauai in 1992. A macadamia-nut plantation, reduced by floods and high winds to a mess of leafless jackstraws, had slipped the grasp of its ruined owners. Makoto won the bidding, but it was Barbara who closed the deal. Barbara had wafted her ethereal way to the local equivalent of Tara, assembled the heartbroken Hawaiian farmers, and performed a faultless slack-key rendition of the sentimental local classic, "Pupu Hinuhinu." Grandma, still clutching her termite-eaten land grant from the royal court of Liliuokalani, had burst into tears of relief. The clan had escaped unbearable ritual humiliation. Because Makoto and Barbara were *artists*. They could *sing*.

As it happened, although Barbara was a major-league Japanese pop star, Barbara was not technically Japanese. Barbara was a Sino-Irish-Polish-Filipino girl, the daughter of two U.S. State Department translators. She'd been born in Kuala Lumpur, and raised in Warsaw, Brussels, Singapore, and Zurich. Barbara was a rarity, a true native of Imperial America's offshore diaspora. Until gently washing up on the white beaches of Hawaii, Barbara had never lived in even a single one of the United States.

Starlitz had no problem understanding Makoto. Starlitz got along fine with Makoto. Makoto was probably the most technically accomplished pop musician in the world, but as long as you didn't ask Makoto to explain his music, the guy's means, motives, and tactics were perfectly comprehensible. Makoto was a Japanese hippie studio producer. Being Japanese made him a tad inscrutable, being a hippie was plenty weird, and his career in the music biz was somewhat unusual. But these three aspects of Makoto's personality were almost always overshadowed by the fact that Makoto was a multimillionaire.

By stark contrast Starlitz found Barbara to be truly unearthly. Starlitz was a little vague about the intensely private boy-meets-girl history there, but apparently Makoto had discovered Barbara idly dawdling in some New Wave dive in Shibuya, wearing a tight sweater and sipping a malted soymilk, existing about eight million light-years away from anybody's idea of a national heritage. Like a lot of pretty girls who had once been too tall and thin, Barbara was a big modelesque mess. She had been lounging in her private thicket of thorns, the slumbering pop princess of the Pacific Rim.

Then Makoto arrived on her scene, sniffed the somnolent air, and said unto her, "Baby, Be Magic." Barbara awoke, blinked, had her hair, lips, and nails done over, and exploded on the stage. To become magic was the first sincere demand that anyone had ever made of Barbara. Barbara was perfectly willing to be magic. There was nothing else to be done about her.

Starlitz wasn't the kind of guy to get all sentimental about a chick who could sing. But he'd never met any human being so fully vested in her rapturous girly divahood as Barbara. Barbara was a hundred and five percent diva: east, west, north, and south, even straight up and down. There just wasn't a lot of conventional human being inside the global diva construct there. Likely there hadn't been a whole lot to Barbara to begin with. Maybe the height, the bone structure, and the vocal cords.

Barbara had no detectable ego. Public adulation meant nothing to her. She was Makoto's shining star, the beloved muse of a musical genius; she was like a guitar that could eat, sleep, and kiss him. Makoto himself was never the star. Makoto could play onstage, he could make a band drive, he could solo even, but Makoto was a bespectacled Japanese hipster with long hair washed in borax and a head like a soccer ball. With Makoto in reach, however, Barbara could perform absolutely anything. There seemed to be no end to the woman's musical flexibility. She could remain in soft focus under an eight-hundred-watt klieg light. Barbara could empty her nonexistent heart to every lonely human being in a packed stadium through an amp stack at eighty decibels, and leave them convinced that perfect romance existed and would always elude them. And, perhaps most to the point, Barbara could flawlessly enunciate Japanese synth-pop, Indonesian kroncong and dangdut, Hong Kong canto-pop, Jamaican reggae, and six regional varieties of Eurodisco.

Makoto and Barbara—they'd had a number of band identities, since they kept spinning sidemen in and out of the stables at Toshiba-EMI and Sony-Epic—had never broken a hit in the United States. They had been huge in the seventies in Brazil, Indonesia, Malaysia, Thailand, New Zealand, Norway, and Finland. In the eighties they'd been mega in Portugal, Goa, Macao, Malta, Ibiza, Korea, Sweden, Hong Kong, Taiwan, and Singapore. They'd scored one-off top-ten hits in France, Spain, Holland, Italy, and Greece. Makoto and Barbara were infallibly big in Japan—even Makoto's spin-off bands were big in Japan. But they had never dented the American market. Never ever. Even though they both spoke mostly English, lived in America, and had every Elvis Presley record ever made.

Starlitz and Zeta arrived at Makoto's dream home just after noon mid-Pacific time. The mogul's mansion couldn't properly be described as "sprawling"—it was properly huge, all right, but it resembled an exquisite, fragile Japanese box kite that had tumbled from a great height onto the vivid green hillside of Kauai's North Shore. The angular flutter of precisely sited walls was surrounded by fragrant trellises, lanai porches, swirling wooden walkways, and melancholy, bougainvillea-shrouded satellite dishes.

Entering the house was like being swallowed whole by an origami crane. The mansion's highly peculiar walls—*membranes* was a better term—were made of a slick, spongeable, Tyvek-like substance. The angular expanses of roof were full of great yawning patio holes, where the luminous Hawaiian moon could gaze in onto uncanny interior vistas of Perspex and pahoehoe lava. The floors and door frames were made of spotted, honey-colored "plyboo," a postmodern laminate of split bamboo and plastic adhesive.

The mansion looked like a stiff Pacific breeze could blow it out to sea with the local whales, but it housed twenty people and had cost somewhere north of three million dollars. No local builder in Kauai was remotely skilled enough to create such a fabulous structure. They'd had to fly in hard-bitten multinational subcontractors who'd worked on the L.A. Getty Museum and that unspeakable Frank Gehry creation in Bilbao. The cost would have crippled anybody but an arty zillionaire who had spontaneous attacks of narcolepsy whenever he met an accountant. Constructing his Kauai palace had even crippled Makoto, but Makoto uncrippled rather deftly. Cost overruns never much bothered Makoto. Given enough pakalolo marijuana, the guy was the essence of indulgent good cheer.

"Hey, Dad."

"What?"

"Hey, Dad."

"Huh?"

"Hey, Dad, how come this rich guy doesn't have any rooms inside his house?"

"Honey, this is one of those way-cool, open-plan, flow-through, shoji-screen things they've got going on in here," Starlitz explained. "Besides, it never gets hot or cold in Hawaii. People here can get away with any kind of loony crap they want."

A local staffer made her yawning appearance. Makoto had recruited his house groupies from the staff of former elevator operators at the Yellow Magic Orchestra shoe-and-software superstore. Makoto's house girl wore a dampproof, rose-pink polyester uniform. Starlitz was pretty sure it was designed by Jean-Paul Gaultier. Only Gaultier could make pink polyester look quite that fuzzy.

Traipsing along in heavy-lidded Hawaiian tempo, the staffer escorted them down an obscure series of damp, slanting, plasticized halls. The walls had been carelessly hung with gold albums and gushing celebrity testimonials. "I wish more American kids could see us getting down to your soulful music—your fans forever, Tipper and Al." "You may say I'm a dreamer, but so are you, baby—Yoko and Sean." "From Ted and Jane to Makoto and Barbara—thanks for the help on the yacht! Call us anytime you're in Atlanta!"

Makoto was standing barefoot in one of his kitchens, eating breakfast. To judge by the look and smell, it was the very same stuff Makoto had been eating for years: potted meat and buckwheat noodles.

"Reggae!" he cried. They embraced.

There was more gray in Makoto's hair. He was thicker around the waist. And were those round specs really bifocals? Yes, they were.

"Eat Spam," Makoto said kindly, proffering his wok. "Come from can on mainland. Good for you."

"We ate at the hotel," Starlitz said.

" 'Hotel!' But, Reggae!" Makoto protested. "You have guest suite here at house. We put you in Mariko Mori room. You know Mariko Mori?"

"Uhm, yeah, no, maybe. Mariko Mori is the daughter of the guy who builds the biggest skyscrapers in the world. She takes art photos of herself, dressed up in Mylar spacesuits, inside the Tokyo subway."

Makoto nodded eagerly. "What sweet girl, huh? Super talented! So cute!"

"Does Mariko Mori have any idea how far out she's been getting lately?"

"Oh, sure! Mariko major artist! Big sale in New York Sotheby's." Makoto gazed down at Zeta, beaming unaffectedly. "Who this fan girl? She wear great shoes!"

"This is my daughter, Zenobia. Zenobia Boadicea Hypatia McMillen."

Zeta and Makoto traded long, guarded, transcontinental stares.

"You like 'Dragonball'?" Makoto offered at last.

"Yeah," Zeta muttered, "Dragonball is pretty good."

"You like 'Sailor Moon'?"

She perked up. "Sure!"

" 'Pokémon'? 'Hello Kitty'?"

"*Everybody* likes those! Who can't like those? They'd have to be *stupid!*"

"This girl all right!" Makoto pronounced. "You hungry, Zen Obeah? You like udon noodle?"

"Are they *white* udon noodles?"

"Very, very white."

"Great. Make me some. Make me some *now*. 'Cause I'm starving."

Makoto filled a badly scorched soup pan from a gurgling jug of appallingly expensive imported spring water. "Young American girl grow up tall and strong eat udon noodle," opined Makoto, wandering among his tropical hardwood cabinets and yanking knobs at random. Two huge tropical cockroaches, the size of his guitar-strumming thumb, jumped out from the pantry. Makoto ducked their clattering flight with a tolerant Hawaiian wince. Eventually he discovered a piled bonanza of plastic-wrapped Nipponese noodle product.

"I boil them," he announced, clicking on his electric stove. "No microwave of tasty noodle. We cook it old-fashion, one-love, natural, i-rie way, mon."

They watched the pot boil in comfortable silence.

Makoto gave Zeta a thoughtful look. "What you like better, Nintendo or Sega?"

"Sega is dead now. Like, totally."

"Yes. You right. I keep telling them, use some Tokyo DJ, but no, no, Propellerheads, Prodigy, every damn time! British techno guy have corner on game soundtrack market."

It was unlike Makoto to mention business before several hours of hospitable Nipponese feel-good touchie-feelie, but clearly the videogame issue had been preying on Makoto's mind. Makoto was over the fact that he would never be big in America, but he was lethally serious about the British pop scene. It was a bone-deep competitive thing for him. Britain was the European Japan.

"Hear anything from Eno lately?" Starlitz prodded.

"I know him back in Roxy Music," Makoto said by reflex. "I know Brian Eno when he wear makeup and feathers."

"D'you read his new book? The one about a year in the 1990s?"

"Professor Eno very good writer," Makoto admitted sourly. He rolled his tongue inside his mouth and slowly emitted a quote. " 'Not doing the thing that nobody had ever thought of not doing.' "

Starlitz pondered this remark. Not many Europeans could have written that sentence. "Eno is heavy, man."

"I keep diary for year 1999 now. 'Oblique Strategy.' " Makoto looked up, stirring the noodle pot languidly. "You keep diary, Reggae?"

"Kind of a principle with me not to leave any paper trails."

"You always on the road. You settle down, better for you. Got little girl, she happier with big house."

"Look, man, don't tell me that. That's what I told *you*, remember? Not me. *You*."

Makoto offered a sphinxlike grin. "We very balance here."

Two of Makoto's staffers drifted in, uniformed, tidy, and blissed out to the eyeballs. "We found another centipede in the sofa, chief," one of them offered in Japanese.

"Well, tell me," Makoto replied in Japanese, "was it a large, sluggish brown one, or one of those little electric-blue toxic bastards?"

"Big brown one, chief."

"Stop fretting. The geckos will eat it."

"You gettum plenty bug here?" Starlitz offered, in his execrable Japanese.

Makoto nodded sharply. "Like you wouldn't believe, brother! It's the damp. We sponge the mold off these plastic walls every week or so, but the bugs live under the house on the pilings. They breed inside those dead macadamia stumps." Makoto scratched thoughtfully at his round, fluffy head. "The worst part of living here is the constant salt breezes. Ate all my studio equipment. Cars, computers, tape drives, you can pretty well name it: it just goes."

The staffers drifted to a rust-spotted refrigerator and began removing fruit. They moved silently, but with amazing languor, as if under light hypnosis. One of them sliced through a big fleshy mango with a ceramic Nipponese blade the color of crab meat. The other started up a spavined Braun food processor. Someone in a remote area of the house put on a bonging tape of Balinese gamelan.

"That rust trouble too bad. Big shame," Starlitz sympathized.

"Houseplants, though," Makoto offered suavely. "This island has the best volcanic soil in the world. I have a bonsai on our back porch that's three meters tall."

"A bonsai? So big?"

"It's a *joke*."

"Sorry, my Japanese plenty rusty now."

"Reggae, trust me, that illiterate crap you were speaking in that bar in Roppongi, that was never Japanese. That was your own unique personal dialect. That was Reggae-ese."

Makoto drained the pot and poured the noodles into a spotless tapered ceramic bowl. "You eat noodle!" he told Zeta in English. "Enjoy!"

Zeta grinned. "Gimme some chopsticks, guy!"

Supplied with sticks, Zeta began vacuuming her noodles with many piercing slurps.

Makoto eased himself onto a padded chrome stool. "I didn't think she resembled you at first, but now I can perceive a strong family trait."

Starlitz nodded. *"Hai."*

"It's very pleasant to meet this young lady. I heard you mention your daughter before, but I thought it was one of those impossible American divorce and custody things. Not that I mean to pry."

Starlitz lowered his head in a jittery half-bow. "I'm sorry about leaving the act. About G-7. My fault. *Gomen nasai.*"

"Reggae, my brother, trust me, I understand. This is one of

those *giri* and *ninjo* problems. It's either *giri*, or it's *ninjo*. That is human life. A man has to make his own karma, understand me? Either way is fine with me."

Zeta looked up with a scowl from her rapidly vanishing noodles. "Stop talking so much Japanese! And especially stop talking so much Japanese about *me*."

"You like to shop?" said Makoto artlessly.

"Spending money? Sure!"

"Your dad and I, we talk some business now. Kats take you to cool surf shop in Lihue. You buy everything groovy." Makoto turned to a smoothie-guzzling staffer and spoke. "Katsu, take this haole kid downtown. Show her every clip joint on the beach. And use the MasterCard this time. It's got the entertainment account."

"Is the Lexus running, chief?"

"Sort of."

"Okay."

"They know us in Lihue," said Makoto, polishing off a final chunk of Spam. "Everybody knows everybody, on a small island like this. You bring a crew of twenty in from Tokyo, you run a big tab at Taisho's down on the South Shore—that's the only sushi joint in Kauai that has fresh squid—well, people get to know all about you. People look after each other around here. Even the Anglos have Asian values. So your daughter will be okay."

Zeta emptied her bowl. "I need to use the bathroom, Dad."

Makoto gestured silently at a speckled plyboo exit.

They left. Then Zeta looked up at him candidly. "Is Makoto a nice guy, Dad?"

"He's very rich."

"But he's kind of nice, right? He's not mad at you about the band. Those were good noodles."

"Yeah. Okay. Ten or twelve layers down, under the contracts, and the record deals, and the touring, and all the times he got screwed over, and all the trouble he has to take to be one of the hippest sons of bitches in the world—yeah, Makoto's a nice guy."

They got lost in the nexus of interlocking flow-spaces, and emerged somehow in Makoto's master bedroom. There were two floral-printed beds in there, amid a private maze of sandalwood screens. The place had a damp sexual reek of patchouli, musk, and wheat germ.

Starlitz noted that Makoto's bedtime reading was a dog-eared copy of Haruki Murakami's *Norwegian Wood*.

Makoto was obsessed with the novelist. He had read all the guy's books with fanatical faithfulness, *Wild Sheep Chase, Dance Dance Dance, Hard-Boiled Wonderland,* even the bug-crushing *Wind-Up Bird Chronicles,* which read like fifty kilos of boiled radishes if you weren't Japanese, but if you *were* Japanese, it was a scarifying, transformative cultural experience.

Norwegian Wood, Murakami's first novel, was the narrative keystone of the Murakami oeuvre, in that it was all about an appallingly hip, soulful, and sensitive Japanese dude, with tremendously good taste in clothing and music, who is way too good for this sorry world, and is right on the verge of deciding to kill himself—but then, his girlfriend obligingly kills herself first. Only people who weren't Japanese could be crass enough to find this story line funny. From a Japanese perspective this was a tale of total sexual, political, and existential authenticity.

There had been one crucial, Suntory-whiskey-and-Gekkeikan-sake-drenched night in Goruden Gai when, over the drunken bellowing of the sweating, tightly packed crowd in an ultrahip bar the size of a phone booth, Makoto had been getting this crucial narrative point across to Starlitz.

Starlitz had listened with great care. It was always worth talking to Makoto. The guy was a great listener, he had astounding ears. Makoto's ears were the best-looking things on his head. Makoto could hear things that scarcely any human being on earth could hear.

So Starlitz had remarked: "Makoto, I definitely see why

the girlfriend has to go. That is a totally dramatic and moving resolution of the story line. By hanging herself she's validating the hero's unspoken anguish. But let's just assume—for argument's sake—that the protagonist has a higher-level grasp of his existential situation. He *knows* that he is an arty intellectual having a lethal identity crisis in his highly conflicted, ultracommercial Japanese society. So, as an act of deliberate perversity he arranges that the girlfriend *doesn't* kill herself. Instead, the girlfriend is well fed, properly exercised, looked after, respected, and pampered in every conceivable way."

"Reggae, that would be a lousy novel."

"Of course it would, but listen to me, man: *Norwegian Wood* is only forty-five thousand words long. That is a fucking *short book*, Makoto. If you swallow that fishhook, you and the girlfriend are gonna choke on your own vomit like Hendrix and Joplin. But if you somehow break that master narrative, you're gonna be rolling in royalties when every other tortured artist who is the voice of his fucking Japanese generation is stuck in a fucking cremation urn."

This was a rather involved debate, but Starlitz's Japanese always improved radically when everyone around him had been drinking heavily. Makoto heard what he was told, and something important broke inside of him. Makoto had to elbow his way out of the bar and into a Tokyo alley, to throw up everything he understood.

After that incident Makoto had stopped writing his own incredible, idiosyncratic songs, which nobody comprehended anyway, and started writing brilliant global-pop pastiches that generated large sums of money on a regular basis.

"Dad, is this a bathroom?"

"Yeah. I think this must be Barbara's bathroom."

"Dad, can you come in there with me? I'm kind of scared."

It was a very scary bathroom. Glaring stage mirrors and big fluffy carpets. Scented candles. Incense. Peacock feathers. Oils. A walk-in makeup arsenal. Terry-cloth shower sarongs in eight shades of tropical pastel. Barbara's eyelash curlers looked like Swiss quark-smashing equipment from CERN in Geneva. There was a highly polished bronze Kali in the corner with big gleaming seashell eye-whites.

"Dad, what is *that* thing?"

"That's called a bidet, honey."

"She doesn't have any toilet in here, Dad."

It was true. The diva possessed no toilet. "Uh, we'll try Makoto's bathroom instead. He's pretty much bound to have a toilet."

Makoto had a low, crouching Japanese toilet surrounded by gently mildewing stacks of *Metropolis* and *I-D*.

Zeta set her lips firmly, in grim feminine commitment. "I can't go here. I'll just wait."

"You sure you can wait all the way to Lihue?"

She nodded. "I guess I have to."

AFTER ZETA'S SLOUCHING DEPARTURE IN THE LEXUS, STAR-litz and Makoto met over honeysuckle-ginseng tea in a lava-lined conversation pit. Makoto's low coffee table had the black lacquered gleam of a concert Steinway. The walls here were hung with exquisite ukiyo-e Masami Teraoka originals, from the Hawaiian artist's legendary "McDonald's Hamburgers Invading Japan" series. Makoto had put his manifold charity plaques on display: his involvement in African river worm blindness campaigns, Caribbean AIDS testing, free flak jackets for UNICEF workers. Outside the sliding Perspex doors lurked a pebbled Zen garden, with a raked sea of symbolic pebbles washing against six large concrete chunks of the demolished Berlin Wall.

"*Tabako?*" offered Makoto.

"I quit again."

"Me too," Makoto lied. With feigned indifference he tossed aside a pack of imported Seven Stars. Then he opened a mahogany box and lit a tightly rolled reefer. He dropped the match in a massive onyx tray.

"One of these days the Big Boom will return to Nippon," he offered tangentially.

"That's what they say. There's bound to be a boom for every bubble."

"When Japan rich and happy again, then I go back to live. I go back often, you know. For studio work. But . . . it's like spirit die in Japan. Everything smell of decay."

"Smelled Russia lately?"

Makoto laughed. "Russia drink too much, never work. Of course they are broke. But why are *Japanese* broke? Japanese work very hard every day! Why, Reggae?"

"You tell me, man. Why should I have all the answers?"

Makoto sniffed fragrant resinous smoke, cracked his solid guitar-playing knuckles, and switched to Japanese. "It's true: you don't have all the answers. That's obvious to both of us now. Because you lost the bet."

"That's right."

"The French One died. Snorting smack. In some crap hotel in the middle of Asia."

Starlitz said nothing.

"I thought you'd win that bet, Reggae. Not that I cared. It was a crazy bet. Why would you want to make a bet like that? You win the bet, you get a little money. You lose that bet: you have to be magic, baby. Magic."

Starlitz spoke in English. "I wouldn't call three hundred million yen tax-free 'a little money.' I would have had some major use for that kind of bread. On the far side of Y2K a fat stack of yen would have been handy."

"It isn't much money," shrugged Makoto. "First hundred million yen is hardest. But now, you lost. Right?" He looked at Starlitz candidly, vague interest dawning.

Starlitz shrugged mournfully. "Yeah. So I'll be magic, man. I'll be magic for you real soon now."

"Where did it go wrong?" said Makoto.

"Well, man, I've been thinking about that. Seriously. It would be easy to say that I blew off the gig for personal reasons. Because of my little girl, and the *giri* and the *ninjo* obligations, and all that. Yeah, I dropped the G-7 gig, I gave it up. But if it wasn't my daughter showing up, it just would have been somethin' else. It was just dumb of me to think that we could create a multinational pop act that would make us a shitload of money, but that had absolutely no talent, soul, inspiration, or musical sincerity whatsoever."

"It make good sense. Basic modern trend of the industry."

Starlitz spread his hands. "Sure, sure. I mean, of course you and I could create a successful global pop act. We had the capital, we had the know-how, we had the contacts. But I couldn't *get away* with that. The world only *looks* that fucking cynical. I was violating a major narrative. I should have *known* some girl would end up getting dramatically killed over G-7, even though the act was totally bogus and meant absolutely nothing." Starlitz sighed. "And it was the *French One* too. That clinches it for sure, man. See, the French One was the very best one, she understood the whole G-7 pitch, she knew we were creating a scene that was a total precession of the simulacrum with no real signifiers. Besides, she was the only one who could sing."

"G-7 making very good money now," Makoto offered. "G-7 making *lots* more money."

"Well, *that's* not surprising."

"*Hai,*" said Makoto intently, "this Turkish gentleman friend of yours, Mehmet Ozbey-san . . . He seems to be very businesslike, quite an accomplished manager. The money's coming in like clockwork, every week. In Turkish government bonds, no less. Inside a diplomatic parcel!" Makoto examined a burning run on his joint and dampened it with a licked fingertip. "Our old G-7 accountant—what was his name?"

" 'Nick.' "

" 'Nick.' " Makoto puffed smoke and switched back to English. "The British police, they arrest your Nick. In Istanbul. Interpol grab him. I'm afraid your friend Nick, not very honest accountant."

"Damn. I'm sorry about that. For Nick, I mean." Starlitz shook his head. "I might have known Nick would crash. Or more likely, get pushed. Nick was important to me, but for Ozbey, Nick was in the way." Starlitz scratched at his jawline, irritated. "That was a delicate arrangement. There weren't a lot of guys with Nick's unique talents who wanted in on such a crap deal."

Makoto stubbed out his joint. "Indonesia in currency crash," he said firmly. "Malaysia very sick financially. Japan in steady recession, eight, nine year. Hong Kong scene have hand over mouth from new China bosses. But Central Asia, much oil money, no pop-music penetration. I write G-7 one special song. Just for fun."

"Oh, no!" Starlitz blurted, stunned. "Tell me you didn't write them a good song!"

Sheepishly, Makoto switched to Japanese. "Listen to me, Reggae," he said reasonably, "I know I promised you that I would never give the act any decent tunes. That was part of the bet. But once that girl was dead, our previous arrangement was off. So, I admit it; I wrote a new song for G-7. Kind of a cool, Central Asian, Tuvan-throat-singing treatment. And it's a hit, brother. Biggest pop hit ever to premiere in Tashkent."

Starlitz struggled back to English. "Why are you pushing this thing? You're all playing with fire. You know that, don't you?"

"G-7 my best commercial act now. Besides"—Makoto scowled—"hot DJ kid in London write them good song anyway."

"You're kidding. Which DJ kid would that be?"

"The new DJ kids all the same! Electronica kid in London

have stupid computer in bed-sit, can't even read music, play guitar!"

"Which DJ kid was it? I need a name."

" 'DJ Dead White Eurocentric.' "

Starlitz winced. "Oh, man, that's scary! You're scaring me here. What the hell is he doing writing tunes for G-7? He's got Madonna hammering his door with her baby over her arm."

Makoto rubbed the broad bridge of his nose. "G-7 are hot. He smells them burning. Just like me." Makoto looked glumly into the prescient gleam of his tabletop. "G-7 is very hot. Because the bombs are falling. It is culture war."

MAKOTO AND STARLITZ SPENT A SLOW AFTERNOON WANDER-ing the palace grounds. Makoto showed Starlitz the dog kennel, the hang gliders, the surfboards, the Aqua-Lungs, and the trimaran. Ritually showing off his Kauai digs was something Makoto did quite a lot of, these days.

Makoto was exhibiting this courtesy just to show that he bore Starlitz no hard feelings. Yes, the two of them had failed to see out the century in full commercial control of the world's least important pop group, but what the hell, it was just the music business. The pop biz had its ups and downs. It wasn't something two sane men should take personally.

"Look at my new roses," Makoto offered in Japanese.

"Hai?" The plants looked unexceptional; the leaves were small, the vines were crooked, they had no blooms.

"They are 'BGM.' "

" 'Back-Ground Music'?"

" 'Benchmarked Genetic Modification.' They can't reproduce outside the lab. Every pot comes with a copyright." Makoto dug in the rich dark earth with the toe of his zori. "They have firefly genes inside them, so they glow in the dark. Just out of the lab, in time for the new century. Barbara hates them. The staff hates them. They're just not natural. They're mutant monsters from Babylon. I tried, but I can't get them to bloom."

"Why you buy these things? Never buy the alpha rollout."

"It was one of those one-click Website things." Makoto ducked his head. "I was surfing stoned. . . . I shouldn't do that anymore. I should just shut up and pay other people to deal with my weird decisions. . . . You wouldn't want the job, would you?"

Starlitz shrugged, surprised. "Maybe. Not many jobs in Kauai."

"Kauai is the 'Garden Island.' It's mid-Pacific service and tourist economics. Lot of bar jobs here, like your old days in Roppongi." Makoto threw his arm over Starlitz's shoulder. "Reggae, let me confide something here. There is no harm in gardening. It's good. It's honorable. The sensei Borutaro, he said that to mind your own garden is a very good idea."

" 'Borutaro'? Some Zen guy?"

" 'Voltaire.' "

"Oh, yeah. Him." Starlitz examined the rosebushes. "I'm thinking about this proposal. Seriously."

Makoto chuckled. "I see the future, my brother. I have no fear of Y2K. The years roll by, I just get fatter, and older, and richer. Maybe I get a little better at playing my guitar. But I have less and less to say. Eventually I approach perfect mastery—but I have no reason to play anymore. And *then*, they can cremate me."

"It's better to fade away than to burn out."

"Yes, surely, but it's not *much* better—and that's why I'm going to get away with it."

IN THE LUMINOUS TROPICAL EVENING, BARBARA RETURNED from teaching her hula hulau class. Barbara had once been a mere hula student. She had taken a properly humble part in Hawaiian hoi'ke recitals. She had put in respectful dues at a local hula dojo. Then Barbara had made one obligatory public performance at the Koke'e Banana Poka Festival.

Barbara was not an authentic hula dancer. Authentic hula was a preindustrial cultural act by regional ethnics who lacked metals and practiced human sacrifice.

But Barbara's hula blew everyone else off the stage. Barbara danced the hula that Hawaii would have created if Hawaii had been a mid-Pacific Polynesian superpower with aircraft-carrier canoes. Barbara danced a hula that knew that it was 1999. It was a bright, fully rendered, safe-sex, steroid and gym-shoes hula.

Now Barbara was Kauai's postmodern hula guru. Barbara had her own hula school now, and she had a student claque of two dozen worshipful, liberal, middle-aged Anglo women who believed in her utterly and would do absolutely anything she said.

Starlitz watched from a safe distance as Barbara glided barefoot from her Mercedes. Barbara wore a wrapped cotton skirt of explosive floral print, a tight strapless bandeau, a white floral handwoven headdress. Barbara drifted nonchalantly across forty feet of red, mossy mud, and arrived with feet so clean that they might have just been steamed and toweled.

"Leggy," Barbara said, blinking her vast, tapering, head-lamp eyes. "Aloha, dude."

"How's it goin'."

Barbara printed her lips on Starlitz's upper right cheek-bone. Starlitz was astonished. Normally, being air-kissed by Barbara was like being tapped by a No mask. But this had been an unfeigned moment of genuine mammalian body contact.

"Where you been so long?" crooned Barbara, in her best chummy, intimate, bantering stage-voice. "I was afraid you didn't love us anymore."

"Lotta business," Starlitz muttered.

"Leggy, stay with us awhile. Welcome to Paradise." Barbara split the air with expressive fingertips. " '*Anuanua o te heiti nehenehe to tino e.*' "

"Uh, yeah, no, maybe." Starlitz was trying not to stare. No man who hadn't known her for years would have been able to tell this, but Barbara was growing old. Very, very gracefully—but old. There were little nips and tucks out of Barbara's creamy toned expanse. An epidermal crinkle here and there. The awesome coconut-oil sheen to her glossy locks looked a hell of a lot like coconut oil, but not a whole hell of a lot like hair.

Sun. Salt water. Surfboards. There might even be three or four spare pounds of extra roast pork on Barbara's frame.

Barbara drifted inside her home. Starlitz followed, kicking off his sandals at the door.

"How's life been treating you, babe?"

"People are nice to me here."

"Yeah?"

"In Kauai I'm a home girl. I'm *ohana*. The people at the florist shop. At the noodle shop. They *like* me." Several languid heartbeats passed. "You know?"

"Yeah, Barbara, I get it, I'm with the program. You mean the pop celebrity thing isn't a burden to you here. Because these simple, multiracial island people can see through the image, to your own true, delightful inner spirit."

Barbara nodded delicately. "I could talk just like that, if I wanted to."

Starlitz shrugged. "Barbara, I have to ask you for a favor."

Barbara smiled broadly, reached out, gave his shoulder a playful hula-style kung-fu jab. "Oh, you!"

"There was this bet Makoto and I had, and I lost it. You know about that?"

Barbara nodded solemnly. "Magic."

"Yeah. I wonder if you'd mind coming with us out to the Waialua River. I need a magic volunteer. You'd be so perfect."

———

JET LAG FELLED HIM EARLY. NEXT MORNING STARLITZ AND
Zeta rose with the cries of the birds, borrowed a car from the
compound's garage, and drove to Lihue for a series of purchases. Tiki torches. Smoke bombs. Flash paper. Mirrors.

Zeta's skin was bright purple. It was one of those new and
very paranoid sunscreens, a postindustrial reaction to the
planet's tattered ozone layer. The game plan was to visibly wax
down one's entire child, so as to avoid possible eruptions of
bleeding epidermal cancers in the depths of the twenty-first
century. The purple tone faded after a while, but it ensured
that you hadn't missed a spot. For her own part Zeta just enjoyed being a purple girl, so she slopped the stuff on three
times an hour.

Zeta's trip to the Lihue tourist traps had been quite a success. She wore a foam sun visor, a cropped tank shirt with a
batik gecko, and drawstring cotton beach pants with decorative cartoon schools of the colorful Hawaiian state fish, the
mellifluous humuhumunukunukuapua'a.

"Boy, Dad. No more stinkin' school. We're in Hawaii. You
are just the coolest, Dad."

"I hear the junior high schools around here really suck."

"Dad, they've got *soaping shoes,*" Zeta insisted, lifting her
newly shod feet. "At my lame school in Colorado the kids
barely even *heard* of soaping shoes!"

Starlitz took a dappled mountain turn, squinting at the
potholed road. "Give me the pitch there."

" 'The Fader' is the most sophisticated soaping shoe in the
line!" declared Zeta, whacking her metal feet on the car's
sandy floorboards with an ominous ringing sound. "Made of
'Meat Is Murder' vegan pleather, this sporting shoe combines
old-fashioned pinpoint mesh with radiator mesh for enhanced
breathability. For better highway vision the Fader is high-
lighted using 3M reflective piping!"

"So what's the 'soap' schtick, exactly?"

"Well, you know how skater guys, like, grind down
handrails on their skateboard axles?"

"Oh, yeah," nodded Starlitz, "lip tricks, burly air, three-sixties, seven-twenties, decal sponsorship, I'm hip."

"Well, the soapers just put stainless steel plates in your shoe. So you can jump on anything, and just kinda skid."

"No skateboard left? Built it right into the shoe?"

"Yeah, Dad."

No board left, just the tricks. "Not doing the things that nobody had ever thought of not doing." Starlitz patted his daughter's slimy purple shoulder. "Kid, this extracurricular thing is definitely working out for you."

STARLITZ AND ZETA SCOUTED OUT THE WAIALUA RIVERBANK, found a conveniently secluded locale in the dripping bush, and carefully planted the necessary magic props. They then returned to the mansion, where Starlitz briefed his patron on the upcoming ritual.

"I'm not saying just any woman would be good material for this," Starlitz said. "Barbara, though, is ideal. But just in case anything turns a little . . . you know . . . freaky . . . keep in mind that she volunteered for this."

"To break the law of gravity?"

"Look," Starlitz said, pained, "don't put it that way. I mean, yes, technically speaking, Barbara is going to 'break the law of gravity.' But this is not a fucking NASA project here, okay? She's doing this for *you*. This is a totally *spiritual* thing. She's going to be *set free*, okay? She's going to become . . . unearthly. Untouched. Transcendent."

"You're serious about this?"

Starlitz frowned. "We *shook hands* on this, man. It was a *bet*. A woman *died* over this. You've known me a long time. You know I can do things like this. You've seen me do a lot of stuff that is . . . inexplicable."

"Float in midair? Not like *that*."

"Look, these are very strange times, man. You asked for magic, and I came here specifically to do it, and now you are going to get it. You, me, and the house crew are going to an ancient Polynesian taboo site. You can stop grinning just anytime, because this outing is not the fucking Tokyo Disneyland, pal. This is straight-out voodoo necromancy. If you've got the nerve to witness this, this is gonna transform your life."

Makoto blinked. "Will Barbara be all right?"

Starlitz slapped Makoto's shoulder. "Y'know . . . I admit, I had real reservations about invoking this kind of primeval energy. . . . But you asking me that, that makes it much easier for me. Because I trust you, man. Your girlfriend should be all right—as long as she is not disturbed during the ceremony in even the slightest way. The *feng shui* energy in a Polynesian ritual site . . . That's a place and a process of *enormous, ancient, supernatural earth power*, you understand me? It is *kame*, it is *mana*. If there's anyone you don't trust completely and totally, do not bring them to this ceremony."

Makoto scratched his head. Makoto had bought it. Makoto was with the program all the way. "What *should* I bring?"

"Well," said Starlitz, "bring a whole shitload of pakalolo."

PREPARING THE RITUAL REQUIRED THREE DAYS. TO DEMON-strate the gravity of the event the participants were required to fast, meditate, and ritually purge themselves. This requirement immediately weeded out half of Makoto's staffers, people who had concluded from the get-go that it had to be another lame scam.

The remainder were made of more adventurous stuff, and after a three-day regimen of white rice, fish broth, and Kauai marijuana, they were primed for anything.

Starlitz led them on a dramatic seven-mile evening hike through the Waialua state park.

"Everyone gather round," Starlitz finally announced. He was reading from a sheet of prepared phonetic Japanese. "As you can see, I was here earlier, blessing the site and setting up these tiki torches. But—and this is absolutely critical—we must all unite to remove *all traces of the twentieth century* from this sacred ground! This place must become eternal and timeless, the way it was and will be, before and after science. That means *all physical traces*: not one cigarette butt, not a pull-tab from a can, no spiritual pollutants, nothing from any factory, no product of any machine. If you see the footprint of a modern shoe, erase it. We need purity. The natural, the unsullied. So get on your hands and knees. Gaze carefully at *every centimeter*. This is a kind of prayer."

Starlitz retired to the fragrant shadows at the overgrown fringe of the clearing, where he eased his aching feet and had a cigarette.

Zeta watched the Japanese staff crawling enthusiastically through the damp undergrowth, sniffing and meticulously pinching up everything that resembled litter. "Dad, they look really, really stupid."

"Wait till I make 'em cover themselves with mud."

Zeta giggled.

"Honey, you promised not to laugh. If you have to laugh, you're gonna have to go lock yourself in the rental car."

"I'll be okay, Dad. Can I have some more granola now?"

After some considerable time Starlitz returned to the meticulously groomed prayer site. "Now, I'm sure you've all been wondering—what about myself? Am *I* sufficiently pure for this ritual? Is my own heart pure? Is my own soul pure? Well, of course you are not pure! All those clothes you wear are twentieth-century products! They must be *destroyed*. Into the fire with them!"

"But what'll we wear back to the house?"

"Be more trust," Starlitz barked, ad-libbing. He returned to his prepared script. "You must cover yourselves completely with this sacred Waialua red earth. I can't be responsible for the consequences if you leave any patch of skin exposed to the unearthly forces."

When he returned again, the devotees were naked and smeared with mud. It was rather pleasant mud, actually. The effect could feel quite soothing. Starlitz himself had donned a feather cloak, a bark-and-grass breechclout, and a towering Hawaiian tribal helmet, all from a local crafts store.

"The moment approaches," he intoned. "You seem to be naked and pure now. But you've forgotten one thing. Do you know what that is?"

The Japanese muttered among themselves at some length. They were clueless.

"Your *contact lenses*! They are alien devices, and in your ignorance you are gazing through them at this very moment, while you cannot see them! I will now circulate among you to remove and store these contaminants."

After half blinding the audience, Starlitz closed in on Makoto, with a tom-tom dragged from the underbrush. "Here you go, man. You've got a central shamanic role here. Start it up with the ritual drumming."

Makoto blinked myopically and thumped experimentally at the taut leather skin. "Hey! This drum is a cheap piece of shit!"

"That is hand-cut wood, Makoto. Natural leather and blood for glue. You think New Guinea tribesmen are gonna tune a drum to middle C? That is a totally natural musical instrument, so of course it's a piece of shit! Get after it, man, play the moment, play what you feel."

Smoke gathered as the sun set, with tropical speed. A spectral oozing of dry ice began to curl along the ground. From her concealed position Zeta yanked long silent threads attached to various limbs and bushes. The outskirts of the clearing swiftly came alive with uncanny presences. The mud-smeared Japanese, reduced to the filthy, half-starved condition of the world's last Stone Age tribe, were utterly petrified.

Starlitz adjusted his headdress and feather cape. Then he

led Barbara, naked like everyone else, to her central wooden pedestal.

"I'm so scared," she hissed.

"Sit here in lotus position. Be calm. Rise above."

"But I'm naked! And I gained five kilos."

"That's Makoto playing, isn't it? You're giving Makoto his heart's desire. Just be magic."

Starlitz made his final arrangements. Then he clapped his hands. The drumming rose to a crescendo. "Good-bye, cruel world," he said.

The pedestal vanished.

There were cries of awestruck wonder. Barbara lifted her shapely arms, white hands unfolding like a pair of calla lilies. She was a trans-Pacific boddhisattva, floating on a cloud of fire.

The torches shot sparks and died. In the double gust of bright and dark Barbara sank gently to earth. Starlitz rushed forward at once, brandishing a second cape.

He wrapped her up and delivered her to the crowd.

"Was I magic?" she muttered.

"Don't ask me. Ask your public."

And her public wept. They believed in her, completely, every one.

THE PUBLIC WADED INTO THE WAIALUA TO WASH THEMSELVES free of red mud. Starlitz thoughtfully produced a dozen sets of shorts, T-shirts, and zoris. Trembling with hunger and amazement, the celebrants hiked a quarter mile downriver. A previously prepared set of taxis were waiting there, meters ticking and headlights blazing. The cars took the crowd back to the mansion grounds, where Starlitz had seen to it that a roaring, fully catered luau was already in progress. He knew they would welcome it. They were freaked, munchie-stricken, and starving.

Working alone by the hearty glow of two big magnum

flashlights, Starlitz and Zeta put out the bonfires, gathered up all the doctored tiki torches, shoveled in the stage hole under the fake pedestal, removed every one of the ropes, strings, and hinges, smashed the large stage mirrors to bits with a ball peen hammer, shoved the whole mess of wreckage into a heavy-duty drawstring canvas bag, and threw it all into the bottom of a ravine. Then they drove their hidden rental car to a cheap hotel room in Princeville, where they bought some Chinese takeout and a fifth of Kentucky bourbon.

Later, bloated with pale shrimp-fried rice and wontons, Zeta picked at the laces of her soaping shoes, in front of the silent, flickering cable TV. "Dad, why do you have to drink that whiskey stuff?"

"In Hawaii it's cheaper than the gasoline." Starlitz was tired.

"Is she really magic, Dad? She sure looked magic. She's like a goddess."

Starlitz looked at his child wearily, and stirred himself. Nobody else was going to be able to tell her the truth. He owed it to her. She was just a little kid. "Honey, we scammed them. It was a confidence trick. But in pop that is the legitimate method. As the great Eno declares in one of his many sacred works, pop music doesn't work on any lame fine-arts model where inspired individual genius presents a masterpiece to an inert public. Pop is very popular. All important changes in the pop world are created by little scenes of people, blindly conspiring with their circumstances, to create something cool that they can't understand." He had a long chug of bourbon. "Eno said it, I believe it, and that oughta be good enough for us."

"So Barbara can't really fly, right?"

"Look, that doesn't matter. Really. That's just not the point."

Zeta scowled. "I still don't get it, Dad."

"Then I'll put it another way, okay? Those people are hippies! As long as they think that the cops and the priests don't approve of it, they'll believe anything! They'll swallow any loony, irrational crap you want to hand them."

Zeta tied the loose lace of her soaping shoe and climbed up on the hotel bed. "Well, let me try, Dad. I think *I* can float in midair." She began energetically jumping up and down on the hotel bed.

"That's a cheap bed, honey. Don't do that."

"Look at me, I'm soaping, Dad." Zeta screeched along the metal edge of the bedframe, poised on one foot. "Look, Dad, I'm moon-walking."

"Give it a rest."

"I'm not tired! Ha ha ha!" Zeta jumped up onto the headboard with a violent crash. "You can't catch me, Dad!"

Starlitz scowled. "You heard me! Don't make me come over there."

Zeta flung herself like a dandelion seed to the top of the window frame. She slid along the top of the window, spun slowly across the ceiling, and fetched up light as a cobweb, in the corner of the ceiling. "Can't catch me! You can't come over! You can't get me down! Look, Dad, I'm being impossible! Ha ha ha!"

"Zeta, you're getting all worked up."

"Look, I'm flying in midair! Ha ha ha!"

More in sorrow than anger Starlitz reached into his bag and produced a throwaway camera. "Zeta, come down from there! Don't make me use this."

Head inverted and pigtails dangling, Zeta began jumping up and down on the ceiling. Hard. Plaster cracked and fell like chunks of macaroni. Starlitz lifted the camera, aimed the lens. Light flashed. Zeta tumbled to the hotel floor with a shattering crash. She began shrieking in pain and rage, clutching her bruised knees and rolling back and forth histrionically.

It had been a long day for both of them.

———

EVEN AFTER ZETA HAD FALLEN INTO A TWITCHING SLEEP, Starlitz found himself jet-lagged and detached from all comfort. The room smelled funny. Why was he drunk now, in some shitty hotel, stinking of smoke and bone weary, in the middle of Paradise? He could feel heartburn gas from bad moo goo gai pan. Maybe it was a clogged artery. A hot little corroded wire of visceral weariness there. A small but lethal promise of future coronary misbehavior. He was exhausted, he'd had too many cigs.

Maybe this had nothing to do with anything in Hawaii. Something had gone wrong with him. With the room; with the town; with the island; with the planet, with the universe. There was a very bad vibe loose somewhere. There was no escaping it; he could feel it rolling in from some stinking rim of the cosmos. He could smell it. The neon sun sinks in a sharp chlorine smell of junk. The vacant rooms and rubble and the chemical gardens . . . the cold blue pool . . . eyes upturned to last cold bubbles, lipstick like iced grease . . . Bad needle jones . . .

Starlitz reached for the phone and dialed.

"*Shtoh vy khoteti?*"

"Viktor? It's Lekhi Starlits."

"Are you in Cyprus?"

"No. I'm in Hawaii."

"Hawaii? TV police thriller? Dark-haired man, many car chases, villains, handguns?"

"Yeah, no, maybe. About the band, Viktor."

"Can you get me a green card?"

"Viktor, has something happened to the band?"

"Oh. Yeah." Viktor smacked his lips. "One of them died."

"Yeah, you told me that. The French One."

"Who, her? No, now the *Italian* One's dead."

"You're kidding. The Italian One's dead?"

"Facedown in a hotel pool. Drugs, swimming . . . the usual."

"Where is the band now? Where is Ozbey?"

"Mehmet Ozbey is in Istanbul. He's training a new Italian One. His Albanian Muslim emigré Italian One."

Starlitz groaned. "Is your uncle around? Put him on the line."

"What are you, drunk? You sound drunk! My uncle's still dead, Lekhi. He was in a Belgrade air base on the first night of NATO strikes. Remember?"

"He's not dead."

"Even if Pulat Romanevich was *alive* you couldn't talk to him. NATO is blowing up all the power plants and telephones, in a corrupt assault against a sovereign socialist nation."

"Forget about it. Air strikes always look better on paper than they do when you blow up real phones."

"Even if my uncle was alive, and the Yugoslav phones were working, my uncle wouldn't talk to you, because my uncle would be heroically engaged in defending the democratically elected president of a Slavic nation, Slobodan Milosevic."

"Tell it to Zhirinovsky, kid. How many missions have the Yugo Air Force been flying against NATO? I've been a little out of touch."

"Not very many," Viktor admitted.

"Then our flying ace is probably not very dead," said Starlitz.

Zeta sat up in bed. "Who is that, Dad? Is it my mom?"

"No."

Zeta sniffled sulkily. Her face looked drawn and wan. "I want to talk to my mom."

"Last I heard of Vanna, she was in Cyprus. I'm calling Cyprus now."

"Is it about the band?"

"Yup."

"Is G-7 gonna die, Dad?"

"No, no, the band does great. It's just the girls that are gonna die."

"You have to save them, Dad."

"Why should I do that?"

"I don't know why. But you have to, Dad. You just have to save them."

STARLITZ WENT BACK TO THE MANSION TO CADGE SOME MONEY from Makoto. Makoto wasn't taking visitors. Instead, Starlitz was corralled by a staffer, who followed his orders and took Starlitz and Zeta to meet Barbara.

Barbara was lounging in the garden in a McDonough ply-boo lawn-chair. She was overseeing the staffers as they languidly ripped up the mutant rosebushes.

"What a nice little girl," Barbara said, looking down at Zeta in her logoed tank top and pedal pushers.

"Mahalo," Zeta said. "Can I have some of that coconut milk? It smells great!"

Barbara languidly beckoned another staffer and had her take Zeta to the kitchen.

"Makoto's laying down some studio tracks today," Barbara told him. "He's not seeing anybody. Especially you."

"Makoto's not all freaked out or anything, is he?"

"No . . . but we never did get our contact lenses sorted properly."

Starlitz said nothing.

"Am I cursed now?" Barbara said. "Makoto said I was supernatural. Did I go too far? Am I doomed now?"

Starlitz shrugged. "No more than anybody else."

"Was I really magic? Is that the real truth?"

"The truth is that you're an idol, Barbara."

"He's not happy," Barbara said, lower lip trembling. "We have little idol problems, sometimes."

"Look, you're shacked up with a crazy musician, babe. Get over it."

"I'm an idol. Is he going to break me?"

"Why do you say that?"

"He's going to break me, isn't he? He always wants me to read those stupid books of his where perfect women die."

"I guess Makoto could break you, but no, I'm pretty sure he won't."

"Then will he leave me? For some other goddess?" Barbara pursed her lips below the sunglasses.

"Yeah, he'll leave you. When you bury him. Then he'll be gone a long, long time."

"But not for some other goddess."

"No."

"Well." She seemed much happier now.

"Look, Barbara, stop fretting. The situation has advantages, okay? Makoto doesn't see you getting old. He doesn't see you changing at all. Because he never fuckin' saw you in the first place. He can only see the magic." Starlitz drew a breath. "People love idols because of the stars in front of their own eyes. Your boyfriend is your biggest fan. It's a drag in some ways, but live with it."

"I always have to live on a pedestal."

"Yeah, sure, but just till he's dead."

Barbara scratched at her cheek.

"Think about that. You're doing hula aerobics three times a week, while Mr. Ukelele Boy is in there chowing on Spam and huffing pakalolo unfiltereds. There's only one end to that story line. The odds say you outlive Makoto by twenty, twenty-five years. Then you get everything, whatever's left. No more idol. No more crowds. So then it's just you. A little old lady. No sex appeal, no flashbulbs, no wolf whistles, no encores. When you're an old woman with lots of money of your own, it's a very different life. There's not a man on earth that can tell you to do a damned thing—men don't give you orders anymore, because men don't even *notice* you. That's when you come totally into your own. Whatever you are, whoever you are, under there."

"That's my future? They say you can tell the future."

"Give me your hand, to make sure." Hiding a yawn, Star-litz looked cursorily into the lines of her palm. "Oh, yeah. That's it, all right."

Barbara pulled her hand back and rubbed it uneasily. "I'll have to think about that."

"Yeah, I would advise that. Think pretty hard. It's way hard to become yourself when you've been pleasing other people all your life."

Barbara gazed at the garden. The conversation was taxing her heavily. "I hate these evil roses. They're the future, but they're not *my* future. I'm glad I killed them all."

Starlitz nodded silently.

Barbara caught his eye. "If I give you some money, would you go away, and not come back here for a long, long time?"

EIGHT

ON THEIR ARRIVAL AT ATATÜRK INTERNA-
tional in Istanbul, Ozbey had them met by a
government limo. The leather upholstery had
been smoothed sleek by the rumps of high-
ranking Turkish bureaucrats. It reeked of chain
smoking and generous three-raki lunches.

Zeta flung her G-7 backpack on the limo's
floor and slumped fitfully behind the nicotine-
yellowed lace curtains.

Worn out from repeated jet flights, Starlitz
stared murkily out his curtained window.

So it was back to Istanbul, finally. He'd
never meant to spend so much time here. The
place had a fatal attraction for him. It had
been so much stronger than he was, so far beyond his ability to help. The city was neck
deep, chin deep, nose deep, in the darkest
sumps of history. Istanbul was the unspoken
capital of many submerged empires: it had
called itself Byzantium, Vizant, Novi Roma,
Anthusa, Tsargrad, Constantinople. . . .

Stuck in dense Turkish traffic, their driver clicked on his radio and began to curse a soccer game. The variant districts of Galata, Pera, Beshiktas, and Ortakoy inched beyond the bumpers. It was the Moslem London, the Islamic New York, crammed neighborhoods of millions with as much regional variety as Bloomsbury or The Bronx.

Istanbul. Crumbling ivy-grown Byzantine aqueducts with Turkish NO PARKING signs. Smog-breathing streetside vendors with ring-shaped breadrolls on sticks. Rubber-tired yellow bulldozers parked under the carved stone eaves of mosques.

Tourist-trap nightclubs featuring potbellied Ukrainian dancers. Vast sunshine-yellow billboards imploring bored Turkish housewives to learn English. Cash-card bank machines in prefab kiosks, built to mimic minarets. Pudding shops. Chestnut trees. Spotted wild dogs of premedieval lineage on their timeless garbage patrol.

Istanbul had more vitality than Sofia, or Belgrade, or Baghdad. Despite its best efforts, the twentieth century had not been able to beat the place down. Istanbul had lost its capitalship, but Istanbul had always walked on its own sore feet. It had not been crushed, conquered, and carpet bombed, it had never been forced to exist at the sufferance of others.

This had everything to do with the scary omnipresence of Turkey's own native version of the Twentieth Century Personified. He was a bizarre, anomalous entity self-named Kemal Atatürk. He was a jackbooted, pistol-packing generalissimo. He had founded the Turkish Republic, kicked out the pashas, shot the Greeks dead in heaps on the battlefield, given Turkey a new name, a new alphabet, new constitution, a new flag. He was a Moslem Mussolini who made the local trains run, but somehow, miraculously, refused to debase himself with fascist crap.

Therefore, in a lethal century thick with the rust of tinpot personality cults—Nasser, Ceauşescu, Díaz, Pol Pot, about a hundred and five others—Atatürk was the lone psychic survivor. Atatürk was the only one of the twentieth century's strutting throng of self-appointed Saviors of the Nation who had no reason at all to flinch at Y2K. The grateful Turks would not rename his streets, bulldoze his airport, topple his ten thousand bronze busts and his macho equestrian statues. Atatürk's steely glare would scan the dark recesses of the nation's psychic landscape for decades to come. Atatürk simply wasn't over yet, not by a long chalk.

At length the limo arrived at a glorious rose-colored palace, perched like a jewel on the Asian coast of the Bosphorus.

This traditional summer retreat, locally known as a *yali*, had been built by a nineteenth-century Ottoman vizier. Atatürk had been no fan of decadent royal fripperies, so Turkey's twentieth century had been rather unkind to this little seaside palace. Marauding Greek soldiers had looted it after World War I. In the 1930s Kim Philby had roomed upstairs. In the forties it had been a party headquarters for a sinister Turkish-German friendship bund. Through the fifties and sixties it had been a gloomy hostel for paranoid Soviet commercial travelers. In the seventies and eighties the imperial relic seemed finally and fatally outdated. Its elegant cantilevered porches had sagged like a dowager's chin. The barge dock had rotted out. The roof, swarming with bats, had shed a generous scattering of its handsome curvilinear tiles.

However, Ozbey's Uncle the Minister had decided that the ever-expanding business affairs of Turkish Intelligence required a silent safe house that could handle high-speed boats. The Black Sea of the 1990s was the Black Market Sea, washing the maphiya-ridden shores of Bulgaria, Romania, Ukraine, Georgia, and Russia. Not a single one of these several nations had any idea how an honest government functioned. Their populations had scarcely a shred of respect for a customs agent, a tax man, a narc, or a gun-control officer.

Buoyed by this fabulous newfound opportunity, the withering Ottoman yali suddenly blossomed anew. A fantastic wealth of narco-spook dope and arms wealth had boated deftly through it. As its secret masters prospered and grew bold, so did the spry little palace. It had sprung back to flourishing life, glowing in the nouveau-riche light of a fin de siècle sunset, its sturdy walls freshly stuccoed in the dusky, traditional "Ottoman Rose." Ornate iron railings, crowned with security videocams, surrounded the palace grounds. Uniformed Turkish paratroopers, crisply attired in white helmets, white chin straps, white dress gloves, flanked its electrified gates.

The gates opened and shut around the passing limousine with an automatic clang.

Starlitz and Zeta clambered out, hefted their bags, and worked their way past the gleaming facades of a vintage Aston Martin, a monstrous armored Mercedes, and a fire-engine-red little sports car.

Starlitz and Zeta trudged wearily through twin inlaid doors into a palatial reception room of nigh-hallucinogenic elegance. The walls were towering spans of dizzying arabesque wallpaper, all poppy-red and gilt. Red velvet sofas. Blue silk divans. Octagonal coffee tables of tortoiseshell and faience. A secretary toiled over a vast rosewood escritoire, with inlaid mandalas of glimmering mother-of-pearl.

The secretary discreetly ushered the two of them into a side alcove, a bay-windowed nook with slender columns and carved balustrades, gilt mirrors, and a tiled ceramic ceiling as rich as marzipan. He supplied them with a silver Turkish coffee service, with dainty cups and heaps of sweetmeats.

To his muted astonishment Starlitz suddenly recognized their attendant as Drey, Ozbey's favorite street thug. Drey was a strapping peasant kid from some one-mule burg in upper Anatolia, a sharecropper with big scarred mitts best suited to a pair of pliers or a skinning knife. Yet here was Drey, all kitted out to the nines in a tailored Italian suit, his jowls shaved, his teeth capped, and his hair oiled, just like a parliamentary attaché. Strangest of all, Drey seemed perfectly cozy about all this, as if putting casino owners into cement was the straight-and-narrow ladder to a cushy sinecure as an aristo flunky.

Drey silently accepted Starlitz's business card and vanished down a carpeted hall. Starlitz found himself distinctly embarrassed. The card's long stay on his ass in his wallet hadn't done the typography much good.

Hunching miserably on the sofa, Starlitz slurped the coffee. It did not revive him, but on top of sleeplessness and jet lag it turned his head sideways. That rich taste of cardamom, Cairo style. This was truly excellent coffee. It was much better coffee than he deserved.

Time crawled past them as they awaited any word from the great man. Zeta was in a state of abject collapse. Her nose was running. Her unbrushed hair was clumped and filthy. She fitfully knocked the heel of her soaping shoe against the meticulously carved and polished rosewood leg of her settee.

Starlitz's skin itched fiercely. His morale was crumbling utterly. He knew it would be fatal to kick up any kind of fuss. They were back on Turkish time. Rising from the couch with heroic effort, he convinced Drey to bring Zeta an orange Fanta. Zeta rapidly consumed her pop bottle, with a glug, a belch, and a final slurp, then dropped the sticky empty on the Trebizond hand-dyed carpet. Paralyzed with soul-devouring preteen boredom, she collapsed in a boneless heap. She was a dead ringer for an adolescent savage, purchased from the wilds of the Caucasus and dragged before an indifferent Sultan.

A levered silver handle turned on an inlaid door. A superstar came out, with a billionaire in hot pursuit.

Zeta sat up alertly. "It's her!" she blurted.

Gonca Utz wore drop earrings, bombe glacée upswept hair, and a peachy Alexander McQueen ballgown of taffeta with chain mail. The gentleman in pursuit was a sturdy, suntanned fellow with rose-colored aviator glasses, a linen banker's suit, and a Windsor-knotted industrialist's tie.

"You," said the billionaire, beckoning to Starlitz. "Young man."

"Yes?" said Starlitz, stunned to be called "young."

"Do you speak Turkish or French?"

Zeta volunteered eagerly. "Hey, I know some French! I took home-school classes!"

"Hello, Gonca," said Starlitz, half rising.

Gonca Utz studied him with Olympian pity.

"You *know* Miss Utz?" said the man with incredulity.

"We met. Some time ago."

"And are you in television?"

"Pop music. I used to run a band. . . ."

"Aha," said the billionaire, nodding in crisp relief. "Very well, tell Miss Utz—I have a jet waiting. She must fly with me to São Paolo. Tonight."

With much backtracking, fractured grammar, and hand waving, Zeta managed to convey this message. Gonca put her tapered hand to her lips and emitted a musical laugh.

"She is wasting her time in that Turkish game show," the Brazilian insisted tautly. "In Brazil we are *very big* in global television. Sponsored by soaps. We are international. Number one domestic program in Moscow. Number two in Taipei. Brazilian soaps are huge in Beirut and Cairo. Tell that to Miss Utz. Make sure she understands."

Zeta gamely began another translation effort, but Gonca turned her glamorous back and fled into the palace gardens. The media mogul fled in pursuit, arms outstretched like a kiln-fired lover on a Keatsian urn. After a moment Zeta and Starlitz heard Gonca fire up her sports car with a Jaguar snarl. The stucco walls near their head emitted a machine-gun rattle as the car's sturdy tires shot gravel.

Starlitz sat down. Somehow his clothing had stained the silk divan.

"She didn't even say hi to me," Zeta said, her sunburnt face crumpling. "And she signed my arm once, and everything. She is such a star! I *loved* her."

A loud military tramping came down a swirling flight of stairs.

"Jesus, you're a pair of sad sacks."

Starlitz looked up, twitching. The American One had landed. She wore a blue beret, a spangled leopard halter top, and ultrabaggy chemical-warfare drawstring pants.

"American One!" Zeta blurted, overcome with joy. "Dad, look! We're saved!"

"Hi, kid," said the American One. "Leggy, what are you doing here?"

"Waitin' on the Man," Starlitz muttered.

"Get up," she ordered. The American One stuck out a sinewy coffee-colored hand, put a handcuff pincer-grip around his wrist, and yanked him from the divan. "Before you talk to Ozbey, *we* gotta talk. Seriously. Time for a high-level diplomatic conferral, homeboy."

The American One herded Starlitz up the stairs. Zeta tagged behind. The three of them stepped through a shuttered door into the sunlight of a second-story palace balcony. Starlitz felt his jet-lagged pupils shrink in pain. He gripped the ornate wooden edge of the railing and gazed over the peacock-blue Bosphorus, a noble body of water with a slight irremovable sheen of spilled crude.

The American One absorbed a fresh deep breath and tucked a hair extension under the leather rim of her beret. "I bet you feel a lot better now, right?"

"Yeah, no, maybe. Thanks, American One."

"It's *Betsy*, remember?" she said. "Betsy Ross." Mrs. Ross plucked a Marlboro from the red cardboard pack tucked in her drawstring waist. She tore off the cigarette's filter, lit the stump, and leaned over the balcony. As an afterthought she held out the pack to Zeta. "Want one, kid?"

"Uh, no, thanks!" said Zeta, beaming with pride at the offer.

With a negligent backswing of her gym-toned leg, Mrs. Ross kicked the rose-colored palace wall. "This joint sure ain't our usual crap G-7 road hotel. I mean, all that classy glass-ware, and tile, and the crystal chandeliers and stuff. . . . This place fuckin' does your head in."

"Yeah, it does." Starlitz understood the overpowering spell of the palace, now that he was standing outside the building's paralyzing semiotic grip.

"This is the most beautiful building I ever saw. Ever. It's another world in there, it is fantastic. I thought Graceland was high class, before I saw this place. Boy, what a cheap hick I used to be." Mrs. Ross puffed at her ruptured cigarette, lids narrowing beneath their vivid sheen of cobra-green eye shadow. "Some very heavy shit goes down inside there, though. You don't wanna see the basement of this place. It's haunted."

A Glastron speedboat approached the yali, its catenary bow cresting the water.

"This place is, like, Gonca's little harem, man. We G-7 chicks are like just passin' through here, but Gonca hangs out here, it's home for her, they're lettin' her redecorate all the bed-rooms with shit she buys down at the Covered Bazaar. Y'know something? Gonca's *special*. Compared to her, we suck."

"Well . . ." Starlitz hedged.

"Don't bullshit me, man. We suck. We do. I know it. That's like our job. We make a career of it. Those Moslem hillbillies on the road, they can't imagine how good we are at that. We suck in ways that are, like, totally beyond their understanding. We fuckin' break them and bury them with how bad we suck. That's what I understand about the pop business now. I never got that part before, but now I really get it." Mrs. Ross turned to stare at him, her eyes like the lambent flames from two Kuwaiti oilfields. "It's a genius fuckin' scam, man. It's a world beater. I'm all for it."

Starlitz said nothing.

"Not that you're any prize, either, man. You're in this shit right up to your neck. You stink of it to high heaven."

Zeta, who had been listening with jaw-dropped astonishment to the solemn pronouncements of adults, flinched in anguish at this attack. She fled to the far end of the balcony, where she pretended great interest as the speedboat tied up at the dock below them.

Mrs. Ross edged nearer to Starlitz, lowering her voice. "But you know what? You *get it*. I *knew* you got it, the first time I saw you. I said to myself, Betsy, I said, this bad mofo here is your ticket out of the barracks, girl. You should listen to the recruiter here. *Be all you can be*. Know what I'm saying?"

"Absolutely, babe." Starlitz felt obscurely proud.

"I'm not sayin' G-7 is a good act, Leggy. It's a shit act. But you know what? I'm new at the pop biz, so I had to pay some dues, and a shit job like G-7 was just what I needed. Now I can sing. I mean, I'm never gonna be Mahalia Jackson, but I get the drill. I know what a chord is. I know what key to use. It's not all that hard."

Starlitz nodded. She was right. Great music was hard. Music that wasn't all that musical wasn't really all that hard.

Her voice vibrated with passion. She looked like she was about to burst out of her clothes, maybe right out of her skin. "Leggy, I need to be bigger than this. A big star for the whole wide world. Super big. Huge. I want to be a monster."

"You know what that means, right, Betsy?"

"Yeah, it probably means I die young, fat, hooked, and stupid. But let me tell you something. I've been around the block with G-7. I just got off a pop tour through half of fuckin' Islam. I've seen these solemn sons of bitches in their Ayatollah beards. I went eyeball to eyeball with them. I know what they mean. They are fuckin' medieval. They're a bunch of friggin' tribal morons. There's not room enough in the world for me and them. If I'm gonna be all I can be, those fuckin' losers have got to shut up shop and go."

She tossed her cigarette into the Bosphorus. "It's not half

enough just to nuke 'em—they've got to *lose everything they believe.* I know they hate me. There's nothing they hate worse than an uppity bitch. Bein' an uppity bitch, I got myself one truly effective attack—I strip down to my scanties and *sit on their face.* Just put my butt-naked ass right into their satellite TV screen, man. Just straddle their big, beardy, Koran-quotin' lips. That scares the shit out of 'em. They're brave, they can give a shit about air strikes from Russia or NATO, but this"— she slapped her left buttock—"this is the one thing they know they can't survive."

"Betsy, you ever heard of a national-security pitch called 'Clash of Civilizations'?"

"I don't read much." She scowled. "So are you gonna help me out with my culture war here, or am I gonna have to settle your fucking hash too?"

"Yeah, no, maybe. I'm definitely with your basic story line. It's way next-century."

"Listen: I'm telling you this, 'cause I want you to know where I'm comin' from. I am comin' down hard on every channel. I am raining down out the sky, *everywhere.* This isn't quite my time just yet, but I am what's next. After Y2K the Whore of Babylon is on her fuckin' way, Jack. And I don't come to bring peace. Because I am a bombshell."

Starlitz nodded helpfully. "What's your career game plan, exactly?"

"Well, step one is to ditch Ozbey Effendi in there. I mean, Mehmetcik is a cool guy and all, he has great dope connections, his security guys take no shit from anybody, I admire all that. He's super polite to me since I fucked his uncle the minister. But I need some solo career space here."

"Betsy, you need a manager, a publicist, an accountant, and a lawyer. And somewhere down the list you need some hit music."

"I got this DJ kid in Britain," she said reluctantly, "he wrote me a love song."

"DJ Dead White Eurocentric?"

She laughed. "Yeah. Him. Little Limey knob-twiddler. . . .
I had a couple days off after Kyrgyzstan, so I flew over to his
studio and I kinda introduced myself to him, and I kind of,
uh . . . well, I blew him. Okay? Dumb little fuck wants to
marry me now. But he's a good musician, though, right? The
guy's got a lame-ass stage name, but he can chart dance hits."

"Yep. You can pick 'em. That guy is a studio wizard. He
could turn you into a monster."

"That's good. That's just great. I knew you would know
about stuff like that." Mrs. Ross scratched her armpit languidly. "I don't think Mehmetcik's gonna fuss too much if I
take a powder from his rockin' little regional scene here. I
mean, I get his picture all right. The French One snorted
horse, so he got himself a French Arab girl. The Italian One
had herself a nasty accident, so he got this Italian Albanian
refugee. . . ."

"Go with the flow, babe." Starlitz plucked a fountain pen
from his jacket, ignoring the fact that airplane cabin pressure
had caused it to hemorrhage ink down his shirt. "It so happens
that I got the perfect promo guy for you. Big network guy. Super photographer. Name is Tim."

"Tim what?"

"Tim from ECHELON."

"How come people in this business never have real
names?" Betsy accepted the phone number on a crumpled
bank slip.

Attracted by a sudden bustle below, Starlitz peered over
the balcony railing. The crew of the speedboat were unloading
its contents. They were overseen by Mehmet Ozbey, who had
arrived on the dock in spotless deck shoes, white duck
trousers, and a double-breasted blue yachting blazer.

The narrow fiberglass hull of the speedboat was packed
with a seemingly endless cargo of white calfskin valises. The
valises were all the same shape and size, and they were com-

ing out of the boat with smooth, industrial, machinelike regularity. There were dozens of valises, every one with the unique shoulder-wrenching heft of tightly packed cash. How on earth had Ozbey gotten so many white calfskin valises? Maybe he owned the factory.

"If I split tonight," said Betsy cagily, "can you cover for me?"

"Yeah. I'm up for that."

"See you around, then."

Mrs. Ross tossed her glossy mane and turned to go. Zeta hurried over, face tight with anxiety. "Hey, wait! Don't leave!"

Mrs. Ross hitched her pants. "Huh? Why not?"

"Because you're from G-7! G-7 is like my favorite band, my favorite band in the whole world!"

Mrs. Ross looked at her with amused pity. "Okay, kid. I get the picture. So what do you want from me? My autograph?" She patted her leopard-dotted torso. "I got no pen on me. Tell you what. I'll give you my favorite push-up bra."

"I just want . . ." Half panicked with star worship, Zeta's eyes filled with tears. "You're the star! I just want you to be the star for me! Tell me what it's all about!"

Betsy paused with her leopard top half-lifted. "What *what* is all about?" she said guardedly, skinning her top back down. "What *pop music*'s all about?"

"Yeah! Sure! Okay! That'll do!"

"Okay." She nodded. "Stand close to me and I'll tell you. I'll tell you the one big secret. I'll tell you the one thing we pop stars ever say that really, really matters." Betsy leaned down, tall, shining eyed, and impossibly confident, and kissed Zeta on the forehead. *"You don't have to be like your parents."*

Then she kicked her way through the doors and strode off, with never a glance back.

"Wow." Zeta was stunned.

Starlitz scratched his head. "Honey, that's not really that big a revelation."

"It is to *me*," Zeta said. "Nobody ever told *me* that before."
Zeta began to cry with joy, tears streaking the corners of her
gappy smile. "I'm so happy that somebody finally told *me*."

STARLITZ WANDERED THE UPPER FLOOR OF THE YALI UNTIL
he located another G-7 girl. She happened to be the German
One, who was sitting alone in a former harem boudoir, watching Deutsche Welt satellite coverage of the Balkan War, and
nervously gnawing at her lacquered nails. The German One
was wearing a Turkish bathrobe and her blond hair was in
curlers. She had a sliced apple and half a salad.

"Betsy's walking out," Starlitz announced. "Looks like I've
lost us another American One."

"Oh, you, you," grumbled the German One, her bloodshot
blue eyes riveted to the screen. "What does one girl matter
now, when there are thousands of war refugees in Europe,
children and poor people thrown from their homes, with no
place to sleep." The German One was both grave and jittery.
"Every one of those dirty loafers wants to take the first bus to
Berlin! I hope Joschka Fischer can handle this terrible crisis,
that big Green hippie."

Starlitz put his hands on his daughter's quaking shoulders.
"Where is Mrs. Dinsmore?"

"Who?"

"Mrs. Dinsmore. Tamara. Tamara the G-7 Chaperone."

"Oh, her," said the German One, nodding absently. "We
had to leave her in Azerbaijan. She had bad problems there
with her passport."

Starlitz swallowed this dire news with gloom, but without
much surprise. "Listen, German One, the kid here is all worn
out. Can you keep her company a little while? I need a word
downstairs with Mr. Ozbey."

The German One looked at Zeta indifferently. "Okay. If
she stops crying. I hate it when they cry."

"Are you the German One?" Zeta ventured bravely.

"*Ja. Ich bin.* So far."

"You're the *original* German One! I have your plastic action figure! I have your platform shoes and your lollipop! I think I even know your real name."

The German One perked up. She patted the side of the sofa. "Okay. Sit here. Would you like a nice lamb salad?"

Starlitz left.

The palace lost most of its tenacious grip on his soul, if he just marched resolutely through it with his eyes half shut. The place was unbelievably lovely. It would be fatally easy to stick around in the palace for quite a while, maybe for several languid, corrupt Ottoman centuries.

He heard Ozbey's voice, barking reassuringly into a telephone. Starlitz knocked at the door. Ozbey shouted a welcome in Turkish.

Starlitz stepped inside. Ozbey hung up the phone at once, slapping it down as if a vital state secret might escape through the earpiece.

"Good to see you, Mehmetcik."

"What a sight you are," said Ozbey thoughtfully, looking him up and down. Ozbey's new office was truly spectacular. The place had framed Ottoman decrees inscribed by left-handed craftsman-calligraphers. Hand-smithed copper banquet plates. A wall-mounted collection of curved Janissary daggers.

Ozbey placed one hand on his natty blue lapel, vaguely in the area of his heart. "I swear I've missed you."

"That's kind of you, man. I appreciate that sentiment."

"I thought you'd never return."

"Well, I had no choice. It was part of the narrative arrangement, basically."

"I'm not surprised," said Ozbey, nodding. "I thought that problem might bring you back to haunt us. The Dead One, you know."

"The *two* Dead Ones, man."

Ozbey winced. "I was just on the telephone now, and . . ."

"You're kidding. Which one is it this time?"

"She is not dead, Leggy. She'll come out of her coma, they say. They promise she will walk again. Not dance . . . but she'll walk."

"Oh, which one was it this time?" said Starlitz, stricken. "Please don't tell me it was the British One. The British One had such a great propaganda line. You could always talk sense to the British One."

"Oh, this development is very bad, I don't want to hide that from you," said Ozbey stoutly, rising from his designer office chair behind the rosewood desk. He opened a stained-glass liquor cabinet and retrieved a silver cocktail shaker. "It was the Japanese One. Too many pills. A suicide attempt. She was being too Japanese."

Starlitz said nothing.

"I don't know what to *do* about the Japanese One. Replacing the other ones is so much easier. There is no oppressed Moslem minority inside Japan. Is there?"

Starlitz thought about it from Ozbey's point of view. It was a dead-easy thing to do, once you were inside the yali palace. Inside the palace the story line made a hell of a lot of sense. "Actually, there's a pretty large diaspora of Iranian guest workers in Japan. Tokyo, mostly. Undocumented labor and all."

"Truly?" said Ozbey, brightening. "Maybe it was fated."

"I'm sorry about the way this situation has played out, man. Maybe I'm not the guy to ask for advice just now. Because I just lost you the American One."

Ozbey was nonplussed. "I can't believe you killed the *American One*."

"She's not dead, man."

"How could she be dead? She was huge, she was tough, she had a handgun. How could you kill her? How is that even possible?"

"She's not dead, Mehmetcik. Solo career."

"Oh." Ozbey removed a cut-glass decanter of Cypriot brandy and a lemon mixer. "That bigmouthed Yankee cop. Well, she was tiresome, with all her rants about women and minorities. . . . I have to say I expected her to lose patience with us. Tell me, do you know any Black Muslims in America? They seem awfully stiff for American black people, with those little bow ties. Are they truly Muslims? Can they dance and sing?"

"Wait a sec," said Starlitz, touching his forehead. "I'm getting a brain wave here. Pakistani Silicon Valley girl. Dad's a circuit engineer for Intel, or Motorola. There's fuckin' thousands of 'em."

Ozbey broke into a sunny smile. "Excellent! You see, that angle would never have occurred to me. An American Cyber-Moslem. Of course! And from California. That couldn't be better!"

"Might be a waste of time head-hunting one. Y2K is so close now, and all."

With an evasive grin Ozbey began agitating his shaker. "Sit down, please. You need a drink."

"I could go for a Cyprus brandy sour in a big way," Starlitz admitted. "You wouldn't have a cigarette around here, would you?"

"I have a humidor. Fine Cuban cigars. Where is it?"

They searched the desk's extensive perimeter. Starlitz fell to his knees to peer in the cavity beneath the desk. He retrieved the fallen humidor, and a pair of abandoned Manolo Blahnik spike heels.

Ozbey winced a bit as Starlitz produced the shoes. "Gonca's been looking for those."

He offered Starlitz a crystal glass. Starlitz had a healthy slug. "Now, that's a bracer," Starlitz said. "I'm jet-lagged to hell and gone. I misplaced my soul in Hawaii. My personal time ghost is still flying somewhere over the mid-Pacific." Starlitz lit his cigar from a porcelain desk lighter. Life became very gratifying suddenly. Starlitz had to sit down.

Ozbey tasted his drink and set it aside. "I like to mix drinks," he said, lighting a cigar. "I like to collect the drink toys, the best decanters, and the nicest little swizzle sticks. . . . But I don't like to drink anymore. I can't get drunk. There is always a midnight phone call. Or a gunshot, or a siren. I can't relax with a drink and be myself. I'm not myself anymore, that's the truth of it." Ozbey looked up mournfully. "Even my boys aren't themselves anymore."

"It's the price of success, man. Money changes everything."

Ozbey reached into his jacket pocket and produced a tinfoil pinch of cocaine. "This still works. Cocaine expands the personality. Cocaine makes you larger than life." He dug in the foil with a manicured thumbnail and sniffed.

"When you left me with the band," Ozbey said, rubbing his sinuses thoughtfully, "I shook your hand. Remember? I swore I would protect those girls. Now I confess to you: I did not protect the girls. The girls died. They will all die. I don't care. The man who told you that they mattered, that man wasn't me. The girls don't matter. *I* matter." He looked around his splendid office. "*This* matters."

Starlitz tapped clean white ash from the tip of his cigar. "It's a point of view," he admitted.

"You said to me once, that I had to decide who I was. It was a wise thing to say. But it's not easy. My name's not Mehmet Ozbey," Ozbey said. "My name is Abdullah Oktem."

Starlitz lifted his brows sympathetically. "Is that supposed to make some kind of big difference to me?"

"Do you know a Turkish Cypriot named Alparslan Turkes? A military man? The former head of Turkish State Security? Did you ever hear of General Alparslan Turkes? He was one of the greatest men in the world. He was like a father to me."

"Sorry, man, can't say I ever knew him."

"I saw him mobbed by crowds in Turkish Cyprus. In Turkmenistan and Azerbaijan they kissed his hands and wept. He had nine children, that man. He was the father of the Gray Wolves."

"Okay."

"Do you have nine children, Starlitz?"

"Nope."

"I have four children."

"That's a pretty good start."

"I don't know what to say to my own sons. Their family name is Oktem. They are the sons of Abdullah Oktem, not the sons of Mehmet Ozbey. How do I tell them that their father's friends are men with names like 'Terminator,' who work for organizations like the 'Turkish Revenge Brigade'?"

Ozbey sat at his desk, opened a drawer, and removed a gilt-framed photo. He propped it on the desktop and observed it, his eyes large, wet, and melancholy. "Poor little Merel . . . when she married me, I was a youth brigade leader. We used to go camping in the woods, singing, with the Gray Wolf Youth. Target shooting. Patriotic Turkish songs. We used to tie knots, and build campfires, and beat up labor demonstrators. It was a modest life, very devoted to the nation. Merel gave me sons . . . but it's no wonder that I outgrew her."

"I've never been able to make that work out either," Starlitz admitted. "I've never seen it done. You know something? I'm pretty sure that men and women with a happy home life can never even fuckin' *meet* me."

"I *knew* you would understand this," Ozbey told him, deeply gratified. "Because you are a philosopher. The only time in my life when I was serious about philosophy . . . I took courses in the American University, but . . . well, it was that seven-year sentence in the Swiss jail. Four kilos of heroin in our bags at the Zurich airport. The enemy informed against us. ASALA, the Armenian Secret Army. We were busy liquidating them at the time."

"The Swiss busted you? And after you testified in Italy at the Mehmet Ali Ağca trial? Man, that took a lot of nerve."

"They arrested Mehmet Sener first. But he never talked. I never talked. He's a very good man, Mehmet Sener. A patriot, a man you can trust. I still see him socially, though he has another name now. Not one word did we give to those Swiss bastards. A year. Two years. Three years. Four years. Five years, and finally the CIA comes through for us, and puts us back into their GLADIO system. I was a boy when I went into that prison. Fresh out of university. Prison hardened me. Prison made me a hard man."

"That's the truth about prison," Starlitz mused. "Václav Havel said that too."

"I think about those five years in prison," said Ozbey. "When I have Gonca Utz—on that divan there, commonly— she moves her bottom for me, she moves her pretty legs, she cries out in that sweet voice. . . . I spent five years in jail, as a very lonely man, looking forward to a moment like that. And now, I take that moment from Gonca whenever I please, but . . . I have to say this . . . I'm never quite there in that moment. I'm the man who is planning that moment. I'm the man boasting of it afterward. But I never seem to be the man *who is there and enjoying that moment*. Where did I lose myself, eh? Life seems so perfect. Where did the story go wrong? Why am I like this, Starlitz? What has the world done to me? Can you tell me that?"

"There are a lot of guys who would kill to have a story like that."

"*I* killed to have that story," Ozbey insisted gravely. "That part about regret and guilt, that part of the story was always a lie. I have no regrets. You plant a bomb, bad people die. You shoot up a restaurant, bad people die. . . . I don't like to kill *colleagues* of mine, like Oral Celik, after he betrayed us. I have to say that incident hurt my feelings. But the killing is not the story. We Turks have these two rival government death squads, you see, JITEM and OHP . . . well, I'm sure you don't want to hear about that, it's regional bureaucracy, it's rather boring. . . . My own sympathies are mostly with JITEM, but you know, when I kill enemies of the state for JITEM, I don't take it seriously."

Ozbey tapped cigar ash and put his feet on the desk. "I mean, of course we still kill the state's enemies, because they're still Turkey's enemies, but that's not the central part of my career. Nowadays we build the new black market. We sell drugs, we sell guns. We build casinos and hotels throughout the Turkish-speaking world. We buy television stations, and newspapers. We finance the Kurdish War, and we finance political parties. We are very prosperous. Since the end of the Cold War we are *rich*. So don't call me a hired killer, a political extremist, mafioso, and heroin trafficker. Those words can't contain me anymore, not here at the end of the century. I'm a corporate officer in oil corporations. I'm on the board of three banks. I make the money that an Arab sheik makes. And I gamble it in my own casinos, so that I win even when I lose."

Starlitz rubbed his double chin. "I think I'm getting a fuller picture here, man. This is good material. Go on."

"You can't *pay* me enough to kill an enemy of the state! I have to do that for patriotism, for the sheer love of it. Mostly, when I'm not on the road, I sit at my comfortable desk, here at the JITEM palace safe house. I make phone calls, on secure diplomatic lines. For instance, I recently sold five million dollars' worth of jeeps and mortars to the Kosovo Liberation Army. The KLA earned that war chest by selling heroin in Switzerland, just as we Turks used to do, when we were young and stupid. They sell heroin that *we gave to them*. So we make money *both ways. Three* ways. *Five or six* ways. We can make money *any* way, as long as the money is black."

"That can't be much of a business constraint nowadays. Especially with a war on."

"The best part is, this is NATO's first real war, and *we* are NATO. Can you believe that? We are winning the war! The Turks are winning a Moslem war inside Europe for the first time in three hundred years! To have lived to see this day! There are times when I think my life is just too good to be true."

Starlitz nodded thoughtfully. "There is a new world coming, isn't there? It takes your breath away sometimes."

Ozbey's dilated eyes gleamed with enthusiasm. "Is the Turkish Army winning that war? The Turkish Air Force? No my friend, it is Turkish *covert operations* that is winning that war. When we captured Abdullah Ocallan in Kenya, that was the greatest Turkish victory in fifty years. Three men in black hoods kidnapped Ocallan in Africa. I know those men in black hoods. They are personal friends of mine. I get them girls and cars. They run a tab in my uncle's casinos. Those men are like princes now."

"I am so with that," said Starlitz, around his cigar. He took it out and waved it. "You know what I admire about your setup here? I like it that this is an actual fucking *palace.* I mean, it's not like some five-eighths-scale Disney World palace, for mass consumption by the tourist trade. This is a no-kidding, fully authentic Ottoman scene you've got going down here, Mehmetcik. There's like fabulous wealth, and masked executioners, and secret palace cabals, and grand viziers, and bribes, and shakedowns, and guys getting their throats cut in dark alleys. And you've even got a whole international harem full of dancing girls up there, eating sherbets and getting their toenails done. It's a no-kidding privilege to see this thing done this way. I live for moments like this."

"I hadn't thought of it that way," said Ozbey slowly. Some crucial junction had kicked over inside his head, or maybe the coke rush was on top of him. "Perhaps that's a part of my identity problem." He glowered.

"Mmm."

"I consider myself quite a Western modernizer. Not an Ottoman. This is troublesome to me."

"Uh, well," said Starlitz tentatively, "that's just my input, man. Sometimes it takes an outside consultant to see these minor things for us."

"You know," said Ozbey, "when you telephoned ahead to say that you were coming back, I made plans to have you killed."

Starlitz said nothing.

"I was thinking of sewing you into a bag, and dropping you into the Bosphorus. It's the traditional way. How hard could that be? There are thousands of unsolved political murders in Turkey. I feel sure that I could make you disappear into deep water—but there is another problem. Because I don't believe that would *kill* you."

"Uh, why do you say that, man?"

"Because I rehearsed that story line to myself. I looked into one of these palace mirrors, I told it to myself aloud. I said, 'I killed Leggy Starlitz. I shot him several times. I threw him into the sea in a bag with many heavy chains. . . .' That story just didn't sound plausible. It was very unconvincing. It had a very false feeling about it. Do you know that feeling? You *must* know it. When you're torturing a man and he's hiding something from you, there's a sound in his story that you learn to recognize. A false note in the story. . . ."

Starlitz tapped cigar ash.

"But listen to this: 'Leggy Starlitz died on New Year's Day 2000.'"

Starlitz's hand froze.

"'Starlitz simply vanished. Starlitz was all over. Starlitz was all wrapped up, he was put away forever. Leggy Starlitz ceased to be. There was a last tick of the clock for the sordid creature called Starlitz. The new world had no more use for Starlitz. In a new millennium he served no narrative purpose.'"

"Shut up, man."

Ozbey laughed triumphantly. "Now I'm talking your language." He went to the wall, removed a short and nasty-looking poignard from its pearl-sewn scabbard. "I don't pretend that I can kill you with this knife. I know better than that. I could scar you, maybe. Cut off your finger, or even a hand. But not kill you." Ozbey set the blade on his desk and pulled off his yachting jacket. He threw the jacket deftly over his chair. "Here. Take that knife, and kill me."

"No, thanks, man."

"Wait a moment. How stupid of me." Ozbey removed his shirt and ripped the Velcro tabs on a light undervest of NATO-issued bulletproof Kevlar. "Here. Try. Go ahead. Kill me. I live close to death every day. I gamble my life, I snort cocaine, I race fast cars, I have unprotected sex with glamorous, promiscuous women. I'm an international playboy spy. Go ahead, stab me to death. Right in the heart, eh?" He pounded his chest. "Come on."

"Mehmetcik, this is not my style." Starlitz set his glass carefully aside. "I mean, you're all coked out and winging it way outside the script here, and this is such a great carpet you've got on your beautiful hardwood floor. . . ."

"Don't make excuses. You *can't*. That is the deeper reality. You *can't*. It's not in your power. What would happen? The narrative would not allow it. Drey would come in suddenly to stop you. The knife would break. I can't be killed by you. Because I am great. I know I am great. I am a lion of the Turkish nation. I can't be merely killed: I can only be martyred. I can't die like the common man I once was. Because I'm no longer myself. I'm not entirely here. I'm not entirely now. I exist below the shallow reality of daily life. I have achieved a true mastery, Starlitz. I am powerful, yet unspeakable. Events pass through me, and into the fabric of history, without ever taking place."

"You've got to drop this and step back, Mehmetcik. You're spreading yourself way too thin here. You're all over the map.

The master narrative can't take that cheap, gratuitous shit. You can be the Ascended Guru Master, or the Dapper Don with the showgirls, or the Secret Spymaster with the smack, but you can't be all of those at once and stay sustainable."

"That is *your* version of the narrative, not mine."

"We are *in* my narrative, man."

"No, we're not. You are in *my* homeland and *my* culture, and this is *my* narrative."

Starlitz groaned. "I *hate* this kind of shit, okay?" He snatched up the knife and drove its curved blade deep into the desktop. "Maybe I can't stab you. But not because you say so. You can't say squat to me. You can't dominate my fucking narrative, because we *are speaking fucking English*. Listen to yourself. You've got nothing more to say. I'm telling you that *none of this actually happened*. You can't argue with me, because *my language defines the terms*. You can't discuss it any further, because it never took place."

Ozbey stared at Starlitz in dazed astonishment, then in a growing rage. His face flushed and grew congested. He opened his mouth, and struggled for his confounded words with a distant, muted squeak.

Ozbey turned and spat on the carpet. He clenched his fists, beet-red with rage, trying to rush forward.

Something snapped in the realm of the unspeakable. Ozbey bent double in silent pain. His knees buckled in their tailored naval whites. He began to heave.

With a vomiting rasp a fifty-caliber bullet fell wetly to the carpet. Then came another. They were huge things, with thumb-sized slugs and big brass mil-spec cartridges. This was bad, but the big wet bags of heroin were worse. These weren't the standard balloon or condom courier bags that human mules would eat and shit out. These were serious, tape-and-poly, kilo smack bags, big fat bricks with the dense, slightly yellow look of window putty. Ozbey was heaving and wheezing them up from his visceral core, with the hair plastered to his forehead and the uncanny look of a starved ghost.

"Okay, I'm with the story here," said Starlitz alertly. He pounded heartily on Ozbey's back with the solid butt of the knife. "It's something we all go through."

Ozbey coughed, spat, sobbed for breath, and heaved again. The atmosphere in the room had become extremely bad. There was a subterranean smell to it, a graveyard, a sewer. A smell far worse than death—it was the smell of very real and genuine things that were explicitly forbidden to exist. Great deeds of valor in a bad cause. Heroic sacrifice in the single-minded service of evil. Adult acts torn from the half-grown souls of children. The mud-caked skeletons of rewritten histories with the luminous teeth of gulag ghosts. Apocalyptic chaos in the service of New World Orders. Villages burnt to ash in order to save them, intellectuals shot in the service of greater understanding.

Starlitz tucked his solid hands beneath Ozbey's armpits, and hauled Ozbey from the rippling, preternatural office. He kicked a door open with an expensive-sounding crack. He found a toilet. He left Ozbey near it.

After six minutes Ozbey emerged into reality. He had washed his face, combed his hair, buttoned his shirt.

"What do you have to say now?" Starlitz asked him formally.

Ozbey carefully tested his sore lips and jaw. "All right. That did not happen."

"That's better. Let's talk like professionals now. It's a far, far better thing." Starlitz threw a collegial arm over Ozbey's sweating shoulder. "Mehmetcik, what do you hear from the pop business lately?"

They walked unsteadily together into the palace's waiting room. Seeing Ozbey's wracked expression, Drey looked up in alarm. Ozbey forestalled him with a lifted hand.

"Have you heard of a new girl group named 'Huda'?" Ozbey croaked.

"Tell me about them," Starlitz said.

Ozbey was regaining his fluency. "They're a Malaysian

Islamic girl group. Four girls. No, four women—married women, with children. They wear the Moslem headscarf. And they wear lipstick. And platform shoes. They sing and dance."

"No kidding. Damn. When did they premiere?"

"Nineteen ninety-seven. They're charting in Singapore and Kuala Lumpur. Koranic lyrics exclusively. And they make religious pop videos. Love for Allah. Positive role models for Moslem children. . . ."

"You know the manager's name?"

"His name is Faraddin Abdul Fattah."

"That guy's a friggin' genius, man. I don't suppose there's any likelihood of this guy getting whacked." Starlitz paused hastily. "Forget I said that."

"Let me show you a new car," Ozbey hedged.

"Great idea. I'm all for that."

They left the palace together for its parking lot, which had crushed and paved the remnants of some preindustrial tulip garden. The sun was setting slowly over Europe in the West.

Starlitz stopped unbidden by a silver-gray Aston Martin DB5. The car's fishlike lines and dual mirrors looked uncannily familiar to him. Then he had it: the Aston Martin had been a Corgi toy in 1964, one of the world's first movie-related action collectibles. The toy car was still in production and still on the market, because the silver-gray Aston Martin DB5 had starred in *Goldfinger, Thunderball,* and *On Her Majesty's Secret Service.*

Half the planet's population had seen those films. They were a truly planetary cinema, the harbinger of Free World domination. Toward the end of the century the property had even adopted the native cinematic structure of Third World chop-socky epics. It had abandoned merely Modernist plot structure for a steady, rhythmic round of stunt violence, expensive sets, and a hot babe. Sadism, Snobbery, and Sex, a Free World formula that was the twentieth century's catnip for the masses.

The car's presence in Ozbey's lot was distinctly *unheimlich.* Starlitz hadn't seen a car with so much panache since he had discovered that subsonic Salt Lake rocket-racer in the basement of the Utah State Capitol. The Aston Martin's front headlamps looked distinctly loose, as if they might flip up at any second for the dual phallic probes of perforated rapid-firing vintage Brownings.

Could this be the actual car itself? Starlitz recalled with awe that the movie car had been mysteriously stolen from the aircraft hangar of an American collector.

"It's pretty, but you can't keep that car in repair," said Ozbey dismissively.

"Oh."

"It's not about the British anymore. Not at all. And the gadgets never work. Forget the shoe-heel telephones, and the exploding fountain pens. Get a real gun."

"Mmmph."

"Mercedes limo, very specialized," said Ozbey, beckoning him over. "This is a true Eurocar. Manufactured in twelve different countries. Digital instruments. Global positioning. Modern armor plating. A private arsenal inside the trunk."

Starlitz stepped closer to the vehicle. The thing wasn't even made of metal. It was all about spun carbon, foamed aluminum, and just-in-time CAD-CAM manufacturing. "She's a beauty," he admitted.

"It's a gift," said Ozbey proudly. "A gift for my friend, Mr. Sedat Severik, the parliamentarian." Ozbey leaned against the gleaming bumper. "Foreigners say that all Turks hate all Kurds. It's a lie. They don't know the good, decent Kurds of this country as I do. They've never been to Sanliurfa, Gaziantep, Adana, where Turkey's simple mountain people are trying to make a peaceful life, without any politics or Communists. Severik Bey, he's a fine old country gentleman. I'm proud to call him my friend."

Ozbey patted the hood affectionately. "He has his own

plantations, olive groves, kilim weavers, hundreds of personal soldiers. . . . He likes things quiet on his own estates. That man enjoys the good things in life, hospitality, horses, young women . . . and he needs a fine car. Traitors and terrorists hate that man. The Kurdish traitors spend most of their time and energy killing decent Kurds. Severik Bey . . . for the cause of our national unity he has given many cousins. But a Mercedes armored limo"—Ozbey smiled—"I would bet on this fine car against an Iraqi tank."

"Can the old guy drive?"

"Does that matter? He can crush anything in his path!"

"I've got to give you credit, Mehmetcik—when you do it, you do it up brown. You're a very generous guy."

"Thank you. Your Japanese boss in Hawaii—does he have any complaints about me?"

"Well, except for the Dead Ones, he thinks the world of you, man."

Ozbey nodded. "I treasure his good opinion. And yours, of course. Why don't you stay at the palace tonight? We're having a little video party. Some members of Parliament from the True Path party and the MHP, some bankers and their mistresses. . . . When we captured Ocallan, there were Kurdish riots all over the world. Kurdish traitors publicly set themselves on fire!"

Ozbey spread his hands, a little sheepishly. "I know it seems unusual, but when terrorist Kurds, on fire, attacked and seized that Greek Embassy . . . well, I have to say it was one of the most fulfilling moments of my life. No—it was one of the great moments of the whole twentieth century. I have all of the highlights on videotape: CNN, Deutsche Welt, Brazilian Globo News, all the clippings. I have to say that the boys and I never tire of them. We show them to diplomats, politicians, secret police . . . all through Turkish high society. It never fails to raise a smile."

Starlitz considered the offer. He had no baby-sitter. "I'm afraid I have to miss it. Got other plans."

"We'll be going out to the dump later, to shoot rats with pearl-handled revolvers."

"Got another engagement, man. Sorry."

"You don't fit in," decided Ozbey, with finality. "I can't make you fit into the coming world. I'm sorry, Starlitz, but I don't want to see you anymore. It doesn't suit either of us. Before I understood my own destiny, I could tolerate having you in the same reality. But not anymore. You have the smell of doom."

"What about the band?"

"I am breaking your number-one rule. They are useful to me, and they matter. After Y2K they will only matter more. I am turning them into my own weapon."

"You break that number-one rule, pal, and you are dead in Y2K."

"No, Starlitz. You're just projecting your own Westernized assumptions. *You* are dead in Y2K."

"I'm promising you, right now—you drop the band, or *you* are dead in Y2K."

"I'm not dead in Y2K. I'm just getting started. *You* are dead."

"Ozbey, wake up, man. You have already got two and a half Dead Ones. You can't keep piling them up. Do you think smack is Coca-Cola? They're both addictive, but it's a matter of degree *and* kind."

"I'm Turkish! Am I supposed to be afraid of heroin? It's what we have! The Afghans won their freedom with heroin! The Albanians are fighting to the death with heroin! I don't want to have this argument!" Ozbey sighed. "I just don't want to have it. So, be quiet. I'll buy you. That settles it. Money talks in every language. I have a valise in the office that is full of Bulgarian currency . . . what do they call it?"

"Forints?" Starlitz offered.

"No."

"Koruna?"

"No."

"The Bulgarian lev?"

"That's it. Nice new bills. Crisp. Hardly used, because Bulgaria is barely capitalist. Take that valise, go to Cyprus, launder it. Go vanish. Wink out. You cannot save me. You can't even save yourself."

"You expect me to write off my obligation to those girls for a single leather satchel full of cheap Bulgarian cash? After all I did for them? After all my plans?"

"Yes. That's my expectation. Take it or leave it."

Starlitz scratched his head. "How about two satchels? I have a traveling companion."

STARLITZ WAS FED UP WITH AIRCRAFT TRAVEL. It was too clean, inhuman, and anesthetizing. He rented a cheap car in Istanbul and cheerfully drove across Turkey, through crazed, high-speed, packed traffic, on many very bad roads.

Zeta had passed out from hunger, jet lag, and star worship inside the German One's room. A calming childish nap had done her a lot of good. She happily drummed the flats of her hands on her personal calfskin valise. "Dad, it's cool to have lots of cash, right?"

"Absolutely."

"When does the German One get her million dollars?"

Starlitz cleared his throat. "The German One is talent, honey. She gets limos, and big, screaming crowds. But as for the talent keeping any of the money, well, pop's rich tapestry is never much with that."

"Dad, she told me being a star isn't that

great, Dad. She says that people think stars wear nice clothes and go to parties all the time. But she works super hard, Dad. She's always in the gym, and she never gets enough to eat. She says she's gonna make it to Y2K, and get her stupid million dollars, and go home to Bremen, and sleep for five years. I mean, that was the deal."

"Maybe that could still happen somehow, but it's not our problem anymore. The G-7 scene is past repair. The scene got stuck inside Turkey, and it is violently mutating, and it is gonna blow. So if somebody's gonna tie off the narrative and scram with the loot, reasonably speaking, it's got to be us."

Zeta fell into thoughtful silence, which wavered, over the passing kilometers, into a carsick sulk.

They slept in a seaside hotel in Antalya. They drove the rental car onto the morning car ferry to Turkish Cyprus. After disembarking, green with pitching seas and the ferry's diesel fumes, they drove across the island into the cramped medieval streets of Lefkosa.

They found Viktor in a working-class section of the Turkish Cypriot capital. Viktor had come to favor a grimy restaurant, in the ground floor of a bullet-pocked 1960s housing project. Viktor's favorite dive had a cozy, bunkerlike feeling, for the walls were thick cement, the northern windows were small and curtained, and the restaurant had only one door left. The building had once had an exit and a view to the south, but the southern wall was smack against the Green Line, facing Greek Cyprus. So the whole southern face of the building had been entirely bricked up.

Viktor wore a floral shirt, tinted shades, tailored khaki trousers, and Turkish-pirated pseudo-Italian shoes. It was lunchtime, and Viktor was wolfing down a red, murky lamb soup, next to a table with a quartet of UN troops. These soldiers were mustached, booted Argentines, wearing camo and baby-blue berets. They were devouring spiced kebabs and chatting in Spanish about the local hookers. The Argentines had the wary eyes of guys who worried a lot about where the crosshairs might be centered, but they didn't look too unhappy about their UN military assignment. There weren't many circumstances in the world where Falklands campaign veterans were treated like humanitarians.

The diner's owner sidled over in his stained apron. He had a cast in one eye, and looked about as crooked as it was possible for a humble cook to look. Starlitz examined the diner's semiliterate, polyglot menu. He had badly missed the excellent Cypriot cuisine during his travels. He joyfully ordered sautéed brains, diced fried liver, and grilled kidneys. Zeta had a white rice soup.

"I love the UN, don't you?" said Viktor in Russian, with a lingering sidelong glance. "They seem so much kinder than NATO."

Starlitz ripped up a pita bread and dipped it in chickpea sauce.

Viktor sighed theatrically. "I love the UN because they're not democratic. They're not advanced, and market driven, and high tech. They're crooked. One never imagined a badly organized, clumsy, crooked, squalid World Government. Yet here they are at the end of the century, see them there?—chain-smoking, and eating goats."

Viktor set down his tarnished spoon and steepled his fingers. "By its rhetorical nature 'World Government' seems pure, abstract, utopian. But this is not a merely conceptual World Government. This is an *actual* World Government we are eating lunch with here. A government with bored soldiers from Ukraine and Sri Lanka, who pass their careers in rotting zones of warlords and piracy. The UN is a global empire, but it's a weak empire of corruption, pretense, smoldering rebellion. It's very like the empire of the Ottoman sultans. Or the Russian czars."

Zeta stared raptly at Viktor, eyes shining. She understood not a word of Russian, but Viktor's basic message seemed to be coming across to her with thrilling immediacy.

"As Pelevin points out in his novel *Lives of the Insects*," said Viktor analytically, "we live like vermin. Why is that? Because we prefer it that way. Law, order, justice, those vast abstractions are too smooth and modernist for human beings who still possess souls. Most people in this world live like rats in the cracks in the walls. Crooked empires contain more cracks. There may be more killing, but there are also more places to hide."

"I'm with that," grunted Starlitz. "Russian theory is a beautiful thing. But since they busted Nick the G-7 Accountant, all my favorite banks around here are full of mousetraps. Therefore, I got a hands-on, practical problem, Viktor. Disposing of my two valises here."

Viktor grinned around his spoon. "Another trip with your luggage through the Green Line, Mr. Starlitz?"

"Viktor, I need a money laundry in *Greek* Cyprus. Turkish Cyprus is over, it's yesterday. I want you to mule my cash to a laundry over the border. If the banks in Greek Cyprus are good enough for the Milosevic family, they're bound to be good enough for me."

Starlitz and Viktor entered into direct negotiations. Young Viktor had enjoyed an eventful year. He had certainly not been wasting his time in the absence of Starlitz and Khoklov. On the contrary: the lack of adult oversight had fully unleashed Viktor's entrepreneurial instincts. Viktor had built a thriving career for himself, silently sneaking back and forth through the Cyprus Green Line.

The ethnic apartheid had created a tremendous osmotic pressure between the little island's two economies. Conventional goods couldn't make it to market through the ethnic-hate taboo, so Viktor had come to specialize in transporting women. In the prosperous Greek half of Cyprus, an Orthodox Slavic hooker was worth five or six times what she could pull in Turkish territories. Entering Turkish Cyprus required few formalities, but formally entering Greek Cyprus by ship or aircraft required annoying documentation. So Viktor was a grow-

ing expert in moving illegal female flesh directly through the
mud, the searchlights, and the barbed wire. There was always
good money in this practice, but rarely so much money as in
the year 1999. Severe political disruption always produced a
much better class of hooker.

Viktor excused himself for a cigarette and a cell-phone
call.

"What was Viktor saying, Dad?"

"We're discussing Viktor's percentage. And the safety and
liquidity of the funds."

"Dad, is Viktor a nice guy?"

"No."

"I *knew* that," said Zeta triumphantly. "I just knew it. I
mean, I *get it* about Viktor now. Viktor is the guy that Mom
One and Mom Two never wanted me to meet. Right?"

"Right."

"I mean, besides you, Dad. Mom and Mom sure didn't
want me to meet you, but they *totally* didn't want me to meet
Viktor."

"I'm glad you get it about Viktor. You should have a good
look at Viktor. He's every mother's nightmare."

Zeta put her elbows on the table, clasped her hands, and
rolled her wrists around loosely. "Dad, can I tell you something? Viktor is just *the coolest guy,* Dad. I used to think guys
in rock bands were cool, but Viktor Bilibin is just the coolest,
dreamiest, gangster guy. He has just such amazing eyes. They
look just like my pet snake's."

Starlitz considered this artless confession. At first glance
this was a very alarming development, but she wasn't his
own child for nothing. "You don't need Viktor," Starlitz informed her carefully. "I got you a fully legal American passport, in your own name. The whole world is yours, babe,
except for Cuba, Libya, North Korea, Iraq, Serbia, and Montenegro."

Viktor returned, sat down, and ordered Turkish coffee. "I

think we can do biznis," he said in Russian. "As long as the bills are not bogus."

"The bills are fine. I don't think Ozbey Effendi would be passing me any bogus Bulgarian."

"Mehmet Ozbey?" said Viktor, sitting up in alarm.

"Yeah, him. Who else do you know with white calfskin valises full of cash?"

"But Mehmet Ozbey is dead."

Starlitz laughed. "You're fuckin' delusionary, pal. I saw Ozbey last night. He was throwing a video party with flaming Kurds and lingerie models."

Viktor went pale. "I know he's dead. I had Ozbey hit," he insisted. "*Nobody* could have survived that."

Starlitz looked around the little grill. The temperature in the establishment had dropped by ten degrees, but no one else seemed to notice. Conversations including an eleven-year-old child rarely attracted sinister eavesdroppers.

"Dad," Zeta said thoughtfully, "did Viktor kill somebody?"

"No."

"He thinks he killed somebody."

"There's a big difference."

Viktor lifted his right hand with two fingers outstretched and his thumb as a revolver hammer. "I killed somebody," he told her in English, his voice gone resonant and spooky. "He wanted to kill me, because I know too much. He put me on his hit list. So, I took revenge on him. I had him liquidated. Boom-boom-bang."

"Wow," Zeta marveled, eyes like saucers and goose bumps all over her arms. "That's so corrupt!"

"It was the naked justice of the streets," Viktor intoned.

"He's full of it," Starlitz said, and switched to Russian. "Viktor, I thought you were keeping a low profile here. You can't have that guy hit. You're a teenage punk, and he's in Istanbul in a fucking palace walking around like a minister. If you're strutting around in some doped stupor claiming that you took out Mehmet Ozbey, you are fucking radioactive. I don't want to be anywhere near you."

Viktor was wounded. "I didn't shoot him myself! I never claimed that! But I know when Ozbey comes to Cyprus—because *everybody* knows when Ozbey comes to Cyprus. So I followed Ozbey. I watched his movements. I squealed on him. I ratted him out. I fingered him to a multinational apparatus of elite killer agents. And they blew him to pieces." Viktor smiled triumphantly.

"What? Who? How? Like, you've got contacts with hitsquad superninjas of some kind?"

"Exactly."

Starlitz leaned back. "You're mental."

"I'm not! Why would I make this up? They were secret agents from Guh-ooh-am."

"From *what*?"

"From Guh-ooh-am. I'll write it down for you." Viktor produced a cheap pen from a Greek Nicosia hotel and scribbled on a badly stained napkin.

"This is Cyrillic and it's not a Russian word," Starlitz complained.

"I'll write it in Roman capitals." Viktor carefully printed GUUAM.

"Guam?" Starlitz hazarded. "I've been to Guam."

"No," Viktor said stubbornly, "it's a multinational league of formerly Soviet countries. Georgia, Ukraine, Uzbekistan, Azerbaijan, and Moldova. GUUAM."

"What the hell are you on?" Starlitz scoffed. "They're a bunch of basket cases!"

"They hate Ozbey in GUUAM. Ozbey is on the rampage across their territories. Ozbey blackmailed the son of the president of Azerbaijan. Ozbey car-bombed the junior defense minister of Uzbekistan. They know that Ozbey is dangerous, and who is supposed to help them? NATO? Ozbey is NATO! Russia? The people in GUUAM are nationalists, they all hate Russia."

Viktor's soup bowl jumped as he banged the table. "I can't help it if you've never heard of GUUAM! GUUAM exists! GU-UAM is huge. GUUAM is as big as Europe, almost! Are they supposed to act like a bunch of faggots when some Turk is fucking with them?"

"You're telling me that Moldova runs offshore hit squads? They don't even have a functional stock market!"

"They're in GUUAM! They can split the expenses five ways."

Starlitz narrowed his eyes. "Mmmph."

"GUUAM can fight! Those countries have armies and navies. They have thousands of Red Army veterans, who never had a chance to fight under their own flag."

Starlitz thought about the proposition. Though totally unprecedented, it didn't seem, on the face of it, out of the question. After all, this was 1999. The planet was busting its strangeness budget.

"Where did this hit go down?" he said.

"I can show you."

"We'd better go look," Starlitz agreed.

They paid up, bought a dozen grape-wrapped dolmades and a gooey chunk of baklava for the road. They picked up Starlitz's Japanese rental car in the shadow of a Lefkosa mosque. The mosque had once been a French Crusader cathedral; it was an offshore Notre Dame, retrofitted with minarets.

A pleasant forty-minute drive took them to a ruined village near the Green Line. The backwoods of Turkish Cyprus were dotted with little ghost towns. Their natural roads had been cut, their Greek inhabitants had fled in terror, and years of economic embargo had finally finished them off.

Viktor nervously directed them down a dirt road, overhung with untrimmed trees, toward an old textile mill. The mill's corrugated metal sides were rust streaked, and the walls were thickly shrouded by thriving subtropical shrubbery. The place had the eerie, Faulknerian look of an abandoned cotton gin. "Why the hell would Ozbey come out here?" Starlitz said.

"I don't know. But he comes here often. He brings his men, sometimes he brings his girlfriend. . . . I assumed they were processing heroin in there."

"That would make sense."

"What's that burning smell?" Zeta said, lifting her chin from the toothmarked rim of her white valise.

Starlitz locked the two valises in the boot of the rental car and pocketed the keys. "You got a gun?" he asked Viktor.

"No, you?"

"I got an Iridium satellite phone," Starlitz offered, hefting it from beneath the seat. Its tough case and monster battery gave it the heft of a blackjack.

"Let's go buy some big guns!" Zeta suggested chirpily. "We've got lots of money."

The little mill village had not been entirely deserted. There were trimmed orange trees here and there, stone walls still kept up, a couple of modest truck farms. Since it was broad daylight—late afternoon, breezy, partly cloudy, full of whole-some Mediterranean clarity—it seemed ridiculous to skulk. Besides, an eleven-year-old girl attempting to skulk was among the most flaunting and melodramatic spectacles known to man.

Matters swiftly complicated themselves. A helicopter had tumbled out of the sky and fallen into the hillside woods, quite near the old industrial mill. This was no small helicopter. The aircraft was almost the size of a London double-decker, with big rubber landing wheels and a vast five-bladed rotor. The oblong hull was done in typically Soviet "sand-and-spinach" camouflage, but it had no national colors and no registry numerals.

"Hey, Dad, Dad, hey, Dad, don't look inside there," Zeta quavered. "Hey, Dad, what if there's *dead people* in there!"

"Maybe you better go back to the car, honey."

Zeta wasn't having any of it. They crept silently into the trees and undergrowth. "Ooh, Dad, Dad," she whispered, "what if it's really gruesome. What if somebody got their arm cut off." Zeta swallowed noisily as a damp wind rustled the treetops. "Ooh, Dad, what if there was like a cut-off guy's arm in there. What if it was a dead guy's arm, and it had like a really cool *watch* on it, but you couldn't touch it because, ooh, ugh, yuck!"

Viktor stopped dead, clutching a branch. "Why did we bring her?"

"Hey, Dad," Zeta babbled, "I couldn't touch a dead guy's arm if it was *cut off*. No way! Not ever! Yuck! Unless it had, like, a collector Beanie Baby in it. Like 'Peanuts,' the royal-blue Elephant Beanie Baby. That one's worth like five thousand dollars!"

"Zeta, I'm trying to think." Starlitz patted her scrawny back reassuringly. "Viktor, where the hell did this chopper come from? How could former Soviets fly this far south? Turkey's crawling with NATO radars."

"Syria," Viktor said. He pointed due east. "Syria is very near."

Starlitz considered this. His interior conception of the planet had just spun ninety degrees. "You're telling me that Hafez al-Assad . . . lets some confederacy that nobody ever heard of . . . launch paramilitary assaults . . . from Damascus airspace . . . against Turkish client states?"

"Wake up, old man. The Cold War ended when I was nine years old. Everybody hates everybody now."

"Yeah, no, maybe," muttered Starlitz.

The chopper lay in the crushed trees at a canted angle, its blades snapped like the dragonfly wings on the wipers of a high-speed car. The chopper had no obvious antiaircraft damage. The loss of a military craft this big, ugly, and powerful usually required heat-seeking missiles. Or multiple ack-ack ground-fire cannon holes. Perhaps its thirty-year-old, piece-

of-shit, analog, Russian-made, Cold War engines had finally
given out.

But such was not the case. Starlitz hoisted himself up the
grainy, paint-peeling, armored wall of the toppled aircraft,
and discovered that someone had deftly shot the helicopter's
pilot in the head. The pilot had been killed with a light-
caliber small arm, derisively small civilian bullets that had
somehow pierced through military bulletproof Perspex, and
through the pilot's armored radio helmet. Then the chopper
had obligingly coasted into the hillside and the crash had
killed the copilot.

"It just can't be," Starlitz muttered, sliding down and spitting thoughtfully into a shrub.

But there was much worse to come, for the dead chopper
had only two corpses inside it. A workhorse chopper like the
Mi-8 could carry up to twenty-four troops. The pilot had
landed his troops successfully. When shot down, he had been
coming back in a desperate effort to *rescue* his troops.

The walls of the silent barn had grown distinctly uncanny.
"Stay here on lookout," Starlitz told Zeta. "If you see any locals
showing up, whistle real loud, then look cute and act lost."

Someone had emptied an AK clip into the broken padlock
and chain on the factory door. Starlitz and Viktor crept inside
the place.

The abandoned factory radiated fatal theater. Ozbey had
set the place up as some kind of paramilitary training gym, a
handy place to keep the good old superspy reflexes trained.
There were weight-lifting benches, barbells, and big broken
sheets of bullet-stenciled mirror. Workout bags dangled next
to green army cots and padlocked gunmetal lockers. There
was a private pistol range. There were a few dead bales of vintage Cypriot wool here and there, looking distinctly bogus and
decorative, but the cavernous, overlit factory resembled nothing so much as a rust-spotted Disneyland thrill ride. Massive
cranes overhead featured conveniently dangling hooks. There

were working conveyor belts still in place. Exposed rafters with handy spools of rope. Giant hollow cargo drums, most of them graphically stenciled with rapid-fire bullet holes.

Someone had driven a flying sports car through the wood and sheet metal of the far wall, leaving a perfect, airborne cartoon outline of a car's silhouette.

An utterly bizarre event had occurred within the structure. It could not be properly described as a firefight. Actual firefights could not possibly lead to one guy killing fifteen armed soldiers. This had not been a battle, but some kind of heroic, semiotic ballet.

The assassins had apparently shown up in good faith. They were traditional, Spetsnaz-style "diversionary troops," rapid-deployment heavies who were trained to eliminate enemy leaders. They wore tropical camo, helmets, and flak vests. They carried serious, soldierly, functional, AKS-74 full-auto assault rifles, a plethora of belt-mounted hand grenades, big spooky silenced pistols, head-mounted burst-transmission radio sets.

One of the squad, a young dead man with a particularly surprised and unhappy expression, was equipped with an SA-7 antitank launcher.

Starlitz and Viktor migrated from corpse to corpse in a dual silent vigil. The dead men had not merely been killed, but killed in particularly extravagant and spectacular ways. They had been blown backward through disintegrating boards. Flung headlong into collapsing stacks of tumbling barrels. While firing their assault rifles helplessly into midair, they'd been blinded with paint and shot dead. One of them had died swatting and stumbling in a full-body burn.

Actual dead people in conventional gunfights tended to have a certain classic, sack-of-meat, Matthew Brady, battlefield look. These dead guys had died in fabulous, balletic sprawls: tumbled onto their backs, their booted legs picturesquely propped up; spinning in midair to crumple to earth like broken puppets; knocked against walls with their necks slumped at theatrical dead-guy angles.

Amazingly, a couple of the assailants had come back to life, or at least regained consciousness, in the latter stages of the event. Ozbey, somehow deprived of the unerring handgun that had killed most of the others, had climactically beaten them to death with his feet and fists.

With a stricken expression Viktor bent and plucked up loose ropes and a scarf of orange chiffon. He sniffed at its perfume, and silently caught Starlitz's eye.

So it had been a trap all along. There were *two* of them. Ozbey had had Gonca Utz inside the place. But no, it was worse than that; the *bad guys* had seized the girl. Ozbey had rescued her.

Ozbey and the girl had left the scene together, triumphantly, in the very same sports car that had previously flown through the air and smashed entirely through the wall. The rocketing car hadn't lost any of its glass, not so much as a paint chip. But its burnt-rubber tire tracks were all over the place.

Their flesh creeping, Starlitz and Viktor silently exited the building. There was nothing to say. This was a crisis beyond description. No mere words, in either Russian or English, could alter the fatal, unnatural tang of the enormity they had just witnessed.

Birds twittered in the trees. Zeta, who had been patiently keeping watch, looked at Starlitz and went pale at the sight. "Dad," she said plaintively, "Dad, what happened in there?"

Starlitz struggled to speak. There was nothing. He had no words. He would never have words again.

Starlitz heard his satellite phone ring. Starlitz found that he was able to move his hand. He was able to push the answer button. He was able to emit one ritual utterance.

"Hello?"

"Deus ex machina." The voice on the phone had a distant,

flattened tang. The sonic highs and lows had been clipped off through compression.

"What's that?" Starlitz asked.

"Try to say it. Speak aloud. Say 'deus ex machina.' "

"Why?" Starlitz asked warily.

"Because that is my story line, man. 'Deus ex machina,' the spook in the machine. You're stuck in the thematics, Starlitz. You're in a crisis of the master narrative. You can't go forward, can't go backward, no way out. That is your situation on the ground there. So then, the god comes down out of the divine sky-car and saves your bacon. And that's me. That's where I have to come in. You with the story yet?"

"Uh, yeah."

"So here I am, man."

Starlitz scratched his dazed and sweating head. "This is Tim from ECHELON, right?"

"Yep! I'm here in the flesh!"

Starlitz looked around himself. Viktor was staring at him with puzzlement, existential horror, and vague dawning hope. Zeta was looking fixedly into the trees with her jaw slack and her shoulders hunched.

"I don't see any 'flesh' here, Tim."

"Look up," Tim suggested.

Starlitz examined the blue sky. Satellite surveillance? Could that be it?

"Look down."

Starlitz looked at the earth. Motion detectors? Seismographs?

"Look all around." Vidcams?

"Your pants are falling down," said Tim triumphantly. "Left caret grin right caret. Semicolon hyphen right parenthesis."

"Hey, Dad," said Zeta. She pointed hesitantly into the empty air. "Who is this guy? What does he want?"

"What does he look like?" Starlitz parried.

"He looks like Bill Gates, sort of. If Bill Gates had thicker glasses and a shitty government job."

"Ha ha ha," said Tim through the phone. "What a sense of humor. Let me shake your hand, little girl. You can call me Uncle Tim."

"He says he wants to shake your hand," Starlitz said. "He says his name is Tim."

"Well, okay, I can hear him," said Zeta. She clasped the empty air and shook it vigorously. Then she winced in disgust as invisible fingers tousled the top of her head.

"Moments like this make it all worse while," Tim recited mechanically into the phone. "Protecting America's vulnerable youth from the threat of international terrorism. That's what I'm all about."

"What the hell is going on?" Viktor demanded suddenly. "What is that ugly black shadow out of the depths of the forest?"

"He says he's come to help us," Starlitz said.

Viktor jumped a foot, clutching his backside with a shriek. Suddenly Viktor's wallet hung in midair, yawning open and disgorging business cards and various forms of currency into the tall grass.

"Hey!" Viktor demanded, clenching his fists. "Tell it to stop!"

"Tim," Starlitz said into the phone, "my associate's kind of upset that you're going through his private business affairs there."

"Fuck him," Tim said cheerfully, in the same flat voice. "What's he gonna do about it? This Russian punk's got no fucking options." Tim tossed the wallet aside. "He's broke. And he's small time. He's not of major surveillant interest."

A look of frantic desperation entered Viktor's eyes. He wasn't taking this at all well.

"Viktor, chill out," Starlitz said. "Let me pass you the word, man. This is ECHELON."

"Did you say ECHELON?" said Viktor.

"Ever heard of it? Shall I spell it for you?"

"Of course I've heard of ECHELON!" Viktor protested. "ECHELON is the legendary capitalist global surveillance system. It's the worldwide signals intelligence directorate! ECHELON is the crown jewel of the antiprogressive Dark Forces!"

"Uh, yeah. That would be the alleged phenomenon."

"ECHELON is run by the UK, USA, Australia, and New Zealand. It uses undersea-cable taps, and surveillance satellites like 'Aquacade,' 'Rhyolite,' and 'Magnum.' It taps the Internet through its major routing centers and does comprehensive word searches on e-mail traffic."

"Hey, shut up," Tim protested over the satellite phone. "That's all totally classified."

Starlitz put the phone on his shoulder and squinted in the sunlight. "Can you actually *see* Tim, Viktor? I can hear him over this satellite phone, but I can't see a damn thing. It's like the guy's installed at hardware level and totally user transparent."

"I can see a kind of black, hideous, paranoid shape," Viktor reported. "It's like some faceless, oozing nightmare that covers the whole earth."

"What do *you* see, Zeta?"

"I can see him fine. I can hear him too. I can even smell him. He doesn't change his clothes very much."

"I'm a busy guy," Tim complained.

"He looks just like my geeky math teacher. You know, that math guy who used to go out during recess and look up our skirts."

"Girls don't like math," Tim grumbled. "Colon hyphen left parenthesis."

"I like math fine, Tim. I just don't like *you*."

"Look, I don't have much time to waste here," said Tim, obviously irritated. "I got eighteen acres of vintage Crays under a hill in Fort Meade, and we're way behind on our comprehensive Y2K upgrades."

"Oh, yeah." Starlitz nodded. "I mighta known."

"Why did you bring a little girl to a Level Three national-security incident? That's not professional. You clowns are lucky that I even showed up."

"You're not supposed to show up, Tim. I never called you. I don't know why you're here." Starlitz shrugged.

"Well, then let me get *you* up to speed, newbie," said Tim briskly. "I mean, you can't even *see* me, because in most circumstances I am, like, light-years beyond your shabby, street-level, hard-boiled little discourse. Because ECHELON is, like, the Olympus of networked globalization. We're so far beyond your mental grasp that we're literally unspeakable. Mere mundane user dorks like you can't even *raise the topic* of ECHELON in any discussion of contemporary reality. Because at ECHELON we're huge, omniscient, omnipresent, and totally technically capable. We've been secretly saving the bacon of the Anglo-American empire since Alan Turing was blowing guys in bus stations. We're always taping everything, but we Never Say Anything. You get me so far?"

"Yeah, no, maybe."

"So that means that a guy like me has no conventional path into the narrative. None at all. I'm *always* the deus ex machina. I mean, the twentieth-century master narrative just doesn't work, unless I remain way behind the curtain, and always super secret. If ECHELON's abilities and activities become common knowledge and a public issue, the whole world is transformed. Outing ECHELON disrupts all the basic political and social assumptions. It throws the whole twentieth-century story straight off the rails. It's like you're filming some kind of BBC British teatime drama, and a giant wrathing kraken comes up out of the Thames."

"Cut to the chase, Tim. So, why do we have the honor?"

"Oh, Betsy called me. We had a nice talk."

"Aha." Starlitz thought this over. It was falling into place after all. Maybe it wasn't that bad. "What exactly can we do for you, Tim?"

"Well," said Tim, "being a deus ex machina by trade and nature, I'm sure I can resolve your nasty little incident here. I've been hitting my databases, and I think I've got a handle on the basic parameters of the problem. We got this Turkish superspy running loose who thinks the twenty-first century actually looks Turkish. He's turning himself into some kind of paradigmatic culture hero. You with my diagnosis so far?"

"Yep."

"Well, we can't have that, man. It's way too disruptive to the totalizing, globalizing trend of the master narrative. It's like an errant subroutine taking up valuable processing cycles. NATO's busy demonizing Milosevic now, we can't waste time and attention on any Turkish spooky domestic weirdness. If this sideshow leaks out and hits CNN, then NATO's finest hour gets upstaged."

"What is the hideous dark force saying to you?" Viktor demanded nervously.

"I think he's recruiting us as a cover-up squad," Starlitz reported.

"That's right," said Tim. "You should never have become involved in such delicate affairs of state. But now that you're stuck in this situation, the narrative allows you only one legitimate role. 'Consequence management.' "

"We're lousy scum, so we have to be Ozbey's garbagemen," Starlitz reported.

Viktor's face fell. One could see right away that he had been somehow expecting this.

"You'll have to remove all traces of objective evidence," said Tim firmly. "I see from satellite photos that the local villagers have some tractors and backhoes. Tell the locals that Ozbey sent you. Borrow their equipment and bury everything and everyone. Then set fire to the building."

"What about the chopper?"

"Tell the locals to pull the rotors and ailerons off it. They can turn the fuselage into a shish-kebab parlor."

"That sure is a lot of work," Starlitz grumbled. "Why should I do all that?"

There was an ominous silence on the line. Then Tim spoke up. "Starlitz, I understand that you don't much care for videocams."

"Why do you say that?" Starlitz hedged.

"How would you like to have a globally networked, forty-eight-million-dollar, telescopic orbiting videocam trained on your head, personally?"

"Don't do that," Starlitz said.

"You would turn into a puff of fucking soot, pal. You would blow away on the breeze like an Industrial Light and Magic particle animation."

"I get the message, Tim. I'll look after the problem, okay?"

"That's better," said Tim.

"Is he paying us?" Viktor asked hopefully.

"*Nyet.*"

"Shit. I knew it."

The uncanny strain of Tim's presence was beginning to tell on Starlitz's nerves. Starlitz was eager to get over the thematic disruption and back to something predictable and much lower key. "Is there anything else we can do for you, Tim?"

"Yeah," said Tim, lowering his timbre and removing some treble from his signal. "Let me ooze a little closer, so this little kid can't overhear me. Okay. Now. Tell me all about Betsy Ross, okay? Because Betsy is hot. She is *so* hot. Does she give head?"

"Ask her yourself."

"But you *know*, right? I'm putting her in alt dot nude dot celebrity. I'm jpegging Betsy into alt dot binaries dot erotica dot voyeur. I got rid of my Monica Lewinsky screensaver. I installed a new Betsy." Tim sighed from the depths of his flat-tened soul. "Someday, I might even *touch* Betsy."

"Why is that a problem for you, Tim? Betsy Ross wants to be everybody's darling. She wants to cover the whole earth. You can't do that and be real fastidious."

"It's because *I'm in government,* bubba! I never got an ini-tial public offering! I got no Internet boom stocks in my port-folio. I'm not one of these glamorous zillionaire geeks, I'm a strictly noncommercial spook geek. What do I have that a hot babe like Betsy would want?"

"Power."

"Oh, yeah," said Tim, all cheered up. "*That.* Okay. Right. Great. I get it. Be seeing you." He clicked off.

THE ELDERLY CYPRIOTS STILL DWELLING IN THE VILLAGE were not too surprised to meet Viktor and Starlitz. They were even less surprised when Starlitz announced their errand. The locals were very cooperative and asked very few questions. The vest-wearing granddad greased up the elderly backhoe, and silently indicated a nearby lemon grove.

While Zeta enjoyed a tall lemonade from kerchief-headed Grandmom, Viktor and Starlitz drove the creaking machine to the orchard. There they discovered a long series of man-sized weedgrown lumps, in various ages and sizes.

These were the disappeared. The people under the lumps had wandered a little too far out of Ozbey's Turkish narrative consensus. Into the Communist party. Or the drowned and nonexistent nation of Kurdistan. Maybe into some glittery-eyed Shi'ite martyrdom cult. So they just weren't around any-more. No ID. No obit. No headstone. No mourners. No nothing.

"Ever work a backhoe?" said Starlitz to Viktor.

"No."

"Want to learn?"

"Do I look like a peasant?"

"Okay, hotshot; then I guess you'll be hauling the bodies out."

Viktor and Starlitz toiled well into the evening. Starlitz, who was quite a whiz at backhoes, deftly scooped an entire lane of holes in the next row of the orchard.

With the growing darkness the character of Ozbey's scene was transforming. The stiffening dead soldiers did not come back to their youth and strength and health and life, for that would have been far, far too much to ask. But they lost their uncanny glossiness. They took on the reassuring appearance of victims of an actual shoot-out. Instead of neat round bullet holes precisely placed in their vital organs, the corpses exhibited the standard results of actual bullets smashing actual human flesh. Floppy hunks of meat torn through exit wounds. Nasty interior ricochets and nasty bone-tunneling effects. Enormous, hideous, hydrostatic bruises. It was hard to be reassured by this, but it meant that their labor was working. The anomaly was draining away. The quotidian was finally reasserting itself. The system was once again functional.

Toward sunset toothless Granny thoughtfully brought them some mutton, milk, and falafels. The locals were kindly people. There was certainly no faulting them for hospitality.

"How can you eat?" Viktor demanded, his dirt-smeared hands shaking in agitation.

"This is hard work, man. I'm hungry."

The naked job had taken a terrible toll on Viktor. Viktor had the flaky, denuded look of a young junkie. His elegant shirt was cheaper. His handsome shoes had burst at the seams. His skin was dotted with acne and septic fleabites. He seemed to have lost a tooth without noticing it.

"I should not be here doing this, Starlitz. I wasn't meant to do this. This is not my role in life."

Starlitz squatted on his haunches. He was by no means happy, but he was far more at ease with himself than he had been earlier. "It's a mass grave. Get used to it. Twentieth century's full of 'em. They're common as dirt."

"But that's you, not me. You *look* like a gravedigger. You feel like one. You've become some kind of troll. Look at yourself. You're like some ugly creature that lives under bridges to kill the innocent. You disgust me."

"I kind of like it here at rock bottom, kid. It's good to know the system still has one. Even in 1999."

"Why are we burying dead men for that monster Ozbey? I never got a chance to bury my own beloved uncle! Why am I doing this filthy work on some stupid Turkish island? Where is my nobility of spirit? In Yugoslavia the heroic Slavic people are standing on their bridges, singing in unison, and bravely defying the NATO oppressor!"

"Kid, you're living in total denial. Yugoslavia is this scene in spades."

"Yugoslavia is a brave, outnumbered people, asserting their own identity against an evil oppressor."

"Asserting identity by burning IDs and stealing license plates? Yeah, sure."

"Starlitz, listen. You must see the truth. We've been reduced to something vile and ugly. Ozbey and Tim are somehow acting together, against all sense, tradition, and reason. We can't let ourselves be historically humiliated! We must rally, unite, and fight against this cruel unilateral globalist dictatorship!"

Starlitz yawned indifferently. "You're just sick of honest work."

"It's for the sake of the living soul of the next century! We can't let the great Orthodox culture, the heir of lost Byzantium, be crushed between Moslems and NATO. The Slavic world is the only real world in the world!"

Starlitz stood up and leaned wearily on his shovel. "So what are you proposing, exactly? Give me the pitch."

"Well—it's not safe for me here in Cyprus. I must leave

this island before Ozbey comes back to kill me. That's for certain. I don't want to go to Belgrade under the bombing but . . . well . . . I've been thinking seriously about Budapest."

"You don't want to miss the fun part tonight, Viktor. After we shovel under the last stiff, I'm gonna torch Ozbey's dojo there. You've probably never seen a major act of arson, but there's a real art to it. You should get hip to this. It's a useful skill."

"Starlitz, stop talking like a dirty beast. I have a glorious vision of the future—it came to me in a rush suddenly, as we were bulldozing that Ukrainian. There are five million Serbian women. Serbian women are even more desperate than Russian women. They need money worse. They have fewer scruples. And Serbian women are very pretty. That means amazing commercial opportunity, for the first entrepreneur to get in on the ground floor."

"You're spoiling a great moment here," Starlitz complained. "Sure, we're filthy, we stink, my hair's falling out and you're losing your teeth, but there's a lot of narrative elbow room when you're right at the edge of genocidal chaos. If we get a little careless with the kerosene, we could set fire to half this fucking village. That sorry fucker Tim would see the flames crackling, straight out of orbit. Serve him right too."

Viktor closed his eyes, shuddered dramatically, and opened them again. They were full of lucid Slavic conviction. "You've finally lost your mind."

"No; actually, *you* are insane, Viktor. Not that I hold that against you."

"No, Starlitz, you're insane; you've lost all sense of proper proportion. Y2K is coming, and you're at the end of your rope. You've lost all sense of restraint and decency. You're going to pop and disappear, just like a stock-market bubble."

"Viktor, don't tell me I'm insane, okay? I've got a child and a nice reputation in the industry. But *you*—you wouldn't know an honest job if it carpet-bombed you. You're a young guy, and you're like a hundred-and-ten-percent shakedown problems."

"All right," sniffed Viktor, "that does it! I knew that eventually you'd insult me unforgivably. Well, someday, when you get over your ugly greed for dollars and your mindless technology worship, you'll be sorry you tried to crush the fine spirit of Viktor Bilibin."

"Great," said Starlitz, "go ahead, walk out on the job at hand. See how far it gets you."

Viktor rose, turned on his heel, and scampered into the cricket-shrieking Cypriot darkness. He was so happy to go that he could barely stop himself from capering.

Starlitz worked alone after that. This didn't bother him much. When the work at hand was unspeakable, it was pleasant not to have to talk to anyone.

Around midnight he set fire to the training hall.

As the flames rose, Zeta stepped out of the gloom and joined him.

"Hey, Dad."

"What?"

"Hey, Dad."

"What is it?"

"Hey, Dad, how come you're so ugly now?"

"Am I ugly now?"

"Yeah, Dad. You're covered with ugly paint. You smell like smoke and blood." She kicked at the dirt with the toe of her shoe. "You got a big bald patch on the back of your head."

Starlitz clamped his hand to the back of his skull. It was true. He had lost his hair. "Zenobia, I don't know exactly how to tell you this, but there are certain things that grown-ups have to do, and—"

"Dad, listen. While I was sitting in there with those old people, watching war coverage and soccer on their satellite TV, I had like, this . . . new feeling. Okay? Like, a feeling in my heart. I think I know what I want to be when I grow up."

"You do, huh?"

"Yeah, Dad! I know all about that now. I want to be a lot like you."

"Oh, brother." Starlitz sighed.

"But it's true, Dad! I want to spend a lot of my time in cars and airplanes. Going to obscure, dirty places. Where terrible things are happening. And most people don't know about them. But they're important anyway. Even though nobody knows or cares much. That's gonna be my life. My life's work."

"You don't say," Starlitz said. The flames were climbing steadily.

"I do say, Dad. 'Cause I really get it about you now. Because I'm your daughter, and I finally got to know my dad. My good old dad. Except, even though you're pretty old, you're not much *good*, Dad. You're bad."

Starlitz watched as a wall collapsed in a massive flurry of sparks. "Am I bad, Zeta?"

"Absolutely, Dad! I mean, you're not actively *evil*—you're just, like, totally provisional and completely without morality. You can personify the trends of your day, but you *never get ahead of trends*. You never make the world any better. You're not strong enough for that, you just don't have it in you. But the thing is—I'm *not* bad. I'm *good*. I'm a good person. I can feel it inside. I want to be genuinely farsighted, and giving, and wise. A powerful force for good."

"Well, I suppose you'll be wanting to go back to your moms, then. And drop old Dad by the wayside."

"Well, no. Because now that I've been away from them awhile, I get them too. I don't want to be like them. No way. Because they're full of lame hippie crap. They're petty crooks, and they're high on drugs. They're all over, Dad. They're yesterday. See, I'm already past Y2K. The twentieth century is already over in my heart."

Starlitz said nothing.

"The twentieth century was never as important as you

thought it was, Dad. It was a dirty century. It was a cheap, sleazy century. The second the twentieth century finally went under the carpet, everybody forgot about it right away. In the twenty-first century we don't have your crude, lousy problems. We've got *serious, sophisticated* problems."

Zeta looked over the crashing roof as it slowly tumbled in foul gouts of flame. "I'm glad I saw this, because this is, like, my initiation. I'm going to be spending a lot of my life in situations just like this. Just like you spend your life. The difference between you and me is, when *I* show up on the scene, people are *glad to see me*. Because when Zeta Starlitz shows up, people get a bath. They get latrines. They get some decent food, their skin stops itching. The children stop screaming. The panic and the terror goes away."

"Did you just say 'Zeta Starlitz'?" said Starlitz, lifting his brows. "So it's gonna be 'Zeta Starlitz,' huh?"

"Yeah, Dad, that's gonna be my name. That's the name I want. I mean, you can't expect people to say 'Zenobia B. H. McMillen is here with the emergency choppers.' But 'Zeta Starlitz,' that's a great, CNN-style, mover-and-shaker name. Plus, I start and I end with a Z. Pretty cool, huh?"

Starlitz rubbed his greasy, dirt-smeared chin. "So, basically, we're talking some kind of a humanitarian bureaucrat, Médecins Sans Frontières–type thing."

"Yeah. That's it. Very high-level, Dad. I speak like nine or ten languages. I wear tailored safari suits. I've got a medical degree, and all kinds of ribbons and medals from Swedish do-gooder committees."

"Kind of making your old dad pretty proud there."

Zeta sighed. "Actually, Dad, it's all kinda based on being as far away from you as possible." She looked up. "I don't mean physically far. I mean, like, in some very distant part of the narrative."

"I see. Well, I'm glad you told me this, Zeta. It makes a lot of sense. It's very plausible. I guess that's how it's got to be."

"So, Dad, how do I do that? I mean, there's a good way to do that, right? I don't quite get that part yet."

Starlitz nodded resignedly. "Swiss finishing school."

"What's that mean?"

"Oh, it's some elite European academy for children of diplomats and rich mafiosi. I put you in an expensive Swiss boarding school. They teach you lame aristo ladylike shit, like proper posture, and violin playing. Then I guess, later, it's an elite med school and lots of . . . ugh . . . humanities courses."

"Wow, that sounds perfect, Dad. Let's do it right now. Let's take our money straight to a Swiss bank, without any of this dirty Cyprus laundry mess."

"No, honey—*you* go to Switzerland. Not me. After this you don't see much of me anymore. Maybe you see me at Christmas. Well, not this Christmas. Not the Y2K Christmas. Definitely not the Y2K Christmas. Maybe the next Christmas. If I'm around. Some Christmases in the next century. If I'm available, I'll try to show up. I'll bring you some nice consumer thing. Okay?"

Her cheeks lit by firelight, Zeta began to cry.

THERE WERE EYES ON HIM FROM THE FAR SIDE OF THE DINER. A Turk in his sixties, bespectacled and weary. He looked like a retired lawyer, or a teacher waiting to die. Starlitz ignored him and continued to eat. Pitas. Lamb casserole. Doner kebab. Mincemeat. Sweetbreads in herbs. Bottle after bottle of Efes Pilsner. Now that Starlitz was alone, he couldn't get enough of it. He had to devour it all. Until there was nothing left.

The man abandoned his shot glass of raki, rose, and placed his snap-brim hat over his vest-covered chest. "You are Mr. Starlitz. Yes?"

Starlitz looked up, belched, and brushed back greasy ringlets from his sweater collar. "What's it to ya?"

"My name is Jelal Kashmas. I'm a newspaper columnist. For *Milliyet*. You've heard of my newspaper, of course."

"Yeah."

"Because you bribed our fashion correspondent. To gush about the clothes worn by your dancing girls."

"Aw, that was ages ago, Mr. Kashmas. I'm not in the pop business now. I'm running a trucking firm."

"I thought you once promised," Jelal said precisely, "that the G-7 band would cease to exist on New Year's Day 2000."

"You want some of these stuffed eggplants, man? I got plenty."

"Instead, the G-7 seem to be preparing for a very ambitious tour in 2000. Morocco. Tunisia. Algeria. Egypt. Pakistan. Malaysia."

"The act is under new management."

"Why should that matter? If you gave your word."

Starlitz hunched his shoulders, blinking. "He turned the whole deal inside out, man. Ozbey turned the story line on its head. The story was that the girls were all going to live. And the band would just vanish like a soap bubble. Instead, the *band* is going to live. The G-7 act will be huge. While the girls die. One by one."

"That's very . . . droll."

"It's not a joke, pal."

Kashmas pulled out a wooden chair and sat. "Do you ever read my columns? 'The Day the Bosphorus Dried Up'? 'How I Lost Myself in the Mirror'? My many romantic stories of gangsters in Beyoglu? A columnist always needs new material."

"I don't read Turkish."

"Do you ever read the Turkish author Orhan Pamuk? He has been widely translated. He wrote *The White Castle* and *The Black Book*."

"I think I've seen his billboards."

"Pamuk understands the Turks. Our noble, tormented, secular Turkish Republic. With her many remembrances, and her great forgetfulness. He's a young artist, but he's the equal of Calvino or García Márquez."

"Calvino is dead, and García Márquez is in the fucking hospital."

"Then perhaps, in the next century, it's time for the world to listen to Turkey for a while."

"I'm all for that," Starlitz grunted.

Kashmas put his tweedy elbow on the table and scratched the side of his head. "What are you doing in this part of my country? Why are you in the stronghold of Severik Bey? Didn't your State Department warn you about this?"

"I'm not a tourist. I run a trucking company. I'm moving goods and products. Fuck the State Department."

"You have no more fondness for music? For Miss Gonca Utz, maybe. This is her hometown. She was born near the Syrian border. They're very proud of her here. You must have seen her many posters. Her CDs. Her videos. They're everywhere."

Starlitz said nothing.

"What about Mr. Mehmet Ozbey? How well do you know him?"

"Well enough."

"Why does he have no childhood?"

"What?" Starlitz said.

"There are records of his public appearances. There are records of his many business engagements. People flock to his social events. But Mehmet Ozbey has no childhood. I have looked. He has no school records. No parents. No background. If you investigate beyond a certain year, Mehmet Ozbey ceases to exist."

Starlitz put his fork down. "Look, pal. It's true that I ripped off your *Milliyet* newspaper—like, ten or twelve times, actually—so I'm gonna tell you this, just fuckin' once. You don't want to investigate Mehmet Ozbey. You'll be a chalk outline on the fucking pavement. Even if you did investigate

Ozbey, you sure as hell wouldn't want to investigate him in Gonca Utz's hometown. Because Severik Bey owns this place, and he is a mountain bandit. He's a straight-out robber baron of the old medieval school. He's a kidnapper, an extortionist, a car thief, and a major-league smack racketeer. Plus he owns his own TV station. Journalists who ask questions here end up handcuffed in stolen cars and dumped in a lake."

Kashmas shrugged wearily. "Do you think this is news to a Turkish newsman? This country is my home. I've lived here all my life. It's in my blood and bones."

"Hmmmph."

"Severik Bey is a famous government loyalist. He's in Parliament. In the ruling party. He gives speeches on secularism and technical education."

"Goodie."

"Am I boring you, Mr. Starlitz? It's tiring for strangers to talk Turkish politics. It's nothing but dervishes, shootings, and scandals. I want to know *your* story."

"Don't have one anymore."

"I see in your face that you have an interesting story. Some people read coffee grounds, but I read faces."

"I'm old and tired, and I smoke too much. End of story."

"Is it true that you ride your own trucks throughout Turkey, crying out to people to trade 'new lamps for old'?"

"Yeah. Sure. You bet. There's a big collectors' market overseas for vintage Turkish copperware."

"I've talked to the men that drive your trucks," said Kashmas, his baggy eyes warm and confiding. "They tell strange stories about you. For months you've roamed the haunted streets of Istanbul and Ankara. Under mosques with broken minarets. In the old ruins. In homes wrecked by fire and earthquake. In abandoned dervish lodges. Wearing dirty clothes, behind mirrored glasses. Looking for dirty dealings, strange local mysteries, the ghosts of dead swindlers and dope fiends. Always in a hurry. A haunted man. A man with his clock running out. Your face is pale, your eyes are restless. The nights in Istanbul are endless, aren't they?"

"Look, Scheherezade, lemme tell you something about Turkish truckers. They're ignorant as dirt. Sure, you *bet* I watch the clock. I'm bringing modern efficiency to your country's crappy shipping services. I'm doing just-in-time delivery, and overnight package service, in a country with lousy roads and no traffic signs. It's a *science*, okay? It's all about putting trucks in *exactly* the right place, in *exactly* the right moment. With global positioning. And software tracking."

"How very mysterious and poetic. Why here, Mr. Starlitz?"

"I like the food here. Come here all the time. I'm a regular. This is my favorite café."

"I mean, why this small Turkish border town? There's no great business here. The town is cheap, and boring. Policemen retire here. Policemen who retire on half pay. Because they preferred traditional torture methods to the new international ones."

"I like antiquing," Starlitz said. He rose from his table to stare out the curtained window.

Down the steep, winding road came one of his trucks. Carrying its usual payload. A few obligatory packages that he'd hired on at a loss. And that other payload, nailed into a sealed and silent crate.

"Don't think that I want trouble," said Kashmas. "I don't want to cause you trouble. Who reads newspapers? It's not like it was in the sixties. I'm a miserable crank. A pop intellectual. A scribbler with big ideas, who writes in a minor language. There are times when I smell of death, even to myself."

A distant high-pitched roar was coming down the mountain.

"I can tell that about people, sometimes," said Kashmas. "It's a kind of gift."

Gonca's red sports car came out of a sharp turn with a tortured scream of rubber. Starlitz stared out the window, his shoulders hunched, forehead touching the glass. Gonca wore a whipping Isadora Duncan chiffon scarf, big starlet's sunglasses.

She drew up on the lumbering cargo truck with the speed of a cruise missile. At the last instant she veered past it with a mad screech of the horn, a sudden red flash like the slash of a razor blade.

"I can't believe it," Starlitz breathed. "I never thought she'd make it."

A larger car came in hot pursuit. It was the massive armored limo of Severik Bey, with the feudal lord commanding the wheel, grinning like a madman as he floored it.

Without so much as twitch to the right or left, the beautiful saloon plowed into the rear of the truck, at top speed. There was a comprehensive smash, like a sudden mortar barrage. The bulletproof glass did not shatter; it bent and buckled. The high-tech armor did not dent; it warped and ruptured. The huge truck flew up on its hind axle with a heavy-metal scream of protest, and it sat on the smashed hood of the Mercedes limo, a dying elephant impaled on a sharp-horned rhino.

Starlitz tossed cash on the table and left the roadside diner without a word. Kashmas followed quickly, drawing a notepad and a camera from his voluminous tweed pockets.

They reached the wreckage, where hot, ruptured metal popped and groaned. Kashmas muttered aloud in astonished Turkish, stamping his feet and staring through windows. "Help me with him," he said in English.

The driver's airbag had inflated. Severik Bey was bleeding profusely, but he was still alive. Kashmas waved his tweedy arms to stop the traffic as Starlitz laid the Kurdish leader on the crumbling asphalt. Severik Bey wasn't quite out; his shoulder was broken, his ribs were cracked, but the old bandit was tough as nails, he was clawing at the dirt, spitting blood, and slowly cursing his fate.

The other two men were far less lucky. The man in the

passenger seat had gone straight into the armored windshield; he was a bloody sack of meat in a policeman's suit.

And in the back was Ozbey, who never bothered with seat belts. If Ozbey had been at the wheel, the contretemps could never have happened. But Ozbey had been a minor figure here in Kurdistan, killing time to amuse his friends. Lolling in the seat with a martini and a cigarette, he'd been flung against the roof like a rag doll.

The panicked driver emerged from the shipping truck. He was shaken, bruised, but mobile. He stood in the road amid the gathering traffic, with the paralyzed look that people always had at traffic fatalities.

Starlitz walked up to him to clap him on the back. "You're a hero," he said.

The stricken driver saw blood in the road. He cried out in Turkish and began to sob.

"Sorry," said Starlitz, "I mean they'll call you a hero. Next year. Once the story's out in Parliament."

"Isn't that Mehmet Ozbey, the very man we were just speaking of?" said Kashmas.

Starlitz was properly cautious. "Is he still breathing?"

With his loafered foot and both his shoulders Kashmas forced open the car's rear door. Ozbey flopped down and hung off the edge of the seat, arms limp as wax in his tailored jacket, his muscular neck like the snapped stalk of a dandelion, blood leaking demurely from both his handsome nostrils. "No. He's not breathing. He's dead."

"You're sure?"

"Yes."

"Absolutely positive?"

"I'm not a doctor. But I've been to many crime scenes. This man is dead."

"Take his picture. Take a lot of them."

"Good idea." Kashmas fired off several snapshots with his sturdy, road-worn German automatic.

"Your camera's working?" Starlitz said.

"Of course!"

"Okay, then that's Mehmet Ozbey," said Starlitz finally. "Or rather, Abdullah Oktem."

"Mehmet Ozbey has two identities?"

"He has at least six identities. Check him for passports."

Another driver came forward, from his stopped car. He was a tubby Turkish businessman with a dazed, good-Samaritan look. The trunk of the Mercedes had snapped open from the impact of the crash. The would-be rescuer was babbling aloud, waving his hands in amazement. He had noticed that the limo's trunk was chockful of machine guns.

"Do you know who this policeman is?" called Kashmas.

"Uh, yeah, I do. That would be the assistant head of the Turkish National Police Academy. Specialist in psychological warfare and counterinsurgency. I forget the guy's name." Starlitz climbed up into the back of the truck. Cantilevered on the ruptured hood of the Mercedes, it moved with a screech under his weight. Starlitz put his hands on the deadly sealed crate that was its special cargo.

Copper jugs. Old discontinued cartons of Bafra cigarettes. Turkish kids' alphabet books from the teens and twenties, with zebras and zeppelins. Ancient state lottery tickets, never redeemed. Pink Turkish lira from before the hyperinflation. Herbal toothache remedies. Spare parts for American-imported Packards and De Sotos. Vacuum jars of quince and sour-cherry preserves. Rose-scented bubble bath in powder-leaking canisters. Minty toothpastes and liqueur-filled chocolates turned to stone in their foil wrappers. Yellowed mosquito netting. Tinted postcards with blushing teenage brides. Dried figs in sacks of burlap. Massive black telephones and moth-eaten red fezzes.

Suggestively shaped bottles of Yorgi Tomatis brand cologne. Spaghetti-western kids' photo-novels called *Texas* and *Tom Mix*. Cracked backgammon boards with pink dice. Coffee-stained card decks, greasy with use. Pistol-shaped cigarette lighters and mother-of-pearl cigarette holders. Eyeglass frames. Cummerbunds. The bookworm-eaten memoirs of Safiye Ayla, the twenties café chanteuse who rightfully boasted of giving her womanly all to Kemal Atatürk.

It had taken him so long to put it all together just right. Those heartbreaking mementos of Turkey's twentieth century, the period's descent into its final banality and decay. The century's *inevitable* descent, oh, how very inevitable. Starlitz had thought to take all the physical evidence with him somehow, to erase it from the scene just as time had erased its meaning, but the truck was wrecked now, and his precious crate was too heavy to budge.

Leave it all, then. Draw two lines under it, just write it off. Bury all that is dead within us.

Now Gonca arrived on the scene, with a screech of rubber and a long honk. She flung open her scarlet door and raced forward headlong. She thrust herself through the gathering crowd, her sunglasses flying and her shoulder straps slipping.

Raising both hands with a vivid keen of anguish, she fell to one knee by the corpse of her lover. She threw her braceleted slim arms and ringed fingers around Ozbey's broken head. For one terrible moment it seemed that such devotion was unstoppable, that Ozbey was sure to pop back up with a smirk and a suave wink, but then Gonca opened her throat and released a cry of such power and desolation that a woman fainted and two men burst into tears.

"This is quite a story," said Kashmas thoughtfully. "Do you have a telephone?"

BY THE TIME THE SCANDAL BROKE FULLY IN TURKEY'S SLUG-gish press, Starlitz had already sold the trucking business. Repeated official attempts were made to dismiss the scandal, but it was just too undismissable, too eager to tell itself. A heroin smuggler, still wanted by Interpol after breaking from Swiss prison. With a top-ranking police officer, the former body-guard of the Turkish ambassador to Washington. With a Kurd-ish warlord, who was still alive, and stoutly refusing to talk. All tied to a comely pop star on a TV game show. There was just no way to swerve around a story like that.

Starlitz left Turkey. In the final weeks and months of the century, he moved his base of operations to Switzerland. It was a Y2K thing; they had gold there, and cash laundries, and fallout shelters. Starlitz bought into a small software company, and radically increased its profits by the cunning process of "value subtraction."

Many software merchants made the profound mistake of selling the best software they could make. Luckily, a study of strategies for information pricing had made it clear that this was not the best source of revenue in a true Information Economy. People became nervous and unhappy if they were sold decent software at a decent price. Decent software should only be offered at a terrifically high, premium price, and loaded down with extras and unnecessary but psychologi-cally reassuring bells and whistles. Then, the middle tier of the market should be offered a cheaper, but still expensive, crippled version of the original software. And newbies and stu-dents and bottom feeders, in their many sorry thousands, were to be sold a barely functional, piece-of-shit, value-subtracted version of the product.

So Starlitz engaged in the software's deliberate ruination, and the market lavishly blessed him. Every other weekend he would sneak out to his daughter's boarding school. He never spoke to Zeta, but he would take occasional snapshots with telephoto lenses. In her prim little uniform Zeta was actually showing up on camera now, a very good sign, considering her career intentions. Starlitz compiled extensive dossiers on her teachers. It was a form of subtle revenge on them, for turning his daughter into an upwardly mobile princess who would come to think of her dad as some kind of antique grease-monkey hick.

Spying and stalking left him a hollow man without a life, but this situation had its rewards. He was getting along fine, at continental distance, with Mom One and Mom Two. Vanna and Judy were still on the splits and not speaking to each other, but they both seemed to be down with the Swiss-boarding-school notion, probably because it was so utterly unlike him. They read his periodic e-mail and studied his photograph jpeg enclosures with unfeigned interest. It seemed that the gender power struggle between them was fading with the last ticking months of the year. Because they were all too old now, thought Starlitz. They had lost their bloom and their youth, so the stakes were too low to fight over anymore. They were all too old to be attracted to people that they couldn't stand.

Judy even made an effort to rise from her wheelchair and generate some revenue. She bought a Body Shop franchise in Oregon, to help support Zeta's demanding educational habits. Zeta was doing well in the school. Her classes were full of neurotic, neglected rich kids that she could totally dominate. After all, Zeta had unchallengeable twelve-year-old cool, because Zeta knew people in pop music. And she could prove it too. Betsy Ross answered Zeta's fan mail.

This was farsighted of Betsy. Zeta, or someone much like her, was going to be the person who would mercifully sign Betsy into a dry-out clinic. Zeta had a core of steel. The good died young, but Zeta was the kind of good who was too tight-lipped and practical to die young. Mere survival wasn't good enough for Zeta; she was the type who prevailed. Zeta was bound to bury almost everyone she knew.

When the fatal Y2K moment came, Starlitz met it in a crowd. Descending mirror balls, schmaltzy public singing, entirely predictable. Just another face, another particle in the public wave. A fat drunk in a nothing suit in a town he didn't know. It would never find him here.

But the moment came and got him. It searched him up like a pursuing fury. It struck Starlitz from the inside out. Hot wire seized his heart. His shoulder was full of pain. He fell like a gutshot deer and tumbled silently into the red and the black.

"AT LEAST YOU PICKED THE PROPER COUNTRY FOR A HEART attack," said Khoklov.

"Oh, yeah," said Starlitz hoarsely. "When it comes to CPR and EMS, Switzerland's second to none."

"How do you feel now?"

"I just had a major coronary. I feel like hammered shit." Starlitz leaned across the chrome tubing of his hospital bed to sniff at Khoklov's massive bouquet. "It's good of you to take the trouble to look in on me, Pulat Romanevich. And flowers too! I didn't expect that of you."

"I kind of picked them up on the way in," said Khoklov. "There's a dead nuclear physicist just down the hall."

Starlitz nodded. "They're common as rabbits in Switzerland. It's that CERN setup in Geneva."

"The nuke professor's stone dead. Right at the tick of the clock."

"Tough break for the hard-science maven. He must have been some special kind of atom guy. Swell bouquet, though." Starlitz scratched at the itching intravenous drip. "So, catch me up on things. What brings you to the land of secret gnomes?"

"Well," said Khoklov, "it's a very odd business. You see, at the hour of Balkan crisis I flew my radar-transparent escape craft to the rescue of Milosevic. He was very glad to see me. Grateful. His lovely daughter was grateful too. So, I was doing tune-ups for a possible family flight to Greece, and . . . Somehow I became ground zero in a Belgrade military airport. On the very first night of NATO strikes. Apparently I was standing directly beneath a million-dollar cruise missile."

"I wouldn't brag about that to just anybody, if I were you."

"There seems to have been a kind of . . . news blackout. A hiss on the tape. Something snapped, you see? Something ran out. I think it's because I'm Russian. I've had an eventful life. Russia has had a very great deal of twentieth century. Russia had much more twentieth century than most other countries. I believe I overdrew the bank account of twentieth century, somehow. There wasn't quite enough twentieth century left to get me all the way through."

"Okay. I can accept that."

"They discovered me much later. At the Prishtina airport, in Kosovo. When the first Russian troops rushed in to seize the airstrip, ahead of NATO. Apparently I was packed up in a kind of coffin, along with the aircraft. Very neatly folded. A hermetic seal, or something like that."

"What happened to the airplane?"

"They confiscated it. Sent it back to Moscow for study, along with the crashed American Stealth bomber. They were nice about it. I have a claim check somewhere."

"Tough break, Pulat."

"Anyway, I do feel better now. I think that—involuntary retirement—did my morale some good. I rejoined my nephew in Budapest—he has some very interesting biznis deals going on there—and I recovered my health. When the actual Y2K day came along, I just breezed right through it. Not a problem. Who cares? Just another day on the calendar. How about you, Starlits?" Khoklov placed his hands along his scarred ribs. "I don't envy a man in a hospital."

"Well, man, I've been lying here thinking deep thoughts. Tell me something, Pulat. Why is it that when people do evil things, they get psychoanalyzed forever? There's always some lame explanation out of their background, or their genetics, or their impoverished upbringing, or their mood disorders, or some such crap. Whereas, if you do amazing, freakish *good* things, nobody ever CAT-scans you."

"It's good to see you turning to philosophy again. In suffering is the beginning of wisdom."

"Check this out, man, I've got a theory. A good person can subsume the narrative of a bad person. Because it's easy for a good person to imagine being bad. But a bad person can't subsume the narrative of a good person. Because they have no understanding what that's like. It's just beyond them, it's beyond their language."

"I like that theory," said Khoklov. "It's mathematical. It's about surface areas, basically. It's a kind of moral topology."

Starlitz nodded silently. Pilots were good at math. Russians were very good at math. Russian pilots really had it on the ball, mathwise.

"It reminds me of the history of the unfortunate G-7," said Khoklov, "which came to such a muddled end. Half the girls dead . . ."

"Half of them alive," offered Starlitz.

"Canceled tours, fired staffers, a scandalous Turkish manager . . . A pop act as dead as mutton. Yesterday's news, completely defunct. It was a lovely concept originally, though."

"Outlived its proper time, man. You really don't want to push history when it's past. It turns right into farce. Or it's fatal. Or it's both."

"Yes, but if you think about the problem with some intellectual rigor," said Khoklov sternly, "far from your usual arty mush and cheap double-talk . . . What was the core G-7 concept? Seven trashy girls, from seven famous, powerful nations, singing stupid popular music, and doomed to rapidly vanish."

"Right. That was it exactly."

"What if we reversed the polarity? Turned the concept inside out, for the far side of Y2K. Seven very talented girls, from seven troubled, totally obscure nations. Singing fabulous, honest, and authentic music. Determined to last as long as possible."

"Why seven girls?"

"Why not? Good number. Dead easy. Let's say: East Timor, Chechnya, Kashmir, Kurdistan, Kosovo, and, oh . . . maybe a Basque girl and a Miskito Indian from embattled socialist Nicaragua."

Starlitz pondered the pitch. It had a solid backing but a nice kind of twist. "And they sing, what, like, in their own, obscure, teeny-tiny languages? And on native instruments? Like gamelans maybe? Assuming they have gamelans in East Timor?"

"Yes, Starlits, but they sing good music. The best music we can get. And they mean it when they sing it. And we tour the globe with the world's least globalizable women. We get huge moral credit with every bleeding-heart critic in the world."

"No commercial potential, man. It wouldn't make any money."

"Lekhi, this is the keystone of the scheme. We don't make any money. We're beyond that now. Why should we care about budgets? After what the twentieth century put us through, we probably don't even have souls. We *lose* money. *Other people's* money. We have an infinite supply of bad conscience! They fall all over themselves to make us lose their money."

Starlitz sat bolt upright in his bed. "Absolutely! That is it! Brother, I am so with this! I can't wait to get started! This is the Spirit of Now!" He grinned from ear to ear. "It's a very, very happening thing."